FUGITIVE

ALSO BY PHILLIP MARGOLIN
Executive Privilege
Lost Lake
Sleeping Beauty
The Associate
The Undertaker's Widow
The Burning Man
After Dark
Gone, but Not Forgotten
The Last Innocent Man
Heartstone

AMANDA JAFFE NOVELS
Wild Justice
Ties That Bind
Proof Positive

A NOVEL

FUGITIVE

PHILLIP MARGOLIN

**Doubleday Large Print
Home Library Edition**

FOR MARISSA,
THE NEWEST MEMBER OF THE
MARGOLIN FAMILY.
WELCOME TO THE WORLD.

FOR MARISSA,
THE NEWEST MEMBER OF THE
MARGOLIN FAMILY.
WELCOME TO THE WORLD.

"Where's Charlie?"
1997

Mr. Burdett, notify me when you've made up your mind," the Honorable Dagmar Hansen said. "We'll be in recess until I hear from you."

Amanda Jaffe rose with the rest of the spectators in the courtroom when Judge Hansen left the bench, but her eyes weren't on the judge. They were watching the intense conference between her father and his client. Frank Jaffe's lips were inches from Sally Pope's ear and he was speaking rapidly. Mrs. Pope's hand rested on her father's forearm and her brow knit as she concentrated on what he was saying.

Amanda frowned, because she sensed more intimacy than was normal between a lawyer and his client.

Karl Burdett, the Washington County district attorney, looked furious as he stormed through the courtroom doors with his two assistants in tow. Frank Jaffe and Mrs. Pope followed a moment later. Just before the courtroom door closed behind him, Frank gave Amanda a quick thumbs-up. This morning, before leaving for court, Frank had hinted at a major development in the case. Amanda was dying to know what had happened in chambers, but she knew better than to bother her father when he was in the middle of a trial.

Amanda decided to take the stairs to the lobby. The walk would probably be the only exercise she would get today and she felt a twinge of guilt. Amanda had been training furiously this summer while she was home from college. As a junior, she had won the 200 freestyle for Berkeley at the PAC-10 championships and had placed sixth at Nationals. If she shaved a few seconds off her best time, she could place in the top three at Nationals as a senior and have an outside chance of making the 2000 Olympic team. Breakthroughs like that didn't happen if you missed too many practices, but she couldn't pass up a chance to watch her father try the nation's most publicized murder case.

Frank Jaffe was one of the best criminal defense attorneys in Oregon, and Amanda had wanted to follow in his footsteps since she was in elementary school. When other girls were reading fashion magazines, she was reading *Perry Mason*. While other girls dreamed of going to the prom, she dreamed of trying homicide cases, and there had been no Oregon case in recent history that had been as highly publicized as the trial of Sally Pope for the murder of her husband, United States Congressman Arnold Pope Jr. Adding to the buzz was the aura surrounding Sally Pope's codefendant, Charlie Marsh, aka the Guru Gabriel Sun, whose rise from petty criminal to national hero and New Age guru had captured the country's imagination.

Amanda was carrying a copy of *The Light Within You*, Marsh's autobiography, in which he bared his soul about the abuse he'd suffered as a child and told how this psychic damage had led him to a life filled with violence. What made the book special was Marsh's account of his amazing religious conversion, which occurred at the moment he risked his life to save a prison guard from the attack of an insane prisoner.

Amanda looked at the photo of Marsh on the back of the book. It was no mystery why women flocked to the guru's seminars, where he taught his flock the way to find the inner light that had suffused him during his near-death experience. Marsh had the blond, blue-eyed good looks of a movie idol, but his violent past hinted at a devil within. Sally Pope was one of the most beautiful and self-possessed women Amanda had ever met, but even she had fallen under Marsh's spell, if you believed the tabloids.

Sally Pope's case had sex, celebrity, and violent death. Only one thing was missing—Charlie. "WHERE IS THE GURU?" screamed the headlines in the national press on the day the trial opened. The question led off every television news hour. Charlie Marsh had disappeared from the Westmont Country Club the instant Arnold Pope Jr. was shot. Like everyone else in America, Amanda wondered where he was now and what he was doing.

PART I

The Happy Warrior 2009

1

It is coming soon, it is coming soon!" Jean-Claude Baptiste, President for Life of the People's Republic of Batanga, told Charlie Marsh in the singsong English spoken by Africans who had been raised speaking a tribal dialect. Like most of the other men at the state banquet, Charlie was wearing a tuxedo. President Baptiste, who had never held a rank higher than sergeant, was commander in chief of the Batangan army and dressed in the uniform of a five-star general.

"Watch closely!" the president said with gleeful anticipation as he jabbed a finger at one of the many huge flat-screen televisions that were mounted along the walls of the banquet hall in the executive mansion. The massive chamber was longer than a football field and was modeled after the Las Vegas casino where Baptiste had won his most important fight. Using flat-screen TVs as wall hangings would have been out of place at Versailles, but they looked perfectly natural amid the mirrored walls, bright lights, and velvet paintings that gave the banquet hall the ambience of a sports bar.

"Now, look," the president said excitedly. On all of the screens mounted along the walls, a younger Baptiste was laughing as he drove Vladimir Topalov, the number two–ranked heavyweight in the world, into a corner of the ring. This Baptiste stood six foot six and weighed two hundred and sixty pounds. His skin was as black as ink and the lights in the arena reflected off his smooth, shaved skull. The present-day version of Jean-Claude looked vaguely like the boxer on the screen, but weighed more than three hundred pounds and gave the impression of being two large men who had been glued together.

"Look Charlie, it comes now," Baptiste told the blue-eyed man with blond hair and tanned, weathered skin who sat to his left at the end of a teak banquet table that easily sat fifty. Charlie feigned exuberant interest, as did the thirty other guests. Anyone giving the impression that he was not completely enthralled with Baptiste's fistic skills risked an attitude adjustment session in the basement of the mansion, from which few emerged alive.

On the screen, Baptiste's opponent staggered back a few steps. Blood from a deep cut over his right eye was blinding him. The future president of Batanga feinted with a jab before landing a crushing hook to his victim's temple. As Topalov sank to the canvas, both the boxing and presidential Baptistes threw back their heads and laughed uproariously. Though the sound was off, everyone at the banquet knew that Baptiste's many fans were chanting "ho, ho, ho," as they always did when "The Happy Warrior" knocked down an opponent. Baptiste had earned his nickname by laughing delightedly whenever he subjected a foe to a particularly awful beating.

Topalov had been hospitalized after the bout. The man who had ruled Batanga before Baptiste had not been so lucky. After his knockout of the Russian, Baptiste returned to Batanga for a victory parade followed by a dinner in his honor given by the previous president of the republic. During dinner, a squad of army officers, bribed with money from Baptiste's fight purse, stormed the banquet hall and engineered a coup. Rumor had it that Baptiste had made several excellent jokes while eating the heart of the ex-president in a Juju ceremony that was supposed to infuse him with the deceased's spiritual essence.

Baptiste smiled, displaying a perfect set of pearly white teeth. "Was that not a wonderful punch, Charlie?"

"Very powerful, Mr. President," answered Marsh. Charlie was a foot shorter and roughly one hundred and fifty pounds lighter than his host. Because he lacked Baptiste's courage and vicious temperament, it had taken a considerable effort to hide his terror during dinner. Now he gathered what little nerve he possessed and raised the subject curiosity had prodded him to explore ever since Jean-Claude had invited him to sit in the chair usually occupied by Bernadette Baptiste, the only one of the president's wives to bear him a child.

"Madam Bernadette would have enjoyed your display of virility, Mr. President."

Baptiste nodded agreement. "Women want a powerful man, Charlie. They know your power will bring them great pleasure in bed, not so?"

Charlie looked down the table at Bernadette's child, five-year-old Alfonse, who sat next to his nanny.

"I see your charming son is here, but where is your lovely wife?"

Baptiste's smile faded. "Sadly, she could not join us this evening, but she told me to say hello to you if you asked about her."

Charlie's heart seized and it took every ounce of his energy to keep from throwing up.

"Ah, dessert," Baptiste sighed as a servant rolled a pastry cart next to his ornate high-backed chair. The benevolent and all-powerful ruler of Batanga loved to eat almost as much as he loved to inflict pain, and he scanned the cart eagerly. It was laden with all of the president's favorites, most of which he'd sampled for the first time in the fast-food restaurants and sumptuous casino buffets of Las Vegas.

"That one and that one, I think," he said, indicating a huge piece of German chocolate cake and a three-scoop ice cream sundae heaped high with whipped cream, sprinkled with nuts, dotted with Maraschino cherries, and covered with caramel, strawberry, and chocolate sauces.

The president turned to Charlie. He was smiling broadly. "Eat up, my friend."

Charlie had no appetite but he knew better than to disobey any presidential command, even one as benign as an order to eat dessert. As soon as the waiter placed an enormous slice of cherry cheesecake on Charlie's plate, Baptiste leaned close to Charlie's ear and whispered conspiratorially:

"I will tell you a secret, but tell no one else or it will spoil the surprise. After dinner, I have an interesting entertainment planned."

"Oh?"

"Yes," Baptiste responded happily. "Its nature is known only to me and Nathan."

Charlie cast a nervous glance at Nathan Tuazama, who was sitting halfway down the banquet table, next to the wife of the Syrian ambassador. Tuazama was the head of the National Education Bureau, Baptiste's secret police. The cadaverous black man's head rotated slowly in Charlie's direction at the same time Charlie turned toward him, as if Tuazama had read his mind. There were rumors that Tuazama had supernatural powers, and Charlie had not discounted these rumors completely. Tuazama's thin, bloodless lips displayed none of the president's joy. Unlike his master, Tuazama had no sense of humor. Charlie wasn't even sure that he had any emotions.

"After dinner, you will be invited to join me in a most unusual and unforgettable experience," Baptiste said, flashing his bright smile. "But enough talk. Come, Charlie, enjoy your cake."

THE BANQUET DRAGGED on for another hour as Baptiste subjected his guests to replays of his favorite fights. Then, a little after one in the morning, he bid a merciful farewell to all but a select group, who had been instructed to stay. Charlie scanned the chosen few and found they included Nathan Tuazama; Alfonse (who could barely keep his eyes open); Madam O'Doulou, the child's nanny; a justice of the Batangan Supreme Court who'd had the temerity to dissent in a case Baptiste wanted decided in a certain way; and an army general who was rumored to have criticized his commander-in-chief.

"Come, my friends," Baptiste said cheerfully. "I want to show you something very exciting and much fun."

Baptiste chuckled and his massive stomach shook. "Much fun, indeed," he assured everyone.

A failure to laugh when the president said something he deemed amusing amounted to treason, so everyone smiled, except the exhausted Alfonse. As the heir to Batanga, Alfonse was—at least for the near future—exempt from Baptiste's homicidal whims. When several Batangan Special Forces troops surrounded the group, it took an effort for Charlie to maintain his smile and it took a supreme act of will to look happy when Baptiste led the group to the special elevator that only went to the basement. The elevator's walls glistened because they were cleaned daily to remove the blood and gore that frequently stained them. No one spoke as the elevator descended. Charlie prayed during the ride and he suspected that he wasn't the only one begging the Lord to let him return to the surface in one piece or, at least, to die with a minimum of suffering.

The banquet hall's casino-like décor had been insanely cheerful. Now the elevator doors opened on a dark and joyless world. Flickering low-watt bulbs cast sections of the damp, gray hallway in a sickly yellow glow, while leaving other parts in shadow. Mold grew on the walls and there was a faint smell of feces and disinfectant in the air. Solid steel doors spaced at intervals broke up the monotony of the corridor. As they exited the car, a scream shattered the silence. Alfonse's eyes widened and Baptiste took him by the hand.

"Do not worry, my lovely child. You are quite safe with Papa. No one will hurt you."

Baptiste led the procession to a door halfway down the narrow hall. Then he knelt so his face was close to his son's.

"What happens to boys and girls when they are bad?" Baptiste asked.

Alfonse, who was very tired, looked confused.

"Come, come, my jewel. You know the answer to this simple question."

"They are punished?" Alfonse answered tentatively.

Baptiste smiled broadly. "Is he not the most intelligent child?" he asked.

Charlie nodded, as the mention of punishment sent his heart rate up.

"Well, Alfonse," Baptiste said, "your mommy was bad. She was cheating, and you know it is very bad to cheat. It is dishonest, is that not so?"

Alfonse nodded, but none of the adults moved or breathed.

"Do you want to see how we punish a mommy who cheats?" Baptiste asked Alfonse.

His son looked concerned but Baptiste did not wait for an answer. He stood up and nodded to Tuazama, who inserted a key in the lock. When the door opened, Charlie stared into total darkness. Then he felt an automatic weapon press into his back as he was herded into the room.

"Surprise!" yelled Baptiste as Tuazama flipped a light switch.

The nanny fainted. The Supreme Court justice threw up. The general was too stunned to do anything but stare. Alfonse shrieked. Baptiste's deep, rolling belly laugh almost drowned out the child's screams.

When the lights flashed on, Charlie's eyes were drawn to a long metal table that was the room's only furniture. Bernadette was lying on it on her stomach. She was naked and her long, smooth legs had been spread apart, exposing her to everyone. It took Charlie's paralyzed mind a moment to figure out what—in addition to his lover being dead—was wrong with the scene. When he realized that the toes of Bernadette's feet were pointing up and she was staring at him, even though she was on her stomach, Charlie's knees buckled and he almost passed out.

"There, there, my friend," Baptiste said as he wrapped one of his huge arms around his guest to keep him from sinking to the floor.

Charlie wished he could faint, but all he could do was stare into Bernadette's dead eyes; a feat made possible by sewing her decapitated head on backward and propping it up on a pillow. Her legs had also been amputated and switched.

Alfonse's unconscious nanny was no help with the hysterical child. Baptiste ignored him and focused all of his attention on Charlie.

"Are you okay, my friend?" he asked.

Charlie was so terrified he couldn't speak.

"I tell you, it hurt me to do this," the president continued, "but I discovered something terrible." Baptiste's huge arm pulled Charlie so close Charlie could smell the president's sweat. "You will not believe this of my dear Bernadette, but Alfonse's mother was having an affair." Baptiste shook his head sadly. "What do you think of that?"

"It's not possible, Mr. President," Charlie croaked. "What woman would ever cheat on you?"

"Yes, yes, I know it makes no sense, but, sadly, it is true. But, you know, there is a mystery here. I do not know the name of the culprit who seduced her, yet. Have you any idea who it might be?"

Charlie felt his bowels loosen. There was no way Bernadette would have held up under torture.

"No, Mr. President, I never heard anyone say anything bad about Bernadette."

Baptiste shook his head slowly. "She and her lover were very careful. They were very clever. But Nathan is working on this problem and I have complete confidence that he will ferret out the identity of the foul person who tempted my beloved Bernadette into breaking her marriage vows."

Then the president smiled. "But come, everyone. It is late."

He released Charlie and bent down to pick up his terrified son. "Now, now, Alfonse, you must be a man. A man does not cry when he confronts death. Enough of this."

Baptiste stepped over the nanny's body. "Revive Madam O'Doulou and bring her to Alfonse's room," he told the soldier in charge of the Special Forces squad.

"And this one?" the soldier asked, pointing at the judge, who was doubled over after a second round of vomiting.

"Leave him with Bernadette. I will decide what to do with him later."

CHAPTER **2**

The executive mansion was a six-story, concave monstrosity that resembled a stereo speaker. The exterior was covered by gold disks that reflected the sunlight in the daytime and deflected bullets anytime. Baptiste's palace was set back from the road behind a spear-topped, wrought-iron electrified fence. A driveway curved past the front entrance, which was entered by climbing a set of steep marble steps. This enabled soldiers standing at the top to shoot down on anyone who tried to storm the mansion from the front.

Charlie staggered down the steps of the

mansion in a daze, ripping off his bow tie, opening his shirt collar, and gulping in fresh air as he went. He squeezed his eyes shut and shook his head from side to side but, try as he might, Charlie could not get the image of the soles of Bernadette's feet out of his head. Positioned as she was, she'd seemed so vulnerable.

A limousine provided by Baptiste had driven Charlie to the executive mansion but no car waited at the bottom of the stairs to take him back to his apartment.

"Where is my car?" Charlie asked one of the soldiers standing guard duty.

"All cars gone," the soldier answered tersely.

"Then bring a car for me."

The soldier's smile was cold. "President Baptiste say no more cars tonight."

Before this evening, Charlie would have reported the soldier for being insolent and would have demanded a car, but he was too upset and frightened to argue. There was a slim possibility that he could locate a minor functionary who would rustle up a car for him, but no power on earth could make him go back inside the mansion to find one.

The absence of his limousine and the soldier's insolence were proof beyond a reasonable doubt that Baptiste knew he was Bernadette's lover. The last time he'd been this frightened was twelve years ago, on the evening he'd fled from the parking lot of the Westmont Country Club after the congressman was shot. He'd stayed terrified until several weeks after his arrival in Batanga. Charlie remembered the moment the fear had lifted. He had been walking on the white sand behind his house, watching the waves sweep in. Emerald green palm trees had been swaying in the breeze and there wasn't a cloud in the sky. Charlie had breathed in the clear, clean air and exhaled. Then he'd smiled and said, out loud, "I'm safe." It didn't take long for him to discover that what he thought was safety was only an illusion.

Charlie's fear drove him down the long driveway to the guard house. Moments after the guard opened the gate, he was trudging toward town along Baptiste Boulevard. Cabs drove by and so did open-backed "money buses" that took passengers around the city on a set route for a dime, but Charlie's apartment was only two miles from the mansion and he needed to walk to clear his head.

The back of the mansion faced the ocean and the cool breeze that blew inland at night chased away the thick, moist heat that folded over the inhabitants of equatorial West Africa most days. Charlie liked the heat. When he thought about it, Charlie realized that the beach weather was one of the few good things about Batanga. Most everything else was shit. Its president was a maniac and most of its citizens lived in fear and abject poverty. Even the rich Batangans lived at the whim of their insane ruler, and the rainy season was long and depressing.

Another good thing about Batanga, from Charlie's point of view, was the absence of an extradition treaty with the United States or anywhere else. Batanga was a favorite sanctuary for deposed dictators, terrorists on the run, and wanted criminals. Baptiste extended the hand of friendship to them all, for a price. Twelve years ago, Charlie had fled to Batanga after being indicted for the murder of United States Congressman Arnold Pope Jr. When he had arrived, he had been rich from the royalties earned by

his best-selling autobiography, *The Light
Within You*, and the money he'd embezzled
from Inner Light, Inc. In those early days,
everything seemed rosy and he'd been
treated like a prince. The people Charlie
met were rich. They ran Batanga, lived in
big houses, ate well, and threw wonderful
parties. And the women . . . ! They had
dangled like ripe fruit, there for the taking
and eager to share his bed because he
was the president's favorite. Charlie's only
contacts with the poor of Batanga were his
houseboy and cook, who knew better than
to say anything negative about their country or their president in a nation where anyone could be a spy, and where the secret
police routinely made people disappear for
any reason or no reason at all.

The changes had come so slowly that
he didn't realize anything was wrong until
it was too late. For the first four years,
Charlie had lived in a beautiful house with
an ocean view, owned by the president.
The rent was steep, but Charlie had several million dollars in his Swiss account,
so it seemed like peanuts. So did the taxes
he was required to pay for the privilege of
living in a country that would not extradite

him. Charlie spent lavishly because he was expected to throw the type of parties to which he had been invited. And there were those gifts for the ladies. All of these expenses were no big deal while his book topped the charts, fueled by the publicity surrounding his murder charge. Then another American celebrity killed someone and Charlie was no longer the flavor of the month. His book royalties were paid twice a year at six-month intervals, so it was almost a year before he was aware that something was amiss. The first time he learned that his income was shrinking, he wasn't overly concerned. When the amount in the next statement was even smaller, Charlie started to panic.

Manipulating people was President Baptiste's hobby, and he engineered Charlie's slow descent from honored guest to lap dog with true genius. When a deposed African dictator fled to Batanga after looting millions from his country's treasury, Baptiste asked Charlie if he would mind moving to a smaller house that was not on the beach. Charlie, who thought he was untouchable, ignored the suggestion. The president could have had Charlie shot or arrested, but he loved slow torture. The next day, Charlie's servants, cook, and gardeners did not show up for work and they never returned. When Charlie complained, Baptiste again suggested that it would be best if Charlie watched his expenses by moving to a smaller place. Charlie stubbornly insisted that he could manage the cost of the villa. The following day, Charlie's electricity was cut off and a government official informed him that his rent had been raised. Charlie suddenly saw the big picture. A week later, he was living in a smaller house with only a houseboy, who doubled as his cook. Twelve years after his escape from America, Charlie lived in a squalid apartment and drove a broken-down Volkswagen Bug.

Charlie knew that he was still alive because he amused Baptiste. The president brought him to parties, where he was frequently the foil of the dictator's practical jokes. Sometimes Baptiste displayed his pet American on Batanga's only television station or at banquets for visiting dignitaries from countries with anti-American policies. Most of the time Baptiste ignored Charlie, which was a good thing.

The route from the mansion to Charlie's apartment led through the heart of Baptisteville. The shops were locked and shuttered for the night and the activity in the bars was winding down. Elderly watchmen sat on upturned wooden crates, guarding gated entrances for Lebanese merchants. Packs of emaciated feral dogs roaming the streets in search of food growled at the rare passerby. And there were the ever-present soldiers. Charlie knew that his white skin was no protection from the psychotic teenagers who formed Baptiste's terror squads, but Charlie was not afraid of the soldiers, because he carried a presidential pass. Those who didn't have a pass cut a wide swath around the young men toting automatic weapons, who were always unpredictable.

Charlie's fear had not abated as he walked downhill toward Waterside. If anything, hurrying along the deserted streets made him more afraid. He imagined one of the black Mercedes favored by the secret police suddenly screeching to a halt beside him. Armed men would grab his arms, a black hood would be thrown over his head, and he'd be returned to the mansion to face whatever fate Baptiste held in store for him.

When he reached the bottom of the hill, Charlie heard the sea sweeping into shore behind the native market. The soothing sound accompanied him for another quarter-mile until he arrived at the Kamal S. Dean brick factory, which took up the ground floor of his three-story apartment building. Charlie walked through an arch at the side. As he climbed the partially enclosed stairway, the wind blew the salty smell of sea air at him and he could just make out the white foam on the crest of the waves that broke on the narrow beach below. Charlie was about to step onto the landing in front of his door when a man materialized out of the shadows. Charlie jumped back and threw up his hands to ward off a blow.

"It's me, Pierre," the man whispered. Pierre Girard, Bernadette's brother, was wearing a tie-dyed dashiki and tan slacks. He was slender and bookish, with sad brown eyes magnified by the thick lenses of his tortoiseshell glasses.

Charlie collapsed with relief. "Oh, Pierre," he said, his voice halfway between a sob and a sigh. "Have you heard?"

Bernadette's brother nodded but his face showed no emotion.

"I'm so sorry," Charlie said.

"There's no time for sorrow. Baptiste knows you and Bernadette were lovers. He's toying with you now but our president has a short attention span. When he tires of his head games he'll send Nathan. You must leave Batanga."

Pierre put a hand on Charlie's shoulder. "Bernadette told me how kind you were to her. She loved you, Charlie."

"Thank you for letting me know that."

"There's something else you should know. Bernadette wasn't killed because she was cheating on Baptiste, although that must have made her pain more enjoyable for the bastard. She was tortured for information."

"I don't understand."

"There are Batangans who want Baptiste dead or gone. She was helping us."

Pierre squeezed Charlie's shoulder. "Do you want to avenge my sister's death?"

"Of course, but what can I do? I can barely help myself."

"You know Rebecca, the bartender at the Mauna Loa?"

Charlie nodded.

"She can put you in touch with a man who can get you out of the country. He is a mercenary and it will be expensive."

Charlie knew that he would probably die a horrible death if he stayed in Batanga. Even if Baptiste let him live, the best he could hope for was a life of fear in which every breath he took was dependent on the whim of a sadistic, homicidal lunatic. If he returned to the States, he would have to stand trial for murder, but twelve years had passed. Could the state even mount a case after all this time? The bottom line for Charlie was that even if he was convicted he would be better off on death row than in Batanga. In Oregon, the condemned experienced a quick death by lethal injection. In Batanga, the president liked to hear you scream for as long as possible.

"I think I know a way to manage it," he told Pierre.

"Good. When everything is in place Rebecca will get in touch with you and she will give you something to take with you that Bernadette entrusted to me."

"What thing?" asked Charlie, who was

naturally suspicious and terrified of being caught helping the rebels.

"Diamonds, Charlie, many diamonds. We need you to carry them to America. We will take them from you there and use them to buy weapons for our people."

"I don't know . . ."

"Did you love my sister?"

Charlie's eyes misted and he nodded, too choked with emotion to speak.

"Then don't let her death be in vain."

Charlie looked past Pierre to the sea. The odds were that he'd be dead before he could help anyone, but if he survived he could finally do something worthwhile with his life by helping Pierre.

"All right, I'm in."

Pierre smiled. "Bernadette knew we could count on you. Thank you, Charlie."

They spoke for a few minutes more. Then Pierre embraced Charlie before slipping over the side of the building and rappelling to the beach down the rope he'd used to climb to the landing.

Charlie's front door opened into a narrow hall flanked by a kitchen and bedroom on one side and a living room and the spare room he used as a study on the ocean side. He turned on a lamp that stood on a cheap wooden desk in his study. Luckily, there was electricity tonight. Charlie booted up his laptop and logged on to his e-mail provider. He assumed that the police would read any e-mail he sent, so he phrased this one carefully. It was addressed to Martha Brice, the editor in chief of *World News*, an ultraconservative magazine with a main office in New York.

"Dear Ms. Brice: My name is Charlie Marsh. You probably knew me as the Guru Gabriel Sun, author of the inspirational autobiography *The Light Within You*, an international best-seller. Twelve years ago I was framed for the murder of Congressman Arnold Pope Jr. and was forced to flee from the United States. Since leaving America, I have been living in the wonderful country of Batanga under the protection of its benevolent ruler, President Jean-Claude Baptiste. President Baptiste is a source of enlightenment and a true father to his people. The Western press has falsely labeled him a dictator. I have not given an interview in some time, but I wish to do so now to set the record straight

about this courageous leader, who has been so unjustly maligned.

"I've seen you interviewed on TV and I've followed your career. I believe that the articles in *World News* present an unbiased view of world affairs. Would your excellent magazine be interested in sending a reporter to write an article that would tell the American people about the wonderful things President Baptiste is doing for the people of Batanga? If so, please contact me so we can arrange the details."

Charlie read the e-mail twice before sending it. If Baptiste saw it he might hold off killing Charlie in the hope that the interview would be published. This would buy Charlie some time, and time was his most important ally. Time would give Charlie a chance to survive; a slim chance, but a chance nonetheless, and Charlie had always been a man who seized an opportunity when he saw it.

Charlie had drunk a lot at the banquet but the horror in the basement had sobered him. He doubted he could sleep, even though it was almost three in the morning. He poured a glass of scotch and carried it to his balcony, which was the best thing about his dingy apartment. Before sunset, he could watch the native fishermen surf the waves in their canoes as they brought their catch in to shore. After dark, the stars would shine bright in the African sky and he would gaze at the lights of ships anchored in the Freeport. During the rainy season he was presented with lightning storms that were as dramatic as a fireworks display.

Charlie took a stiff drink and tried to imagine what Bernadette had suffered before death had shown her mercy. A tear trickled down his cheek and he brushed it away. The tear was as much for himself as for his dead lover.

THE HEAT OF the sun woke Charlie. He opened his eyes and stared at the sea, wondering why he was outside. There was a chair next to Charlie. In the second after waking he thought he saw Bernadette out of the corner of his eye, sitting beside him, laughing in that way of hers that lit up any room she was in. Then Charlie remembered the events at the mansion and suppressed a sob.

Six years ago, Baptiste had introduced

his fourth wife to Batangan high society. Charlie had been taken by her elegant beauty and warm smile but he knew she was untouchable and soon forgot her. Over the next few years, he saw Bernadette from a distance at state dinners and a party or two. He remembered the way her pregnancy suffused her features with a maternal glow and the way she smiled when she gazed at Alfonse. But she wasn't smiling the first time he was alone with her.

A little over a year ago, the secretary of state had hosted a party for a visiting dignitary from Ghana. Charlie was bored by the company, annoyed by the noise, and tired of just about everything else that was going on. A set of stairs led down to the beach from the patio of the secretary's house. Charlie set off along the shore and found Bernadette sitting on a thick log that had washed up in the tide. It was dark and neither the moonshine nor the ambient light from the house were strong enough to breach the shadows that obscured Bernadette's face. When he drew closer, as well as tears glistening on her ebony cheeks, Charlie saw a split lip and a swollen eye. The darkness and the damage to Bernadette's face prevented Charlie from recognizing her right away or he would have fled. God knew what Baptiste would do to a man found alone with his wife. By the time he realized who she was, Bernadette's head was on his shoulder and her tears were dampening his shirt.

Bernadette had given up on kindness and now she'd met someone who was tender and compassionate. When she stopped crying and began to think clearly, Bernadette realized the threat she posed to Charlie. She thanked him, squeezed his hand, and left him alone on the beach. But then, a month later, while the president was in Las Vegas, gambling and whoring, Bernadette saw Charlie at a gala at the Batanga Palace, the country's only luxury hotel. This time she lost her heart to him.

At first, Charlie resisted his desire to be with Bernadette, because he didn't want to be cut into tiny pieces by a chainsaw or slowly turned into barbecue by a blowtorch, two of the president's favorite methods of execution. But Charlie had never been in love before and he was stunned by the depth of his feeling for this beautiful lost soul. They began meeting in a room at the hotel, which Charlie rented under an assumed name. During their first tryst, Bernadette confided that the all-powerful ruler of the Batangan people was anything but in the sack. Charlie learned that Baptiste blamed Bernadette for his many failures in bed and beat her when he was unable to perform. The beatings had gotten so bad that she'd begun to fear for her life.

Bernadette and Charlie talked of escape and a life together, even though they should have known that the affair and their dreams were insane. But people in love lose touch with reality. Charlie never asked himself how it was possible for their trysts to go undiscovered in a country where everyone was a spy and the one person most likely to be the subject of surveillance was the supreme ruler's wife. Now Charlie knew that Baptiste had always been aware of every move they'd made.

Charlie wept quietly as he wondered how it was possible for someone as wonderful as Bernadette to be dead. When he'd exhausted his tears, he closed his eyes, leaned his head back, and felt the sun on his face and the caress of a sea breeze. Waves were washing over the rocky beach below his apartment as they did every minute of every day. The world continued its beat and Charlie was alive to enjoy it. And as long as he was alive, there was a chance he would survive and win some measure of revenge for his lost love.

CHAPTER 3

Four days after his escape from the mansion, at a little after eight in the evening, Charlie walked through the milling Waterside crowds. The dusky air was filled with the competing rhythms of native drummers and radios blaring hip-hop and African highlife. Smoke from cooking fires curled into the night sky. The fires had been built in front of tumbledown shacks made of corrugated tin and other junk. They were stacked one against the other near open sewers. Women wrapped in rainbow-colored cloth sold fish fresh from the canoes of the fishermen while other vendors squatted on low stools beside small grills, hawking roasted yams.

Charlie passed bands of bare-chested boys wearing ragged shorts. They played in the dust near open-front stores protected by thick metal gates. These children believed that all white men were rich, so they approached Charlie with hands outstretched, crying, "Papa, papa, gimme five cents." Many had distended bellies. One boy dragged a horribly mangled foot behind him. Another had a large lump on his stomach and sat in the road, his dull eyes staring. Older beggars with missing limbs or blind eyes pleaded for alms more quietly, thrusting rusty tin cups out when he walked by.

Charlie ignored the children and the beggars as he struggled up the hill toward the center of Baptisteville. At the top was Main Street, divided by a tree-shaded center island that stretched the length of the city. On either side were Western-style drugstores, movie theaters, restaurants, and gift shops that catered to wealthy Batangans, expatriates, and the rare tourist. The evening crowds were smaller here, because the European or Middle Eastern owners had closed their stores, but the streets were still crowded with taxis and money buses. Charlie crossed the road and turned into Lafayette Street, the center of Batanga's nightlife. Here were the Cave, the Peacock, the Mauna Loa, and other brightly colored shack bars where bar girls hustled a mostly white clientele to the incessant beat of rock and hip-hop.

Charlie maneuvered past several Batangan men in shorts and ripped T-shirts who sat on the curb outside the Mauna Loa, joking, arguing, and drinking from bottles filled with warm beer. A cigarette vendor tried to interest Charlie in one of the packs that rested on a tray he'd balanced on a wooden stand. Several beautiful African girls in tight, flashy, low-cut dresses leaned against the outside wall of the bar. Charlie greeted the women, who knew him by name. One girl promised him a night of ecstasy unlike any ever experienced by mortal man. Charlie begged off, claiming that a night with any one of them would end with him dead from pleasure. The women were laughing when Charlie entered the shack.

Expatriate white men and African

women sat along a wooden bar or at the few small tables that took up most of the floor space. Charlie edged past two Batangan girls who were dancing with each other to the Rolling Stones' "Brown Sugar," and took the only empty stool at the bar.

"Eh, Charlie, why you not come more?" asked the bartender.

"Rebecca, you know I love you too much," he answered. "If I come too much, I will say you must marry me."

"Maybe I will say yes, eh?" she answered coyly.

Charlie shook his head, feigning sadness. "I can hope, but I know you will break my heart."

Rebecca laughed raucously. "I say, Charlie, you bullshit me too much."

Charlie smiled. "Do you think you can find me a cold Heineken?"

Almost everyone in Batanga lived from day to day. Baptiste's secret police exploited their destitution by paying for information. Charlie had learned that it was wise to trust no one, but Pierre had told Charlie that he could trust Rebecca, a beautiful Batangan woman who had once been the mistress of the cabinet minister, who owned the Mauna Loa. Charlie frequented the bars on Lafayette Street and knew Rebecca. He had never heard her utter a subversive thought or discuss politics, and he was shocked to learn that she was part of the underground.

Bartenders meet a wide range of people and Rebecca had acquaintances, Batangan and otherwise, up and down the social ladder. Pierre had told Charlie that Rebecca would find someone who would help him escape from Batanga. This morning, a small boy had begged him for money using a code phrase. While Charlie was giving him a quarter, the boy told Charlie to come to the Mauna Loa at eight thirty.

Rebecca set a frosted green bottle on the bar, while Charlie casually scanned the room. The men in the bar were in groups or chatting up women. None looked the least bit interested in him. When he swiveled back, a white man who'd been sitting two stools away leaned across the bar girl who sat between them.

"I know you," he proclaimed so loudly that he could be heard over the music.

"I don't think so," said Charlie, who could

smell the booze on his breath from the distance of two barstools.

The man was broad-shouldered, big through the chest, and spoke with a southern accent. Charlie figured him for six two and two hundred. He was bald with a ruddy complexion and faint traces of boyhood acne and looked like he could handle himself in a fight.

"No, no, don't tell me. It'll come to me," the drunk insisted. He gazed into space for a moment then snapped his fingers. "TV! I've seen you on TV."

Charlie held his breath.

"You're that guru. Tell me I'm wrong."

"No, you got it." Charlie sighed.

"Hey, honey," the man said to the bar girl who sat between him and Charlie, "would you mind switching places? I'll buy you another to make it worth your while."

The bar girl surrendered her stool and the man moved next to Charlie.

"Hope you don't mind but it's not every day I bump into a celebrity in this place. Brad and Angelina don't pop in here much," he said with a braying laugh that set Charlie's teeth on edge.

"Chauncey Evers," the man said, reaching out a large hand. Charlie shook it reluctantly.

"Charlie Marsh," Charlie answered as he tried to figure out how to get away. His contact was never going to approach him while he was with this clown.

"I have to apologize upfront. I haven't read your book. I meant to but I haven't. But I did see you on TV during the thing at the prison when you saved the prison guard's life. That was something."

Two men and two women vacated a table. Evers picked up his glass.

"Let's grab that table and you can tell me all about the standoff at the prison."

"That's okay," Charlie said, desperate to beg off. "I'm supposed to meet someone."

"Well, you can drink with me until *she* gets here," Evers said with an exaggerated wink, "and the drinks are on me. It ain't often I get to meet a genuine hero who was on television and wrote a book." Evers lowered his voice. "And wants to escape from this hellhole."

"You're . . ." Charlie started, but Evers had turned away and was weaving unsteadily through the close-packed tables.

As soon as he was seated, he thrust a pen and a napkin at Charlie.

"Can I get your autograph for my girl-friend?" he asked loudly.

"Can you get me out of here?" Charlie said as he leaned over the napkin.

"That's easy," Evers assured him.

"How soon can you do it?"

"As soon as you pay me seventy-five thousand dollars."

"Seventy-five?" Charlie repeated anxiously.

"And it's got to be in cash. I don't take checks. Is that a problem?"

"No," Charlie said.

World News had agreed to do the interview, so Charlie would ask Rebecca to get a message asking for the seventy-five-thousand-dollar fee to Martha Brice through Pierre Girard and the rebels.

"What I want to know," Charlie said, "is how you're going to deal with Baptiste's secret police?"

"You mean that guy over by the wall?" Evers said as he kept his eyes on Charlie, a big smile on his face. "I spotted that clown as soon as he walked in."

"Yeah, well, don't be so smug. I spotted

him too. He tailed me from my apartment and he didn't try to hide the fact that he was following me. There are people outside my place every minute I'm at home and someone on my ass whenever I go out. Baptiste wants me to know he's having me shadowed. His secret police are very good. They can make themselves invisible if they want to. This is Baptiste's way of telling me I'm on a short leash. What I want to know is how you're going to deal with these guys."

"Don't worry about it," Evers said confidently. "You get me the money and I'll get you out."

"Why should I believe you?"

Evers shrugged. "Beats me. But you're the guy who sent for me. So," the mercenary asked, "what did you do to get Baptiste's panties in a bunch?"

Charlie hesitated. If Evers found out that the president had a personal grudge against him he might change his mind about taking him home. An American passport went only so far as protection, in Batanga.

"Come on, Charlie. If I'm going to risk my neck to get you out of here I have to know what I'm dealing with."

Charlie looked down at the tabletop. "I had an affair with one of Baptiste's wives."

Evers whistled.

"He tortured her to death and showed me the results. Then he pretended he didn't know who her lover was, but he knows," Charlie said bitterly.

"Man, you are in a heap of trouble. But never fear. Chauncey Evers will come to the rescue."

"What do I do next?" Charlie asked as he handed the autographed napkin to Evers.

"Get the money. Tell Rebecca when you have it and she'll tell me. Then you do exactly what I tell you to do and you'll be back in the good old US of A before you know it."

CHAPTER **4**

Some people said that God was good and merciful, but Dennis Levy knew that was not true. One had only to turn on the television news to see evidence of gross injustice in the world. One percent of the Earth's population skied at Gstaad and lay on the beaches of Nevis while millions starved in Africa. And what about AIDS and Katrina and the poor in India, who lived in the streets and scavenged in garbage dumps for their meals? Closer to home, there were undeserving people who held positions of power and worked in luxurious offices with views of Central Park because they had married money, while those with real talent—like Dennis Levy—slaved away in a cubicle and had to kowtow to them.

These were some of the things Dennis was thinking about as he trudged from his cubicle to the luxurious office of Martha Brice, his boss at *World News.* Levy had grown up lower-middle-class on Long Island and had worked like a dog in high school to earn a scholarship to an Ivy League university. While he bused tables in the cafeteria at Princeton, the legacy morons in his class received a weekly allowance from dear old dad. When Levy was studying into the wee hours and graduating with a three-point-fucking-eight GPA, the sons and daughters of the rich were getting drunk and stoned and screwing anything that moved, safe in the knowledge that plum jobs in their parents' firms or corporations waited for them regardless of their grades. Where was the justice in that, and what had all his hard work and sterling academic career gotten him? His rich classmates were raking it in as stockbrokers and lawyers; people who couldn't write their way out of a paper bag got the choice assignments at *World News* while he was making peanuts reporting on stories that would never earn him the reputation he deserved.

Levy forced himself to smile when he announced his presence to Brice's so-called executive assistant, Daphne St. John; though he was willing to bet this was not her real name. Daphne was a stuck-up bitch, who had turned down Dennis's offer of a drink shortly after she was hired. Memories of her incredulous refusal still burned, but he was damned if he'd let Brice's glorified receptionist know it.

"Mrs. Brice is on an *important* call," Daphne told him, clearly implying that Brice's meeting with him was not important. "Take a seat and I'll tell you when she's ready to see you."

Dennis planted himself on a sofa and fumed silently while he leafed through the latest issue of *World News*. He had just finished mentally editing another article on the Middle East poorly written by one of the senior hacks when Daphne told him he could enter Brice's inner sanctum.

Dennis was tall and gangly, with the pasty complexion low-paid reporters have when they only make enough to subsist on fast foods. His black hair was curly and his blue eyes were intense. He always seemed to be on edge and—though he was obviously very smart—he was slow to get jokes, because he lacked a sense of humor. Dennis was also socially inept. He had no sense of style and never felt comfortable in a restaurant that rated stars or at a function where a tuxedo was required.

Martha Brice was completely at home at Le Bernardin or a society gala. Dennis grudgingly conceded that she had a first-class mind, as evidenced by the diplomas from Yale and the Columbia University School of Journalism that hung on her wall, but she couldn't have been more than ten years older than he was and she was already the editor in chief of a major news magazine. What really bugged Dennis was that she'd gotten her position by marrying Harvey Brice, who owned *World News* and was at least twenty years her senior. Dennis couldn't really argue that she wasn't a good executive, but he felt that he was as qualified to run a major magazine as she was, and might be sitting in Martha's chair if he'd had the good fortune to be born to wealthy parents instead of the owner of a dry-cleaning establishment and a first-grade teacher.

Dennis also had to concede that Martha Brice was glamorous if, in his opinion, a bit overweight. Her heart-shaped face was framed by jet-black hair shaped in a bob, and she'd applied bright red lipstick to her thick, pouty lips. The lustrous hair and fire-engine mouth contrasted sharply with her pale white skin. Today, she was wearing a black Armani pants suit with a cream, man-tailored shirt. Tasteful black pearl teardrop earrings and a matching necklace told you that she was loaded but didn't have to broadcast the fact.

"Good to see you, Dennis," Brice said as she motioned him into a chair. "How are you getting along?"

Dennis had no idea what she was asking about. Did she want to know about his private life, or how he liked his job? He decided to play it safe.

"Fine," he answered.

"I've been keeping an eye on you and I'm very pleased with your work."

Dennis blushed. He was not used to praise.

"I know you haven't been given the most

challenging assignments," Brice continued, "but one way I gauge how dedicated
and competent my reporters are is to see
how they handle assignments I know won't
necessarily interest them. Now it's time for
you to take a step up. Are you interested?"

"Definitely," Dennis answered, sitting up
straight without realizing he was doing so.

"How old are you, Dennis?"

"Twenty-five."

"You would have been thirteen, twelve
years ago," Brice said, more to herself than
Dennis. "Do the names Charlie Marsh or
Gabriel Sun mean anything to you?"

Dennis frowned. "Didn't he start some
kind of New Age religion and then get
charged with murder?"

The editor nodded. "The press called
him 'Satan's Guru' and the case was plastered on the front page of every newspaper in America. Mr. Marsh first gained
notoriety during a prison standoff at the
state penitentiary when he saved a prison
guard's life. He was rewarded with an early
release and wrote a best-selling autobiography called *The Light Within You*, which
attributed his miraculous conversion from
petty criminal to hero and alleged humani-

tarian to the discovery of God's light within himself. The TV talk shows ate it up.

"Marsh started calling himself Gabriel Sun and hawking self-revelation and salvation through Inner Light seminars, which he held all over the country. Twelve years ago, United States congressman Arnold Pope Jr. was shot at one of these seminars. Marsh and the congressman's wife were charged with the murder and Marsh fled the country."

Brice slid a thick folder across her desk.

"This is background on the guru. It will give you enough information to conduct an interview with him."

Dennis flipped through the file, which was crammed with newspaper clippings and computer printouts.

"Marsh is hiding out in Africa, isn't he?" he asked, starting to remember facts about the subject of his story.

Brice nodded. "He's in Batanga."

Dennis frowned. "Isn't that the country that's ruled by a cannibal?"

"Those rumors about President Baptiste eating the ex-president's heart have never been verified. I suspect he spread them himself to scare the dickens out of anyone who was thinking of opposing him. But you can ask Mr. Marsh. I hear he knows the president very well."

"So, how am I doing this interview, by phone?"

Brice smiled warmly. "You know that's not how we conduct business at *World News*. I've booked you on a flight to Lagos, Nigeria, that leaves at seven tonight from JFK."

"This evening?"

"That's not a problem, is it?"

"No, no. I can leave tonight."

"Good. It's a short hop from Lagos to Baptisteville."

Dennis was stunned by his good fortune. He was flying to Africa to interview an international celebrity in a country ruled by a cannibal. How cool was that! And though he knew next to nothing about Charlie Marsh, he was a quick study. By the time he landed in Baptisteville, he'd be ready to rock and roll.

"Is there anything special you want me to discuss in the interview?" Dennis asked.

"Don't worry about the interview. Mr. Marsh will be returning to the States with you and you'll have plenty of time to talk to him."

Dennis frowned. "Isn't he still under indictment for murder?"

"Yes. That's why he's returning. He's always claimed he was innocent of the charges and he wants to clear his name."

"Wow! So this could be a really big story?"

"It *will* be a really big story, and it will be your story. Do you think you can handle it?"

"Definitely!"

"There could be a book in this, too. You'll see what I mean when you read through the file."

A book! A huge story and a book! Dennis was having trouble breathing.

"There is one thing, though," Martha said. She reached behind her desk and pulled out a valise that looked like it had gone through the wars. "When you pack I want you to use this suitcase."

"I have a nice valise at home."

"I'm sure it's much nicer than this but it doesn't have seventy-five thousand dollars concealed in it, does it?"

"Seventy-five . . ."

"Mr. Marsh is in great danger. He could be dead by the time you land, tomorrow. Hopefully, he'll be alive and you can give him this money, which will be used to aid his escape."

"This sounds dangerous," Dennis said warily.

"It is dangerous, but so is reporting in a war zone or flying into the eye of a hurricane. Top reporters court danger. I had you pegged as someone who would welcome the chance to take risks to land a story that could win a Pulitzer Prize. Was I wrong? If you think this is too big for you . . ."

"No, no, I can handle it, but won't Mr. Marsh be arrested when he lands in the States? Don't they check to see if you're a wanted criminal on the computers at Immigration when you fly in from a foreign country?"

Brice nodded. "That's why he'll be using a passport with another name."

"But that's illegal."

"Probably."

"I'll be arrested if I help him sneak into the country illegally."

"Perhaps, but we'd hire the best lawyers

for you. Besides, I suspect you'll be protected by the First Amendment."

"Is that true? Have you asked a lawyer
about that?"

"There wasn't any time. Mr. Marsh's life
is hanging by a thread. Do you want to
chance his being arrested, tortured, and
killed while we seek a legal opinion?"

"Of course not."

"Are you my man, Dennis, or should I
give this assignment to Shelby Pike?"

Shelby and Dennis had started at *World
News* at the same time. Dennis was of the
opinion that Pike was a talentless suck-up.
There was no way he was giving up this
chance at fame and fortune to Shelby Pike.

"I'm in, Mrs. Brice."

"Then you'd better hurry home and pack,"
Brice said.

BARBARA WALTERS: Why did you change your name to Gabriel Sun after you were released from prison?

CHARLIE MARSH: In the Bible, Gabriel is an angel who serves as a messenger from God and I felt that a greater power, be it God or Allah or whatever, had chosen me to be His messenger when Crazy Freddy tried to murder the hostages. And, of course, the sun is a symbol of the inner light that consumed me at my moment of truth.

WALTERS: What were you feeling when

Freddy stabbed you? Were you afraid you'd die?

MARSH: To the contrary. When Freddy stabbed me I was filled by my inner light and I was completely at peace. There was no fear, only love. And it's this experience that I want others to have so they can know that they have the power to change themselves for the better.

WALTERS: Many of the hostages said that you were able to convince Mr. Clayton, who was one of the most violent prisoners in the penitentiary, to stop his assault on the guard by telling him you loved him.

MARSH: That's true, Barbara. When I was infused by my inner light I learned that Love is the most powerful force in the universe, and that Love can overcome violence. And it isn't just violence that can be overcome once we learn how to turn on and harness our inner light, Barbara. As I explain in my seminars, when our inner light is on, it fuels the self-confidence that can make us successful in business, personal relationships, and every other aspect of life. And I'm very excited about the opportunities my seminars give me to help so many people succeed by learning how to harness this power that is in each and every one of us.

The seat-belt light flashed and a flight attendant announced the descent into Baptisteville International Airport. Dennis put the transcript of the twelve-year-old *Barbara Walters Special* interview back in Marsh's file, put the file in his flight bag, and glanced out the window. Wisps of vapor thickened into billowy, opaque clouds that hid the ocean from view. Then they were through the clouds and the plane swept over a vast expanse of clear blue water, a white sand beach, and a thick stand of emerald green palm trees. After a series of sharp bumps, the plane coasted to a stop in front of a long, one-story terminal.

A blast of thick, hot air struck Dennis when he stepped out of the plane and descended the portable staircase to the runway. As he crossed the tarmac, his shoes stuck to the asphalt and the humidity made his shirt cling to his body. Moving in the African heat was like swimming through glue, and he prayed that the terminal was air-conditioned.

The sun was so bright that Dennis was forced to shade his eyes. When he could see, he was overwhelmed by an onslaught of color. He had never seen so much green or a sky so blue, and everyone was black. The airline mechanics, the pilots and the flight attendants, and most of the passengers were black. So were the soldiers with their automatic weapons and the vast majority of the people waiting behind the plateglass windows in the arrivals area. Dennis was the oddly colored person here, and it made him feel a little uncomfortable.

The outside of the terminal had been painted a drab brown and the middle of one wall was taken up by a larger-than-life image of Jean-Claude Baptiste's smiling face, above which was the greeting, WELCOME TO BATANGA. The president's eyes seemed to focus on Dennis when he approached the building, as if Baptiste knew he was smuggling in money and a forged passport to help Charlie Marsh escape his grasp. Dennis had read stories about the atrocities committed in Batanga, and he felt sick and a little disoriented as he waited to go through customs. He imagined being taken from the line to a windowless, soundproof room where he would be strapped to an uncomfortable wooden chair by terrifying, steely-eyed interrogators and confronted with the money that had been found in the lining of his suitcase. But when it was his turn, a bored customs inspector asked him a few perfunctory questions before stamping his passport and waving him on.

Dennis hurried to reclaim his suitcase. He tried to stay calm as he waited for the baggage handlers to bring it from the plane but he found it difficult to keep from shifting in place and impossible to keep his head from swiveling this way and that looking for the policemen he felt certain were closing in on him. He also checked the crowd in the baggage claim area for Charlie Marsh, who was supposed to meet him at the airport and drive him to his hotel, but he saw no one who resembled the smiling, dreamy-eyed swami he'd seen in the photographs in the file.

Dennis spotted his suitcase and grabbed it, expecting to be pounced on any minute. When there was no pouncing, he carried the valise to the front of the terminal where groups of Batangans and a few expatriates were greeting his fellow travelers. A man detached himself from the wall and walked toward Dennis. He wore dark glasses, khaki pants, a sweat-stained T-shirt advertising Guinness Stout, sandals, and a baseball cap.

"You from *World News*?" he asked.

"Dennis Levy," Dennis answered with a smile of relief. He extended his hand. Charlie hesitated, then glanced around anxiously as he shook it. Charlie's grip was limp and disinterested and his palm was sweaty.

"Let's get out of here," he said, and headed for the door.

Dennis caught up with Charlie when he stopped at a rusty, dented, dirt-stained Volkswagen standing at the curb in a no-parking zone. Two policemen were standing next to the car. Dennis froze, certain that they were about to be arrested. Then Charlie slipped each cop some money and Dennis realized that they had been paid to watch the car. Charlie opened the trunk so Dennis could put his suitcase in it.

"Do you have the money?" Charlie asked as soon as they were in the car.

"Yes. It's in the lining of my suitcase."

"The full seventy-five?"

"It's all there."

"Thank God," Charlie intoned, closing his eyes briefly.

Moments later, they were careening down a two-lane highway just as the sun was starting to disappear behind a row of low green hills. Dennis waited for Charlie to say something else, but the subject of his future best-seller was concentrating on the road and seemed to have forgotten that there was a passenger in his car.

"Are we going to my hotel, Mr. Sun?" Dennis asked in an attempt to get a conversation going.

"Marsh, Charlie Marsh. Call me by my right name."

"So, you don't go by Gabriel Sun anymore?"

Charlie glared at him for a second before returning his eyes to the road in time to veer around a stray goat.

"Forget about all that Sun shit," he said when they were out of peril. "That's way in the past."

"Okay."

The Volkswagen drove by an outdoor market that had been set up in a clearing at the side of the road. Dennis shifted in his seat to take in the scene. Native women wrapped in multicolored cloth carried babies strapped to their backs while balancing baskets of fruit, rice, and fish on their heads. Men in khaki shorts and disintegrating T-shirts that hung in shreds from their well-muscled backs passed in front of wooden stalls selling red, yellow, and blue tins and boxes. Oddly, the goods in each stall appeared to be identical. Children played among the stalls. Some of the people on the roadside smiled and waved when the car flashed by. Dennis waved back. Marsh ignored them, jamming the heel of his hand on the horn if someone got too close, but never decreasing his speed.

"Look at those dumb bastards," he muttered.

Dennis gave Charlie an odd look. This wasn't going the way he'd expected. Marsh appeared to be an angry and frustrated man. Dennis wondered if he should make the reason for Marsh's anger and frustration the central theme of his interview. If Charlie Marsh had gone through a spiritual transformation during his years in Africa, Dennis's book would be even more interesting. He'd read the articles Martha Brice had included in the file, about the exciting prison standoff, Charlie's affair with the congressman's wife, and the murder case, so he knew the book would have sex, politics, and violence, but this could add a whole new intellectual layer to the biography that would engage the critics and those who voted for literary prizes.

AS THEY NEARED Baptisteville, clusters of huts constructed from mud and tin started to appear at uneven intervals. Occasionally, Dennis spotted a house built with concrete blocks, which vaguely resembled the ranch houses he'd grown up with in the suburbs. Behind the buildings, grassland stretched to the horizon. The foreign landscape captured Dennis's attention and he found himself asking Charlie questions about what he was seeing. Charlie answered his questions grudgingly and deflected any questions about subjects Dennis could use for the interview.

Dennis guessed that they'd reached the outskirts of the city when they passed the executive mansion, which reminded him of a casino he'd visited in Atlantic City. A few minutes later, the Volkswagen was stalled in traffic on a narrow, one-way street lined with two-story buildings. Balconies shaded the street-level stores. Through the open fronts, Dennis glimpsed shelves and display cases stocked with bolts of cloth and canned goods.

Throngs of people crowded the side-walks but it was rare to spot a white face. Horns honked and beggars supported by wooden staffs limped by. The traffic moved and the car drove out of the business district onto a sea-cliff drive. In the distance, at the top of the cliff was the fifteen-story Batanga Palace hotel, a stark, modern edifice that was the tallest building in the city.

"I'm going to tell you the facts of life," Charlie said as the hotel driveway came into view. "In Batanga everyone is a spy. You can't trust a soul. The average Batangan will sell his mother to the secret police for a few dollars. So, you don't talk to anyone about anything. Not the bellboy or the desk clerk, not anyone.

"Now, we've been followed since we left the airport. No, don't turn around. You won't be able to pick them out. When we pull up to the hotel, act natural. You're going to want to hang on to your suitcase, but that would be like waving a big sign that says, 'I've got something hidden in here.' So you let the bell man take the suitcase up to your room. Then you take the money out and put it in that flight bag you're carrying. After you do that, have a shower, which is the first thing a white man who hasn't been in Africa before would do when he got to his hotel. But keep your flight bag with you in the bathroom. As soon as you're changed, go down to the bar. Bring your flight bag with you. If you leave it in your room it's going to be searched."

"Are you going to meet me?"

"No. I'm out of here as soon as I drop you off. Now listen up. A big, bald white man will contact you. His name is Evers. You give him the money. He's going to fly us out of here, tonight."

"Tonight! But I just got here."

"And you're just going to leave. Evers is a mercenary. He's got a plane coming in on a bush airstrip a few miles outside the city. As soon as you give him the money he'll contact his partner and we'll all meet up at the strip."

"Is Evers going to take me there?"

"Hell, no. You don't want Baptiste's men

seeing you two together. All he's taking is the money."

"Then how will I get there?" Dennis asked anxiously.

"Ask the doorman at the hotel where the nightlife is, then have the doorman get you a taxi."

"Should I bring my suitcase?"

"Are you stupid? Who brings a suitcase to a bar? No, you don't bring your suitcase. You leave it in your room so no one thinks you're skipping out."

"Hey, back off, Charlie. I'm new to this cloak-and-dagger stuff."

"You'd better be a fast learner because one stupid move could cost you your life. Now pay attention. As soon as you're away from the hotel, tell the driver you've changed your mind and want to see an old friend. Give him these directions," Charlie said, slipping Dennis a piece of paper. "This will take you to the expatriate compound so it will look like you're visiting a white friend. When you get to the gate of the compound tell the driver to go two more miles. If he balks, slip him five dollars. He'll take you to the moon for that kind of tip. Watch the odometer. Just before it hits two miles, you'll see a dirt road off to the right. Take it a mile in and we'll be there."

"I don't know about this," Dennis said nervously.

"You have two choices. Do what I just told you and get out of this hellhole tonight, or use your return ticket to fly out tomorrow. The problem with choice number two is that you'll have to be in Batanga in the morning, by which time President Baptiste will know that I've flown the coop.

"Now ask yourself, who is the last person with whom I was seen and who do you think will be questioned about where I've gone? While the secret police are adjusting the voltage to the electrodes attached to your testicles, I'll be flying to freedom and you'll be wondering why you aren't with me."

"Attaching electrodes! They can't do that, can they? I'm an American citizen."

"You think Baptiste gives a shit? When he finds out I've escaped, he's going to want to hurt someone, and you're going to be the only one here."

6

The shower felt great. The cold water washed away the fatigue of travel and the layer of sweat that had caked his body ever since Dennis had stepped out of the plane into the African sun. The mere fact that he was in Africa was astonishing to someone who had never been farther than the East Coast of the United States. As Dennis toweled off, he thought about everything that had happened since he'd landed in Batanga. The events of the past hour both scared him to death and exhilarated him. The exhilarating part involved mercenaries, secret police, and the possibility of a thrilling escape in the night. The scary part involved the possibility that the escape would be thwarted by the secret police and he would end up with electrodes attached to his testicles. Dennis was terrified of being tortured, but he was more frightened of losing the most important story and the greatest professional opportunity of his life.

After he changed into fresh clothes, Dennis carried his money-filled flight bag to the bar, which was packed with expatriates and wealthy Batangans. Charlie had told him to order a piña colada, which would identify him to Evers as the person with the cash. Dennis found a table and put his flight bag between his feet so he could touch it. He was halfway through his drink when a gorgeous black woman in a short red dress sat next to him.

"That's an interesting drink you have there. What is it?" she asked.

"It's a piña colada."

"You like that drink?" she asked.

"Yes, I do. It's good."

"Is it sweet?"

"A little."

He felt a sudden pressure on his left

knee and the heat rose in his cheeks when he realized it was caused by the woman's hand.

"I can be good too and I'm sweeter than your drink. Do you want to taste me?"

Sweat formed on Dennis's brow, even though the hotel was heavily air-conditioned. He had very little sexual experience and a situation like this had never before presented itself. Every nerve in his body was urging him to answer in the affirmative and whisk this stunning woman up to his room. Then he remembered his Pulitzer Prize and why he was in the bar.

"If I wasn't meeting someone I'd gladly accept your offer. Maybe another night."

Rebecca leaned in close and lowered her voice. "Mr. Evers wants you to go to the garden by the pool after you finish your drink. Take the path that leads to the hut bar."

Dennis started to say something, but the woman touched his lips gently with her fingers.

"Maybe we will meet again tomorrow night, yes?" she said loud enough to be heard by anyone who was listening. Then Rebecca walked away, her hips swaying rhythmically in a manner calculated to attract the attention of every man in the bar. While all eyes were on Rebecca's backside, Dennis worked on his drink, hoping the alcohol would help him calm down. When he'd drained the glass dry, he left the bar through the door that led to the pool.

The temperature was in the eighties, but the air seemed cool in comparison to the 100-plus degree heat that had greeted Dennis at the airport. The back of the hotel was a tropical paradise. Lights illuminated oversize ferns, palm trees, a spectacular array of flowers, and several paths that led away from the pool into a garden. At the start of one path, a sign pointed toward a hut without walls that was covered by a thatched roof. A bar took up the center of the hut. Dennis was halfway down the path when he heard someone behind him. Before he could turn, a hand clamped down on the wrist that held the flight bag. Dennis's blood pressure skyrocketed.

"I'm Evers. Don't say a word. Just give me the bag and keep moving. Have a drink at the bar then head to the rendezvous."

Dennis released the bag and a huge,

bald man walked past him and disappeared into the garden. Dennis was still shaking when he sat at the bar. A stiff scotch helped him relax a little. When he'd finished it, he went to the front of the hotel and asked the doorman where to find some action in town. As soon as he was given the name of a few bars and the street they were on, Dennis asked the doorman to get him a cab. The doorman blew a whistle and a taxi pulled up. The cabbie was a big man wearing a dashiki decorated with a picture of Jean-Claude Baptiste. When Dennis got into the taxi, he turned his head toward the backseat.

"Where to, my friend?" he asked with a jovial grin.

"Lafayette Street."

"Ah, you are looking for fine Batangan women," the cabbie said with a knowing shake of his head.

"Maybe," Dennis answered nervously.

"I show you the best bars."

"Great."

"You are American?"

"Yes," Dennis answered tersely, remembering Charlie's admonition to talk to no one.

"Not too many Americans come Batanga way."

When Dennis didn't respond, the driver said, "I like Americans. They tip big." Then he laughed.

Dennis cast a few surreptitious glances out the back window of the taxi as it sped into town. He didn't see any cars following him.

"I've changed my mind," Dennis said. "I want to go to Idi Amin Beach."

"That trip more money," the cabbie said.

"That's okay."

The beach had originally been named after Batanga's first president, but President Baptiste had rechristened it in the name of his boyhood idol. The compound where many of the expatriates lived backed on it. The driver cut through a few side streets before turning onto Baptiste Boulevard, the main road out of the city.

"What kind work you do in America?" the driver asked.

"I write for a magazine."

"Ah, *Penthouse*, *Playboy*, they are good magazines."

"Actually, it's a news magazine. We report what's happening in the world."

The cabbie shook his head. "That's a good thing. It is wise to know about the world. Have you come to Batanga to write about our great country?"

"Uh, yes. The American people want very much to learn about Batanga."

"That's good. Batangans know much about America. We see the movies. Many gunfights and car chases. Have you ever been in a gunfight or a car chase?"

"That doesn't really happen. I mean, not often. They just put those in the movies to make them exciting. Most days of the year, it's pretty boring in America. Americans just get up and work and watch television and go to sleep. There's not much exciting going on."

"I would like a television. It would be a good thing to have. They show our great football team on TV."

The streetlights disappeared a mile past the executive mansion and the only hole in the dark night was created by the cab's headlights. By the time they were close to the expatriate compound, Dennis was starting to feel confident that he would escape from Batanga. The cabbie kept up a constant chatter and Dennis found himself talking too, because it helped him relieve his tension. When Dennis saw the wall that sealed off the expatriates from Batanga, he told the cabbie to go on for another two miles. The driver asked for more money and Dennis gave him five dollars as Charlie had instructed. The driver responded with a big grin and drove on. He almost missed the turnoff, but Dennis spotted it. The cab backed up and began to bounce as it moved slowly along the unpaved road.

Dennis began to worry when he didn't see anything that resembled an airstrip. Then the trees disappeared and Dennis spotted a Land Rover and Charlie's Volkswagen parked in the middle of an open field.

"Stop here," Dennis said.

The cab stopped and Dennis handed the driver the fare and a big tip.

"You want me to wait for you?" the driver asked.

"No, thanks. I've got a ride back to town."

Dennis got out and Charlie walked out of the shadows.

"So you decided to come along on our little adventure," he said to Dennis.

"I've never walked away from a story

yet," Dennis said, trying to sound like a hard-as-nails veteran reporter.

Charlie started to say something else when he noticed that the taxi had not moved.

"Did you tell him to go back to town?" he asked just as the cabbie stepped out of the taxi with a gun in his hand.

"Down on the ground," the driver commanded.

"Who . . . ?" Dennis started to ask just as the cabbie clubbed him with the gun.

"On the ground," the cabbie barked. Charlie dropped to the dirt and Dennis collapsed, dazed by the blow.

"Is anyone else here?" the cabbie asked as he scanned the darkness. Before Charlie could answer, the taxi driver's head exploded and red mist fanned out behind him.

"Fuck!" Charlie said as Chauncey Evers appeared, cradling a high-powered rifle outfitted with a night-vision scope.

Evers grabbed Dennis by the arm. As the mercenary pulled him to his feet, Dennis gawked at the dead cabbie. Then he threw up.

"Get your shit together," Evers said,

tightening the grip on Dennis's bicep. "Baptiste's men will be here any moment.

"Turn on the car lights and light the flares," Evers told Charlie. "We don't know how close the other bastards are and our ride is on its approach."

Evers released Dennis's arm. Dennis staggered a few steps. He felt woozy from the blow to his head. Something trickled down his cheek. When he took his hand away, it was covered with blood.

"I'm bleeding."

"For Christ's sake, grow up. Do you want to die here?"

Dennis stared at Evers.

"Well, you're going to if you don't get your ass in gear. There are a series of flares on either side of the runway and we've got to get them lit."

Charlie had already turned on the headlights of the Volkswagen and the Rover. He was lighting his second flare on one side of a narrow dirt airstrip when Dennis set off his first. Dennis was still nauseated from the blow to his head but he pushed through the pain and kept moving. Just after he set off the next flare he heard the faint sound of an aircraft approaching.

Seconds after all the flares were lit, a small plane dropped out of the sky. It didn't look much bigger than a pickup truck, and Dennis, who had flown infrequently and always in a commercial airliner, had trouble believing that this toy would be able to fly four grown men out of the jungle.

The makeshift runway was about 2,000 feet long and the plane bounced along the ground when it hit the dirt. As soon as it reached the end of the strip it made a U-turn.

Headlights appeared from the direction of the main road and Dennis heard car engines racing.

"Move," Evers barked. Dennis jumped into one of the two rear seats, next to Charlie. Seconds later, Evers was sitting next to the pilot and they were taxiing toward freedom.

Two black Mercedes burst onto the runway and followed the plane down the dirt strip. A gun poked out of the rear window of the lead car and Dennis saw a flash.

"Up!" Evers shouted.

The nose of the plane jerked skyward and they began a steep climb. Dennis was pinned to his seat and thought he would throw up again. Then they were in the clouds and Charlie was laughing hysterically.

"Thank you, thank you," he hollered, "and God bless America."

CHAPTER 7

At the height of her agony, Rebecca cried out to Jesus. Jean-Claude Baptiste nodded his approval. In addition to practicing an animistic tribal religion, the president of the republic hedged his bets by attending Roman Catholic mass regularly, and he approved of a woman who kept her faith under trying circumstances. The interrogator asked the bartender from the Mauna Loa another question. When he found her answer unsatisfactory he did something that caused her to scream again.

There was a knock on the door to his office and Baptiste turned down the intercom that was transmitting the interrogation from the basement. Baptiste liked to conduct his own question-and-answer sessions in person when he could, but his position as president didn't leave him much free time, so he'd learned to delegate and made do with listening to important interrogations over the intercom.

The door opened and Nathan Tuazama entered. He was dressed in a tan business suit, a light blue silk shirt, and a forest green tie. Most men trembled in Baptiste's presence but Tuazama was a man whom Baptiste feared. This was due to a dream Baptiste had had many years ago that featured him and Tuazama. In it, both men were being menaced by a lion in a clearing in the jungle, but the lion appeared to be unable to choose between them. Every time the lion headed toward Baptiste he grew confused, changed direction, and headed for Tuazama. Then, just as he was about to pounce on Nathan, he would again grow confused and start toward the president. In the dream, the lion was never able to make a decision about which Batangan would be his dinner.

Baptiste had told Nathan about the

dream. Then he had consulted an old man in his village, who was a magician. The day before the consultation, Tuazama paid the old man twenty dollars. The Juju man listened intently as the president recounted his dream. Then he read the entrails of a goat and revealed that the fates of Baptiste and Tuazama were inextricably entwined. Since then Baptiste had been very solicitous of Tuazama's well-being and Tuazama had done everything he could to encourage Baptiste in the belief that he would stay alive as long as the chief of his secret police was well cared for.

"Sit down and listen for a few moments, Nathan."

There was another scream followed by another plea to Jesus for mercy.

"She is strong," Baptiste said.

Tuazama shrugged. "That's true, but she'll tell us what we want to know eventually. In any event, this interrogation may be unnecessary. I believe I've figured out what happened and where Charlie has gone."

Baptiste leaned forward, eager for the information.

"The night of the banquet at the mansion, Charlie sent an e-mail to *World News*, an American magazine, offering to give an interview. A few days later, a mercenary named Chauncey Evers met with Charlie in the Mauna Loa, where the bartender works. The man who saw this thought that Evers was a harmless drunk and didn't bother to report the meeting. He has been dealt with.

"Yesterday, Charlie picked up an American journalist named Dennis Levy at the airport. Levy works for *World News* and he was on the plane that flew Charlie out of the country. After driving in from the airport, Charlie dropped Levy at the Batanga Palace, where Evers was staying. My guess is that the bartender put Charlie in touch with Evers and Charlie arranged to have Evers take him to the United States."

"But Charlie's a wanted man in America."

"He's not stupid, Mr. President. He had to know you'd figured out that he was Bernadette's lover. He knows what would have happened to him if you decided to punish his transgression. I'm guessing he chose American justice over yours. And then, of course, there is the matter of the diamonds. A child went to Marsh's apartment yesterday. I suspect Rebecca will eventually confess that she sent the child to Charlie with the diamonds."

"Where does this Levy fit in?"

"Charlie is running out of money. I've checked. Evers doesn't come cheap. I'm guessing that *World News* paid Charlie for the interview and he used the fee to pay Evers. Levy probably smuggled the money into the country."

Baptiste stared straight ahead and Tuazama waited patiently.

"I underestimated Charlie," the president said. "I should have given him to you sooner. I want you to handle this matter personally. Go to America and bring back the diamonds."

"And Charlie?"

"Charlie's not important. He's nothing to me anymore. It's the principle of the thing now, Nathan. If I let Charlie get away with this everyone will think I am weak. So, find what he's taken then make an example of him that will grab the attention of the next traitor who thinks about crossing me."

CHAPTER

8

Amanda Jaffe's phone woke her out of a deep sleep. She groped for it after the third ring.

"Hello," she mumbled groggily as soon as she located the receiver.

"Is this Amanda Jaffe?"

"Who is this?"

"My name is Martha Brice. I'm the editor in chief of *World News*."

Shit, a reporter, Amanda thought as she swung her legs over the side of the bed and brushed her long black hair away from her face. Amanda's boyfriend, Mike Greene, the chief criminal deputy at the Multnomah

County District Attorney's office, had spent the night with her at her condo because neither of them had a meeting or court appearance until noon. Amanda had been looking forward to sleeping in, for a change.

"Do you know what time it is, Ms. Brice?"

"That's Mrs. Brice, and since its seven a.m. in New York, it must be four where you are," the woman answered calmly.

"Is there some reason you couldn't call me at my office at a civilized hour?"

"Actually, there is. I'm in my corporate jet headed for Oregon. I should be at the airport in four hours. I want to meet with you as soon as I land."

Brice's imperious tone acted like a double shot of espresso.

"Look, Mrs. Brice," Amanda snapped, "I don't try my cases in the press, and if you think the best way to get an interview with me is to wake me up in the middle of the night, you should take a refresher course at whatever journalism school you attended."

"You must not have understood me, Ms. Jaffe. I'll chalk that up to my waking you. I'm not a reporter. I am *the* editor in chief of *World News*. I run the magazine. I don't conduct interviews. I'm flying to Portland to hire you to work on a case; one that I'm certain you'll want to handle."

"What case?"

"I don't wish to discuss the particulars over the phone."

Amanda was quiet for a moment. She didn't like Brice's attitude, but she was intrigued.

"I'll be in my office by the time you land," she said.

"I won't have time to drive into town. I have an important meeting in New York, later today. I'd like you to meet me at my plane. There's a conference area on board. There's also a galley, so I can provide breakfast. Am I correct that you're partial to blueberry pancakes?"

Amanda's mouth opened in surprise. "If that was meant to impress me, you've succeeded."

"I'm afraid you're too easily impressed. One of my assistants Googled you. I obtained that piece of information from an interview you gave to one of my competitors after the *Cardoni* case."

"That was a few years ago."

"Don't tell me you're on a diet."

Amanda laughed. "No, Mrs. Brice, and your offer of blueberry pancakes has served its purpose. I'll need the carbs to get me through the day, since I'm going to be sleep-deprived."

"Come to the Flightcraft FBO at eight."

"FBO?"

"It means fixed base operator. Think terminal. Jennifer Gates, my administrative assistant, will be waiting in the lounge and she'll escort you on board. One more thing. Don't tell anyone about our meeting."

"You don't want anyone to know you're coming to Portland?"

"That is correct. You'll understand why when I tell you about the case," Brice answered just before she broke the connection.

Amanda flopped onto her back so she could gather the strength to get up and get dressed. She found Mike lying on his side, watching her. As chief criminal deputy in the Multnomah County District Attorney's office, Mike had led many of the county's high-profile murder cases and they'd met when he prosecuted the *Cardoni* case, which almost cost Amanda her life. They'd had an on-again, off-again relationship ever since.

If they weren't so busy, she and Mike might have had time to figure out where that relationship was going.

Mike had blue eyes, curly black hair, and a shaggy mustache. Because he was a bulky six-five, he was frequently mistaken for someone who played college football or basketball—sports in which the cerebral DA had never engaged. Instead, Amanda's boyfriend competed in chess tournaments and was good enough on the tenor sax to play professionally.

"I guess we're not eating breakfast together," Mike said.

"Sorry," Amanda said, "duty calls."

"A new case?"

"Yup."

"What's it about?"

"I don't know, and I can't tell you the identity of the client, so don't ask."

"*Mrs. Brice* must be rich," Mike said with a grin.

"Please forget you heard that name or I will not have sex with you until the next millennium."

Mike laughed.

"And how did you know she was rich?"

"Yours truly knows what an FBO is. Don't

forget, I practiced law in LA. So, she's flying in on a private jet, huh."

"Mike," Amanda warned.

Greene laughed again. Then he looked at the clock on the nightstand. "What time do you have to be at the airport?"

"Eight."

Mike snaked an arm across Amanda's stomach. "I'm going to have trouble getting back to sleep," he said as his hand moved slowly to Amanda's breast.

Amanda rolled toward Mike. Being jerked out of sleep always jangled her nerves and she did have plenty of time to shower and dress.

"All men are pigs who only think about one thing," she said.

Mike grinned and answered with the most valuable phrase he'd learned in law school: "Assuming that's true, what's wrong with it?"

IT WAS HOT for a Portland summer and Amanda had the air conditioning cranked up as she drove along the freeway to Airport Way, the road that led to Portland International Airport. Just before the road curved toward the parking garage for the

main terminal and the arrivals and depar-
tures areas, she saw a sign that read BUSI-
NESS AVIATION and turned into a parking lot
that fronted the Flightcraft FBO, a one-story
steel-and-glass building that acted as the
terminal for private aircraft. Inside were a
few rows of seats and a check-in desk.
When Amanda entered, an attractive brunette with bouncy, shoulder-length hair
stood up. She was wearing a blue pinstripe
pants suit, a white silk shirt, and a strand of
white pearls and looked very businesslike
as well as very elegant.

Amanda was good-looking, but no one
would call her elegant. Years of competitive swimming had given her broad shoulders and a muscular build she kept hard
by continuing the workouts that had made
her a PAC-10 champion and given her a
shot at an Olympic berth. Her figure was
nothing like that of a fashion model, but it
still attracted men.

"Ms. Jaffe?"

Amanda nodded. The woman held out
her hand and they shook.

"I'm Jennifer Gates, Mrs. Brice's assistant. Mrs. Brice is waiting for you."

"Pleased to meet you, Jennifer. Lead on."

A sleek white Gulfstream G550 with the *World News* logo stenciled on its fuselage waited on the tarmac a short distance from the terminal. Amanda climbed a set of steps and walked into an interior unlike that of any plane in which she'd ever flown. The floor was covered with a deep beige carpet you'd expect to find in a Manhattan penthouse and the walls were paneled in dark wood. There were fourteen roomy seats upholstered in tan leather, one of which had been converted into a neatly made bed. Midway back from the cockpit was an oak conference table with a single place setting consisting of a monogrammed linen napkin, a crystal glass filled with ice water, another glass for the orange juice in a crystal pitcher, and silverware that Amanda was willing to bet was real silver.

Amanda had gone to college in the Bay Area and law school in Manhattan, so she wasn't totally ignorant of fashion, but the woman sitting across from the solitary setting was obviously an expert. She wore black Manolo Blahnik slingback pumps, black crepe pants, and a gray tweed Donna

Karan belted jacket with black trim. A gold link necklace graced her neck, gold earrings dangled from her ears, and she told time on a Cartier tank watch. Next to her on an empty seat was a large black leather Prada hobo bag. Brice's nails were manicured, her makeup was perfect, and her hair looked as if a stylist had just worked on it. No one would ever guess that she'd flown a redeye cross-country.

"Thank you for coming, Ms. Jaffe," Brice said.

"Nifty wheels," Amanda answered as she completed her survey of the Gulfstream's interior.

"I like it. Can I offer you orange juice, coffee?"

Amanda slid into the seat with the place setting. "Orange juice would be great, and I bet your chef can whip up a latte."

"Single or double?" Brice asked as an amused smile creased her lips.

Amanda smiled back. "A double, please."

Brice looked up at Jennifer Gates, who poured Amanda a glass of orange juice then walked to the back of the plane to place her order for a latte.

"Now that I'm suitably impressed, do you want to tell me what's going on?"

"Do the names Gabriel Sun or Charlie Marsh mean anything to you?"

"Satan's Guru! Of course I know who he is. The trial of Sally Pope was my father's biggest case."

"Mr. Marsh is returning to Oregon to face the charge that he murdered Congressman Arnold Pope Jr. I would like you to represent him. You'll be paid a five-hundred-thousand-dollar retainer. If the retainer is insufficient to cover your time, additional fees will be provided."

Amanda had been given some large retainers, but nothing like this. It took all of her courtroom training to keep her excitement from showing.

"Why is *World News* willing to fund Gabriel Sun's defense?" she asked.

"It's not. Do you remember Mr. Marsh's best-seller?"

"*The Light Within You*? Of course. I was in college when my father defended Sally Pope. I'll bet every student at Berkeley read that book."

"I've negotiated a contract with Charlie's old publisher on his behalf for a new book;

an autobiography that will take up where his first book left off. Charlie will tell all about the shooting at the Westmont Country Club, his flight to Africa, his life in Batanga, and his trial—the trial you will conduct."

Brice leaned forward slightly and locked eyes with Amanda.

"There's no question that Charlie's new book will be a best-seller. Everyone in America will read it, and you will become the best-known criminal defense attorney in the country. Are you interested, Ms. Jaffe?"

Brice leaned back and let her pronouncement sink in.

"Of course I'm interested," Amanda said just as Brice's chef appeared with her pancakes. Jennifer Gates was following a few steps behind, carrying Amanda's latte.

The *Pope* case had made her father's reputation. The trial of Sally Pope and the continuing saga of Charlie Marsh's flight to Africa had dominated the airwaves for more than a year. Amanda was already famous in Oregon—and she was known in professional circles outside of the state—but she would become a household name in every state in the Union if she defended Satan's Guru.

"What's your relationship to Charlie Marsh?" Amanda asked as she poured hot maple syrup over the stack.

"It's strictly professional."

"Then what are you getting out of this?" Amanda asked before taking her first bite.

"Exclusive access. He's agreed to speak only to *World News* and to permit us to embed one of our reporters in your defense team during the trial."

Amanda lowered her fork. "Whoa, wait a minute. What would this reporter be doing?"

"His name is Dennis Levy. He's a very competent young man. I think you'll like him."

"You haven't answered my question, Mrs. Brice. What do you envision Levy doing during the trial?"

"I envision him being a fly on the wall. He'll be present in court, of course, but he'll also sit in on strategy meetings, your conferences with Mr. Marsh, interviews with witnesses. Then he'll also do one-on-one interviews with you and your team. We'll have an edge on every other newspaper, magazine, and TV news program."

"We may have a problem. I can't have your reporter setting out my strategy in your magazine for everyone in the DA's office to read."

"Of course not. Dennis won't do anything to compromise Mr. Marsh's case."

"And he's not going to be able to sit in on my meetings with Mr. Marsh. He's not an attorney so he's not covered by the attorney-client privilege. If a third party is present during a conversation I have with Mr. Marsh, the privilege disappears. Your reporter could be called as a prosecution witness and be forced to testify about everything Mr. Marsh said to me in confidence."

"What about his First Amendment protections as a member of the press?"

"I'm not an expert in this area, but I'm pretty certain the courts have held that the First Amendment doesn't protect a reporter in these circumstances."

"I'll have my legal staff look into the question. Again, I'm not going to do anything that could hurt Mr. Marsh's chances at an acquittal."

"Mr. Levy would have to follow my instructions. I'm going to want to review his articles before they're published to make sure nothing he writes will tip our hand or reveal a confidence."

"I think we can work that out. So, are you on board?"

"I'm definitely interested, but I may have a conflict. You know that my father—Frank Jaffe—represented Sally Pope, Mr. Marsh's codefendant?"

Brice nodded.

"As I said, I was in college when the trial was held, but we're partners now and I have to make certain that no conflict exists."

"Mrs. Pope was acquitted, wasn't she?"

"The case was dismissed with prejudice, in the middle of the trial. The legal effect is the same."

"So where's the problem?"

"There may not be one, but I have to make certain. If there is none, I'll definitely take the case. That is, if Mr. Marsh wants me as his lawyer. You understand that you won't be my client, he will. If he wants me, I'm in."

"Good."

"Where is Mr. Marsh now?"

"En route to New York. He'll stay in an apartment *World News* owns."

"You're not going to announce his return,

are you? I don't want the district attorney to know where he is. He'd have him arrested."

"I have no intention of letting anyone know that Mr. Marsh is back in the States until you tell me it's okay."

"Good. The first thing I'll do, as soon as I'm certain I can take the case, is to arrange Mr. Marsh's voluntary surrender. This will give me time to set up a bail hearing. I don't want him in jail while we're preparing for trial if I can prevent it."

Brice reached into her hobo bag and pulled out an envelope. She handed it to Amanda.

"This is your retainer and a list of phone numbers that will reach me. Let me know as soon as possible about the conflict problem."

"I'll want to speak to Mr. Marsh immediately, once I'm on board."

"I'll send the jet for you and you can meet in New York, if you'd like."

Amanda ran her hand over the leather-upholstered seat. "I might just take you up on that if you throw in another free breakfast. These pancakes are delicious."

CHAPTER

9

Amanda could barely contain her excitement as she drove to her office. She'd been involved in some big cases that had gained national attention, like *Cardoni*—the serial killer case—and the *Dupre* matter, which had involved the murder of a United States senator. But the attention *State v. Charles Marsh* would garner would be on a whole different plane. Her life would be turned upside down, but it would be worth it for the chance to be part of history.

Then there was the personal reason for taking the case. What a coup it would be if she cleared Marsh's name the same way her father had cleared Sally Pope's.

Amanda parked in her lot and walked through the waves of rolling heat to the Stockman Building, a fourteen-story office building in the heart of downtown Portland. Jaffe, Katz, Lehane and Brindisi leased the entire eighth floor. As soon as Amanda checked for messages at the front desk, she went to her father's office.

Frank Jaffe was a big man in his late fifties, with a ruddy complexion and curly hair that was starting to show more gray than black. His nose had been broken twice in his youth during brawls, and he looked more like a criminal than a doctor of jurisprudence. Frank's spacious corner office was decorated with antiques and dominated by a huge desk he'd bought at an auction soon after opening his practice. Over the years, the desk top had been scarred by cigarette burns, paper-clip scratches, and coffee stains that were hard to spot, because almost every inch was covered by law books, stacks of paper, or files.

Amanda announced herself by tapping on Frank's doorjamb. He looked up from the draft of the legal memo on which he was working.

"What's the reason for the smile that's plastered across your puss?" Frank asked.

Amanda plopped herself down on one of the two client chairs that stood on the other side of Frank's desk.

"Why do you think I was given this?" Amanda asked, tossing the retainer check toward Frank. He stared at the check for a moment. Then he whistled. Amanda's smile widened.

"Did you win the lottery?" he asked.

"Sort of. I've just been hired to defend the case of the century."

"Enough already," Frank said, unable to contain a grin. "Out with it. What case is big enough to warrant this type of retainer?"

"Charlie Marsh is returning home to stand trial for the murder of Arnold Pope Jr."

Frank stopped smiling. "You're kidding!"

"I'm dead serious. He's on his way back to the States from Africa as we speak. *World News* magazine is going to put him up in New York until I can arrange for his surrender."

"How is he paying you?"

Amanda told her father about the book

deal and Martha Brice's expectations regarding *World News*' exclusive coverage of the case. When his daughter finished, Frank frowned.

"I don't like this business with the reporter."

"Me either, but I can control him, and Brice agreed to my restrictions."

"Or said she did. From what you've told me, she's the type who will promise the world and not mean a word of it. She'll count on you not being able to give up a half million dollars once it's in your account. When she has you involved she'll push the envelope."

"Or try to. I made it clear that Charlie is my client, not she. And I hope you know I can handle the Martha Brices of this world."

"That I do, but it won't be easy, and you've never been involved in a media circus like the one you're about to encounter. It can be intoxicating. How many world-class lawyers have you seen turn into fools as soon as they were given a chance to pontificate on national television?"

"Point taken, but you forget that I'll have a wise old mentor to guide me while I'm on my journey along the yellow brick road. I'm sure I can count on you to pour a bucket of cold water on me if I start acting like a jackass."

Frank smiled. He'd have the bucket ready, but—knowing his daughter as he did—he doubted he'd ever have to use it.

"I have two requests, Dad," Amanda said. "Can you fill me in on the *Pope* case? I read the papers and saw some of it while you were trying it, and we talked a little, but that was twelve years ago and I could do with a refresher course."

"You want me to do that now?"

"Give it a shot."

"I don't know if I can, off the top of my head. Look, I do have to finish this memo. So why don't we order in and talk in the conference room at lunch? I'll have the file brought up from storage. That will give me time to think."

"Fair enough."

"You said you had two requests. What the second?"

"It dawned on me that we might have a conflict problem. I haven't talked to the bar yet, but I'll be representing a codefendant of someone you represented. She can't be charged again, but I can still imagine problems. So, I wondered if you would get Sally Pope to sign a waiver."

"That shouldn't be a problem," Frank said, his face displaying none of the emotions that the thought of seeing Sally Pope evoked.

Frank and Amanda talked for a while more. Then Frank told her that he needed to get back to his memo and she went to her office. Frank did have to finish the memo but he really wanted time alone to deal with the possibility that he would have to see Sally Pope again. She'd been out of his life for a long time but there were still scars.

Frank leaned back in his chair and stared out of his window at the green hills that towered over downtown Portland. The sky was clear and blue and dotted with white clouds; a tranquil scene that was at odds with the emotions boiling up inside him. Thinking about Sally Pope was painful, so Frank turned his attention to Charlie Marsh. Frank's client may have been Sally Pope but the trial had always been about Marsh, and Charlie's story began with the prison standoff.

PART II

*State of Oregon
v. Sally Pope* 1996–1997

10

Minutes before Crazy Freddy Clayton started his hare-brained attempt to escape from the state prison, he and Charlie Marsh were working on a writ of habeas corpus at a table in the rickety wooden stacks that held the prison library's woefully inadequate collection of legal texts. The cellmates were best friends and a truly odd couple. They were dressed in identical prison Levi's and blue work shirts, and they were both a shade under six feet but that was where the similarities ended.

Charlie had blond hair and no tattoos. Freddy had shaved his head and resembled an art gallery when naked. Charlie was looking at parole in a few weeks on a three-year sentence for credit card fraud. Crazy Freddy was serving consecutive twenty-year terms for attempted murder and armed robbery and would be using a walker by the time he left the prison. Charlie had pumped a little iron since beginning his incarceration but the muscle he'd added to his slender frame was difficult to discern. During his many incarcerations, Freddy had developed bulging, well-defined lats, abs, pecs, and biceps by following a workout regime that bordered on the psychotic. Crazy Freddy *was* psychotic so the effort hadn't cost him much.

While Freddy lived for violence, Charlie was a pacifist for practical reasons; he was a coward who had lost almost every fight in which he'd been involved. In fact, if it weren't for Freddy, Charlie would have been one of the most picked-on boys in school and someone's bitch in the prison. But Freddy had grown up next door to Charlie and they'd been best friends since elementary school. Charlie hid Freddy in his house whenever Clayton's drunken father went on a rampage, and he'd helped

Freddy—who was not too bright—with his schoolwork from day one. Freddy reciprocated by beating the crap out of anyone who dared to pick on his friend. It was amazing, but Freddy—a true paranoid—trusted Charlie. When he found out Charlie was headed for his lockup, he'd made certain that the inmates knew that his pal was off-limits and he had arranged to bunk with him.

Like most sociopaths, Freddy was convinced that he was highly intelligent and he was constantly coming up with "brilliant" ideas for overturning his convictions. These were the kind of ideas that never held up under close scrutiny, but Freddy rarely had his ideas scrutinized, because no one had the courage to argue with him. Debate was useless anyway, since Freddy would pound his critic into pulp when Freddy grew frustrated over his inability to understand the critic's logic. Charlie never suggested directly that his friend's ideas were stupid. Freddy had never touched him in anger during all the years they'd been pals, but it was always better to play it safe where Freddy was concerned.

"I'm not finding anything," Charlie said.

He'd been reading cases in which the courts overturned convictions because of incompetence of counsel.

"Look harder. There's gotta be something about it in them books."

"I don't know, Freddy," Charlie said cautiously. "I just don't see the Supreme Court overturning your conviction because the guy peed a lot."

"Listen, man, you ever have to go real bad?"

"Sure."

"How well are you thinking when you got to go real bad?"

"It is distracting."

"That's my point. The motherfucker was peeing at every recess, and those court sessions were *long*. How the fuck is he gonna be concentrating on my case when he has to pee so bad? When that snitch motherfucker Jermaine was testifying against me, my lawyer was twitching and wiggling around so much I thought he was gonna fall off his motherfucking chair. I bet he didn't hear a word that lying motherfucker said. Now that's motherfucking incompetence, ain't it?"

"Well, yes, it would be like falling asleep.

There are cases where the courts have held that a defendant didn't receive an adequate defense when his lawyer fell asleep during the trial."

"See, now you're thinking."

"An incontinence defense would certainly be revolutionary."

"A what?"

"Incontinence. It means the guy can't hold it in, he wets himself. This might lead the Supreme Court to order all lawyers to wear Depends."

Freddy smiled. "I like that."

It was at this moment that warden Jeffrey Pulliams entered the library with prison guard Larry Merritt and three librarians from the county library system—Mabel Brooks, Ariel Pierce, and Jackie Schwartz. Warden Pulliams was a chubby, balding optimist who believed in rehabilitation. During his tenure, he had striven to build ties between the prison and the community to aid the transition of ex-convicts from incarceration to a productive life in society. This tour was part of the warden's outreach program. It was his hope that the librarians would not only send books to the prison, but would also help promote the literacy and creative writing courses he had introduced into the prison curriculum.

Freddy Clayton was well known to the warden. They'd had a heart-to-heart talk each time the inmate had been released from solitary. The warden believed in the basic goodness of man and he never gave up on one of his charges. He was very pleased to find Freddy in a library. Of course, Crazy Freddy was not interested in outreach or broadening his mind. His main interest in life was getting out of prison in any way possible. He believed that the fortuitous appearance of the three lady librarians presented him with a faster way of achieving this goal than pursuing a writ of habeas corpus through the courts.

"Ladies," Warden Pulliams said, "I'd like you to meet Frederick Clayton and . . . ?"

"Charles Marsh, sir," Charlie said when it was obvious that the warden had no idea who he was.

"Of course, Mr. Marsh. These women are librarians and I'm giving them a tour of our facility. Would you like to explain how important this library is to you?"

Charlie stood up but Freddy stayed seated.

"A well-stocked library is essential in a prison," Charlie said. "As you may imagine, ladies, prisoners have a lot of idle time, and idle hands are the Devil's workshop. This library enables us to put our idle time to good use."

While Charlie's bullshit answer was enchanting the warden, Freddy bent down and pulled a shiv out of his sock.

"I couldn't have expressed it better, Mr. Marsh," the warden said with a wide smile, which vanished instantly when Freddy yanked Jackie Schwartz away from the group and pressed the razor-sharp blade of his prison-made knife against her jugular vein.

"What are you doing?" Charlie yelled.

"I'm getting me the fuck out of here," Freddy told his friend. Then he turned his attention to the warden.

"I'll gut this bitch if you don't do exactly what I say. Do you understand me, motherfucker?"

"Mr. Clayton . . ." the warden began.

"Shut the fuck up. I do the talking here. Anyone says a word and I start cutting. Now get the fuck over to the storeroom."

Freddy nodded his head toward the far

wall, where a door opened on a storage area that contained cleaning supplies, extra books, and odds and ends.

The guard started sliding his hand toward his nightstick.

"I saw that," Freddy said, sliding his blade an inch to the right. A thin trickle of blood dribbled down the hostage's throat. Mabel Brooks gasped.

"Shut the fuck up, bitch, and you, drop the stick and start moving. Next time you move funny she dies and I just start stabbing until someone brings me down."

The warden had read Clayton's file several times and knew he would kill without remorse.

"Do as he says," Pulliams ordered in a shaky voice as he started walking toward the storage room.

The other inmates who were using the library had heard the commotion and they wandered over as Freddy herded his hostages through the stacks.

"Get out," Freddy commanded. "You don't want to be in here."

The men didn't stop to think. Charlie started to follow them but Freddy stopped him.

"Not you, Charlie. I need you with me, bro."

Charlie's heart sank. He was just weeks away from parole. Now Freddy was making him an accomplice in crimes that could keep him behind bars forever.

As soon as the hostages were inside the storeroom, Freddy looked around. His eyes stopped on a large spool of cord.

"Tie them up, Charlie."

"Maybe we should . . ."

"Nah, we got to tie them up so they won't cause trouble."

Freddy used the shiv to cut several lengths of rope. While Charlie was tying up the hostages, Freddy's eyes roamed the room. When everyone but Jackie Schwartz was secure and seated on the floor, Freddy turned the quivering woman over to Charlie and inspected several cans of paint that were stored in a corner of the room. Next to the paint cans were several tins of paint thinner, which bore labels warning that the product was hazardous and flammable.

Freddy searched the warden and the guard but didn't find what he was looking for. Then he collected the women's handbags and searched through them. He smiled when he found a pack of cigarettes in Mabel Brooks's bag and grinned broadly when he discovered her lighter.

"This is just what I need," Freddy said. He walked over to the painting supplies and carried one of the tins of paint thinner over to the spot against the wall where Charlie had lined up the hostages.

"This here's my insurance," Freddy told Charlie. Then he turned to the hostages. "You all are gonna get a bath. I see anyone try to escape . . ."

Freddy flicked the lighter. Mabel Brooks stared at the tiny flame and started to weep, and Jackie Schwartz was white-faced from shock.

Freddy opened the tin and doused the woman. Then he moved to the next hostage. When he was done, Charlie pulled him aside and whispered so the hostages wouldn't hear him.

"Freddy, this isn't good. Maybe you should stop now. No one's been hurt too badly. Maybe we can convince the warden to let bygones be bygones if you let everyone loose."

"Warden ain't gonna forgive and forget,

are you?" Freddy asked Pulliams. The warden didn't answer.

"That's what I thought. Nah, Charlie, we're in this for the long haul. It'll be freedom or death."

"I got freedom coming up, Freddy. I'm gonna get paroled real soon. How about letting me walk on this?"

"Can't do it, bro. You know I ain't good at expressing myself."

"You talk fine. You're a bright guy."

"Not like you, Charlie. I wouldn't know the words. I'm gonna need you to talk for me."

Charlie glanced over at the women. They were terrified. The guard was trying hard to stay cool, but Warden Pulliams was sweating badly. Charlie felt sorry for them. He also felt sorry for himself and pissed off at Freddy for getting him into this mess.

Charlie's relationship with Freddy was complicated. They were best friends, but Charlie disapproved of almost everything Freddy did. If it weren't for the bonds they'd forged since childhood, Charlie would have stayed miles from Clayton. Still, there was no denying that he would have been badly injured several times if Freddy hadn't protected him, so he did owe Freddy for that. If Freddy released him to negotiate he could run, but that would probably mean that the hostages would die or a SWAT team would come in blazing and Freddy would die, and he didn't want that on his conscience.

"Okay, bro. I'll help you out here, but you have to promise me that you won't hurt anyone."

"Hey, if someone gets out of line, I'll draw the line."

"True enough, but I'll have a hard time selling your program if I can't assure the negotiators that all of the hostages are un-harmed."

"I see your point."

"Great. So, what's your plan?"

This was a difficult question for Freddy to answer, since he had acted on impulse without a strategy.

"Well, we tell the motherfuckers to let us out of here or we kill *these* mother-fuckers."

"Okay, that's a start, but where do you want to go once you're out?"

This was an even tougher question.

Freddy hadn't been too many places besides prison. Then he remembered a television show that had featured a hostage
situation.

"A tropical island, man. I want to go to
a tropical island. And I want a jet and one
million . . . nah, make it two million dollars."

Charlie nodded several times. "That
sounds doable," he lied.

A tentative knock on the storeroom door
startled everyone.

"Get the fuck back, motherfucker, or
I'll start cutting on these bitches," Freddy
yelled.

"It's me, Jack Collins," the trustee librarian answered in a shaky voice. Collins was
a seventy-year-old lifer who had been a
fifty-two-year-old bookstore owner until he
shot his brand-new, twenty-year-old wife
and her lover. "They told me to talk to you,
Freddy."

"What do they want?" Freddy asked.

"They want you to let everyone go. They
won't hurt you if everyone's okay."

"You tell them I ain't letting anyone out
until my demands are met. If they don't
meet my demands, people are gonna die.

I got them all covered with paint thinner. If I don't get what I want we're gonna have an old-fashioned barbecue in here."

"What . . . what do you want?"

"My man, Charlie, knows our demands. Who's out there with you?"

"Nobody. Just me."

"You better be telling the truth or we're gonna have crispy-fried librarian for dinner."

"Don't hurt anyone, Freddy. Okay? I'm the only one in the library."

"I'm sending out Charlie. He'll tell them what we want. And I'd better get it."

"Is Freddy insane?" Collins asked when he and Charlie were far enough from the storeroom so Freddy couldn't hear him through the door.

"Are you referring to his mental state or his plan?" Charlie answered bitterly.

"The question was rhetorical," said Collins, who knew that Freddy was a head case and that Charlie knew what "rhetorical" meant.

"I don't know why Freddy does this shit," Charlie complained. "But then neither does he, half the time."

"Well, you better do something. McDermott's in charge. He's got the prison locked down and SWAT is on the way."

Michael McDermott, the assistant warden, was a deeply religious man, who had started as a guard and worked his way up to his present position as second in command. McDermott despised Warden Pulliams and he hated the inmates. He had no faith in rehabilitation and viewed incarceration as punishment for sin. The assistant warden longed for the good old days when flogging, chain gangs, and sweatboxes were the rage.

McDermott was waiting outside the library door, cradling a shotgun across his massive forearms and glaring down at Charlie from six feet five inches above ground. Several armed guards stood behind him, but none were as big. McDermott was a bull with a thick neck, broad shoulders, and tree-trunk torso and legs.

"Who's this?" McDermott asked Collins.

"Charlie Marsh, sir," answered the trustee, his voice quivering. "He's Clayton's cellmate."

"Okay, Marsh. What's going on here?"

"Mr. McDermott, sir, I just want to say

that I had nothing to do with this. I'm up for parole in . . ."

"Did I ask for your life story, Marsh?" McDermott said in a tone that would have been a bone-chilling growl if it had come from a rottweiler.

"No, sir. I just wanted you to know that this was all Freddy's idea. See, he doesn't think so well at times, and this is one of them. We were working on a legal writ when Warden Pulliams stopped at our table with these three ladies. Next thing I know, Freddy's got a knife and he's threatening to kill one of the women if the warden doesn't do what he says. Now, the warden, the women, and a guard are tied up in the storeroom."

"Let's go in and take him out," suggested a buzz-cut guard who was almost as big as McDermott.

"With all due respect, sir, that might not be wise," Charlie said. "Freddy doused everyone with paint thinner. He'll set them on fire if you storm the room. But listen, I think there's a way out of this."

"Talk," McDermott ordered.

"Freddy and I grew up together. We've been close since elementary school. I know exactly how his mind works. Freddy has a short attention span, real short. He gets crazy ideas and acts on them without thinking, but he loses interest fast. You can get everyone out of this unharmed if you have a little patience."

"What do you have in mind?"

"Freddy's got demands. He wants a jet plane to fly him to a tropical island and two million dollars."

McDermott laughed harshly. "Where'd he get that from, TV?"

"Probably, or some movie. But he's fixed on these demands, and once Freddy is fixed on an idea there's no way to change his mind until he gets bored. So we have to make him think you're trying to put the deal together and let me work on him. I'll try to get as many people out of there as I can, and I'll try to talk Freddy out as soon as I see he's losing interest.

"I don't want anyone hurt. Freddy is my best friend. He had a real rough time growing up and it screwed up his mind. Also, he's not too smart. If it's possible, I want to keep him, the warden, the guard, and those ladies alive."

"What's in this for you?" McDermott asked.

"Nothing. I'm only in on a credit card fraud beef. I'm up for parole real soon. I just want everything back the way it was before Freddy went off on those people."

"All right. Tell Clayton I'm working on getting him the plane and the money."

"The hostages will need food soon, and water."

"I'll see what I can do," McDermott said. "And you're doing the right thing by helping us, Marsh. I remember cons who do the right thing." He paused. "And I particularly remember those who don't."

The assistant warden waited until Charlie reentered the library. Then he turned to the guard with the buzz cut.

"Find out where the SWAT team is and let's get some more men up here."

"Are you going to wait for Marsh to work on his buddy?"

"I'll give him some time, but not much," McDermott answered, his close-set eyes concentrating on the library door as his mind swept through various scenarios, all of which ended with Freddy Clayton's bullet-riddled body being dragged out of the store-room by his heels.

A RABID CONVICT holding three helpless women and a prison warden hostage is the answer to a twenty-four-hour news station's prayers, but there was no television or radio in the library, so Freddy was unaware of the media circus that had sprung up around the prison. Charlie knew about the news coverage because McDermott had given in to requests to let a pool of reporters from the papers and television into the prison. The lights on the TV cameras would flash on whenever he stepped out of the library door to continue his dialogue with McDermott.

During the next two days, Charlie shuffled back and forth between the storeroom and the hall outside the library as Freddy's patience dwindled to almost nothing. As it turned out, the assistant warden and Crazy Freddy had about the same tolerance for inaction. Charlie was constantly talking his friend out of cutting throats and McDermott out of sending in the troops. An arson expert had informed McDermott that the flammable qualities of the paint thinner would dissipate over time, upping the chances that the SWAT team could prevent major injuries if they acted fast enough. Charlie found out about this plan and squelched it by telling McDermott that Freddy kept dousing the hostages with more fluid whenever he grew bored.

The prison standoff came to a head on the third day. The close air in the storeroom stank of sweat, fear, and paint thinner. The hostages were exhausted, frightened, and depressed, and Freddy was at the end of his rope. He hadn't slept for more than twenty minutes at a time since precipitating the hostage crisis and his nerves were completely frayed. Charlie watched him pace back and forth in front of the hostages, the shiv clutched in one hand and the lighter in the other. Freddy would tense every time a "thump-thump-thump" signaled a helicopter passing overhead and grow even more tense when there was silence, which he took as the lull before a SWAT team stormed the storeroom.

"This is it, this is it," Freddy mumbled under his breath. His eyes were bloodshot and his jaw was clenched so hard that his skin was drawn tight across his cheek-bones.

"Be cool, Freddy," Charlie said, trying to sound confident through his exhaustion.

"The motherfuckers are stalling. The SWATs are coming any minute. I can smell them."

"I don't think so. I really believe they're getting the money together."

Freddy stopped pacing and stared at Charlie.

"Bullshit."

Normally, Freddy yelled and ranted, but now his voice was calm and pitched low. His self-possession terrified Charlie.

"They're not sending a plane. They're playing you. It's time to show those motherfuckers I mean business or they'll lose respect for me. Once that happens it's the SWATs for sure."

"They'll definitely send in the troops if you send out a body. You'll be giving them no choice."

Freddy's shoulders sagged and Charlie knew that his friend had given up all hope of lying on the beach of a tropical island.

"I don't give a fuck anymore. The SWATs come in, I'm a dead man. I go out there,

I'm a dead man. You don't think some accident is gonna happen to me somewhere down the line if I survive today? Sending a body out is my only chance."

Freddy turned away from his friend and studied the hostages. Most of them were too tired and hungry to show emotion. Larry Merritt was the only one who had the courage to meet Freddy's eyes. Freddy pointed at the guard.

"I'll slit his throat and you'll drag him out. Tell McDermott that a hostage dies every hour the plane and the money aren't here."

"No, Freddy. Don't do this."

"I gotta, bro. Ain't no other way."

"If you kill him you're killing me, too. They'll come in shooting and no convict is gonna walk out alive."

"You can hide behind that," Freddy said, pointing to a broken, three-legged office desk that canted sideways, one corner touching the floor. "Then you surrender. You're smart. You can talk your way out. Me, I gotta act."

Freddy started toward the guard. "Say good night, mother-fucker."

Freddy started his downward thrust and Charlie hurled himself between the prison guard and Freddy's knife.

"What the fuck!" shouted Freddy as the shiv buried itself in Charlie's shoulder blade. Charlie was sprawled across the startled guard. Freddy jerked the knife out of Charlie's back and Charlie rolled sideways so he could see his cellmate.

"Shit," he groaned. "You stabbed me, Freddy."

"What the fuck were you doing?" asked his shocked friend.

"Saving your life."

Charlie pulled himself into a sitting position and gathered his courage, still keeping his body between Freddy and Merritt. What he wanted to say was hard for a man to express.

"I love you, Freddy."

"What?"

"Not like that. I'm not queer. I love you like a brother. Hell, we are brothers. We don't have the same mother or father, but we're more brothers than natural brothers. You hear what I'm saying?"

Freddy looked stunned. Outside of

bitches in the throes of passion, who he knew were just after his dope or money, no one had ever told him they loved him.

Charlie reached over his back and felt blood leaking from the knife wound. He grimaced.

"You okay?" Freddy asked with genuine concern.

"No, man, I'm not okay. You fucking stabbed me. But I'd let you kill me if it would save your life. That's why I couldn't let you off the guard. If he died, you'd be a dead man for sure."

"You'd die for me?" Freddy said, trying hard to get his mind around the fact that Charlie was willing to take a bullet for him.

"To save you, yeah. Hell, how many times have you rescued me? I can't count them. It's time for me to pay you back."

"Oh, man, you don't owe me shit. You're my friend, Charlie, my only friend."

Freddy's eyes filled with tears, something that hadn't happened since he'd built an iron shell around his feelings to shield himself from his father's vicious abuse.

"Naw, Freddy, you got plenty of friends," Charlie lied, embarrassed by Freddy's unexpected and unprecedented display of emotion.

"You're lying, bro, but I ain't mad. I know you just want me to feel good, but I don't. I know plenty of people fear me, but you're the only one who cares. You protected me from my old man when he, well, when he done that shit."

Charlie felt a spasm of pain and moaned. Freddy knelt next to him and looked at his shoulder. The back of the blue prison-issue shirt was turning red. Freddy helped Charlie take it off, then made a compress by folding the shirt and tying it in place over the wound with his own. As he helped Charlie to his feet, Freddy noticed an empty liter bottle of cola that had rolled against the wall. A wave of strong emotion swept through him as he realized what he had to do. Then he threw his arms around Charlie and hugged him.

"I'm sorry I got you involved in this," Freddy said when he'd released his friend. "I wasn't thinking. You could have been killed, but I was just thinking of myself."

"Hey, man . . ."

"Don't say nothing, Charlie. Let me talk.

You always think about me, man, but I'm a selfish bastard. It's time I did something for you. I'm setting everyone free. You're gonna take them out of here. Tell McDermott I'm gonna surrender and face the music. I fucked up and I gotta pay."

"That's great, Freddy. You're doing the right thing."

"Yeah, bro, I believe I am. Cut them loose and get your ass out of here."

Charlie felt lightheaded from his wound but he knew he had to move fast, before Freddy changed his mind. Charlie used the shiv to cut everyone's bonds. Then he gave it back to Freddy and led the hostages out of the storeroom.

"It's Charlie Marsh, Mr. McDermott," he shouted through the library door. "I've got the hostages with me. They're free and unharmed. Don't shoot, we're coming out."

The door opened and the hostages rushed into the corridor. Some were sobbing; others were too exhausted to show emotion.

"Mr. McDermott, Freddy wants to surrender. If you go in now he'll give up," Charlie managed. He was feeling dizzy from blood loss and the pain was making it hard to think. Suddenly, Charlie staggered and collapsed to the ground next to Warden Pulliams.

"Get a medic," the warden told McDermott. "This man was stabbed saving Larry's life. He's a hero."

The captain of the SWAT team sent a medic over to Charlie. Then he and McDermott and several members of the SWAT team entered the library. The point man led them through the stacks until they could see the door to the storeroom. The captain used hand signals to place his men where they would have a clear shot.

"Mr. Clayton, this is Assistant Warden McDermott. We're grateful that you've released the hostages unharmed. Please come out now and we'll take you into custody. I assure . . ."

The storeroom door burst open to reveal Crazy Freddy Clayton. He was stripped to the waist and his sculpted body gleamed with sweat. In one hand he held his shiv; in the other he held the soda pop bottle. The bottle was filled with paint thinner. A rag had been stuffed through the neck and into the liquid. Bright flames were eating away at the rag.

"FREEDOM OR DEATH!" howled Freddy as three shots fired simultaneously by members of the SWAT team caught him in the chest.

Freddy staggered a step and the Molotov cocktail exploded, bathing him in flames.

CHAPTER 11

Charlie Marsh had always been a nobody; an insignificant member of the human race who had left no mark on history during his time on Earth. Now he was a hero and, as Warden Pulliams was quick to point out to anyone who would listen, walking proof that the warden's theories of rehabilitation worked. What better example could there be than Charlie's willingness to sacrifice his life for that of his jailer?

The warden was wise enough to realize that many convicts would not view Charlie's actions in a positive light and would consider Freddy Clayton, who had died in flames rather than knuckle under to The Man, as the true hero of the prison stand-off. To protect Charlie from those inmates who had not yet turned a moral corner, the warden sent Charlie to the county hospital to recuperate while he arranged for an early release, an appropriate reward for his gallantry.

The first evening Charlie spent on clean sheets in the air-conditioned luxury of his hospital room, the nurse tuned his television to the national news, where the prison standoff was the lead story. It was surreal, watching himself stagger out of the library behind the hostages and collapse to the floor while Mabel Brooks told the world:

"That guard wouldn't be alive if it wasn't for Mr. Marsh. None of us would be alive. He threw himself between that knife and Mr. Merritt. And he kept that animal from setting us on fire. I know we'd all be dead if Mr. Marsh hadn't protected us. God bless him."

Charlie should have felt proud of his heroic actions and elated by his proximity to freedom, but the primary emotion he experienced was guilt. Was he really a hero? Had he thrown himself between Freddy's knife and Larry Merritt's body to save an innocent man or to save himself from being charged as an accessory to murder? And why had he told Freddy he loved him? Had he spoken from the heart or was he trying to distract Freddy to keep himself from being murdered for interfering with his lunatic friend's insane plan? Charlie had been living the con for so long that it was hard at times for him to divine his own motivations.

Life moved quickly for Charlie. While the parole board considered Warden Pulliams's recommendation for early release, he waded through offers from literary agents and movie producers. The offers were a surprise, and the fact that he was going to make a huge profit from Freddy's death increased his guilt. An image of Freddy Clayton in flames seared his brain whenever he thought about the money he was going to make. This image didn't deter him from hiring an agent or accepting a seven-figure movie deal and another seven-figure book deal for his autobiography, but it kept him from experiencing unfettered joy at his sudden reversal of fortune.

Freddy's death was the only downer for

Charlie in the whirlwind that became his life after prison. Within days of his release he was on *Oprah* and the *Today* show, and he learned that Tom Cruise was interested in playing him in the movie. No longer did Charlie sleep in the upper bunk of a prison cell; now he slept on silk sheets in a Manhattan apartment that his publisher let him use while he was working on the book.

Charlie stayed away from drugs, which were offered at the many parties he attended, and he didn't get drunk, because he liked to keep his wits about him, but he did not stay away from the ladies. Charlie could not believe the variety of women who begged him to take them to bed. There were black women, white women, and Asian women. There were blondes, brunettes, and redheads. There were women who were attracted to celebrities; there were women who wanted to have sex with a rich man; and there were women who were fascinated by dangerous felons, which was how Charlie began portraying himself. No one in his new circle of acquaintances had ever heard of him or Freddy before the prison standoff, so they accepted his new and improved version of Charlie Marsh, the extremely violent felon who had experienced a miraculous conversion.

Mickey Keys, his newly acquired agent, a fast-talking, red-haired, freckle-faced man of forty-two who was frenetically cheerful, had given him the idea when he joked that it would help sell books if Charlie had a more exciting name. As soon as his agent made this comment, Charlie realized that not only was his name as dull as the image a marsh conjured, but so was his life story. His parents had been decent, hardworking folks whose only sin was spoiling their only child. Charlie had turned to crime because he was lazy, and the only violence his escapades ever caused occurred when he was beaten up by a mark who caught on to his scam.

On the other hand, Freddy Clayton's life resembled a Shakespearean tragedy or a really good soap opera. Freddy had been an abused child. Television talk show hosts loved that dysfunctional-family shit. Freddy had committed murders and armed robberies. He'd had hairbreadth escapes from the law, and violent fights. Few people beside Charlie knew the facts of Freddy's life—or his, for that matter. Who could contradict him if he took a few incidents from Freddy's saga and claimed them for his own? Their parents were dead, and so were many of the witnesses to Freddy's deeds. Oh, there was the odd living acquaintance, but most of those in the know had prison records. Who would take their word over a hero's, and how many of them had outstanding warrants that would be executed if they stepped forward? Charlie convinced himself that his book would be a homage to Crazy Freddy if he claimed his friend's life as his own.

Most of his interviews had focused on the prison standoff, and Charlie had been vague when an interviewer asked him about his past. He hadn't started working with the ghostwriter who would actually write his book, either, so no one knew what he was going to say in his autobiography. Charlie spent the next month revising the outline his agent had suggested he write. By the time he met the ghostwriter, his autobiography contained accounts of knife fights and bare-fisted brawls, in which Charlie emerged victorious, as well as murders and other illegal endeavors. In his introduction, Charlie explained that the details of these incidents had to be kept vague because of potential criminal liability. There were also hints of a childhood in which he had been physically—and perhaps sexually—abused. Charlie knew that this would make his innocent parents look bad, but they were dead, and anyway, wouldn't a parent be willing to tarnish his or her name a little bit if it helped their child succeed in life after a rocky start?

Of course, the book had an uplifting ending. Charlie talked about the Inner Light™ that had infused him during his near-death experience, and how being filled with this light had led him to renounce crime and vow to help everyone else on earth find their own Inner Light™. Getting a trademark for this phrase was another idea of Mickey Keys's.

There hadn't really been any light, inner or otherwise. Charlie didn't have a clear recollection of what had happened during the insane moment when he'd thrown himself between the guard and the shiv. The inner-light business had been Mickey's suggestion, too. Well, not an outright suggestion, more a "memory" of Charlie's that had been elicited by some very pointed questions, such as "Did you have any religious experience when you were stabbed? You know, some people who've had near-death experiences claim to see a blinding light. Something like that? That would be great, because talk shows love it when you have a religious conversion or a near-death experience."

Charlie announced the formation of Inner Light, Inc., at the press conference heralding the publication of *The Light Within You*, which had been hurried into print while the action at the prison was still fresh in the public's mind. At that conference, Charlie also announced that henceforth he would refer to himself as Gabriel Sun, a new name that would commemorate the death of the bandit Charlie Marsh and his rebirth as a bringer of light.

Charlie's autobiography became an instant best-seller. It began in his deprived childhood, detailed the way poverty and abuse had made him a criminal, and explained how his experience with his Inner Light while saving Larry Merritt—and Warden Jeffrey Pulliams's belief in him—had restored his faith in the goodness of man. Charlie told the attending media representatives how he looked forward to holding seminars in the cities on his book tour so he could help troubled people find their Inner Light. There would be a nominal fee for attendance but, Charlie promised, the benefits to an attendee's personal and spiritual development would far outweigh the price of admission.

The seminars and the concessions that hawked Charlie's book, CDs featuring Charlie's words of wisdom, T-shirts, and other Inner Light paraphernalia produced a river of cash. Charlie had made a living swindling people out of their money, and he found a kindred spirit in Mickey Keys. The agent and his new client began sending the cash in the accounts of Inner Light, Inc., to secret bank accounts in Switzerland as quickly as it came in. Mickey, who had an accounting background, worked up a second set of books for the IRS, and Charlie and Mickey's real financial picture looked very healthy even as it appeared to be anemic in their ledgers.

Charlie held his seminars at each stop on his book tour. They were attended by members of the middle class who longed to be wealthy and successful, and people with wealth who were troubled by their success.

If the opportunity presented itself, he would fuck any rich woman who wished to purge her guilt by servicing an all-wise and dangerous ex-con. On occasion, he would have sex with one of the less well off groupies who hung around his book signings. That's what he was doing after a very lucrative seminar at Yale University when he was startled in mid-thrust by Mickey Keys's unannounced entry into his hotel bedroom.

"What the fuck!" Charlie shouted, furious at being interrupted. The coed he'd been banging was as delicious as a peach and as tight as a drum.

Keys ignored Charlie and turned on the television. "Watch this."

"It better be great."

"It's better than great, Charlie. Now, pay attention."

It was night on the screen. Flames could be seen flicking out of a few barred windows, and the spotlight of a police helicopter illuminated the prison grounds and the National Guard and state troopers massed before the high walls.

"Why did you need to interrupt the best fuck I've had all year to show me a prison? I'm trying to forget prison."

"You'll want to get reacquainted when you hear my idea. This is a shot of the Oregon State Penitentiary. Early this morning, a fight erupted between a Latino gang and members of the Aryan Brotherhood. When guards tried to intervene, several were taken hostage and the fight turned into a full-scale riot."

"What's your point?" Charlie whined, upset that his boner had begun to wilt.

"We're going to Oregon, where you will offer your services as a negotiator to help end the insurrection at the prison."

"Oregon? I don't even know where the fuck that is."

"The national press knows where it is. This is the lead story on every network and all the cable news shows."

"Mickey, you don't know squat about this kind of shit. The authorities aren't going to let me anywhere near the prison."

Mickey smiled. "That's probably true but you'll get tons of free publicity if they do. And if the governor won't let you talk to the rioters, you look like a good guy who's just trying to help. No matter how the riot ends, you come out smelling like a rose and you get tons of free air time."

"What about the book tour?"

"I talked to your publisher. They agree that you should go. They're already setting up a seminar at the home of a lawyer who published a book with them."

Charlie lay back in bed. The coed was clutching a sheet to her chest and listening intently to the conversation.

"All right, when do we leave?"

"In about two hours."

Charlie smiled at the girl. "That gives us enough time to finish what we started, sweet thing.

"Turn off the set and let me get back to my business," Charlie told Keys.

The agent shook his head and left the room. Charlie felt under the sheets until he found a hot, soft place between the coed's legs.

"I see you haven't cooled down."

The coed rolled over until she was breast-to-breast with Charlie.

"Fuck me hard, Charlie," she whispered, "and when you're done, take me with you to Oregon."

"What?" Charlie said, pulling away a little.

A hand wrapped around his penis.

"I'm wasting my time in college. I'm so unhappy here. I want you to teach me the path to inner peace."

Charlie wasn't in the mood for a philosophical discussion. He also didn't want this broad tagging along to Oregon, even if he had been sincere when he praised her sexual abilities to Mickey Keys.

"I hear you, sister, but . . ." Charlie started, when the soft, rhythmic motion of her hand made him forget what he was going to say.

"Please, Charlie, let me come. I'm smart. I can help, and there are other things I can do for you."

Charlie knew he should say no, but the girl ducked beneath the sheets and the touch of her lips banished all knowledge of the English language from his brain.

CHAPTER 12

Dunthorpe was an affluent community on the outskirts of Portland, and Charlie's seminar had been hosted in a Tudor mansion surrounded by several acres of lawn and trees. The mansion was bigger than some he'd been in since he'd become a celebrity and smaller than others. When he was in these penthouses, mansions, and estates, he felt like Alice in Wonderland. He was rich beyond his wildest dreams, but since he'd started holding his seminars he'd met people compared to whom he was a pauper. Where did all this money come from?

There was something else that seemed surreal. Charlie had grown up poor. There were evictions, there were times when there wasn't enough food, and there was violence in his neighborhood and his life. He'd always thought that his problems would be solved if he were rich, but these people were rich and they looked to him for help in finding happiness. He didn't get it.

Charlie was rarely alone during his year and a half in prison or the whirlwind his life had become since regaining his freedom, and he'd come to treasure the rare moments of peace and quiet he was able to salvage from his hectic existence. As soon as he finished signing copies of his book, Charlie slipped through the French windows in the library to get a breath of fresh air. There was a flower garden on the far side of the spacious lawn. Charlie wandered across the manicured grass in its direction. Delmar Epps, a muscular ex-heavyweight boxer Mickey Keys had hired, followed far enough behind to give Charlie the illusion of privacy and close enough to fulfill his duties as a bodyguard.

Everything had gone as Mickey had

predicted. The authorities had refused to let Charlie be involved in the negotiations with the prisoners, so he shared none of the blame when two guards and several inmates died in a bloody shoot-out. Charlie was able to go on television and pontificate about the way things might have ended if he had been allowed to bring inner peace to the rebellious souls of the prisoners. As a result of the publicity, Charlie had packed the convention center for a citywide seminar that had brought in a tidy sum. They had also done well in Dunthorpe at this second seminar aimed at a more select audience.

After initially bitching and moaning about having to fly to the boonies, Charlie had finally conceded that he was glad Mickey had dragged him to Portland. Oregon had been a revelation for a man who had been reared in bleak, urban poverty and had just emerged from the gray of prison to take up residence in the concrete caverns of Manhattan. There were clear blue skies here, emerald green grass, and a never-ending vista of trees and flowers. The summer air was warm and unpolluted, and Charlie breathed it in, savoring a gentle breeze as he crossed the lawn.

A high hedge of arborvitae divided the lawn from the garden and muffled a spirited conversation. Charlie wanted to be alone, so he started to change direction. He stopped when a woman's voice rose in anger. Charlie took a step into the garden and peered around the hedge. A man in tan slacks and a forest green polo shirt was arguing with a woman in a light blue dress held up by spaghetti straps.

The man, who looked to be in his late twenties, was tan and fit, with the wide shoulders and slender waist of an athlete. Charlie didn't recognize him. But the woman was definitely familiar. She'd stood behind most of the guests at the seminar, wearing a bemused smile that told him she wasn't buying one word of his bullshit. Charlie also remembered the woman because she was stunningly beautiful, with caramel-colored, shoulder-length hair and blue eyes that reminded him of the clear Caribbean waters he'd seen in a television commercial.

"You're not listening, Tony," the woman snapped. "I don't want you bothering me.

Do I have to talk to someone at the club to get you to leave me alone?"

The woman started to leave, but Tony grabbed her wrist.

"Brushing me off isn't going to be that easy, Sally."

Sally stopped and turned slowly until her face was inches from his.

"Take your hands off of me," she said, emphasizing each word in an icy tone that would have frozen fire.

Emboldened by Delmar's presence and the possibility of getting in the blonde's pants, Charlie decided to inject himself into this volatile situation.

"Yeah, motherfucker," Charlie said in his best prison don't-fuck-with-me voice. "Unhand the lady."

Tony took one look at Charlie's unimposing appearance and laughed.

"'Motherfucker'? My, my, and here I thought you were in favor of peace and love, Swami."

Thanks to Freddy Clayton, Charlie hadn't been in any fights in prison and very few on the outside, but he'd seen quite a few and had made a mental list of what worked and what didn't. Charlie shot a fast right over Sally's shoulder and connected with the tip of Tony's nose, a very delicate part of the anatomy that hurts like hell when mashed. Tony's hands flew up to his nose just as Delmar imposed his bulk between Charlie and the wounded man. The ex-boxer grabbed the fabric at Tony's neck in one massive fist and twisted.

"This gentleman bothering you, boss?" he asked Charlie as he peeled back his jacket with his free hand so Tony could see the fancy, ivory-handled revolver wedged in his waistband.

"No, he isn't bothering anyone anymore," Charlie answered. "Send the *gentleman* on his way, Delmar, and see to his nose if it's broken."

Delmar dragged Tony out of the garden and Charlie turned toward the woman.

"I'm sorry you had to see that."

"I've seen worse," she answered coolly, "and I'm perfectly capable of taking care of myself."

Charlie was surprised. He'd assumed that a society woman would be terrified and sexually aroused by violence, but this one seemed more amused than horrified. She tilted her head and studied Charlie for a moment.

"I assume these heroics were a prelude to an attempt to fuck me," she said.

"What?!"

"Didn't any of the ninnies at the seminar want to jump in the sack with you after hearing your patter about inner lights and personal peace?"

"I don't . . ."

The woman laughed. "Looks like I've got you rattled."

"Hey, when you've done the things I've done and made it through prison in one piece, nothing rattles you," Charlie said, trying to recapture some of the high ground.

"Do tell, tough guy. Well, we'll see. Witnessing these manly fisticuffs has made me hot," she said in a voice devoid of sexual desire. "Think you're ready to prove how manly you really are or do I have to hunt up someone else?"

"Yeah, okay, I'm with you," was the best he could come back with. Charlie was usually the animal prowling the jungle for pussy. But this woman made him feel like prey.

"Then let's get out of here. Tony's such a

jackass that he might call the cops, so it's better if you're not around." She tossed him her car keys. "These are for my Porsche. You drive."

SALLY POPE'S HOME wasn't as grand as the mansion they'd just left but it wasn't a shack either.

"Nice digs," Charlie said as soon as Sally turned on the lights so he could see the stone entryway and the curved staircase that led to the second floor.

Sally didn't waste time replying. She dropped her purse on a small table near the door and moved in on Charlie. He could feel the firmness of her breasts against his chest. Her hand slid down to his crotch and he was starting to lose it when he noticed a catcher's mitt and a plastic bat lying on the entryway floor.

Sally felt him tense and stepped back. She saw where he was staring.

"That's Kevin's. He's four, and you don't have to worry. He's at a sleepover, so we won't be disturbed."

"What about your husband? Is he at a sleepover, too?"

Sally closed her eyes for a moment and

took a deep breath. "Look, Charlie, do you want to fuck or learn my family history?"

"Hey, sorry, none of my business."

"Let's get this out of the way, okay? My husband is United States Congressman Arnold Pope Jr. and he's in Washington, DC, tonight, saving the country from liberals, abortionists, and criminals like you. Now, if that frightens you so much that you can't get it up, leave. If you're still interested in a roll in the hay, can the questions."

"WHO WAS THAT guy you were arguing with, tonight?" Charlie asked. They were lying in the wreckage of Sally's marital bed, lathered in sweat and resting for round three.

"A nobody, Tony Rose. He's the tennis pro at the Westmont Country Club. He thinks we've been having an affair, but that term is a tad more sophisticated than I'd use to describe what we've been doing."

"Why was he so pissed off?"

"I dumped him and bruised his ego."

"You gonna dump me?" Charlie asked with a grin.

Sally rolled over so she was facing Charlie, and raised herself up on an elbow.

"Let's get this straight, Charlie. You're a

good fuck. If you're game, and the opportunity presents itself, we'll meet again while you're in Portland, but that's it. I love my son and my husband and I'm not going to leave either one."

Charlie was confused. "If you love Arnie Jr., how come you're here with me?"

For the first time that evening, Sally Pope looked flustered. "That's none of your business."

She got out of bed, walked into the bathroom, and slammed the door. Charlie scrambled after her.

"Hey," he said through the locked door, "I'm sorry. I shouldn't be so nosy. Come on out and I won't ask any more questions, promise."

The toilet flushed and the door opened. Sally had regained her composure. She touched Charlie's cheek.

"This has been nice, Charlie, but I'm tired. Do you mind?"

"I'm bushed too," he said, though she'd excited him enough that he wouldn't have minded another tussle in the sack. "I've got TV, radio, and another book signing in Seattle. We're driving up in the morning, so I should get my beauty rest."

Sally took her hand away and smiled, though her eyes were sad.

"You know," Charlie said, "I'm going to be back here after Seattle and I'll have a few days before we go to San Francisco."

Sally looked thoughtful. "How would you like to hold one of your seminars at the most exclusive country club in Oregon?"

"Sounds good."

"Let me work on it. I'll get back to you."

"I'll be at my hotel again on Thursday for a book signing. You want to drop by?"

"I can't be seen with you. You understand that?"

"Sure, but I can fix it so you can slip up without anyone seeing you."

"I assume this is from experience?"

Charlie grinned. "I have a foolproof system. I'm in the penthouse suite and there's a back elevator. Only one who'll know is Delmar, and he's already seen us together."

"Let me think about it."

"Great. Do you have a pen? I'll give you my cell phone number. Call me in Seattle about the seminar and anything else you can think of."

Charlie phoned Delmar and told him to meet him on a corner a quarter-mile from

Sally's house, so no one would see him outside. While he waited in the warm night air for his limo to arrive, Charlie tried to figure out Sally Pope. He decided that she was a sad and bitter woman. Why else would a congressman's wife with money and looks drag him, Tony Rose, and—he guessed—a slew of other men into her bed? He felt sorry for her, but that wasn't going to keep him from enjoying another night in bed with the woman if the opportunity presented itself.

CHAPTER 13

Life was a smooth ride for Charlie until everything went to hell on the day of the seminar at the Westmont. He hit the first bump in the road on a sunny afternoon in a bookstore in Portland. He was sitting at a table piled high with copies of *The Light Within You*. Delmar Epps stood a few steps behind Charlie, trying—and failing—to be inconspicuous. Seated beside Charlie was Mickey Keys, who was dressed in a tan suit, white shirt, and red tie, and looked as happy as can be. It was unusual for him to accompany a client on a book tour but Keys didn't think of Charlie as a client; he thought of him as a gold mine and he wanted to keep a close eye on his mother lode.

In front of the table was a line that stretched around the store. It was composed of excited customers eager to purchase Charlie's book so they could learn how to ignite the light within them and find wealth and inner peace. When a fan reached the head of the line, Charlie would smile and ask to whom he should inscribe the book. Then he would make a cheerful, positive remark while he wrote "Never stop until you've turned on your Inner Light. Peace, Gabriel Sun."

After the first few customers, Charlie went on automatic pilot. That was why it took him a second to recognize the next two men in the line.

"Hey, Charlie, long time no see," said Gary Hass, the late Freddy Clayton's most intelligent criminal associate. Gary was so ordinary-looking that witnesses had a hard time identifying him in a lineup. This made him markedly different from the tattooed, pierced, and steroid-inflated Werner Rollins, who stood at Gary's shoulder and would have been perfectly at home in any barbarian horde. Unfortunately for humanity, Hass's scarred and deformed psyche was the exact opposite of his bland appearance. A slender, if wiry, five foot seven, Gary wasn't physically imposing but he was ruthless and he never forgot a slight, no matter how small. Gary also had the gift of patience. Get the better of him today and he would exact revenge by tying you to your bed and burning down your house long after you'd forgotten you'd ever had a run-in with him.

"Great book," Gary said.

"Glad you liked it."

"I liked it so much I read it more than once; especially the parts about your exciting experiences in the world of crime. Know why I had to read those parts so many times?"

"Uh, no."

"I found them confusing, Charlie. Many of your exploits sounded both familiar and unfamiliar at the same time. I mean, I seemed to remember some of those events but not exactly the way you remembered them. For me, it was like watching a science-fiction movie where people go into a parallel universe that's a lot like the Earth we know, but different. Like where the South wins the Civil War. You know it didn't happen that way but if the writer is very skilled it seems realistic. See what I mean?"

"Not really. Look, it's good seeing you but there's a long line. I'm not supposed to talk to any one customer for more than a few minutes."

"Hey, Werner and I don't want to be a problem so why don't we get together for coffee when you're finished."

"I don't know, Gary. I'm awfully busy."

"I'm cool with that. If you don't have time for coffee we'll fly back East and see if an investigative reporter at the *New York Times* wants to discuss our confusion about the book over a double decaf mocha. To tell the truth though, we'd rather spend our time reminiscing with a pal about the good old days."

Charlie felt sick. A sheen of sweat formed on his forehead. "Maybe I can spare some time when I'm done."

"Great! There's a restaurant two doors down. Werner and I can't wait to hear all about the exciting life you've been leading. See you soon."

"Who were those guys?" Mickey Keys

asked when Gary and Werner left without buying books.

"Acquaintances from the old days. I'm going to grab a cup of coffee with them after the signing."

"Do you want me to come along?"

"No. You and Delmar go back to the hotel."

"You sure you want to be alone with them?"

"Positive. Believe me, Mickey, the less Gary and Werner know about you, the better off you are."

CHARLIE FOUND THE odd couple sitting in a booth in the back of the restaurant. Gary was nursing a cup of black coffee while Werner wolfed down a slab of pie. A plate with the cannibalized remains of a burger and fries was also sitting in front of the Neanderthal.

"My man," Gary said as Charlie slid into the booth. "You not only survived the big house but you're looking prosperous."

Charlie shrugged. "The book's only been out a few weeks. There's no telling what might happen."

"Hey, don't be modest. *Newsweek* reported you got a seven-figure deal for the book and another mil or so for the movie. Say, have you met Tom yet? What's he like in person?"

"That stuff about Tom Cruise is Hollywood bullshit, Gary. They're negotiating. He hasn't committed."

"That fucker can act," Werner opined between mouthfuls of pie.

"Yes, well, how are you? It's been years."

"About five," Gary said. "Werner and I took off after that muffed bank job. What a cluster fuck that was; one dead guard, one dead civilian, and no money."

Gary shook his head sadly. Then he perked up. "You know, there's an incident in your book that vaguely resembles our fiasco. Werner and I got a kick out of the part where you dive behind that car, guns blazing. It reminded me of a scene in a John Woo flick. In fact, it's almost identical to a scene in one of his movies. Funny thing though. Werner and I remember Freddy going into that bank with us but we don't remember seeing you there. Of course, you were probably describing another bank job you pulled with Freddy and some other guys where a guard and a customer were killed."

"Well, you know, I had to disguise the events so the cops couldn't use the book as a basis for an indictment."

"Yeah, I get that. The thing is Werner and I think some big publisher might be interested in our life stories now that your book is selling so well. It can be a whole new genre, *Criminal Confessions*. The only thing holding us back is our concern for you. If we tell our stories, some of our reminiscences might contradict your version of events. We'd feel real bad if our success created difficulties for you."

Charlie sighed. "Okay, Gary. Let's stop fucking around. What do you want?"

"A small piece of the pie, an opportunity to dip a crust of bread into the gravy train, a . . ."

"Can you cut the crap? I get it. What do I have to do to get you and Werner to go away?"

"We don't really want to go away, Charlie. A big star like you should have an entourage."

Charlie snapped his head back and forth. "That's not gonna happen."

"Sure it is. We figure we can testify at these seminars about how we were terrible criminals, corrupt to our very souls, until you helped us find our inner lights."

"No way."

Gary's affable demeanor faded away. "Do you know what plagiarism is? Werner and I feel that you plagiarized our lives. That's a crime, Charlie, and you know what they say: 'If you can't do the time, don't do the crime.' There's also 'Crime does not pay.' It all boils down to the fact that there are consequences for bad acts. The consequence in your case is a tax on profits. You'll pay a bit of it now and we'll tag along to keep an eye on the receipts so we can decide how much the tax will be in the future."

"I'm not gonna do it. You go to the *Times* and see what they say. Who's going to take your word over mine? I'm a hero, Gary. I saved a guard's life.

"And how are you going to prove I made this stuff up? A reporter will want specific facts about murders, armed robberies, and other crimes that would send you away forever. But say they believe you committed these crimes. That wouldn't prove I made up the incidents in the book. I'd just say that my crimes were different from what you say you did. In my introduction I said I made the events vague and changed names and places to protect myself from getting charged with the crimes. So do your worst."

Gary turned red, which meant he was pissed off. Charlie had forgotten for a moment who he was dealing with, but he remembered now. Gary leaned across the table and lowered his voice.

"If you think talking to a reporter is the worst thing I can do to you, you must have forgotten some of the things you've seen me do. Fuck with me and you'll have to sleep with one eye open for the rest of your life."

Gary leaned back and let what he'd said sink in. "I'm going to forget how rude you've just been. We'll see you tonight at your seminar at that fancy country club. That'll give you a few hours to think."

Gary nodded to Werner, who vacuumed down what was left of his pie.

"Pick up the check, will you?" Gary said.

Charlie watched them leave. Then he closed his eyes and exhaled. How could he be so stupid? He'd been so full of himself lately that he'd forgotten what the world was really like. People like Sally Pope lived in Camelot, but he lived in the jungle, where he was prey and people like Gary and Werner were predators.

Are you out of your mind?" Moonbeam asked Charlie, who was in the bedroom of his hotel suite, killing time before the seminar at the Westmont Country Club by quick-drawing a Ruger .357 Magnum Vaquero revolver. The engraved, stainless steel, ivory-handled gun weighed more than two pounds, had a six-inch barrel, and was a gift from the twentysomething wife of a septuagenarian Texas oilman. She had given it to Charlie after a night of intimacy following an Inner Light™ seminar in Austin.

"Relax, Moonbeam," said Charlie, who

almost choked whenever he used her "mystical" name.

When they were in New Haven, Charlie had told "Moonbeam" that she could come to Oregon with his entourage. Now he deeply regretted the words he'd moaned in the heat of passion and he had decided to dump her when they moved on. "Moonbeam" might be great in bed but the rest of the time she was a bossy pain in the ass. The broad had also shaved her head, because she'd concluded—for reasons Charlie never understood—that her hair was impeding her spiritual growth. Charlie was definitely not turned on by bald women and he'd said so.

"You're an ex-con," she persisted. "Having a gun violates the conditions of your parole. What if someone sees you?"

"Do you think I'm stupid enough to carry in public? Delmar totes my piece when I'm out and about and he's licensed to carry."

Charlie's bodyguard was slouched on the sofa reading a sports magazine with an NBA star on the cover.

"Haven't you heard of the right to bear arms, bitch?" Delmar asked without looking up from the article he was reading. "Or didn't you study the Constitution at your fancy Ivy League college?"

Before Moonbeam could answer, the door to the suite opened and a waiter rolled in a serving cart with Charlie's dinner. Charlie froze in mid-draw. The waiter stared at the gun. Charlie whipped it behind his back.

"Don't they teach you to knock?" he shouted at the flustered server.

"I'm sorry, sir. I did knock on the door to the suite. The man said I could . . ."

"Yeah, yeah, just leave it," Charlie said. Mickey Keys was out in the sitting room. "Have my agent sign for this."

"Thank you, sir," the waiter said as he backed out of the bedroom.

"Have I made my point?" Moonbeam asked. "If he talks to your parole officer, you'll be putting on your seminars for the prisoners at the state pen. And there's something else. You have to stop sleeping with that woman."

"Whoa, who I fuck is none of your business. I warned you I wasn't a one-woman man when you insisted on following me out here."

"I know, Charlie, but it doesn't look good. She's married and she has a kid, not to mention that her husband is a powerful politician who can seriously mess you up."

"How do you think we got this gig at the Westmont? I'm just using her for her connections, baby. If you're too jealous to see that, maybe you should just go back to your rich friends."

Moonbeam looked frightened. "Don't send me away, Charlie. I only want to help."

"Well you're not helping by nagging my ass every five minutes."

Moonbeam moved close to Charlie. "I'm sorry. You know I'm just worried about you."

Charlie felt the heat and remembered what the girl looked like naked, hair or no hair. He glanced at the clock and saw that there was still time before they had to leave for the country club. He put his arms around Moonbeam.

"I know you care about me, baby," Charlie said in a voice that oozed concern. "Just don't worry so much."

Moonbeam looked down and Charlie lifted up her chin until he could see her eyes.

"You don't have anything to worry about. Sally can't touch you in bed, and that's what counts between a man and a woman."

Charlie released the girl's chin. "Why don't you take five, Delmar?" he said as he fondled her small, firm breasts.

The bodyguard looked at his watch. "We're heading out in three quarters of an hour."

"That's cool. See you then."

Delmar left. Charlie scooped up Moonbeam in his arms and carried her to the bed. His timing was perfect. When his bodyguard rapped on his door three quarters of an hour later, Charlie was refreshed, fed, and ready to bilk the members of the Westmont Country Club.

15

Shortly after sunset, on the evening Congressman Arnold Pope Jr. was murdered, Sally Pope stood next to John Walsdorf, the manager of the Westmont Country Club, and watched a line of expensive cars drive toward the entrance to the Westmont's sprawling fieldstone clubhouse. The caravan snaked along a wide, tree-lined lane that ran by a few of the golf holes. There was no moon, so the lush emerald green of the fairways was left to the imagination.

Some of the cars turned left at the end of the lane and drove past the pro shop into the outdoor parking lot that bordered the driving range. The rest went right and discharged their passengers at the club entrance after circling a large grass turnaround decorated with flower beds. Illumination from the clubhouse spilled onto the turnaround, fading as it crossed to the far side.

"Can I talk to you for a minute?" Tony Rose asked Sally Pope just as the limousine carrying Charlie Marsh, Delmar Epps, Moonbeam, and Mickey Keys drove into view.

"Not now, Tony. I'm busy," Sally said, annoyed that Rose would pick the moment when the guest of honor arrived to speak to her.

"When, then? We have to talk."

"We don't have anything to talk about," Sally whispered angrily. "And I don't think hashing out any problem you might have in front of John would be a good idea, do you?"

Rose suddenly noticed Walsdorf, who had the power to fire him. Frustration and anger made his face flush. He started to speak, then thought better of it. The tennis pro shot Sally an angry look and walked toward the parking lot just as Charlie's limousine stopped at the clubhouse entrance. The chauffeur ran to Charlie's door. Before he could grip the handle, Werner Rollins stepped in front of him. The driver took one look at the Visigoth and skidded to a stop. This gave Gary Hass the opportunity to open the door to the limo.

"Hey, Charlie," Gary said, flashing a wide smile.

Delmar Epps got out of the limo and put a hand on Gary's chest.

"Step back, sir," Charlie's bodyguard commanded in his most intimidating tone. Werner started toward Delmar but Gary waved him off.

"I'm an old pal, right, Charlie?"

"It's okay, Delmar," Charlie answered nervously as he emerged from the car.

John Walsdorf was uncomfortable with activity that was far better suited to a lower-class tavern than a country club that catered to his refined clientele, but Sally Pope was unfazed. She walked over to the limousine, distracting the testosterone-charged men just as Mickey Keys emerged from the car. Keys took one look at Werner Rollins and edged away from him.

"This is John Walsdorf, Charlie," Sally said. "He manages the club."

Behind the club manager were two hefty security guards dressed in blue blazers, black turtlenecks, and gray slacks. They fixed on Delmar and Werner, who paid no attention to them.

"Pleased to meet you, Mr. Sun," said Walsdorf, a short, balding man with a narrow mustache, whose paunch was hidden under a buttoned suit jacket. He eyed Charlie's bodyguard and Gary's scary companion nervously.

"It's a privilege to be invited to speak at this august institution," Charlie brown-nosed.

"We've already got a good crowd," Walsdorf told him.

"Great," Mickey Keys chimed in.

"Why don't I show you where you're going to speak?" Sally offered.

She started toward the front door of the clubhouse, then froze. Walsdorf followed her gaze and saw a tall, broad-shouldered man bearing down on them from the direction of the parking lot. He recognized him immediately.

United States Congressman Arnold Pope

Jr. was an ex-Marine and he looked like he was still in training. His stride was purposeful and his brown eyes were fixed on his wife. The open top button of his dress shirt, the tie that hung at half-mast, and the congressman's flushed face were hints that Pope was not in full control of his emotions.

"Is this the latest boyfriend?" Pope barked angrily.

Sally stared at him with disdain. "I didn't know you planned to join us, Arnie."

"Caught off guard?" Pope said.

"Not in the least, dear. You know you're always welcome to join me. The only surprise is that you've shown up at something I'm hosting. I see so little of you."

Pope shifted his attention to Charlie. "You're the guru, right?"

Charlie laughed nervously. "That's what the newspapers are calling me."

"What does your religion say about adultery?"

"Pardon?"

"You heard me, you little prick."

"Do we have to do this here?" Sally asked.

"Where do you want to do it, in our bedroom or this punk's hotel room?"

"I don't know what you're talking about," Sally answered coldly.

Pope pulled an envelope from his suit jacket's inside pocket and took a stack of photographs out of it. Pope held up a snapshot that showed Charlie and Sally groping each other in the foyer of the Popes' home. Seconds after Sally realized that the shot had been taken through one of her front windows, Pope threw the photographs at her. Then he punched Charlie in the face.

The limo driver rushed out of the way. Charlie staggered into Delmar. Delmar pulled Charlie behind him and hit the congressman in the solar plexus. Pope dropped to one knee seconds before one of the security guards slammed into Delmar, who brought his knee up between the guard's legs. The guard turned pale and Delmar swung him into his partner, who crashed into Werner Rollins.

John Walsdorf scurried to safety and tripped, tumbling to the ground. Delmar and Werner Rollins were fighting with the security guards in the area between the turnaround and the parking lot. The crowd cleared a space around them. Charlie and

Gary Hass backed around the traffic circle until they were far enough from the fight to be cloaked in shadow. Walsdorf saw Rollins knock one of the guards to the asphalt, making sure the guard was down, before joining Gary and Charlie.

Seconds later, Walsdorf saw Delmar Epps deliver a high karate kick to the head of the other security guard. Delmar watched the guard crumple to the pavement, then joined the group standing in the shadows just as Arnold Pope swore at Charlie and charged.

"Don't, Arnie!" Sally yelled.

The club manager saw flame flash from the general area where Charlie was standing just before Sally reached the congressman. An instant later a gunshot silenced the crowd. Arnold Pope stopped moving. He looked stunned. Then he staggered forward a few paces, wobbled in place, and stared at his shirtfront, which was slowly turning red. Pope dropped to his knees. A woman screamed. Sally ran to her husband. Delmar yelled, "Go, go." Walsdorf heard car doors slam. Seconds later, the limo drove away but Walsdorf didn't look to see where it was going. He was staring at Arnold Pope Jr., who showed no signs of life.

Twenty-five minutes later, John Walsdorf learned that one of the officers had found an ivory-handled Ruger .357 Magnum Vaquero revolver lying in the shadows where Charlie Marsh had been standing.

16

The Westmont Country Club complex straddled two counties. Most of the members lived in populous, urban Multnomah County, but most of the club grounds, including the clubhouse, were in Washington County, where sprawling bedroom communities, high-tech companies, and large areas of farmland coexisted uneasily. Karl Burdett was an athletic thirty-two-year-old with sandy blond hair and a confident smile. The newly elected district attorney for Washington County, a staunch conservative, had narrowly defeated a moderate candidate in last fall's election. His most important backer was Arnold Pope Sr., and Burdett had jumped into his car as soon as the wealthiest man in the county summoned him.

Of course, Pope had not summoned the DA himself. The call had come from Derrick Barclay, Pope's personal assistant, a pompous little man whose presence set Burdett's teeth on edge. Barclay had not told the district attorney why his employer wanted the audience and had not bothered to inquire whether the suggested time was convenient. He had assumed—quite correctly—that Burdett would cancel any conflicting appointments.

Even though Barclay had not stated the reason for the meeting, Burdett knew why Pope wanted to talk to him. The district attorney was charged with convicting Arnold Pope Jr.'s killer, and the old man was going to demand to be involved in the prosecution. Senior would never be put off by the quaint idea that the manipulation of the justice system by a private citizen was highly improper.

Senior had constructed his manor house of slate-gray Tenino sandstone on a high bluff overlooking the Columbia River. With its roof of red tile and parklike grounds, the mansion looked friendly and noble and had none of the personality of its owner. The grounds were surrounded by an ivy-covered brick wall that kept out the riffraff. Burdett used the call box at the gate and was admitted to the grounds. Derrick Barclay was waiting at the carved-oak front door. He was five feet eight, narrow, and had a pale complexion. Barclay's lips were forever pursed, as if to let the world know that he found everything he encountered distasteful.

"Mr. Pope will see you in the study," he said in a clipped, British accent. Burdett was tempted to answer, "Jolly good," until he remembered that Barclay had the ear of his biggest campaign contributor.

Arnold Pope Sr. was pacing back and forth on a Persian rug when Barclay showed the DA into a high-ceilinged, book-lined room. A stone fireplace occupied one wall and a leaded-glass window looked out on a garden. Pope was a bear of a man, who had invested the money he made in timber in several fledgling high-tech companies that were now industry leaders. When the timber industry took a nose dive, Senior didn't blink.

"Do you have him?" Pope asked without preamble.

"No, sir, but every law enforcement agency in the country is looking for Marsh. He won't stay lost long."

"What about that woman? Is she in custody?"

Burdett's brow furrowed. "What woman?"

Pope stopped pacing. "That gold-digging bitch he married, the person who's responsible for my son's murder."

"Sally Pope?" Burdett asked, puzzled by the suggestion that Junior's wife had anything to do with the murder. "A number of very credible witnesses saw her when the congressman was shot. No one saw her with a gun."

Pope glared at the district attorney. "Please don't play stupid, Karl. You do know about 'aiding and abetting' and 'conspiracy,' or didn't you pay attention in your criminal-law class?"

Burdett flushed. "I know you're upset but you don't have to insult me."

"I'll do more than insult you if the people who killed my boy escape justice."

"I can't just arrest Sally, Mr. Pope. There's

no evidence indicating that she's guilty of murder."

"Then you haven't heard about the note?"

"What note?"

"The one found in my son's Washington, DC, office."

"No, I haven't."

"You do know about the photographs?"

"Of course. We collected all of them from the crime scene."

"They were sent to Arnold along with a note. His aide delivered the envelope. My son left the note on his desk when he rushed to the airport. The FBI has it."

Burdett didn't bother to ask how Senior knew about an ongoing FBI investigation about which he—the head law-enforcement official in the county and the person in charge of the murder investigation—knew nothing. Senior didn't just contribute to local political races. His tentacles reached to the top tiers of the Washington hierarchy.

Pope pressed a button on his desk and Barclay hustled in, carrying a fax. Pope nodded toward the district attorney and Barclay handed the document to Burdett. It was a photocopy of a note constructed from letters cut out of magazines and pasted onto a piece of paper. The note read: THEY'LL BE TOGETHER AT THE WESTMONT TOMORROW NIGHT AT THE GURU'S SEMINAR.

"I don't see how this note implicates Sally Pope," Burdett said after studying the fax. "The pictures show her having an illicit relationship with Marsh. Why would she send it?"

Pope smiled, but there was no humor in his smile. "You don't know my daughter-in-law very well, Karl. She is a devious, scheming whore. She knew you would see it this way. Who could suspect her of tipping off her husband about her affair?"

The smile disappeared. "Think, Karl. She used the note and the pictures to enrage Arnold, knowing he would rush back to Oregon to confront her. They set him up to be killed. And she set up Marsh to take the fall for her."

"That's an interesting theory, but I can't arrest Sally without proof."

Pope's smile reappeared. "Oh, there's proof that she was a conspirator in the plot to kill my boy. There's more than enough proof. The FBI found fingerprints on the note. Guess who they belong to?"

17

In his youth, Frank Jaffe had been a brawler and carouser; a man's man with a ruddy complexion and the thick muscles of a stevedore. He believed wholeheartedly that a woman's place was in the home, where she did womanly things like cooking and raising the children. Men, on the other hand, worked long hours to support their families and played with their children when time permitted. Then his world turned upside down.

Samantha was twenty when she died giving birth to Amanda. How did a man raise a baby—and a girl baby at that—when he didn't even know how to change a diaper? That was just one of a thousand questions Frank had asked himself during the grief-filled days that followed his wife's death and his sudden plunge into fatherhood. Frank had to answer these questions quickly. When a baby is screaming there's not much time for in-depth research.

Frank was a great father, even during the insane years when he was attending law school at night, working all day, and thanking God that his parents were overjoyed to babysit Amanda. When he started Jaffe, Katz, Lehane and Brindisi with some classmates from law school, he had nothing in his life except work and his daughter. Frank never remarried, because he'd never had the time for a serious relationship and he'd rarely found anyone who could measure up to Samantha. On the one occasion he'd come close, his devotion to his work and his child had created a rift that could not be mended.

Frank had written off romance by the time he entered the fourth decade of his life. Then his secretary ushered Sally Pope into his office and Frank felt like a virginal teenager who has just been introduced to the head cheerleader.

"I assume you know who I am," Sally said as soon as they were alone.

Frank smiled. "Anyone who watches television or reads a newspaper knows who you are, Mrs. Pope. You are notorious."

Sally laughed and Frank heard church bells chime. Her eyes laughed, too. Her caramel-colored hair shimmered.

"I guess I am notorious," Sally said. "The papers talk about me as if I'm one of those femme fatales from the old black-and-white films."

"Mary Astor in *The Maltese Falcon* or Barbara Stanwyck in *Double Indemnity*," Frank agreed.

Sally looked directly into Frank's eyes. "There is one difference between me and those ladies of the cinema, Mr. Jaffe. I am not a murderer."

"Does someone think you are?"

"My father-in-law, Arnold Pope Sr., is doing everything in his power to see that I'm charged with murdering my husband. And—before we go any further—I need to know if that's a problem."

Frank was confused. "If what's a problem?"

"If you take my case, you'll have to go up against Senior. He's a formidable opponent. I know that from experience. He also owns a lot of people. I need to know if he owns you or if you're afraid of him."

"I barely know Mr. Pope." Frank smiled. "We don't exactly run in the same circles. And, from what I've heard, I doubt I'd like him very much if I did get to know him."

"Then you'll take my case?"

"Is there a case? Have you been charged?"

"Not yet. But I have friends who have friends and I've been warned that Karl Burdett has convened a grand jury with me as its target."

"Have the police or a prosecutor tried to speak to you?" Frank asked.

"I was interviewed at the club when Arnie was shot. It never entered my head that I'd need a lawyer, then. A detective came to my house yesterday but I'd been alerted to the investigation so I refused to talk to him. That's when I asked around and got your name."

"Before we go any further, we need to

discuss the business side of my representation. Are you aware of the expense involved in defending a murder case?"

"I don't care about the expense."

"I'll need a $100,000 retainer for my fees, investigation, and expert witnesses," Frank said. "The case could get even more expensive."

"That won't be a problem. I'll bring in a cashier's check tomorrow."

"Okay. Now that you're officially my client, it's time for me to give you my lawyer speech. I give it to every client and you shouldn't take anything I say personally. But you should take what I say to heart because misunderstanding our relationship as attorney and client can land you in a lot of trouble.

"Now, anything you tell me is confidential with only a few exceptions which we can talk about later. So, if you tell me you did kill your husband . . ."

"Which I did not."

Frank nodded. "But if you did and you confessed to me, I would never tell anyone what you told me. On the other hand, I'm an officer of the court, so I can't let you commit perjury. If you tell me you did kill

Congressman Pope I can't let you get on the stand and swear you were in Idaho at the time of the shooting. I wouldn't tell on you, but—if you refused to recant—I'd be forced to drop your case and I *will* keep your retainer."

"Mr. Jaffe, let's get this out of the way once and for all. I did not kill my husband or have anything to do with his death. Anyone who says I did is lying. If any evidence implicates me, you can be certain it's been fabricated. I am completely, one hundred percent innocent."

"Then why is Karl Burdett convening a grand jury?"

"I honestly don't know. All the newspapers say that Charlie Marsh shot Arnie."

"Maybe Burdett is working on a conspiracy or aiding-and-abetting theory. If Charlie Marsh fired the shot that killed your husband but you assisted him in his plan, the law considers you to be as guilty as the person who fired the shot."

"Charlie and I never discussed murdering my husband."

"Then you know Marsh?"

Sally paused. "I'm not a good person,

Mr. Jaffe. I've cheated on my husband many times. I was cheating on him with Charlie Marsh. But I loved Arnie. I know that sounds contradictory but our relationship was complicated, and Senior is responsible for that."

"Why don't you explain what was going on."

"I'm what people of breeding call trailer trash." Sally laughed bitterly. "The description is pretty accurate. A good part of my early years was spent in trailer parks. My father was someone passing through town, so I have no idea who he is. My mother was a drunk, but in a dark tavern, after a guy had downed a few, she was an attractive enough drunk to catch a few men before they realized how bad a bargain they'd made. Then she'd be out in the cold again, looking for shelter and the next bottle.

"I grew up fast. I know now that I've got a pretty good mind, but while I was growing up the boys were never interested in that part of my anatomy." Sally laughed again, self-consciously. "My mother was my role model. I was the high school slut and a high school dropout, and I used sex to get what I wanted. The one thing I did right was waiting to get knocked up until I met someone with money. And that's where Arnie comes in.

"Senior convinced him to enlist after college because being a Marine would look good when Arnie ran for office—something Senior started working for on the day Arnie was born. But Senior screwed up. When Arnie went into the Marines it was the first time in his life that he was out from under his father's thumb.

"Arnie was at Camp Pendleton completing his Marine Infantry Training. I was working in a restaurant near the base. He came in a few times on leave and we started dating. Freud might say that our courtship was Arnie's way of rebelling against his father. I was a waitress with no education to speak of, someone he knew his father would loathe."

Sally looked very sad. "I told you I'm not a good person. Our marriage is proof of that. As soon as I found out who Arnie was and how much money he had I tricked him into getting me pregnant. It wasn't hard. He said he loved me. I think he did. When I told him I was pregnant he seemed happy. He's the one who said we should get married. I don't think he thought about the consequences."

"Did you tell his father?"

Sally shook her head. "We went to Las Vegas over a weekend. Senior didn't know until it was too late."

"How did he react?"

"Not well. He tried to get the marriage annulled but Arnie stood up to him. It was probably the only time in his life that he showed any backbone. That's when I fell in love with him." She shook her head. "I have to admit, it took me by surprise. I went into the marriage for the money, but Arnie was this big, sweet kid, and I really started looking forward to having a baby."

"Did Arnold Sr. mellow when the baby was born?"

"Not one degree. Senior is relentless when he wants to get his way. When Arnie wouldn't file for divorce, he poisoned him against me by spreading rumors that I was sleeping around; rumors that had no basis until Senior got to me."

"How did he do that?"

"By beating down Arnie until I came to despise both of them. Senior couldn't control me. I was too tough for him. So he wrecked our marriage by constantly making Arnie choose between us. Arnie was so whipped he sided with his father rather than face him like a man. That's when I started sleeping around. I just wanted to wake him up and that was the only way I could think to do it. I never enjoyed the affairs. They were just a way of fighting back. I wanted him to stand up to someone, even if it was me, but he didn't have the guts."

A tear rolled down Sally's cheek. "Until the night he died, that is. That was the first time in a long time that he acted like a man."

Frank's client looked down at her lap, where her clenched fists lay.

"I know I hurt him—and there were times when I despised him—but I really loved him."

Her voice was barely above a whisper. Her suffering brought back the pain Frank had felt when Samantha died.

"Do you want some water?" he asked.

Sally shook her head but she still couldn't speak. Frank waited patiently. When she was calmer he asked a question he hoped would take her mind off her husband.

"Does anyone know where Marsh is?"

"There are rumors that he's somewhere in Africa—a country that doesn't have an extradition treaty with the U.S.—but the rumors haven't been confirmed as far as I know."

Frank made some notes. "I think this is enough for today," he said when he was through. "I guess I don't have to tell you that you shouldn't discuss your case with anyone but me or my investigator—and I mean anyone. No one but me, or someone who works for me, can use the attorney-client privilege to prevent being compelled to testify against you. If a reporter, detective, anyone, approaches you about the case, just tell them your attorney has directed you to refrain from commenting. That's it. Just cut them off.

"Meanwhile, I'm going to let Karl Burdett know that I'm your lawyer and you're off-limits. I'm also going to try to find out what the evidence is that has him believing he can convince a jury beyond a reasonable doubt that you're guilty of murder."

CHAPTER 18

A week after Sally Pope hired Frank, she was charged with murder and conspiracy to commit murder. Two days after Sally's arraignment and release on bail, Frank was cross-referencing phone calls made by a heroin dealer in a federal narcotics case when Herb Cross stuck his head in the door. A few years back, Cross, a slender, bookish African-American, had been mistakenly identified as a robber by a white convenience-store clerk. He told Frank he had an alibi but Frank's investigator was new and inept and had failed to locate any of the people Cross swore could clear him.

Frustrated by the investigator's incompetence, Cross went off on his own and located the men. After the DA dismissed the case, Frank refunded Cross's retainer, fired his investigator, and offered Cross the job.

"I've been through the discovery in *Pope*," Cross said. "You busy or do you want to go through it now?"

Frank rubbed his eyes and leaned back in his chair. He pointed at the paperwork that covered his desk.

"This has to be the most boring case I've ever worked on. I can use the break."

"*Pope* isn't boring," the investigator assured him. "I've got everything spread out in the conference room."

Frank brought his coffee across the hall to a long table covered with photographs, police reports, and files.

"Give me the *Reader's Digest* condensed version," Frank said as he took a sip from his mug. "I'll go through everything myself, later."

"Okay, well, Burdett has Charlie Marsh pegged as the shooter."

"Because?"

"They found a fancy, ivory-handled .357 Magnum at the scene. It's a custom job, very distinctive, and it belongs to Marsh. A waiter at Marsh's hotel saw him playing with it earlier in the evening and his agent, Mickey Keys, saw the gun in the limo that took Marsh and his entourage to the Westmont."

"Was Marsh carrying it?"

"No, Keys told the police that Marsh's bodyguard, Delmar Epps, liked the gun and carried it in his waistband when Marsh was in public. Epps was playing with it in the limo but Keys doesn't know what happened to the gun once Epps got out of the car."

"And the Magnum is definitely the murder weapon?"

Cross nodded. "The lab made a positive match. The bullet that killed the congressman was fired from Marsh's gun."

"Are Marsh's prints on the weapon?"

Cross shook his head. "Someone wiped it down."

"Did someone see Marsh shoot the gun at Pope?"

"They have a witness." Cross handed Frank a crime scene photo. "Marsh was standing in a group on the other side of this turnaround."

Frank wasn't a member of the Westmont but he'd been there several times.
He guessed that the police photographer
had been standing under the portico at
the main entrance and had shot across the
turnaround toward the pro shop. Even
though it was a night shot, Frank could
see the side of the turnaround closest to
the entrance with enough definition to
make out a section of a flower bed that
had been trampled underfoot. But the light
from the club entrance faded out midway
across the turnaround, leaving the far side
in shadow. The pro shop, which was about
twenty-five yards back from the road on
the side away from the club, was almost
impossible to see.

"Where was Marsh supposed to be
standing?" Frank asked.

"See the road leading from the main
street?" Cross asked, pointing at the far side
of the turnaround.

Frank nodded.

"He was a little bit in from where the
road bends toward the parking lot, sort of a
straight line to the edge of the pro shop."

"Okay, I've got it."

Frank studied the picture. "There's not a

lot of light on that spot. How do they put Marsh with the gun?"

"Several witnesses will testify that they saw a muzzle flash from the area where Marsh was standing, but the key witness for the state is Werner Rollins. He's an ex-con and Burdett is holding him on an outstanding warrant. Rollins is an acquaintance of Marsh who was at the seminar with another ex-con, named Gary Hass. A fight broke out after the congressman hit Marsh. Rollins got into it with a security guard. He ended up in the group on the other side of the turnaround. Then he took off when Pope was shot. The police picked him up a few hours later. He's cut a deal with Burdett and he's going to testify that he saw Marsh shoot Pope."

"What does his buddy, Hass, say?"

"He's not in custody but they do have Delmar Epps. It looks like Epps drove Marsh from the scene. He was also involved in the fight. Word is they're cutting a deal with him, too."

"What does he say happened to the gun?"

"He says Hass opened the limo door when the car stopped. When Epps realized the limo driver wasn't opening the door he thought there might be trouble—a fan, paparazzi—so he says he got out to deal with Hass and left the gun on the seat."

"So we have Marsh in the car with the gun."

Cross nodded.

"Where's Marsh now?"

"My latest information is that he's sought asylum in Batanga, which doesn't have an extradition treaty with the United States."

"Doesn't a cannibal run that country?"

"So they say."

"Okay, so we have Marsh as the shooter. Why does Burdett think Mrs. Pope is involved?"

Cross pointed at a Xerox copy of a group of photographs. "The day before he was shot, someone sent these pictures and an anonymous note to the congressman's office. The pictures show our client and Charlie Marsh in compromising positions in her house and they show Mrs. Pope at night going into and out of the elevator that went to Marsh's penthouse hotel suite. The note said that Sally Pope and Marsh were going to be at the Westmont on the following evening. The note was made by pasting letters cut from magazine ads onto a sheet of white paper. Sally Pope's fingerprints are all over the paper and on some of the pasted letters. Mrs. Pope subscribes to the magazine from which the letters were cut. I think Burdett is going to argue that our client lured her husband to the club from DC so Charlie Marsh could shoot him."

"Do we know where the paper is from?"

"Similar paper was found during a search of the Pope residence."

Frank studied the pictures of Marsh and his client in flagrante. He looked troubled for a moment. Then he brightened.

"Someone took the pictures of Marsh and our client making out. Find the photographer, Herb. He's the key to this case."

"Do you have any idea who might have hired the photographer if it wasn't our client?"

"I'll ask her for ideas, but the obvious suspect is Arnold Pope Sr."

Frank told his investigator about Senior's relationship with Junior and his daughter-in-law.

"Do you know—off the top of your head—what law firm Senior uses for his legal work?" Cross asked.

"I think it's Reed, Briggs. Why?"

"Investigators who do surveillance work are a special breed. They're usually loners who earn a living by spending eight to twelve hours a day with their camera staking out workmen's comp claimants or plaintiffs in personal injury cases to see if they can catch them malingering. They're frequently social misfits who can't take regular office work. They don't like routines or bosses looking over their shoulder. Firms don't carry these guys on their payroll like they do in-house investigators, but they have a list of people they'll contract with for odd jobs when the need arises. If Arnold Sr. hired the photographer he may have gotten the name from someone at Reed, Briggs."

"Get on it, then. If we can prove that Senior hired the person who took the photos we'll tear a huge hole in the state's case. Have you found anything else that could cause us problems?"

"I'm not certain. There are two witnesses listed on the indictment who don't match up with a police report."

"Who are they?"

"Otto Jarvis and Anthony Rose."

Frank frowned. "I don't recognize Rose. I'll ask Mrs. Pope if she knows him. Jarvis is a lawyer."

"Is he with a big firm?"

"No, he's a bottom-feeder. He does court-appointed criminal cases, but nothing big. Misdemeanors, shoplifts, drunk drives. I've heard that he does a lot of divorce work. If I'm not mistaken, he's had a few problems with the bar, so check to see if he's had ethics complaints filed against him."

"Will do. Should I see if he's connected with Senior? Maybe he's the one who set him up with the photographer."

"That's a good idea," Frank said. Then he went quiet. When he spoke again he looked worried.

"What concerns me, Herb, is the absence of a police report for these two witnesses. That usually means a DA is setting up a surprise, and I don't like surprises when I'm in trial."

CHAPTER 19

As Highway 26 heads west from Portland toward the Pacific Ocean, the urban landscape gives way quickly to suburban shopping malls and green spaces dominated by sprawling, glass-and-chrome office complexes housing high-tech companies. Frank Jaffe was already in farm country when he took the exit to Hillsboro twenty minutes after leaving the city.

Frank looked forward to the drive to and from the courthouse during the trial, because he was alone with Sally Pope. Much of the time, Frank discussed trial strategy or gave Sally his impressions of the way the trial was going, but sometimes they talked about things that had nothing to do with the law, and those were the times Frank treasured the most. He knew the ethics rules prohibited him from having a romantic relationship with a client, but spending an hour a day alone with Sally was the next best thing.

If Frank had to use one word to describe Sally Pope's demeanor during her trial, it would be "composed." It would definitely not be "serene," because Frank knew that there were times when she was boiling mad, but Sally never let anyone but Frank see this side of her and she only let her emotions show in the privacy of Frank's office or in his car.

The grayish white, neoclassical Washington County courthouse took up a block on the outskirts of city center in Hills-boro. Each morning, when they arrived for court, reporters hurled questions at Frank and his client as he escorted Sally between the fluted columns at the main entrance. And each day they ignored the press and hurried up the stairs to the courtroom of the Honorable Dagmar Hansen in which Mrs. Pope's future was being decided.

Judge Hansen, a dirty-blond, cigarette-smoking hard case in her mid-forties, had made her bones defending insurance companies. She was a political conservative who was very smart and tried to be fair. The judge had made enough money in private practice to be immune to a bribe and she had enough integrity to stand up to a bully. Frank was confident that Arnold Pope Sr. would not be able to get to her.

The courtroom was packed from the first day, and seated directly behind the prosecution table every minute court was in session was Arnold Pope Sr. Sally made a point of ignoring her father-in-law and the hateful stare he directed at her every time she passed him.

It took a week to pick a jury, because of the publicity the case had received. As soon as the jurors were sworn, Karl Burdett gave an opening statement in which he claimed that the evidence would show the defendant had designs on her husband's money from the start and had tricked him into marriage by getting pregnant. The DA displayed a sample of the photographs the congressman had received the day before he died. Then he argued they were the bait the defendant used to lure Junior to his death so she could inherit millions from his estate and collect additional millions from the insurance policy on the congressman's life. During his harangue, Burdett referred to Sally Pope as a gold digger, a black widow, a harlot, and a harridan. Frank wondered if the DA had assigned a deputy to make a list of every derogatory term that could be used to describe a woman.

Frank's opening statement was brief, dwelling on each juror's obligation to wait until all of the evidence was in before drawing any conclusions about guilt or innocence and their obligation to acquit if the prosecution did not prove its case beyond a reasonable doubt.

As soon as court adjourned, Frank summoned Amanda from the back of the courtroom and introduced her to Sally. Frank had urged his daughter to enjoy her summer break by hanging out with her friends, but Amanda was a courtroom junkie who planned to go to law school after college, then practice criminal law, like her dad. There was no way Frank could talk her out of sitting in on the biggest case of his career.

"What did you think of the opening statements?" Frank asked as he packed up his papers.

Amanda cast a nervous eye at Frank's client. "Can I be honest?"

"Please," Sally said.

"Burdett kicked your butt, Dad."

Frank responded with a hearty laugh. Sally seemed amused by Amanda's cheeky reply.

"Out of the mouths of babes," Frank said.

"Hey, I call 'em like I see them."

"You called this one correctly." Frank sighed. "My statement was vague because I'm still in the dark about the state's case and I didn't want to commit to a defense theory that Burdett can destroy."

"I thought the DA outlined his case pretty thoroughly."

"He's holding something back. There are two witnesses on his list who don't have police reports and I'm scared to death of what they're going to say."

"Who are they?"

"Tony Rose and Otto Jarvis. Jarvis is a lawyer. He refused to meet with Herb, and Mrs. Pope has no idea who he is."

"Who's the other witness?"

"Tony Rose, the tennis pro at the West-mont Country Club."

Now it was Frank's turn to hesitate.

"Go ahead, Frank," Sally said. "Your daughter seems pretty savvy."

"Rose and Mrs. Pope had a . . . relationship. That might be why Burdett is going to call him. But Rose refused to talk to Herb even after Herb told him that we knew about the affair. That makes me very nervous."

DURING THE FIRST week of the trial Burdett called witnesses who established that Junior married Sally Pope after she became pregnant. Then he proved that Sally's affair with Charlie Marsh started shortly before Junior was murdered, by using the testimony of Delmar Epps, who told the jury about Marsh's trip to the Pope home on the evening of the Dunthorpe seminar and her visit to Marsh's penthouse suite. Epps corroborated the testimony of the waiter who saw Marsh with the ivory-handled Magnum at the hotel and said he left the gun in the limo when he got out of the car.

Next, Burdett called John Walsdorf, who told the jury how the fight between Congressman Pope and Charlie Marsh started and how Delmar Epps, Werner Rollins, and the security guards were involved. While cross-examining Walsdorf, Frank established that the manager of the Westmont watched his client during the melee and saw her running toward her husband when the shot that killed him was fired.

After Walsdorf testified, the prosecutor proved that Charlie's Magnum fired the fatal bullet. Witnesses from the Westmont told the jury that they had seen Charlie standing in a group on the other side of the turnaround. Some of these witnesses saw a flash come from that area just before they heard a gunshot and saw the congressman collapse. Werner Rollins testified that he was standing near Marsh and saw him fire the murder weapon.

Frank didn't ask many questions during this phase of the case. Charlie had plenty of reasons to shoot Junior that had nothing to do with a complex murder plot. Arnie Jr. had punched him in the face and was running toward him to do more damage when the fatal shot was fired. In closing, Frank planned to argue that Charlie Marsh acted alone.

EARLY ON THE fifth day of trial, Burdett called Otto Jarvis to the stand. Jarvis did not look well. He was fat and sloppy and he had a waxy complexion. His sparse gray hair was arranged in a bad comb-over and his white shirt bore faint coffee stains. Jarvis's hand shook when he was sworn in and the lawyer looked away when Frank tried to make eye contact.

"Mr. Jarvis," Burdett asked, "what is your profession?"

"I am an attorney-at-law," Jarvis said with as much dignity as he could muster.

"How long have you been in practice?"

"Thirty-five years."

"Where is your office?"

"In Portland."

"Do you specialize in any area of law?"

"Yes, sir. About three-quarters of my practice involves family law."

"Does a lawyer who practices family law represent parties who wish to obtain a divorce?"

"Yes, sir."

"Mr. Jarvis, were you acquainted with

the deceased, United States Congressman Arnold Pope Jr.?"

"I was."

"When did you become acquainted with
him?"

"About two weeks before he died," the
lawyer answered.

"Where and when did you meet?"

"We met at three in the afternoon on a
Wednesday in a tavern in Tualatin," Jarvis
said, naming a suburb a short ride from
Portland.

"That seems like an odd place for a
member of the United States Congress to
confer with an attorney."

"Yes, well, Mr. Pope didn't want anyone
to know about the meeting."

"Why is that?"

"He was thinking of getting a divorce
and he didn't want the press—or anyone
else—to find out."

"Was there anything unusual about the
way the congressman was dressed when
he met you?"

"Yes. He was disguised. He wasn't wearing a suit. He had on old, baggy jeans and
a jacket with the collar turned up and sun-
glasses and a baseball cap. He kept on the

jacket, cap, and glasses all the time we were talking."

"Was there one person in particular Congressman Pope wanted kept in the dark about your meeting?"

"His wife."

"The defendant, Sally Pope?" Burdett asked.

"Yes, sir."

"Why didn't he want his wife to know?"

"He was afraid of her . . ."

"Objection," Frank said.

"Goes to state of mind, Your Honor," Burdett said.

"I'll allow the question," Judge Hansen ruled.

"You were saying?" Burdett continued, flashing a smirk at Frank.

"He was afraid of what she would do if she found out he was going to divorce her."

"Was he specific about his concern?"

"Yes, sir. He said he was afraid she would have him killed."

"Objection," Frank boomed.

"Yes, Mr. Burdett," Judge Hansen told the prosecutor. Then she turned her attention to the jury.

"Ladies and gentlemen, I am striking that last answer. You are to disregard it."

Fat chance, Frank thought.

"What happened at the meeting?" the prosecutor asked.

"We talked about the financial ramifications of the divorce and custody. The Popes had a young son."

"Did the congressman make a decision about what he was going to do at the meeting?"

"No. Just before he left he said he'd get back to me."

Burdett turned toward the defense table. "Your witness, Mr. Jaffe."

"Mr. Jarvis, did you tell anyone about this secret meeting with Mr. Pope?"

"No."

"So, only you and the congressman knew about it?"

"I don't know if the congressman told someone about it, but I didn't."

"Mr. Jarvis, how many people are in your firm?"

"I'm a sole practitioner. So it's just me."

"You said that the congressman discussed the financial ramifications of a divorce from Mrs. Pope."

"Yes."

"There would have been several million dollars involved, wouldn't there?"

"Yes."

"How much money were you discussing?"

"Uh, I don't recall exactly."

Frank leaned back and smiled at the witness. "In the past, oh, say, five years, how many divorce cases have you handled involving many millions of dollars?"

Jarvis flushed and looked down. "Uh, I'm not certain."

"Maybe I can help. If I told you that I had my investigator review every divorce case you've filed in the past five years and he told me that he could only find six such cases, all involving sums of less that two million dollars, would that surprise you?"

"Uh, no."

"You don't normally handle big-ticket divorce cases, do you?"

"No, not normally."

"And you don't normally represent prominent members of the Oregon community, do you?"

"No."

"So the congressman would be quite an unusual and exciting client for you, wouldn't he?"

"I . . . yes."

"And the sum of money involved would be way more than you normally deal with, wouldn't it?"

"Yes."

"And you want this jury to believe that you can't remember how many millions of dollars were involved?"

"I, um, it just slips my mind, at the moment."

"Or, perhaps, you don't know how much money was in his estate because you never met with Mr. Pope."

"I definitely met with him. I just don't remember how much money he had."

Frank noticed a few jurors taking notes. He moved on.

"Are there Oregon firms that routinely represent parties in divorces who are wealthy?"

"Yes."

Frank rattled off the names of several law firms in the metropolitan area.

"Any one of those firms would be used

to handling cases with assets in the millions of dollars, wouldn't they?"

"Yes."

"During your years in practice, have you had ten complaints filed against you with the Oregon State Bar?"

Jarvis flushed. "I've had some complaints filed. I don't remember the number."

"Have you been suspended by the state bar from the practice of law for six months on two occasions for ethics violations?"

"Yes," Jarvis answered angrily.

"Mr. Jarvis, do you still want this jury to believe that a man like Arnold Pope Jr., with all the contacts he had, chose to consult about his divorce with a lawyer who has rarely handled a society divorce or a divorce with these kinds of assets and who has bar complaints filed against him and who has been suspended several times for being unethical?"

"I . . . he didn't tell me why he chose me. Maybe he was afraid that it would get back to his wife if he went to one of the big firms."

"How did Mr. Pope arrange to meet you at the tavern?"

"He phoned my office."

"Was there anything that would have prevented Mr. Pope from calling someone at a big firm to arrange a secret meeting at the tavern where you and he allegedly met?"

"No, I guess not."

"Do you bill by the hour, Mr. Jarvis?"

"Yes, sometimes."

"So, you can produce a record of the initial call from the congressman if I subpoenaed it?"

"No. I don't think there is a record."

"There must be a record of the time spent during this conference. You can produce the file, can't you?"

"I didn't make a file. The congressman didn't hire me. We just consulted."

"But he paid you for the consultation? There's a check, isn't there?"

"He . . . he paid me in cash. He didn't want any record of the meeting his wife could discover."

"I assume you recorded the transaction somewhere so you'd remember to report the fee as income on your taxes?" Frank asked with a sweet smile.

Jarvis looked like a deer caught in very

bright headlights. "Uh, I may have forgotten."

"I see," Frank said. "So, let me get this straight: there are no witnesses to this meeting, no records, no proof that it ever happened, except, of course, for your word?"

"Why would I lie?" Jarvis asked, but he sounded desperate.

"Good question. Did Arnold Pope Sr. pay you for your testimony?"

Jarvis shot an involuntary glance at Senior then pulled his eyes away as soon as he realized what he'd done. Frank couldn't see Senior's reaction but he did notice several jurors look in Senior's direction.

"No. That's not true," Jarvis answered.

"Then can you explain where you got the money you used last month to pay off the several thousand dollars in debt on your credit cards?"

"I was in Las Vegas recently and I did very well at the tables," Jarvis answered lamely.

"Did you report your winnings to the IRS, or did you forget to make a note of them like you did the fee Congressman Pope allegedly paid you?"

"I . . . I will at the appropriate time."

"Good for you, Mr. Jarvis. No further questions, Your Honor."

"THE STATE CALLS Anthony Rose, Your Honor," Karl Burdett said as soon as Otto Jarvis fled the courtroom.

While one of Burdett's deputies ducked into the hall to summon the witness, Frank reread the meager investigative report Herb Cross had put together. Rose had gone to high school in Sisters, Oregon, a small town in the center of the state. He'd been a star on the tennis team but his grades weren't good enough for a college scholarship, so he'd enlisted in the army. Rose had made an attempt to get into the Rangers but had not been selected. Herb had talked to a few of Rose's acquaintances, who said he'd told them he'd made jumps from airplanes and excelled in marksmanship but washed out because of a hostile officer. Rose was honorably discharged from the military and enrolled in college at Ohio State, where he'd excelled on the tennis team, making the quarterfinals of the NCAA tournament his senior year. After a brief flirtation with professional tennis, Rose returned to Oregon, where he was hired as the club pro at the Westmont.

The courtroom door opened but Frank waited for his first look at Sally's lover until Rose raised his hand to be sworn. The tennis pro looked like a poster boy for a country club gigolo. He was handsome, athletic, and dressed in a navy blue blazer, neatly pressed tan slacks, and a sky blue shirt that was open at the neck enough to show a tuft of chest hair. Frank noticed that his smile caused the face of every woman on the jury to light up.

"Mr. Rose, are you acquainted with the defendant?" Burdett asked after a few preliminary questions. Rose locked eyes with Sally. With his head turned, the jurors didn't see him smirk.

"You might say that," Rose answered.

"In what capacity have you known her?" the prosecutor asked.

"In several capacities. She was my student—I gave her tennis lessons—I like to think we were friends and we were definitely lovers."

There were murmurs in the spectator section. Frank saw several jurors scrutinize Sally Pope in a distinctly unfriendly manner at the mention of a second extramarital affair.

"How long did your sexual relationship with the deceased's wife go on?"

"A few months."

"Why did it end?"

Rose paused for dramatic effect before answering.

"She wanted me to murder her husband and I refused."

Frank heard gasps from the gallery and saw shocked expressions on more than one juror's face.

"That's a lie," Sally whispered vehemently.

"Can you relate the conversation in which the defendant asked you to kill her husband?" Burdett asked as he struggled successfully to stifle a triumphant smile.

"Certainly. We were at a gathering on an estate in Dunthorpe at which Charlie Marsh, or Guru Gabriel Sun, or whatever he was calling himself, was lecturing about inner peace or some such nonsense. Mrs. Pope asked me to go outside after the lecture. She led me to a secluded spot in the garden. As soon as we were alone and out of the hearing of the other guests, Mrs. Pope asked me if I would like to earn a quarter of a million dollars. I asked her how I could do that. She said her husband was planning to divorce her. There was some kind of contract the congressman's father had insisted Mrs. Pope sign under the threat that he would disinherit his son if she didn't. I don't remember all of the details but the one that worried Mrs. Pope left her in bad shape financially if there was a divorce. But if her husband died before a divorce was final, she would inherit a fortune. She also said there was a life insurance policy for several million dollars. She sounded desperate."

"What did she suggest you do to help her avoid the consequences of a divorce?"

"She wanted me to take care of her husband before he could file."

"What did she mean by 'take care of'?"

"Kill him. Murder him."

"There's no question in your mind about that?"

"None. She said she wanted him dead and how I did it would be left up to me."

"What was your response to Mrs. Pope's

request that you assassinate a member of the United States Congress?"

"I told her she was nuts; that I wasn't going to kill anyone, no matter how much money she offered me. Especially not a member of Congress. I mean, I'd have the whole federal government after me: the FBI, the CIA, the Secret Service.

"To tell the truth, I was also offended that she had such a low opinion of me that she thought I'd kill somebody for money. And it was pretty clear that she was using me. I mean, she acted like she loved me and she hinted that we could get married after Junior was out of the way, but I know she didn't have any real feelings for me."

Rose shrugged. "She was great in bed, but she lost interest as soon as she climaxed, if you know what I mean."

Burdett chose to move on rather than follow up on that topic.

"How did the defendant act after you refused to help her murder her husband?"

"She was very upset. She called me names, insulted my manhood." Rose shrugged again. "Mrs. Pope was used to getting her way with men and I think she was shocked that any man could refuse any request she made, no matter how crazy."

"Did anything happen while you were arguing?"

"Yes, sir. Charlie Marsh showed up. It was obvious that he wanted to impress Mrs. Pope by coming to her rescue."

"What happened?"

"He hit me when I wasn't prepared. Then he had his bodyguard rough me up."

"Did the bodyguard display a weapon?"

"Yeah. I didn't get a good look at it but there was a gun in his waistband. He made sure I saw it."

"Was there anything distinctive about the weapon?"

"I do remember a fancy handle."

Burdett asked permission to approach the witness and showed Rose the murder weapon.

"Is this the gun Mr. Marsh's bodyguard was carrying?"

Rose took the revolver and examined the grip. "I can't be certain," he said. "I only saw the handle for a second. But this could be it."

Burdett returned the exhibit to the table

holding the evidence, before continuing to question the witness.

"Did you hear anything Mr. Marsh said to the defendant or anything she said to him after you fought?"

"No. The bodyguard hauled me away and threatened to beat me up if I didn't leave immediately. To tell the truth, after my conversation with Mrs. Pope I was pretty anxious to get as far from her as possible."

"Did you have any more contact with the defendant after your argument?"

"No, sir. She did cancel her tennis lessons, but she did that with the pro shop."

Burdett consulted his notes. Then he addressed the judge.

"No more questions on direct, Your Honor."

"Mr. Jaffe?" Judge Hansen asked.

Frank had no idea how to cross-examine Rose, so he did the only thing he could think to do.

"It's getting late, Your Honor," Frank said. "I wonder if we can recess for the day?"

Judge Hansen glanced at the clock. It was 4:45. "Very well, Mr. Jaffe. We'll reconvene in the morning."

Frank had maintained a stone face during Rose's devastating testimony. As soon as the jury left the courtroom, he leaned over to his client.

"He made that up," Sally Pope said before Frank could get a word out.

Her voice was tight with anger.

"It's a crime to commit perjury. He could go to prison if I prove he's lying. Why is he doing this?"

"I can think of two reasons he'd lie under oath. One is revenge. When we went into the garden, I told Tony I didn't want to see him anymore. He was upset when I broke it off."

"Rose doesn't strike me as the type who'd lose sleep over a woman telling him their affair was over. No offense, but I'm guessing you're not the first club member he's seduced."

"I know for a fact I'm not. And, for the record, I seduced him. But Tony is used to being the one who breaks off the affair and I think I bruised his ego."

"What's your other idea?"

"Senior got to him just like he got to Jarvis. Tony's not real big on ethics. He'd have no compunction about lying under oath if he was paid enough. Hell, if I *had* offered him a quarter million dollars to kill Arnie I bet he'd have done it."

Frank was about to say something else when Herb Cross pushed through the court-room doors, sporting a wide smile.

"What's up?" Frank asked.

"I found the photographer."

"Great work. Have you talked to him yet?"

"No, but I know where he lives. I figured you'd want to come along."

CHAPTER 20

Hey, is this Jack Rodriguez?" Herb Cross asked as soon as someone answered the phone. Cross was calling from Frank's car, which was parked across the street from a poorly maintained rental home in a rundown section of North Portland. Weeds outnumbered grass in the overgrown postage-stamp front lawn, and the small Cape Cod hadn't seen a new coat of paint in recent memory.

"Who's this?" was the cautious answer.

"Are you the private detective?" Cross asked, trying to sound as paranoid as the man to whom he was speaking.

"Yeah," Rodriguez answered, perkier now that he smelled a buck. "What can I do for you?"

"Look, I don't feel comfortable talking on the phone, if you know what I mean."

"Certainly. I definitely understand the need for confidentiality. So, where do you want to meet?"

"Do you have an office?"

"No, I find it's better not to draw too much attention to myself."

"Oh yeah, that's right. Mr. Jarvis told me you don't have an office. I forgot."

"Who?"

Cross heard panic in the PI's voice.

"Otto Jarvis, the lawyer. He gave me your number. He said you do really good work."

There was dead air. When Rodriguez spoke, he sounded very nervous.

"Here's the thing. I just checked my calendar and I forgot about a project that's going to take me out of town for a while. So I don't think I can do anything for you right now."

"Oh man, that's disappointing, because Mr. Jarvis said you're the go-to guy if someone thinks their wife is, uh, you know what I mean."

"Not really, and I think you have the wrong guy, anyway, because I don't know this Jarvis guy. So, good luck with your wife."

The moment Rodriguez hung up, Cross called Frank, who was stationed near the back door of the PI's house.

"He denied knowing Jarvis, but he got very panicky as soon as I mentioned his name. I figure he'll be coming out any minute. I've got the front."

Cross put the cell phone in his pocket and started across the street. He saw a curtain move. He hoped Rodriguez would make a break for it so they wouldn't have to figure out how to get in his house. He also hoped the PI didn't have a gun.

FRANK HAD SWAPPED his suit for a black leather jacket, a black turtleneck, and black slacks, which—along with his thick upper body and broken nose—made him look like a thug. As soon as he heard the back door open and close, he stepped around the corner of the house and into Rodriguez's path.

"Where you headed, Mr. Rodriguez?" he asked as the PI skidded to a stop. Rodriguez was skinny and about five foot seven. His long black hair was greasy and unkempt and Frank saw acne scars on his sunken cheeks. The lawyer didn't think Rodriguez would try to fight but he looked like he might be fast, so Frank clamped a hand on his forearm.

"Who the fuck are you?" Rodriguez asked, trying to sound tough and failing miserably.

"Why don't we tell you inside," Frank said as Herb Cross walked up behind the PI.

Frank's investigator had his hand stuffed in his jacket pocket as if he were holding a gun. Rodriguez's eyes darted between his captors. While the PI was making up his mind, Herb opened the back door and Frank made the choice for him by pushing Rodriguez inside.

The blinds were down and a low-wattage bulb in a standing lamp cast a sickly pale light over a disgustingly dirty living room. Soiled clothes, skin magazines, and dirty dishes were strewn around. The smell of stale pizza and sweat made Frank wince. He decided that calling the house a pigsty would insult swine everywhere. The only neat spot was a corner of the room given over to a computer, printer, fax, and telephone. Frank guessed that this oasis of cleanliness served as Rodriguez's office.

"How do you live here?" Frank asked.

"Fuck you," the PI answered without much conviction.

Frank shoved Rodriguez onto the couch and stood over him, because he was afraid to sit on any of the furniture.

"What's this all about?" Rodriguez asked.

"We know you took the pictures of Sally Pope with Charlie Marsh," Frank said.

"I don't know what you're talking about," Rodriguez said as he folded his arms across his chest and turned his head so he wouldn't have to look at Frank.

"Explain how he fucked up," Frank said to Cross.

"You made a really amateurish mistake, Jack," Frank's investigator said. He handed the PI one of the photographs that had been shot through the windshield of a car.

"I've never seen this before."

"Then someone stole your ride. A VIN number is a seventeen-character alphanumeric code specific to each vehicle."

"Tell me something I don't know," Rodriguez said, but he was staring at a section of the photo and he'd started to sweat.

"The VIN is mounted on a strip where the dashboard and the windshield meet on the driver's side. Yours is reflected in the picture. Like I said, an amateur's mistake. I traced the VIN back to you, Jack."

"You're in a lot of trouble," Frank said. "I'm sure you know that Sally Pope is on trial for killing her husband."

"What's that have to do with me?"

"Do you know the DA's theory? He thinks your photos were used to lure Congressman Pope to his death. That makes you an accessory to murder."

"Bullshit." Rodriguez hugged himself tighter. "I want a lawyer."

"Cops have to get suspects lawyers. I'm not a cop."

"Then who the fuck are you?"

"Your savior, Jack. The man who can keep you from facing a murder charge."

CHAPTER 21

Karl Burdett was in a great mood when he led his trial assistants into the courtroom the next morning. Frank Jaffe was supposed to be a hot shot but Karl felt that he had him on the ropes. True, Jaffe had scored some points with Otto Jarvis, but he didn't think he'd lay a glove on Tony Rose. If the jurors believed Rose, the case was over.

"Mr. Burdett," Judge Hansen's bailiff said while Karl was swinging his attaché case onto the prosecution table, "the judge wants you in chambers."

"What's up?"

"I don't know, but Judge Hansen, Mr. Jaffe, his client, and two other men are waiting for you."

Karl frowned. He told his assistants to get his files ready and walked toward the judge's chambers. He didn't like surprises.

"Morning, Karl," the judge said. She hadn't donned her robes yet and was wearing a black pants suit and white silk blouse. Even though it was illegal to smoke in a public building, Hansen was on her third cigarette and the room stank from cigarette smoke.

Karl recognized Herb Cross, who was sitting on a couch against the wall next to a scrawny, unkempt man who looked to be in his late twenties and was wearing a sweatshirt, jeans, and running shoes.

Judge Hansen pointed at a chair. It was across the desk from her and next to Frank, who was seated next to his client. The only other person in the room was the judge's court reporter, which meant they weren't going to have an off-the-record chat.

"Mr. Jaffe has brought some very unsettling information to me and I'm trying to figure out the best way to handle the situation," the judge said.

"What situation? I don't know what's going on." The DA cast a quick glance at Jack Rodriguez. "If it involves a new witness, Mr. Jaffe hasn't given me notice as required by the discovery rules."

"It does involve a witness but Mr. Jaffe didn't learn about him until last night. That's why we're meeting. However, before we discuss Mr. Rodriguez's testimony, I want to make certain that I understand your case. You're not going to argue that Mrs. Pope shot her husband, are you?"

"No. Charlie Marsh shot him."

Judge Hansen nodded. "Okay, so, if I've got this right, you're going to argue that Mrs. Pope and Mr. Marsh conspired to kill her husband."

"Right."

"Then Mrs. Pope got someone to take photographs of her and Mr. Marsh in compromising positions and sent these pictures to her husband to make him angry and jealous so he would come to the Westmont Country Club where Mr. Marsh could kill him."

"That's our case."

"Mr. Jaffe, let's put Mr. Rodriguez's testimony on the record," the judge said.

"I object to this . . . this procedure. I really don't . . ."

"Relax, Karl," the judge said. "I'm taking this testimony in chambers so the press won't hear it. That would be pretty embarrassing for you. You'll catch on once you hear what Frank's witness has to say."

Frank turned his chair toward the PI. "The judge swore you earlier, Mr. Rodriguez, and you're still under oath. Understand?"

"Yeah," Rodriguez answered reluctantly.

"Are you a private investigator?"

"Yes."

"Have I shown you state's exhibit thirteen, the photographs that were sent to Congressman Pope?"

"Yes."

"Did you take the pictures?"

"Yes."

"Please tell us why you were following Mrs. Pope and Mr. Marsh and taking photographs of them."

"I got a phone call."

"From who?"

"A man."

"Did he tell you who referred him to you?"

"I do work for the Reed, Briggs law firm every once in a while. He mentioned a lawyer over there."

Frank turned to the judge. "If I may, Your Honor, I'm prepared to prove that the Reed, Briggs firm handles Arnold Pope Sr.'s legal work."

"Whoa, wait a second. What's going on here?" Burdett asked, alarmed by anything that could damage his relationship with his largest contributor.

"Relax and you'll find out," the judge told the DA. "Proceed, Mr. Jaffe."

"Okay. Now, Mr. Rodriguez, was there anything unusual about the voice of the man who contacted you?"

"He had a British accent."

"Did I have you call a number, last night?"

"Yes."

"Who did you call?"

"You said it was the unlisted number a Arnold Pope Sr.'s estate."

"Was there anything familiar about the

voice of the man who answered the phone?"

"Yeah. It was the guy who'd hired me."

"You're certain?"

Rodriguez shrugged. "Well, I never met the guy but it sounded just like him. He had that British accent. And when I told him who I was he got very panicky and refused to put me through to Mr. Pope."

"Did he hang up?"

"Yeah."

"Your Honor," Frank said, "Derrick Barclay, Mr. Pope's personal assistant, has a British accent. I made a recording of the call and Mr. Barclay sounds pretty rattled on it."

"Very well. Go on."

"When you were hired, what were the terms and what were you told to do?" Frank asked.

"The guy with the accent wanted me to follow Mrs. Pope and take pictures if I caught her doing something she shouldn't."

"How were you paid?"

"Upfront into my bank account."

"Did you ever learn the name of the man who paid you?"

"No."

"Did you have more than one conversation with this man?"

"Yeah. He called a little after Mrs. Pope was arrested."

"During that phone conversation did the man ask for the name of a divorce attorney who wouldn't mind bending the rules a little?"

"Yeah. He said he'd heard that I did work for small firms and solos and he said he needed a guy who could use some dough and wasn't picky about what he had to do to earn it."

"Did you give him a name?"

"I told him about Otto."

"Otto Jarvis?"

"Yeah."

"Did you give the pictures that were sent to Congressman Pope to someone?"

"Not exactly."

"What did you do with them?"

"I sent them to a PO box."

"That's all, Your Honor."

"Would everyone but Karl please leave my chambers," Judge Hansen said.

"I don't think . . . " the DA started.

"*I* think it would be better for you if we

talked without an audience," Judge Hansen said. "Mr. Jaffe, you don't mind if Mr. Burdett and I have an ex parte conference, do you?"

"No, Your Honor."

As soon as they were alone, Judge Hansen took a drag on her cigarette. Then she shook her head.

"I thought this case smelled as soon as I heard your theory."

"Those pictures . . ."

"If Mrs. Pope didn't hire Rodriguez to take them, the only thing they prove is that she was set up."

"Marsh could have faked a British accent to make everyone think that Derrick Barclay made the call," Burdett persisted.

Hansen leaned forward and fixed Burdett with a hard stare.

"I've heard the tape of Rodriguez's call and I know how Barclay's voice sounds. I've also heard scuttlebutt around the courthouse that you had no intention of charging Sally Pope until you came back from a meeting with Arnie Sr. Is there any truth to the rumors?"

Burdett shifted uneasily in his seat. "The grand jury found . . ."

"The grand jury will find anything you want them to. We both know that, so don't give me that shit. I have half a mind to haul Derrick Barclay and his boss in front of a grand jury and ask them about those photographs."

The blood drained from Burdett's face.

"Now, I'm going to assume you didn't know that Jarvis was committing perjury before you put him on, but you have to believe that none of the jurors are going to credit his bullshit story about the so-called secret meeting. And Tony Rose is so slimy I'm surprised he didn't slide off the witness chair. The whole prosecution stinks, and the question for you to ponder is who will be in the shit when the smoke clears.

"If you go forward, Frank's going to drag Senior and that little weasel Barclay into court, and I promise you this. If they lie under oath in my court, I will put them in prison along with anyone who was their knowing accomplice. So, here's my suggestion. You ask for a dismissal with prejudice and I'll grant it. Otherwise, you're on your own."

KARL BURDETT TOOK several hours before returning to court to tell the judge that he was going to dismiss the case against Sally with prejudice. Most of that time was spent in his office with Arnold Pope Sr. and Derrick Barclay, trying to explain the consequences they would face if their complicity in luring Arnold Jr. to the Westmont was made public and they had any part in shaping the testimony of Otto Jarvis or Tony Rose. Some of the time was spent weathering Senior's tirades.

As soon as Arnold Pope stormed out of his office, Burdett drew up a motion to dismiss with prejudice. When the paperwork was completed, Judge Hansen ordered the dismissal in open court. Then Frank and the DA held a press conference at which the prosecutor said that evidence had come to light that raised reasonable doubts about Sally Pope's guilt. Burdett refused to answer any questions about the evidence, claiming there was an ongoing investigation that could be jeopardized if he disclosed what he'd learned. At Judge Hansen's urging, Frank agreed that he would not reveal the evidence that had led to his client's exoneration, so Frank simply thanked the prosecutor for having the courage to change his mind when justice demanded it. Burdett claimed the high ground by saying that the prosecution always wins when justice is served.

"I CAN'T BELIEVE it's over," Sally said an hour after Frank drove away from the courthouse. They were seated across from each other in Sally's living room, drinking her scotch. Her son, Kevin, was staying with a friend who had been taking care of him during the trial. "I'm only sorry that the jury didn't say I wasn't guilty."

"A dismissal with prejudice is the same as an acquittal," Frank reminded her. "The DA can never charge you with your husband's murder again."

"There are people who will think I got off on a technicality."

"Those people would always have questions no matter how the case ended. You're just going to have to ignore them."

"That bastard," Sally muttered. "I wish there was some way to get back at him."

"You're going to have to ignore Senior, too."

"That won't be easy. I know him. He'll go after me as long as he's alive. He can tie up Arnie's estate, and he swore he'd try and get custody of Kevin."

"Senior won't succeed if he tries either of those ploys. He could face criminal charges if it came out that he bribed witnesses to lie about you and you'd have one hell of a lawsuit."

"I don't want to file a lawsuit. I just want to be left in peace."

"I'll do my best to see that it happens."

Sally shifted her gaze from her glass to her lawyer. "You've been wonderful."

Frank felt uncomfortable. He wanted to look away but felt he would reveal his emotions if he did. Instead, the blush that colored his cheeks served that purpose.

"It was easy. I believed in you."

Sally didn't speak for several heartbeats. Then she said, "I don't want to be alone tonight."

"What do you mean?"

"You know what I mean. I want you to stay with me."

All of the confidence Frank had demonstrated in court deserted him.

"I can't, Sally."

"Don't tell me you don't want to."

"You're a client. The rules of ethics . . ."

"Don't mean a damn thing if two people care about each other. I've seen the way you look at me. You didn't work as hard as you did to free me just because I paid you."

Frank knew there were a million reasons he should stand up and leave, but he didn't.

PART III

**State of Oregon
v. Charlie Marsh** 2009

CHAPTER

22

The long table that filled the center of the Jaffe, Katz conference room was covered with banker's boxes, transcripts, three-ring binders, and case files. Amanda had cleared a space on one end for her sandwich and coffee mug, and she had finished eating well before Frank finished his recap of the *Pope* case.

"I forgot that Tony Rose was a key witness against Mrs. Pope," Amanda said. "Life sure takes interesting turns."

"That it does," Frank said as he considered the way fortune had favored the former country club tennis pro.

"And I always wondered about what went on in chambers that morning."

"I couldn't tell you or anyone else. Burdett agreed to drop the case if the reason for the dismissal was sealed."

"Did Senior go after Mrs. Pope after the trial?"

Frank nodded. "He's a vindictive prick. He threatened a civil suit for wrongful death, he threatened to contest Junior's will, and he threatened to get custody of his grandson. I put a stop to that at a sit-down with him and his attorney. Once his lawyer saw that there was a good chance I could prove he'd hired Rodriguez to take the pictures and bribed Otto Jarvis to perjure himself, he convinced Senior to back off."

"What happened to Mrs. Pope?" Amanda asked.

"The money Junior left her and the proceeds of the insurance policy made her a wealthy woman. As soon as everything was settled, she moved to Europe with her son to protect him from the publicity. She lived in Italy until recently, when she returned to Oregon so Kevin could finish his education in America."

"Have you seen her since she came back?"

"No. She's a bit of a recluse, and I haven't had a reason to renew our acquaintance," Frank said.

Amanda thought her father sounded a little stiff. She thought she knew why, but decided to ignore his reaction.

"Are you certain Mrs. Pope had nothing to do with her husband's death?" she asked instead.

Frank thought about Amanda's question. "Judge Hansen told me Karl Burdett argued that Charlie Marsh could have faked a British accent to frame Senior in case anyone figured out that Rodriguez took the pictures. It did seem odd to me that Senior would let someone who'd be so easy to identify negotiate with Rodriguez. But I'm fairly certain that Sally Pope is innocent. I even wondered if the bullet that hit Junior was meant for her. Sally was almost next to him when the shot was fired."

Amanda stood up and tossed her trash in the wastebasket. "Will you try to get the waiver for me?"

"I'll call Sally today."

"Thanks, Dad."

"My pleasure."

Frank's shoulders sagged as soon as the door closed behind his daughter. He had told Amanda what she needed to know about the *Pope* case to represent her client, but he hadn't told her anything about his relationship with Sally Pope. There were some things that a father didn't discuss with his children, like the torrid affair that had started the evening Frank had won Sally's case and the way he'd felt when she went to Europe. Frank had been confused, frustrated, and, though he hated to admit it, lovesick. Just thinking about Sally today had resurrected those emotions.

Before she'd left him, Frank had convinced himself that Sally was drawn to him as much as he was attracted to her. There was the way she looked at him, the way she moved so close whenever the occasion permitted intimacy. There was the timbre of her voice when it was late in the evening and he was driving her back to her house. Later, he rationalized making love to her that first time by telling himself that he'd had too much to drink, but he knew he would never pass a polygraph on that one. Plain and simple, except for Samantha, he had never wanted a woman the way he wanted Sally Pope.

The affair had lasted several months. If it had been made public, it could have cost Frank his license to practice law but he was willing to risk it. Then all of Sally's legal affairs were settled. When she told him that she was going away, Frank had felt the bottom drop out of his world. Sally had said all of the right things—she loved him, she would always think of him—but she'd asked him to understand that she had to put Kevin's happiness before her own.

Enough time had gone by for his obsession with Sally to have ended. But he did think about her occasionally, and Amanda's excited revelation about the *Marsh* case had ripped the scab from a wound he thought had healed. Frank would call Sally Pope as promised, but he was not looking forward to seeing her again.

CHAPTER 23

Every morning, Amanda performed a routine of rigorous calisthenics, a remnant of her days as a competitive swimmer. The morning after her father briefed her on the *Pope* case, she was in the middle of a set of pushups when her phone rang. She powered through three more and grabbed the receiver on the fourth ring.

"Thanks for waiting until six-thirty to call," she said as soon as Martha Brice identified herself.

"I assumed you were an early riser," Brice answered, oblivious to Amanda's sarcasm.

"Mr. Marsh is in town," Brice continued.

"Good. I want to meet with him as soon as possible."

"The corporate jet will be in Portland tomorrow morning. Jennifer will call your office with the time."

"Okay. Please keep him incommunicado until I tell you otherwise. No press conferences, no leaks. I'll try to talk the district attorney into letting Mr. Marsh surrender at the bail hearing. But I know Karl Burdett pretty well. If he learns Marsh is in New York, he'll do an end run and have the police arrest him."

"Mr. Marsh will be sequestered until you say otherwise."

"Great. See you tomorrow."

AMANDA SHOWERED, ATE breakfast, and dressed in her most serious business suit before driving to Hillsboro. Karl Burdett's office was in a modern addition to the courthouse that had been built after the *Pope* case was tried. Amanda had called ahead and Burdett's secretary ushered her into his office as soon as she arrived.

The decorations on the DA's walls were clichés. There were the obligatory college and law school diplomas, the plaques from the Elks and the county bar, plus photo ops of Burdett with every politician he'd ever met above the rank of state legislator and any celebrity, regardless of rank. Amanda had seen the photographs before, but today her eye was drawn to one that pictured Burdett and Tony Rose in hunting gear, leaning on their rifles on either side of a six-point buck. Normally, she wouldn't have given a thought to the picture. Tony Rose was a celebrity and a big contributor to Burdett's party. But Rose was also a key witness against Sally Pope.

Amanda certainly wasn't surprised that Burdett was a hunter. The clues were the mounted animal heads that glared down at her from the office walls. The trophies didn't bother her. Many Oregonians, including her father, were hunters. Frank had taken her with him when she was old enough to shoot a rifle. Amanda had never enjoyed killing deer, and had used the excuse of swim practice to beg off as soon as her distaste for hunting outweighed the joy she received from spending time with her father in Oregon's spectacular forests.

Karl Burdett was behind his desk, leaning back casually in his chair. He greeted

Amanda and she turned from the wall decorations. At Sally Pope's trial, the DA had been young, cocky, and recently elected to a post he saw as a launching pad to higher office. Had he sent Sally Pope to death row, Senior would have used all of his influence to make Burdett's dreams come true. But Senior had conveniently ignored his own role in the *Pope* fiasco and blamed Burdett for Sally's acquittal. Since the trial, Senior had kept Burdett in place so he could torment him, dangling a run for attorney general or Congress just out of reach.

Burdett had not aged well. The thirty-two-year-old Karl Burdett had been trim and athletic, with a healthy complexion and a full head of sandy blond hair. The forty-four-year-old version was loose and sallow, with a thinning mane flecked with gray. If Senior unfairly blamed Burdett for losing *Pope*, Burdett saw Frank Jaffe as the root of all the setbacks that had followed his defeat. Frank's daughter was a reminder of his humiliation, and his welcoming smile was as phony as his hearty greeting.

"To what do I owe this visit, Amanda? You were very mysterious on the phone."

"I have an early Christmas present for you, Karl."

"Oh?"

"Charlie Marsh wants to return to Oregon to face the charges against him."

Amanda could see it was taking all of the DA's self-control to keep from bolting upright. Instead he eased forward.

"How do you know that?" Burdett asked, unable to keep a slight tremor from his voice.

"I'm his lawyer."

"Where is he?" Burdett demanded.

"I can't tell you."

"He's a fugitive. You have to tell me where he is."

"Actually I don't if I learned his whereabouts in an attorney-client confidence, but we don't have to get into a pissing contest. Charlie wants to return to Oregon and you want him back. If you promise to let him surrender at a bail hearing, he'll be in Oregon in no time flat."

Burdett hated letting a Jaffe call the shots but he knew that he could get back in Senior's good graces and salvage his career if he convicted Charlie Marsh.

"What do you have to lose?" Amanda

pushed. "If I tell Mr. Marsh you're going to throw him in jail as soon as he sets foot in Oregon he may change his mind about turning himself in. And he'll be in custody if the judge denies bail."

"You're right. I'll agree to a voluntary surrender. When are we talking about?"

"I don't know yet, but it will be soon. I'll call you this week to set a date for the hearing."

"Good, good," Burdett said. "I'll look forward to hearing from you."

I bet you will, Amanda thought as she shook hands and headed out the door.

CHAPTER 24

Karl Burdett had gotten used to the power and prestige that the office of district attorney bestowed. While he would never admit it, subconsciously he knew that he was not talented enough to succeed in private practice and he dreaded the thought of scrambling to make a living at his age. That was why he needed Senior's approval and support almost as much as he needed air.

Minutes after Amanda left his office, Burdett was in his car, headed for the Pope estate to deliver the news of Charlie's return. He was almost there when Tony Rose sped by in a silver-gray Ferrari F43. Burdett was not surprised that Rose was visiting Senior. The tennis pro had been fired by the Westmont soon after Sally Pope's trial. Less than a year later, he'd founded Mercury Enterprises, which had started small, manufacturing tennis equipment, and had grown rapidly when American wunderkind Gary Posner won the U.S. Open playing with a Mercury racket. The sports world was shocked when Posner signed an exclusive contract with Mercury instead of Nike or another monster sporting-goods firm. The terms were never made public but the rumors put Posner's endorsement fee in the neighborhood of Tiger Woods's. The source of Mercury's funding was a tightly held secret but speculation ran wild that Arnold Pope Sr. was Rose's secret backer and the money was Rose's payoff for perjuring himself at Sally Pope's trial. If so, the money was well spent, because Mercury's stock and profits had risen as swiftly as Posner served. The firm now successfully sold hunting, fishing, golf, and basketball equipment and it had a line of clothing and foot gear. The face of Mercury was the handsome Tony

Rose, but Burdett was certain that the brains and the money behind the company was Arnold Pope.

"WHAT'S THIS ABOUT Marsh?" Arnold Pope asked as soon as Burdett walked into his home office.

"He's coming back to stand trial. He'll probably be here within the week."

"How do you know that?"

Senior's excitement increased as Burdett recounted Amanda Jaffe's visit.

"Bring me a copy of the case file," Senior said as soon as Burdett was through.

"It's big. It might . . ."

"I know it's big. Copy it and have it here by tomorrow. And keep me up to date on every single development, no matter how small."

"Yes, sir."

"And Karl."

"Yes, sir."

"In life it is rare to get a second chance. Now you have one."

"I'll do my best."

"No, Karl, you will not simply do your best." Senior locked eyes with Burdett. "Either you or Marsh will be totally destroyed by the end of this case. You decide who will be buried."

Before Burdett was out of the room, Senior had swiveled his chair so he was staring through his window at Mount Hood, but it was not the majestic, snow-covered giant he was seeing. In his imagination, he saw Charlie Marsh sweating out his time on death row as each second brought him closer to a lethal injection. Then he thought about Amanda Jaffe. She was very good. Could she achieve what her father had accomplished? Funny things happened to rock-solid cases when a clever lawyer got in front of a jury. Look at the O. J. Simpson case. An idiot should have been able to convict him but he walked.

Senior had attempted to have Marsh killed shortly after he was granted asylum in Batanga, but the mercenary he'd hired had backed out of the contract. President Baptiste made a lot of money portraying Batanga as a safe haven for the most wanted. It only took a little research for the would-be assassin to learn the fate of those who attempted to end the lives of the fugitives whose safety the president guaranteed. The killers who were caught in-country met a fate too grisly to describe. A Dutchman who had murdered one of Baptiste's guests had been pursued relentlessly by agents of the National Education Bureau. When they caught him, he earned a PhD in torture before his body parts were scattered around the tourist attractions of Amsterdam, guaranteeing that Baptiste's message would be communicated worldwide. Try as he might, Senior could find no one who would risk Baptiste's wrath. Now it appeared that his quarry was coming to him.

Senior pushed himself to his feet. At seventy, his joints were stiffening and his back had tightened up. Walking was a chore but he didn't let anyone see his discomfort, because he never showed weakness. After completing the laborious climb to the second floor, he worked his way slowly and painfully to the room at the far end of the corridor, where Junior had spent his boyhood. Now it was a shrine. The shades were always down in this room and the ceiling fixture was coated with dust. When he flipped the switch, muted light cast a yellowish glow over the pictures on the walls and the trophies, medals, and mementos that filled the shelves. Across the room was a bed whose sheets never needed to be changed.

Senior sat on the bed and stared at a picture of Junior with the first President Bush. Senior was a good friend of the ex-president, who had spoken on Junior's behalf at a fund-raiser during his son's first congressional campaign. Other notable politicians had helped his boy get to Congress. They knew he was the future and they flocked to embrace him. Senior, who almost never cried, felt tears well up as he thought about what might have been had Junior not been cut down in the prime of his life by that . . . He took deep breaths until he was back in control of his emotions.

Pope shifted his attention to another photograph, Junior in his dress uniform shortly before his discharge from the Marines. If ever there was a man who looked like he should be president of this great country, it was Arnold Pope Jr.

Next to the picture of his son in his dress uniform was a picture of Junior holding a child in his hand as he would a football. It had been taken when Arnold Pope III was two weeks old. That bitch had named Junior's boy Kevin out of spite, but his grandson would always be Arnold III to Senior. Just thinking of his only grandchild made Senior's fists clench. Junior's whore had kept Senior away from his grandson with restraining orders and by putting the Atlantic Ocean between them, but he had photographs and videos taken surreptitiously through telescopic lenses. What he did not have was his grandson, the future of the Pope clan and the last of his bloodline.

Junior was dead. Senior faced that fact every day. His boy had been a candle whose light would have guided America to a radiant new day of decency and honor. Charlie Marsh and the whore had snuffed out that candle and they would pay. Senior knew that he could never get his son back, but he could get revenge.

CHAPTER 25

Herb Cross's wife was a CPA in the Portland branch of a national accounting firm. When she was promoted to a position in the firm's national headquarters in Atlanta, Herb regretfully resigned. The regret went both ways. After Herb left, Frank used several investigators but none of them had been satisfactory. Then Amanda told Frank about Kate Ross.

Kate had a degree in computer science from Caltech and had been recruited by the Portland Police Bureau to investigate computer crime. After a few years of pounding a keyboard for a living, Kate had asked for a transfer. While working in Vice and Narcotics, she was involved in a shoot-out at a shopping mall that had left civilians and an informant dead. The Bureau had made Kate the department's scapegoat and she'd been driven off the force.

Kate's computer skills and police background helped her secure a job as an investigator at Oregon's largest law firm. When Daniel Ames, a first-year associate at the firm, was charged with murder, Kate asked Amanda to represent him. After the two women cleared Daniel's name, Jaffe, Katz hired Kate as the firm's investigator and Daniel as an associate, and Kate and Daniel started living together.

Kate was five seven, with a dark complexion, large brown eyes, and long, curly black hair that made her look faintly Middle Eastern. She usually dressed in jeans and man-tailored shirts that showed off her athletic figure. When Amanda returned from her meeting with Karl Burdett, she poked her head into Kate's office. The investigator had her feet up on her desk and was immersed in a police report.

"How would you like to work on the case of the century?" Amanda asked casually.

Kate looked up, her expression blank. "I've gotta pass, Amanda." She held up her police report. "I've pledged my life to helping a dipsomaniac insurance executive avoid conviction for his fourth DUI and I won't rest until he's back on the highway endangering the lives of all of Oregon's citizens."

"Gee, I hate to interfere with your mission, but I'm going to pull rank and insist you give my case priority."

"Okay, if you insist. But you've got to square it with Ernie. This guy is repeat business and he refers a lot of his alcoholic buddies to the firm."

"I'll talk to him."

Kate put her feet on the floor and swiveled her chair in Amanda's direction. "So, what's this big case you want me to work on?"

Amanda told the investigator about her meeting at the airport with Martha Brice and the editor's recent phone call. Kate knew about Charlie Marsh because of his book, but she only had vague memories of

Sally Pope's trial, so Amanda brought her up to speed on the old case.

"I'm flying to New York tomorrow morning to meet with Marsh," Amanda said. "While I'm gone I'd like you to go through the file and start organizing it for trial. Burdett indicted Sally Pope on a conspiracy theory, so, to get a conviction, he had to prove that Marsh murdered Congressman Pope. That means he'll be presenting many of the same witnesses he used in Pope's trial. See if you can have a trial book ready by the time I get back."

As SOON AS Kate finished her work in the drunk-driving case, she carried a mug of coffee and her laptop into the conference room. She sighed when she saw the mass of materials piled high on the long table. Then she booted up her laptop and went to work.

Kate spent the first few hours typing a synopsis of the police, lab, and autopsy reports, witness statements, and trial testimony into her computer. Then she organized the digested materials into categories. When she was through, she went back to the reports and made a list of those that dealt with different time periods or subjects.

One category had to do with testimony concerning the murder weapon. The initial mention of the ivory-handled .357 Magnum was in a statement by Mickey Keys, who said he'd first seen the gun in Texas when Charlie was given the weapon as a gift. He told the police that Charlie played with the gun in his hotel room but never took it out, because he was on parole. The literary agent said that Delmar Epps, Charlie's bodyguard, got a kick out of toting the weapon in public when he was guarding Charlie. Keys remembered seeing Epps with the gun in the limo on the way to the Westmont.

In Tony Rose's report of his run-in with Charlie at the Dunthorpe seminar, Rose told the police that Epps had flashed the gun when the bodyguard was manhandling him. He remembered it because of the fancy grip.

When Kate put Rose's report on top of a stack of items that were pertinent to the Dunthorpe seminar, a photograph caught her attention. She pulled it out of the center of the pile and studied it. The photo showed Charlie and his entourage as they were about to enter the mansion in Dunthorpe. Kate was glad she'd found it, because it put a face to the people about whom she'd been reading.

Charlie sported a great tan and looked like a poor man's John Travolta circa *Saturday Night Fever* in his white jacket, white slacks, and black silk shirt. Gold chains graced his neck and a gold Rolex encircled his wrist. His smile was warm and he appeared to be relaxed and in control. Standing to Charlie's right was a grinning Mickey Keys. Keys wore a navy blue blazer, tan slacks, and an open-necked, emerald green sports shirt that went perfectly with his styled red hair.

Slightly behind Charlie was a massive black man with a shaved head, who Kate assumed was Delmar Epps. On Charlie's left was a young woman who was looking up at Charlie with adoring eyes. Several things about her were odd. Her head was as devoid of hair as the guru's bodyguard's, and while everyone else in Charlie's entourage was dressed in expensive, stylish togs, the girl was wearing a peasant dress and blouse. To Kate's eye, the woman seemed out of place, like a gypsy who had wandered into a night club full of partying movie stars.

A thought occurred to Kate. Epps had testified that he'd left the .357 Magnum in the limo when he'd gotten out at the entrance to the Westmont on the night of the shooting, but no one had corroborated that assertion. What if Epps did have the gun when he left the limo but lied so no one would think he fired the fatal shot? If Epps was carrying the revolver when he left the limo, how could Marsh have gotten it?

Kate studied a photograph of the weapon. Then she went on the Internet and discovered that the Ruger weighed over two pounds. The gun also had a six-inch barrel, so it would be a bit unwieldy. Epps had been fighting with the security guards shortly before the fatal shot was fired. Kate remembered a witness testifying that Epps had knocked down a guard with a karate kick to the head. All that jumping around could have dislodged the gun if the heavy, cumbersome weapon was stuck in Epps's waistband, and anyone in the crowd around the combatants could have picked it up.

Kate found a few photographs that showed both the area on the side of the turnaround where Epps had been fighting and the area between the turnaround and the pro shop where their client had been standing. There wasn't that much space between the two positions. If the gun had dropped out and had been kicked back toward Marsh, he could have rushed forward and gotten it.

Kate tried to remember who had been with Marsh. Werner Rollins had testified that he'd joined Marsh and Gary Hass after he'd decked the guard with whom he'd been fighting. Epps said that he had moved back so he could protect Marsh. Rollins had testified that he saw Marsh fire the shot that killed Arnold Pope Jr.

If Epps and Rollins had lied to the police so they could cut deals, any of the other men standing with Marsh could have fired the shot.

26

Amanda had returned to New York a few times since graduating from law school at NYU, and she had mixed feelings about the city. Manhattan was a wonderful place to visit. It had the best restaurants, great shopping, terrific museums, cutting-edge art, the theater, and a buzz in the air that let you know that big things were happening. But you didn't go to the theater or eat at a four-star restaurant every night when you lived in the city. At heart, Amanda was an Oregon girl. After the initial excitement of a visit wore off, she would miss Portland with its easygoing pace, snow-capped mountains, and gentle, green hills. This, however, was her first day in New York in some time, and she found herself intrigued by the bustling crowds and longing for a real pastrami sandwich when the limo that had picked her up at the airport whisked her past the Carnegie Deli on the way to her meeting with her client.

World News was hiding Charlie Marsh in a corporate condo near Columbus Circle. The driver phoned ahead to alert Dennis Levy that Amanda was on her way. As she rode up in the elevator, Amanda wondered if the real Charlie Marsh would be anything like the Charlie Marsh of her imagination: a swashbuckling bandit who had dramatically cast away his penchant for violence so he could bring enlightenment to mankind. Many people who had been won over by his vivid transformation from evildoer to saint never believed he was guilty of the congressman's murder. Amanda had been enthralled by his autobiography, but she'd learned enough about the failings of career criminals from her father to maintain a healthy skepticism about the guru's claims.

The door to the *World News* condo opened as soon as Amanda knocked. A skinny kid, who looked like he was barely out of adolescence, peeked through a gap in the door and anxiously scanned the corridor beyond Amanda's shoulder as if he was expecting a SWAT team to charge in behind her.

"Miss Jaffe?" he asked nervously.

Amanda nodded. "And you must be Dennis Levy."

"Come on in," Levy said, stepping back enough so Amanda could slip sideways into a large living room with an amazing view of Central Park. Several locks snapped shut behind her. A moment later, Amanda felt the freezing cold air that was blowing through the apartment like a hurricane.

"What's with the air-conditioning?" she asked Levy as she fought an impulse to wrap her arms across her chest.

The reporter, who was bundled up in a heavy sweater, jerked his head toward a slender, blond-haired man in a dark blue warm-up suit, who was perched on the edge of a sofa, channel-surfing on a huge flat-screen TV.

"He says he hates heat and anything else that reminds him of Africa."

Amanda's idea of what Marsh would

look like was based on his author photo on the back of *The Light Within You* and dim memories of the fugitive on television shows. Marsh looked nothing like the confident, dynamic spokesman for self-awareness she remembered. He was emaciated and his skin had the leathery look common to people who spend too much time in the sun with too little sun block.

"Charlie, your lawyer's here," Levy said.

When Marsh heard his name, his head swiveled toward Amanda but his body and the remote stayed pointed at the television.

"I can't get over all these channels," Charlie said. "Did you know you can get porn in your own home for free in high definition?"

"Yes, Mr. Marsh, I'm well aware of that," Amanda said, smiling involuntarily. Her client's wide-eyed awe reminded her that he had been in exile for twelve years.

Marsh turned off the set and stood up. "How come I didn't get your father?"

Amanda took no offense. "He represented Mrs. Pope, your codefendant. It would be a conflict of interest if he represented you, too."

Marsh inspected Amanda. "You look young. Do you have enough experience to handle a case this big?"

"Do you think a major publication like *World News*, with all its resources, would ask me to represent you if they didn't think I was up to the job?" she answered calmly.

"Yeah, point taken. But you can consult with your father, right? I mean, he can be involved in the case even if he can't be my lawyer?"

"I always consult with my father when I have a complex case. And he consults with me when he has one. So you don't have to worry. You'll be getting two lawyers for the price of one."

"Okay. Just checking. Don't get upset. It's my life on the line here."

"I'm well aware of that. Look, Mr. Marsh, you're the client and what you say goes. If you aren't comfortable with me as your attorney you're perfectly free to hire some-one else."

"No, no, that's okay. I'm sure you're good. I was just hoping I could get your dad be-cause he got Sally off. But you're okay, too."

"Now that that's out of the way, there's a

lot to discuss, so we should get started. Where's a good place to talk?"

"We can do it right here," Dennis Levy said. Amanda heard the eagerness in his voice and decided that she couldn't put off setting guidelines for the reporter.

"Mr. Levy, it won't be possible for you to sit in on my conferences with Mr. Marsh."

"Hey, you don't have to worry, I'm on Charlie's side. And don't forget, the more authentic the book I'm writing, the better it will sell, so everyone benefits."

"That may be, but Mr. Marsh will lose the right to assert his attorney-client privilege if a third person is present during our conversations. That means the DA can compel you to tell a jury everything Mr. Marsh thought he was telling me in confidence. I can't permit that."

"You don't understand. This is going to be a *huge* story. We're talking prizewinning journalism here. And you're going to get more publicity from this than you can handle, so why don't you cut me a little slack?" Levy smiled conspiratorially. "Who'll know what went on in this apartment if no one talks?"

"I'd know," Amanda said, "and I wouldn't

lie if I was asked whether you sat in on our conferences. You're a reporter. I understand your desire to cover a story like this, but Mr. Marsh's life is at stake, and I won't do anything to jeopardize it. You may not be present while we talk. Is that understood?"

Levy's face had turned bright red during her lecture.

"Okay, okay, but will you talk to me about things that don't jeopardize the case?"

"Of course, and I'll try to keep you in the loop as much as possible," she said, to mollify Levy, "but Mr. Marsh is my priority."

"Hey, Dennis," Marsh interjected, "can you do me a favor?"

"Sure, Charlie," Levy said, eager to please his meal ticket.

"I'm starving. Can you run out and get me a cheeseburger with bacon? I haven't had a good burger in twelve years."

Levy looked upset at being cast in the role of errand boy but he held his tongue.

"And fries. I want fries and a Coke."

"Okay," Levy said grudgingly.

"How about you, Amanda?" Charlie asked. "Is it okay if I call you Amanda?"

"Sure."

"Then you can call me Charlie. So, how about it? Are you hungry?"

"I've been craving a hot pastrami sandwich on rye ever since I drove by the Carnegie Deli."

"Done. You got that order, Dennis?"

"LEVY'S A REAL pain in the ass," Charlie said as soon as the front door closed behind the reporter.

"He's just excited about his story."

Marsh cocked an eyebrow. "You haven't been trapped with him twenty-four-seven for the past few days."

"Point taken," Amanda said as she walked over to a table that stood next to one of the picture windows overlooking the park. Marsh took a seat on one side and Amanda took a pen and a legal pad out of her attaché case.

"So, what's going to happen to me when I land in Oregon?" Marsh asked. He was trying to act cool but his body language told Amanda a different story.

"I've cut a deal with Karl Burdett, the DA."

"Didn't he prosecute Sally?"

Amanda nodded. "And he's still the DA. Karl has promised me he won't arrest you when you land. You'll be able to surrender voluntarily at the bail hearing."

"Okay, that's good. And I've got the dough to post bail."

"There isn't an automatic right to bail in a murder case, Charlie. The judge can order you held without bail if Burdett convinces him that there's very good evidence that you murdered Congressman Pope."

"But I didn't. I'm innocent."

"Then why did you run?"

"Delmar grabbed me as soon as the shooting started and dragged me to the limo. He was doing his bodyguard thing. We peeled out and he started driving all over the place to lose anyone who was pursuing us. When we finally stopped we were miles away from the country club and I'd had time to think. I'm an ex-con; Pope hit me because I was screwing his wife; and I ran from the scene of the crime. How's that going to look? Guilty, guilty, guilty was the only answer I could come up with. I was certain I'd be the fall guy if I turned myself in, especially after they arrested Sally. So I went to Canada, got myself some false ID, and took a tramp steamer to Batanga. The rest is history."

"I'm curious, Charlie. You know you're facing the death penalty, right?"

Marsh nodded.

"Then why did you come back? You were safe in Batanga."

Marsh laughed. "Amanda, I'd be safer strapped into an electric chair than I was in that mosquito-infested hellhole."

"Why don't you explain that to me?"

"If you don't mind, I'd rather not."

"I get that you had a bad experience over there . . ."

Marsh snorted. "You don't know the half of it."

"It could be important for the bail hearing. You fled the country once and Burdett will argue that's evidence that you'll be a flight risk if the judge sets bail."

"Believe me, I am never going back to Africa; not ever. You won't even catch me watching a Tarzan movie."

"The judge isn't going to take your word that you won't flee, without an explanation."

Marsh spaced out and Amanda let him

think. When he looked at her, his jaw was set.

"I'm going to do this just once, so take good notes and never ask me about Batanga again. But, before I tell you about Batanga, I have something I need you to do for me."

"What's that?"

"I brought something with me from Batanga that I want you to hold for me. When we get to Oregon I want you to put it in a safety-deposit box."

Amanda frowned. "What exactly is this thing?"

"I can't tell you."

"We're not talking drugs here, are we?"

"No. You won't be breaking any laws, but you will be doing something important for a lot of innocent people. I can't say any more. Will you do it?"

Amanda hesitated. She needed to gain Marsh's trust if she was going to be an effective advocate for him. On the other hand, she wasn't going to aid and abet a criminal enterprise.

"You swear you're not asking me to commit a crime?" she asked, knowing full well how ridiculous it was to ask that question of a criminal who had earned his living as a con man.

"Yes."

"All right. Give me the item."

Charlie went into his bedroom and returned shortly with a box wrapped in brown paper and bound with twine. Amanda put it into her large handbag.

"You ready to talk about Africa?" she asked when the box was out of sight.

Charlie sighed. "Let's get this over."

For the next hour, Marsh told his lawyer about his years in exile, concluding with an account of his hairbreadth escape from the makeshift airfield.

"Jesus, Charlie, you're lucky to be alive."

"I want you to keep me that way."

"I'm definitely going to try my best, but tell me, if you didn't kill Pope, who did?"

"I don't know."

"Everyone says the shot was fired near you and the gun was found where you were standing."

"Look, Amanda, it was dark, what with Werner and Delmar fighting and Pope screaming at me and the citizens shrieking, it was like being in the middle of a three-ring circus."

"So you're saying that you don't have any idea who killed Arnold Pope?"

"None whatsoever."

AMANDA WAS DOG-TIRED by the time she checked into her hotel. Her cross-country trip and the lengthy interview with Charlie had been exhausting, and Dennis Levy hadn't made her job any easier. He'd tried to eavesdrop on their conference several times and she'd used a lot of energy fending off his constant attempts to convince her that there would be no real problem if he had better access to her client.

Amanda took a hot shower to banish the chill that the arctic conditions in Charlie's condo had seeded into her bones. There was a message from Martha Brice, who wanted an update. Amanda gave it to her while luxuriating on her bed, wrapped in one of the terry-cloth robes that the hotel provided. She was tempted to call Mike Greene just so she could talk about something other than the case, but she remembered the three-hour time difference between New York and Oregon and realized he'd probably be in court. Instead, she called Karl Burdett to tell him that Marsh would fly back on Wednesday. Burdett agreed to set the bail hearing for Thursday. Amanda had feared that the DA would renege on his promise and she breathed a sigh of relief when she hung up the phone. After the call to Burdett, she phoned her office to see if there was anything that required her attention and spoke briefly with Kate Ross.

When she finished her conversation with Kate, Amanda was a little more relaxed and ready to think about her first impressions of Charlie Marsh. He was definitely not faking his relief at escaping from Batanga. His years there sounded like hell. Amanda couldn't imagine the horror he'd felt when he saw his butchered lover in Baptiste's torture chamber.

Marsh also seemed needy and unsure of himself. He had tried to put on a brave front but Amanda could tell he was scared; a perfectly rational reaction, given his situation. Getting Charlie bail wasn't going to be easy. Neither was keeping him off of death row.

What worried Amanda most was whether Charlie was anxious because he had murdered Arnold Pope Jr. In the American legal system, the state was the only party with a burden at trial. It had to convince the jury beyond a reasonable doubt that a defendant was guilty as charged. A defendant never had a burden of proving anything, so a defense attorney didn't need to know whether her client had committed the crime with which he was charged. That didn't mean that Amanda wasn't as curious about her client's culpability as she was about the contents of the box he'd given her. Charlie's protestations of innocence were convincing, but he was a con man, and con men made their living by lying with a straight face.

CHAPTER **27**

The knot in Frank Jaffe's gut tightened as he drew closer to Sally Pope's estate. The more he wanted to see her, the more he didn't. When Frank promised Amanda that he'd meet with Sally, he honestly thought he could handle seeing her again. Now, he wasn't so sure.

Sally lived in the middle of farm country. Here and there, cattle, sheep, and horses grazed in fenced pastures and a barn or a farmhouse appeared. There were low hills and cultivated squares of yellow and green given over to crops or dark brown patches where the fields had been churned to re-claim the soil for planting.

Frank had arranged the meeting through Jimmy Pavel, the attorney who handled Sally's legal affairs. A few hours after Frank phoned, Pavel called with directions to the estate and a time for the meeting. While he waited for the call, Frank looked up Sally on the Internet. There were numerous references to her before, during, and immediately after the trial. The search results tailed off drastically after she moved to Europe but there were references that linked her to Liam O'Connell, an Irish author who'd been short-listed for the Booker Prize and was a minor celebrity in the U.K. There were very few hits since she'd returned to the States.

A low stone wall marked the boundaries of the estate. It broke to permit access to the grounds along a dirt road that wound through a thicket of trees. After a short distance, the woods gave way to an expanse of well-tended lawn and a view of a white, antebellum plantation home that looked down on new arrivals from its perch on top of a gentle rise. An image flashed through Frank's mind, of hoop-skirted southern belles fanning themselves in the summer heat while their beaus sipped mint juleps on the veranda.

The drive curved in front of a columned portico. Frank parked and got out. A white-and-honey-colored collie trotted toward him, wagging its tail lazily. Frank leaned over to pet the dog, then rang the doorbell. After his *Gone with the Wind* moment, Frank was disappointed when the woman who answered the door was wearing jeans and a light blue T-shirt. She had straight black hair, an engaging smile, and a heavy Italian accent.

"You must be Mr. Jaffe."

Frank nodded.

"I'm Gina, Mrs. Pope's personal assistant. She's expecting you. She's around back. Follow the path. You can't miss her."

Frank followed a trail of irregularly shaped slabs of gray slate around the side of the three-story house. The collie trotted along beside him. Frank heard a splash and laughter and saw three teenage boys playing in a large swimming pool. They were bronzed from hours in the summer sun. Two of the boys had mops of shaggy black hair. Chlorine and sunlight had turned the tallest boy's hair a shiny, copper blond. There was a diving board at the deep end and the boys were taking turns doing silly dives. The blond boy paused at the end of the board. He was lean and muscular. After a few bounces he pushed off and rose gracefully. At the point where a competitive diver would have tucked and somersaulted, he flailed his arms in crazy circles and belly-flopped, creating a tidal wave that soaked his friends. The boys laughed and Frank smiled.

"That's Kevin."

Frank turned. Sally Pope was observing him from beneath a floppy, wide-brimmed straw hat. There were gardening gloves on her hands and she was holding a trowel. Sally was dressed in patched jeans and a short-sleeved shirt stained with dirt. She was not wearing makeup, and perspiration streaked her face. There was a spot of grime on one cheek, where she'd touched it with her glove. With all that, Frank thought she was still one of the most beautiful women he'd ever seen.

"He looks like he's had a few lessons," Frank said as he watched Sally's son swim a lap of butterfly.

Sally grinned and her smile affected him as it had all those years ago.

"He's on the high school team." She pulled off her gloves and wiped her brow. "Let's talk on the patio. And take off your jacket and tie. It's way too hot for formal attire."

Sally led the way to a circular glass table on a large brick patio that was mercifully shaded by an overhang. Frank stripped off his jacket and was loosening his tie when Gina appeared with a pitcher of iced tea. Sally set her hat on a chair and shook out her hair. Despite an occasional strand of gray, her blond hair was still vibrant.

"You look good, Frank."

"I look old."

She smiled. "Not so old. How's Amanda?"

"Great. She's a partner in the firm."

"I tried to keep up on Oregon news when I was living in Italy and I read about some of her big cases."

"She's got another one. That's why I'm here."

"Jimmy said it was about a case, but he also said you refused to explain."

"I wanted to tell you in person. Charlie Marsh is coming back to stand trial."

The color drained from Sally's face.

"I wanted to give you a heads-up before the press learns he's coming home."

"My God, I can't go through that again."

"I'm afraid you won't be able to avoid it. Karl Burdett is bound to call you as a witness."

Sally turned her head toward the pool. "They'll go after Kevin."

"He was too young. He wouldn't know anything Karl could use."

"Not Burdett, the reporters. I've tried to shield him. Now it will all come out about Arnie and me, my affairs."

She looked sick.

"I'm sorry," Frank said, knowing that the tepid sentiment was totally inadequate and would do nothing to disperse the terrible cloud Sally and her son would soon be under.

"Why is he doing this?" Sally asked. "They'll try to get the death penalty. Why come back?"

"I don't know. Amanda is with him now. She'll find out, but she may not be able to tell you."

Sally clenched her fists. She was looking someplace that Frank could not see.

After a few moments she took a deep breath and Frank saw the steely reserve she'd displayed during her trial push aside the other emotions.

"You'll get through this," Frank assured her. "So will Kevin."

"Yes, we will," Sally answered firmly. "So, Frank, did you come out just to warn me?"

Frank took the waiver out of his jacket pocket. "Amanda is cautious and she likes to do everything correctly. Since I represented you and she's my law partner, she asked me to approach you about waiving any conflicts of interest so she can represent Charlie."

"Would there be any danger to Kevin or me if I sign?"

"I don't think so. The attorney-client privilege would still be in effect and you always maintained your innocence. I can't think of anything you confided to me that was incriminating. But you can consult an attorney if you're worried."

"What will happen if I don't sign?"

"Amanda might have to get off the case, but that wouldn't end it. Marsh would just hire a different lawyer."

"Give me a pen," Sally said.

"Thank you. This case means a lot to Amanda."

Sally smiled. "Does she want to prove she's as good as her old man?"

Frank smiled back. "I'm sure that has something to do with it."

"She has a long way to go if that's her goal."

"Not as far as you might think. She's one hell of a lawyer."

Sally's smile faded. She studied the man across the table. "How are you doing, Frank?"

He shrugged. "The practice is going strong."

"That's not what I meant."

"There hasn't been anyone significant in my life since you left, if that's what you're getting at."

"You know it hurt me to go, but I had to put Kevin first. He would have been a constant focus of the tabloids, and there was Senior. He even dogged me in Italy. If I didn't have the money for the best lawyers it would have been worse than it was."

"You don't owe me an explanation."

"I wanted you to know."

"Thank you. I understand you found someone."

Sally nodded. "Liam. He's away teaching a summer course at Berkeley."

"How long have you been together?"

"Five years now. Kevin adores him."

Frank forced a smile. "I'm happy for you."

"It might have been different under different circumstances."

"You and I are old news, Sally."

Sally picked up the pen Frank had placed on the table and signed the waiver.

Frank nodded toward the pool. "How much does Kevin know about what happened to his father?"

"He knows Arnie was a congressman and that he was murdered. He knows I was tried but the charges were dismissed." She paused. "We rarely talk about the case. I guess we'll have to now. He'll read about it in the newspaper, and someone at school will bring it up."

"Is he as tough as his old lady?"

"I think so. I hope so, because this won't be easy."

"What about Charlie Marsh? Do you know anything that can help Amanda?"

"Honestly, I don't. I was focused on Arnie during the fight. I have no idea who shot him."

"If Amanda wants to talk to you, will you see her?"

"Of course."

Frank put the waiver in his attaché and stood up. "It's been good seeing you again, Sally."

"Can't you stay? Gina can make us lunch."

"I wish I could but I have an appointment in town. A client."

Sally studied him, trying to divine if he was telling the truth. Frank showed her the face juries saw, which exhibited no emotion even when events in the courtroom took sudden or terrible turns. She stood and offered him her hand. It was warm and he let the touch linger for a moment more than was necessary for a farewell.

"I'm glad I got a chance to see Kevin," Frank said.

"I'm glad I got to see you again."

Sally walked Frank to his car and waved

as he drove off. When he was out of sight, Frank let out the breath he'd been suppressing along with his emotions. He'd lied to Sally. There was no client waiting for him. Being with her had been hard, and he'd had no desire to prolong the pain.

On Tuesday afternoon, shortly after a brief phone conference with Amanda, Kate Ross called to set up an interview with Tony Rose, never expecting the president of Mercury Enterprises to grant it. Rose was the head of an international business empire and she was an investigator for a small local law firm. When Kate drove into the visitors' parking lot on the Mercury campus, she was still trying to figure out why Rose's assistant had phoned back fifteen minutes after her call to tell her that Mr. Rose would see her in an hour. The only answer she could come up with was that the names Sally Pope and Charlie Marsh were the equivalent of "Open Sesame" where Rose was concerned.

The Mercury Enterprises campus was a sprawling, ecologically friendly collection of glass-and-steel buildings interspersed with tennis courts, soccer fields, outdoor and indoor basketball courts, and a track-and-field complex. Kate saw an indoor, Olympic-size swimming pool through the glass walls of a pyramid-shaped structure she passed on the way to the administration building. Nationally known track-and-field athletes participated in Mercury's famous training program, and the campus was home to basketball camps for budding NBA stars. It didn't take Kate long to conclude that the onetime gigolo and tennis bum had done all right for himself.

The reception area of the administration building with its wide-open spaces, glass walls, and three-story atrium had the feel of a botanical garden. Kate gave her name to the guard at the reception desk. He made a brief phone call before giving her a clip-on visitor's pass and telling her to have a seat. As she thumbed through a copy of *Sports Illustrated*, intense men and women sped by her, obviously on missions of great importance. Everyone, regardless of age, looked terribly fit. Kate made a vow to get back into her workout routine as soon as she returned from the interview. Her interlude of self-castigation was interrupted by the appearance of a stunning brunette in an expensive, tailored business suit, who escorted her to an elevator separate from the main bank.

The car whisked them to the executive offices, where the doors opened on a waiting area decorated with cases displaying medals and trophies won by Mercury-sponsored athletes. The walls were covered with blowups of Mercury advertisements and photographs of athletes in action. Kate recognized most of the featured stars. The brunette ushered Kate past the displays to Tony Rose's inner sanctum.

The office décor was an extension of the waiting room. Trophy cases lined two walls, and photographs of sports figures hung above them. The rest of the walls were glass and gave its occupant a spectacular view of the Columbia River. Tony Rose got up and walked around the side of a large modern desk made of glass and wrought iron. If he'd aged since the *Pope* trial, Kate couldn't tell.

"Thank you for seeing me on such short notice," Kate said as they shook hands.

"When my assistant said you worked for Frank Jaffe's law firm and wanted to see me about Sally Pope and Charlie Marsh, I had to find out what was going on."

Rose motioned Kate into a chair and perched on the edge of the desk, gaining the high ground. He flashed a disarming, boyish smile and Kate saw why the ladies at the Westmont might have found him irresistible.

"So, Ms. Ross, what is going on?"

"Charlie Marsh is returning to Oregon to face the charges against him."

"No kidding? Is Frank Jaffe representing him?"

"He can't. He represented Mrs. Pope, so he has a conflict of interest."

"Too bad. I always wondered how I would have held up if he'd questioned me. I was looking forward to crossing swords with him. So, if Frank isn't Marsh's lawyer, who is?"

"Frank's daughter, Amanda."

Rose nodded. "That's right. She's supposed to be pretty good, too. So, what can I do for you?"

"I wanted to talk to you because Karl Burdett will probably call you as a witness."

"About Sally trying to hire me to kill Junior?"

Kate nodded. "You were also at the Westmont when Congressman Pope was shot, weren't you?"

"Yeah, but I can't help your client."

"Oh?"

"I was some distance from the action in the parking lot, almost at my car, when I heard the shot. I turned around but I couldn't see much because of the people between me and the congressman, and it was dark."

"Why were you at the club that evening?"

"I probably worked late. I had administrative duties connected with being the club pro. But that's a guess. You've got to remember, this was twelve years ago."

"I appreciate that. Maybe I can help you. I've just been through the file, so a lot of this is fresh for me. There was a report that contained the statement Sally Pope gave to the police on the evening of the shooting. She says that you tried to talk to her just as the limo with Marsh and his entourage drove up."

Rose shrugged. "If she said that happened I won't deny it."

"Why did you want to talk to her? I would have thought you wouldn't want to go anywhere near her after she tried to get you to kill the congressman."

"I honestly don't remember talking to her, so I can't help you. Now, will you tell me something?"

"If I can," Kate said.

"What's the deal with Marsh? Why is he coming back after all these years? I thought he was safe and sound in . . . What's the name of the country where he was hiding out?"

"Batanga. And I really don't know why he decided to return."

"Maybe it got to be too much for him," Rose mused. "It happens. You read about these sixties radicals that have been underground for years and they're married and have kids and they get an attack of conscience and turn themselves in."

"Could be," Kate said. "I really don't

know. Getting back to the case, do you still maintain that Sally Pope asked you to kill her husband?"

"That's what happened."

"You're certain about that?"

Rose laughed. "I may not remember some things about that time but you don't forget a person asking you to murder some-one."

"And that was in Dunthorpe at the semi-nar?"

"Right."

"Okay, back to the Westmont. When you were walking to your car, did you notice Mr. Marsh?"

"I may have, but I don't recall."

"How do you feel about Marsh, person-ally?"

"What do you mean?"

"He did break your nose after the semi-nar in Dunthorpe."

Rose laughed. "He didn't break it, he just bloodied it, and that's water under the bridge." Rose swung his hand out in an expansive gesture. "Look around you. You may have noticed that I've got a lot on my plate. As far as I'm concerned, that busi-ness with Sally and the guru is light-years away. When you see him tomorrow, you tell him I'm not holding any grudges."

"Fair enough." Kate stood up. "Thanks for seeing me. I know you're busy, and I appreciate it."

Rose also stood up. "No problem," he said as he walked Kate to the door. She handed him her card.

"If you think of anything, give me a call."

Rose studied the card. "Sure thing," he said. "Allison will take you down."

On her way back to her car, Kate rewound the interview in her mind and concluded that she hadn't learned a thing. But something Rose had said nagged at her during the trip back to the office. Only she couldn't figure out what it was.

CHAPTER 29

Amanda stepped out of the hatch of the Gulfstream G550 and shaded her eyes from the sun. As soon as they adjusted to the glare, Amanda spotted TV vans, a mob of reporters, and Karl Burdett and two policemen standing outside the rear door of the FBO. Amanda stared at Burdett for a second, then turned around and glared at Dennis Levy.

"What are they doing here?"

"We have to start selling Charlie's side of the story if we want to get the public on our side," Levy explained as if his betrayal was the only reasonable course of action.

Amanda shoved Levy back into the interior of the plane, forcing Charlie to take a few steps back.

"You idiot. Did it ever enter that thick skull of yours that one of the reporters might call the district attorney to get his take on the return of Oregon's most wanted fugitive?"

"The DA?"

"Yes, Dennis. He's the gentleman standing with the two policemen. Burdett's probably here to arrest Charlie because he thinks I double-crossed him by calling a press conference to get our side in front of the public before he could."

"I . . . It never . . ." Levy stuttered.

"If you pull something like this again I will have you on the next plane back to New York."

"I don't work for you," Levy answered belligerently.

"That is correct. You work for *World News*. I work for Charlie Marsh and I don't work for *World News*. If you go behind my back one more time I will advise Charlie to give *Newsweek* exclusive access to his story."

Levy paled. "Look, don't do anything

rash. I just thought the publicity would put Charlie in a good light."

"I don't try my cases in the press, Dennis. I try them in court. And I know exactly why you stage-managed this media circus. You want to sell copies of *World News* and promote your book, so don't go all Mother Teresa on me about how you called the media to help Charlie."

"No, no, I really wanted to help Charlie. I mean I know this will help me too, but that wasn't my main motivation."

Amanda decided not to waste any more energy on Levy. She looked over his shoulder at her client.

"Not a word when the cameras start rolling, understood? If we're lucky I'll be able to talk Burdett out of arresting you."

"I'm not talking to anyone," Charlie assured her. "The DA can use anything I say to the press against me."

Amanda stared angrily at Levy. "At least one of you was listening. Now, I'm going to lead us off. You two stay behind me and I'll try to keep Charlie out of jail."

The crowd had surged forward the first time Amanda stepped out of the plane, and they were waiting at the bottom of the stairs that connected the private jet to the tarmac. Amanda paused halfway down so she was above the reporters.

"Good morning. I'm Amanda Jaffe, Charlie Marsh's attorney. I'm glad to see District Attorney Burdett here. I want to thank him for agreeing to let Mr. Marsh voluntarily surrender tomorrow at his bail hearing when he could have taken him into custody today. It's always a pleasure when the defense and the prosecution can operate on a handshake."

Out of the corner of her eye, Amanda saw Burdett's face turn the color of severe sunburn.

"Why has Mr. Marsh waited twelve years to turn himself in?" a reporter called out.

"We're all exhausted from our plane ride and we won't be making any statements right now. I can say on Mr. Marsh's behalf that he's excited to be back in America and he is eager to have his day in court."

"Why did he flee the country, Amanda?" another reporter shouted.

"This venue is an inappropriate place to try Mr. Marsh's case. The district attorney and I will both be in court and we'll have

our say there. Thank you for being understanding."

With that, Amanda led her brood down
the rest of the stairs. Karl Burdett stepped
in front of her.

"I had nothing to do with this, Karl,"
Amanda said before he could get a word
out. She threw a thumb over her shoulder.
"That's Dennis Levy. He's a reporter for
World News. He called the press without
my knowledge."

Burdett was furious but he knew he
couldn't arrest Charlie without looking bad.
Amanda started walking, and Burdett hurried to stay by her side.

"Your client dodged a bullet today, Jaffe.
You'd better not try anything like this
again."

"I'm as upset as you are, Karl."

Amanda pushed through the shouting
reporters, who obviously had not taken
seriously her statement about not answering questions. Several of them followed
her into the terminal. Amanda spotted Kate
waiting at the front door. As soon as the
investigator saw her boss, she left the terminal and started the car that she'd parked
in front.

"I'll see you at the bail hearing, tomorrow," Amanda told Burdett as she left the terminal. "Thanks again for not arresting Marsh."

Amanda held the rear door of Kate's car open for Charlie and Dennis, then jumped in the front passenger seat. The reporters were still shouting questions when they drove away. As soon as she was out of camera range, Amanda leaned back against the headrest and exhaled.

CHAPTER 30

Gary Hass sat on a metal folding chair and looked out the window of the abandoned loft at the Space Needle as he waited for Ivan Mikhailov to revive. It was a beautiful summer night, and the illuminated Seattle landmark stood out against the starry sky, but Gary was not thinking about the beauty of the moment. He was daydreaming about the carnage that would result if the Space Needle were toppled by a set of carefully placed explosives.

The Russian drug dealer groaned. Gary sighed, displeased that his reverie had been interrupted. Mikhailov was naked and secured to an uncomfortable wooden chair by duct tape in such a way that all of the places where Gary might wish to inflict pain were exposed. Gary waited patiently as Mikhailov became conscious and slowly figured out his predicament.

"Good evening," Gary said. "How are you feeling?"

Mikhailov stared stupidly for a moment before his features hardened into an icy stare.

"Do you know who I am?" he asked in a voice that would have turned Gary's blood cold if their positions had been reversed but which he found merely amusing considering that the Russian was naked and helpless.

"You're Bob Smith of Omaha, Nebraska, aren't you?"

Mikhailov gaped at Gary. Then he shouted, "No, you idiot. I am Ivan Mikhailov and you will set me free immediately or I will have you cut into pieces and fed to my dogs."

"Oh, shit," Gary said. "I'm sorry, sir. I thought you were Bob Smith of Omaha. Man, did I fuck up."

"Yes, you did, but you can save yourself

by setting me loose at once," Mikhailov said imperiously.

Gary grinned. "Actually, Ivan, I'm just playing with you. I knew who you were when I killed your men and Tasered you in the parking garage. You're Ivan the Terrible, the violent drug dealer who's been poaching on Julio Dominguez's territory and beating up his dealers. Do I have that right?"

"You won't think you're so funny when I skin you alive."

"Will that be before or after you feed me to your dogs?"

The Russian began struggling against his bonds. Gary watched for a moment before walking over to his captive and slapping him across the face several times. The slaps only stung Mikhailov but they were humiliating, and the ease with which the strikes were delivered emphasized his helplessness.

"Stop that, Ivan. It's unbecoming. Besides, you can't pay attention to what I have to say if you're twitching and jumping up and down."

"Do you want money?"

"Well, duh, who doesn't? But if you're

thinking ransom or a bribe, that's not on my mind. Julio already paid me."

"I'll double what he gave you."

"I'm sure you would, but I wouldn't be able to torture you if I took your bribe, and I'm in this as much for the fun as for the money. I mean, if you don't enjoy your work you should find some other type of employment, right?"

Gary watched the Russian's face. The sweat that suddenly dampened his captive's brow and the way his pupils were snapping back and forth, as if searching for a way out, let Gary know that Mikhailov finally got it.

"See, Ivan, you're affecting Julio's profits and we can't have that. Before you appeared on the scene, Julio had a nice thing going. He's got a supplier in Colombia who's happy with him, a snazzy house, and plenty of pussy, not to mention the biggest television set I've ever seen. If you still had eyes when I finished with you I'd take you over to watch a game. Anyway, Julio wants me to make sure he doesn't have to cancel HBO because your shenanigans are eating into his bottom line."

Gary walked behind Mikhailov and

wrapped tape around his mouth. That was when the Russian started to scream, but the muffled cries were barely audible.

"That's why I gagged you, Ivan," Gary said. "I knew you'd wake the neighbors, and unlike you, I am very considerate of other people."

GARY GREW TIRED of playing with the Russian after a few hours. The so-called tough guy hadn't been so tough after all and had ceased to be a challenge during the preliminaries. Gary would have killed him to stop his whimpering but Julio wanted his rival to suffer, so he'd plugged away, not really enjoying himself but earning his pay.

After tidying up, Gary made an anonymous 911 call to the police. Julio wanted the murder publicized so no one else would try to move into his territory, and he couldn't scare anyone if no one knew what happened to Ivan.

Gary was tired and not particularly satisfied with the evening when he locked the door of his seedy hotel room. The paint was peeling, the mattress sagged, the only window looked out on an air shaft, and the porcelain on the sink was chipped. The room was depressing but it was in a hotel where no one noticed anything, and he would be gone by morning.

After showering in the narrow bathroom, he turned on the television to see if the media knew about his handiwork yet. Gary was fully awake within seconds of seeing the lead story on the late news. Charlie Marsh was back in the US of A only a few hours from Seattle down the I-5. The same Charlie Marsh who had skipped out without paying Gary for the use of his life and who'd been sunbathing on some African beach, sipping piña coladas, while Gary was compelled to scratch out a living getting rid of other people's problems.

Gary walked over to the window and stared down the shaft at the years of accumulated trash. He had no trouble imagining Charlie's broken body rotting down there.

CHAPTER 31

Kate drove Dennis Levy to the bail hearing so Amanda could discuss the case with Charlie, but Charlie didn't feel like talking during the ride to the Washington County courthouse. He spent most of the time staring at the scenery with the window rolled down, even though Amanda's car had air-conditioning. The wind on his face and the smell of fresh air were physical manifestations of the freedom that could be snatched from him later that morning if Amanda couldn't convince the judge to grant him bail. Between his prison stretch and the psychological prison he'd inhabited in Africa,

Charlie realized that he'd enjoyed very little real freedom in the past fifteen years. It made him wonder about the life he'd led.

Amanda worried about fighting her way through the crowd of reporters at the courthouse, but Karl Burdett unintentionally created a diversion by pontificating to the press at the front entrance. That made it easy for Amanda to smuggle Charlie through a little-used side entrance. She could have been angry at the DA for using the media to bias the jury pool, but she couldn't feel too self-righteous after yesterday's fiasco at the airport.

Amanda threw curt "no comments" at the reporters who were camped outside the courtroom door as she hustled her client to the relative sanctuary of their counsel table. Charlie had his head down, so he didn't see the slender African man in the back row of the spectator benches until he turned to watch Karl Burdett and a female district attorney push through the courtroom doors. Charlie experienced a violent urge to rush to the restroom the second he made eye contact with Nathan Tuazama. Then Burdett and his assistant passed between the two men. Charlie turned away quickly and shivered.

"Are you okay?" Amanda asked when she saw Charlie's ash gray complexion.

"I'm just nervous," Charlie lied as he imagined Tuazama's eyes boring through his back into his soul.

"Good morning, Karl," Amanda said as Burdett tossed his attaché case onto the prosecution table.

Burdett nodded but didn't return her greeting. Then he turned his back on Amanda and began organizing his papers. Amanda wondered why the DA looked tense when he had the edge at the bail hearing. Before she could puzzle out the problem, the bailiff rapped his gavel and the Honorable Marshall Berkowitz hurried out of chambers to take the bench. The judge, who was short and grossly over-weight, wheezed as he waddled to his position on the dais.

"Good morning," he said with a friendly nod to both parties. If Judge Berkowitz was intimidated by the large contingent of re-porters in his courtroom and the publicity his case was receiving, he didn't show it.

"Good morning, Your Honor," Burdett said as he rose to address the court. "This is the time set for the bail hearing in *State v. Charles Lee Marsh aka the Guru Gabriel Sun*. Let the record show that the state is represented by Karl Burdett and Rebecca Cromartie. The defendant is present, represented by his attorney, Amanda Jaffe."

"Good morning, Your Honor," Amanda said. "As a preliminary matter, I'd ask the court to strike Mr. Marsh's aka. He took that name years ago to promote his book and seminars and he hasn't used it in over a decade."

"It's how people know him, Judge," Burdett countered. "We'll have witnesses referring to him as Gabriel Sun or the guru. Besides, Miss Jaffe hasn't given me notice so I'm not prepared to argue this issue, this morning."

"I'm inclined to agree with Mr. Burdett," the judge told Amanda, "but you can file a motion with some law if you're concerned."

Amanda wasn't really concerned about the relatively benign aka in the indictment. What did worry her was the possibility that any juror who remembered Charlie's alias would also remember that the tabloids had started calling her client Satan's Guru as soon as he was accused of murder. But she decided to fight that battle another day.

"Let's get to the matter of bail," the judge said.

"I think I can save the court some time," Burdett answered before Amanda could get a word out. "If Mr. Marsh surrenders his passport, the state will not oppose bail in light of his voluntary return to face trial."

Amanda was shocked by Burdett's concession but she was also surprised by his tone. The DA sounded like he regretted giving Charlie a break. If he felt that way, why was he agreeing to bail?

"That seems to take care of your motion, Miss Jaffe," Judge Berkowitz said.

"It does, and I want to thank Mr. Burdett for being so reasonable."

Burdett didn't respond to Amanda. Instead, he told the judge that Charlie would have to be booked into the jail so he could be fingerprinted and have a mug shot taken. Then the DA suggested a bail amount that was well within Charlie's means. Amanda agreed to the sum quickly and the judge told his clerk to prepare the paperwork. As soon as Amanda and Burdett agreed on a trial date, the DA and his assistant left the courtroom, followed by a pack of reporters.

"Am I free?" Charlie asked, unsure of what had just happened.

"As soon as we post bail."

Charlie grinned. Then the grin faded as he remembered Nathan Tuazama. He scanned the crowd but the African was no longer in the courtroom.

"Something wrong?" Amanda asked.

"No, no. I'm just, uh, shocked by how fast everything went."

"That makes two of us."

"I bet you didn't see that coming," Kate said as she and Dennis joined Amanda and Charlie at counsel table.

"No, I didn't," Amanda answered, still confused by Burdett's concession.

A sheriff's deputy walked over to escort Charlie to the courthouse jail for booking.

"Kate, can you go with Charlie?"

"No problem."

"I'll get up to the jail as soon as I post your bail," Amanda told her client. "Do not say anything about your case to anyone, understood?"

"Mum's the word."

"Good. See you in an hour or so."

"I take it that this was unexpected?" Dennis Levy said.

"Very. I thought Burdett would fight to the death to keep Charlie in custody."

"Any idea why he caved?"

"He didn't *cave*, Dennis, and don't you dare put it that way. I don't want to make Karl sorry he gave us a break by making him look like a coward."

"No, no, you're right. I'll write it up as a magnanimous concession."

"Good."

"So, why did he cave?" Levy asked with a grin.

"I have no idea. And now, you have to excuse me. I want Charlie out of custody as soon as possible."

FIFTY-FIVE MINUTES LATER, Amanda escorted Charlie out of the jail and into the sunlight. He paused in the warm summer air to close his eyes and take a deep breath. Amanda noticed a group of reporters moving toward them. Kate was waiting at the curb to drive Amanda to her car. Amanda grabbed Charlie's elbow and hustled him toward the street. They were almost there when Kate's windshield exploded.

Kate threw an arm across her face. Charlie froze. Amanda slammed a shoulder into his back and drove him to the pavement just before another bullet passed through the space where his head had been, before blasting a chunk of concrete from the courthouse facade.

A reporter screamed. Others ducked for cover. A cameraman swung around and foolishly looked for the shooter through his lens. Two sheriff's deputies crouched at the entrance to the courthouse, guns drawn.

"Keep down," Amanda shouted as she pushed her client halfway under the car.

"What happened?" Charlie asked.

"Someone shot at you. Stay still. The shots came from the other side of the car. The chassis will block you from view."

Dennis Levy cowered on the floor in the back of Kate's car. Kate crawled across the glass littering the front seat. She paused long enough to draw her gun before pushing open the passenger door and rolling to the pavement.

"Are you okay?" Amanda asked.

"Yeah."

Amanda heard a siren. Kate got to one knee and peeked over the hood. An ambulance was speeding toward them and the cameraman who had tried to locate the shooter was pointing the police toward a row of two-story commercial buildings several blocks away. When Kate was certain they were safe she signaled Amanda and the women helped Charlie to his feet.

"You saved my life," Charlie told Amanda.

"Jaffe, Katz, Lehane and Brindisi is a full-service law firm," she joked, trying to keep her tone light while she fought the shakes that grew worse as her adrenaline wore off.

"I'm going to need a statement," a police officer told Charlie. Charlie looked at Amanda.

"It's okay," she said. "You're the victim here. Did you see who shot at you?"

"No. I was looking at the car door. I was going to get in when the window exploded. Then you pushed me to the ground."

"I'm afraid I can't add anything to what

Mr. Marsh said. I didn't see a thing. As soon as the window exploded I knocked him down. After that, the car blocked my view."

"I'm going to need you to come inside anyway so the detectives can take a statement," the officer told Amanda.

"That's okay. We'll just be hounded by the reporters if we stay outside," Amanda said just as Karl Burdett raced out of the courthouse followed by some of his staff.

"What happened?" he asked Amanda.

"A sniper took a shot at Mr. Marsh." Burdett turned pale. Amanda pointed to the place where the police had gone. "He was probably on one of those buildings."

"This is terrible," Burdett said, more to himself than Amanda. He looked stricken as he walked over to confer with one of the police officers, leaving Amanda confused by the DA's reaction, which seemed wrong somehow, even given the upsetting event she had just witnessed.

32

Amanda had reserved rooms for Charlie and Dennis in a boutique hotel on the outskirts of downtown Portland. Levy chattered nonstop during the ride to the hotel but Charlie barely uttered a word. Amanda attributed his silence to trauma from the assassination attempt, but Charlie was thinking about Nathan Tuazama.

Charlie was exhausted when Amanda parked at the hotel. Levy invited them into the bar for a drink, but listening to the reporter drone on about himself was more than they could bear. Amanda begged off for both of them by saying that she had several matters to discuss with her client.

When the elevator stopped at Charlie's floor, they walked down the corridor to his room. Charlie was about to slide the key card into the slot when he saw that the door was ajar. His mouth went dry and his pulse accelerated. He should have run but he wasn't thinking straight and he pushed the door open.

The room looked like Hurricane Katrina had whipped through it. The mattress was off the bed and a knife had been taken to it. Stuffing from the mattress mixed with the contents of Charlie's drawers and closet, which were strewn across the floor. The television had been dismantled and the air-conditioner had been ripped from the wall and taken apart.

Amanda phoned the front desk and told them to call the police. When she hung up she turned to her client.

"All right, Charlie, what's going on here and does it have anything to do with the box I just stashed in my new safety-deposit box?"

"Probably," Charlie answered nervously.

"Am I putting myself in danger because I've helped you?"

Before Charlie could answer, Amanda's cell phone rang. She fished it out of her purse and saw that Mike Greene was the caller. Amanda excused herself and walked into the hall.

"I just heard about the shooting at the courthouse. Are you okay?" Mike asked.

Amanda could hear the concern in his voice. This wasn't the first time Amanda had had a brush with death. Mike had been with her right after her hairbreadth escape from the serial killer the press had nicknamed the Surgeon and shortly after she'd survived a home invasion by professional killers while she was representing Jon Dupre. Amanda was glad he'd called. Knowing that Mike cared for her was as calming as a cup of chamomile tea.

"I'm fine. I was shaken up right after the shooting but I wasn't hurt at all."

"Do you want me to come over tonight? I can bring Chinese."

"I think that's a great idea. Look, I'm in the middle of something. Let me call you when I'm through and we'll figure out tonight."

Amanda disconnected just as the manager and hotel security stepped out of the elevator. After a brief look around, the manager told Charlie that he would move him to another room. Shortly after that two Portland Police officers walked in. While they were interviewing Amanda there was another knock on the door. Charlie turned. The man standing in the doorway looked familiar. When he saw Charlie was having trouble placing him, he held his hands out at his sides as if the greater exposure would solve Charlie's problem.

"It's me, Charlie," the man said. "Mickey Keys, your agent."

CHARLIE TOOK A good look at his onetime agent and crime partner as he escorted Keys to the end of the hall, where they would have some privacy. Keys was thin; not in a physically fit way but in the way someone looks when they're not eating well because they can't afford food. The collar of his shirt was frayed and the elbows of his jacket were shiny. There were lines on his face that hadn't been there twelve years ago. His skin had a waxy pallor and there were dark circles under his eyes.

"What are you doing here?" Charlie asked.

"What do you mean, Charlie?" Keys said, flashing a tense smile that made him look desperate. "I'm your agent, your business manager. As soon as I heard you were back in the States, I got on the first plane West. I figured you'd need someone to set up appearances, handle your contracts. You know, like the old days."

"I've already got a contract for a new book. If I'm not on death row, my publisher will handle the bookings."

"You can't cut me out, Charlie. We have a contract, too," Mickey said, pulling a wrinkled and stained sheaf of papers out of his jacket pocket. "This is a copy, in case you lost yours. It makes me your agent."

"Our agreement ended when you cut a deal with the feds."

Keys pushed the papers at Charlie. "There's nothing in our contract that lets you out of our arrangement. I'm entitled to fifteen percent of everything."

Charlie held his hand in the air, refusing to touch the contract. "You're not getting a penny. You sold me out."

"I had to. They were going to make me

do hard time if I didn't come clean about the Inner Light scam and the second set of books. You were in Batanga, protected. I was out on a limb, all by myself."

"A business relationship requires trust, Mickey. How can I trust you after what you did?"

"What I did was three years in a federal lockup while you were getting blow jobs on a tropical beach."

"Hey, man, I'm sorry you went to jail, but Batanga was no cakewalk. I'd have traded places with you in a nanosecond if I'd known what I was getting myself into. Why do you think I'm here facing a death sentence?"

Keys dropped the tough posture and his shoulders sagged.

"Look, Charlie, I'll level with you. I'm desperate. The feds took everything. I've been working as a telemarketer, because no one will hire an ex-con to do anything else. I live in a hotel room with roaches. You've still got the money in your Swiss account and all this new dough. I had to give my money back as part of the plea bargain. I've got nothing."

"I can give you a few bucks, if that's why you're here."

Keys reddened. "I don't want a handout. I want back in the game. I want to be a player, again."

"Then I can't help you."

"I'll hire a lawyer. I'll sue and I'll win."

"Do what you gotta do," Charlie said before walking back to the chaos in his room.

Keys leaned back against the wall. When he had pulled himself together, he started walking to the elevator, his head down, looking utterly defeated.

"Mr. Keys."

Mickey looked up and found Charlie's lawyer blocking the way.

"Can I talk to you?" Amanda asked.

"We'll do our talking in court when I sue your client for breach of contract," Keys answered, trying to sound like the tough negotiator he'd been before his fall.

"I don't know anything about your business problems with Mr. Marsh. I'm his criminal attorney."

"Then what do you want?"

"You were at the Westmont when Congressman Pope was shot, weren't you?"

"Yeah."

"Would you be willing to talk to my investigator?"

"About what?"

"Anything you saw that will help us get a handle on what happened."

Keys looked incredulous. "You want me to help that ungrateful prick after what he just did to me?"

"We just want to hear your version of what happened."

"My version, huh." Keys stopped talking and Amanda could almost see the wheels turning inside his skull. "Well, let's talk about that. My memory is a bit hazy right now. But I might be able to remember more clearly if my financial situation cleared up. So, why don't you have a word with Charlie. When you get back to me—depending on the news—I'll either be talking to your investigator or the DA."

CHAPTER

33

The morning after the sniper attack, Amanda slept late and didn't get to the offices of Jaffe, Katz, Lehane and Brindisi until nine. When she opened the door to the reception area, Dennis Levy was talking excitedly on his cell phone. He broke off his call as soon as he saw Amanda and sprang out of his chair, almost knocking the latte she was holding out of her hand when he thrust a copy of *World News* at her.

"What do you think?" he asked proudly.

"Not much until I've had my coffee," Amanda answered, taking a step back from the keyed-up journalist.

"Look," Levy said, pointing just below the picture of Charlie Marsh that graced the magazine cover, where bright red block letters proclaimed, THE GURU RETURNS. Following the title was the byline, DENNIS LEVY.

"That's my story," Levy declared.

"Congratulations," Amanda told him, impressed despite her dislike for the reporter.

Levy flipped the magazine open to his story and directed Amanda to a column on the second page. "I told you you'd get a lot of publicity out of this," he said.

Amanda read the column. Sure enough, she was prominently featured as the lawyer Charlie had chosen to defend him.

"Mrs. Brice overnighted this copy to me. It is literally hot off the press."

Amanda forced a smile. "It looks like you're on your way, Dennis."

"So, what are we doing this morning?"

"I'm not sure," Amanda lied. "I do have other cases. Why don't you wait out here while I get some caffeine in me and try to figure out my schedule? All that excitement at the courthouse threw it off."

"Sure thing," Dennis said.

As Amanda walked toward Kate's office,

she chanced a quick glance over her shoulder. Levy was smiling like the Cheshire Cat as he reread his magazine article. She couldn't blame him for being proud.

Amanda knocked on Kate's doorjamb. "I have a problem," she told her investigator. "I'm interviewing Sally Pope and I do not want Jimmy Olsen's evil twin tagging along."

"Levy wants to look at the *Pope* file. I can set him up in the conference room and you can sneak out while he's going through it."

"You're brilliant."

"That's why I get the big bucks."

"Just make sure he understands that he has to leave the file the way he found it. I haven't had a chance to go through it yet."

"Will do. I'll also take him with me when I interview Ralph Day."

"Who?"

"He was Junior's challenger in his last election."

"Right. That should keep him out of my hair."

WHILE HE WAITED for the receptionist to bring him coffee, Dennis studied the mountain of information spread across the conference table. The task of going through it was daunting but Levy loved research. He believed that it was his attention to detail that made him superior to the other reporters at *World News*.

Kate's trial book made it easier for Dennis to work through the material. She had explained how she had organized everything from the file into piles relating to different topics. The first items Levy looked at were the autopsy report and photos, because he'd never covered any crime stories and he was curious. He flipped through them with only the tiniest emotional reaction and was pleased with himself. When he was through with the material concerning the cause of death, he pulled over another stack.

An hour later, Dennis squared off a group of reports and stood up. As he stretched, he noticed something sticking out of a pile of witness interviews. He pulled it out and gave it a cursory inspection. He was about to put it back when something caught his eye. He pulled it closer and squinted. Then his eyes grew wide and his heart began to beat rapidly.

. . . .

"So, WHAT'S IT like working for the Jaffes?" Dennis Levy asked as he and Kate drove to Ralph Day's office. The reporter had been talking nonstop since he'd gotten in Kate's car and he couldn't sit still. The constant chatter and twitching was getting on Kate's nerves.

"Most of the time it's just routine stuff. You know, witness interviews, like today. Internet searches."

"It must be pretty exciting when you're investigating a big case, like Charlie's."

"The job has its moments," Kate answered ambiguously, choosing to keep to herself the details of the harrowing situations in which she'd been involved since going to work for Jaffe, Katz, Lehane and Brindisi.

"Any background you can give me on Amanda? Things that aren't public knowledge that might spice up my stories."

"You mean like her affair with Brad Pitt or the identity of the father of her secret love child?" Kate answered, keeping her eyes on the road ahead.

Levy's laugh sounded forced. "That's good. Yeah, that would help sell magazines."

"I'm afraid Amanda doesn't have a lot of secrets and—if she did—she'd have to be the person to tell them to you."

"Oh, come on. There's got to be something."

"What makes you think I'd dish dirt about a good friend?"

"So there is something to tell?" Dennis said eagerly. "You know *World News* could make this worth your while. You don't have to work for a small firm your whole life. The publicity I can give you would definitely help your career."

Kate held her temper. "That's a good point," she said evenly. "I'm certain every major law firm in the country would be eager to hire a private investigator willing to sell out every secret they had. I'll remember to put in my résumé that I can be bought easily."

Dennis colored as he realized that he'd gone too far. "I didn't mean it like that."

"I'm sure you didn't," Kate said, not bothering to mask her distaste.

"Hey, look, I'm sorry if we got off on the wrong foot. I don't know what I was thinking. Let's start over. Why don't you tell me about the witness we're going to interview?"

"*We* aren't interviewing anyone, Dennis. Remember the ground rules? You're just going to listen and you are not going to speak unless I say it's okay."

"Right, right. I get that. It was a figure of speech."

"I'm glad we have that straight. Ralph Day was Junior's opponent in the election. Pope defeated him the first time he ran for Congress but Day won when Junior was killed. Day was also at the Westmont on the evening the murder took place."

"What do you think he can tell us . . . you . . . that will help Charlie's case?"

"I have no idea."

"Speaking of ideas, I got a few when I was going through the *Pope* file."

"Such as?"

"We should talk to Werner Rollins. After he cut a deal with the cops, Rollins said he saw Marsh shoot Pope, but he could have been pressured to finger Charlie. Twelve years have gone by. Who knows what he'd say now. If he retracts his statement it will really help clear Charlie."

Kate had never thought Levy was stupid—just obnoxious—and she was impressed by his insight.

"That's good thinking, Dennis. I've been trying to find Rollins. He may be in Denver. I have a Colorado PI following up on a lead."

"Great! Say, if you find him can I come along?"

"I'll have to ask Amanda."

"Oh, sure. Put in a good word for me, will you? I'd appreciate it."

"I'll do that."

RALPH DAY'S INSURANCE agency was in a strip mall on the outskirts of Hillsboro. Day walked into the waiting room moments after his secretary buzzed him. He was a large, affable man in his early sixties with a little excess weight and a full head of white hair. He wore a charcoal gray suit and a conservative tie and looked the part of a successful insurance salesman. When they were seated in his office, Kate explained Dennis's involvement in the case. The ex-congressman had no objections to having a reporter sit in on the interview.

"I read about the shooting at the court-house," Day said. "Was anyone hurt?"

"We were lucky. The sniper missed with both shots."

"Thank God for that." Day paused. He looked pensive. "Can you tell me why Marsh is coming back after all these years?"

"That's what everyone wants to know," Kate answered.

"I guess it will come out at the trial. So, what did you want to ask me? I don't know what help I can be. This all happened so long ago."

"I guess I should start by asking you about your relationship with Arnold Pope Jr. around the time he was killed."

"That's easy enough. I hated Pope's guts. No, let me amend that. It was his father's guts I hated. Junior didn't have any. He was just the old man's puppet. There were times I actually felt sorry for Junior. He didn't have a mind or life of his own."

"Can you explain that?" Kate asked.

"Sure. Arnie Jr. was the political equivalent of one of those prepackaged boy bands the record companies put together. Senior started grooming him to be president from the moment he was born."

"I've been doing a little research and you credited Senior's money with Junior's victory in your first contest."

"No question. I raised a decent amount for my campaign but I couldn't compete. I couldn't prove it but I know that Senior violated every campaign financing rule on the books. He funneled money through friends, employees, PACs he created with straw men. Hell, I had some money for TV, but you couldn't turn on a set without seeing Junior's smiling face in front of an American flag."

"Would he have won a second term if he wasn't murdered?"

"I'm far enough from the race to give you an honest answer. Junior would have kicked my butt. The boy had no substance but that was a hard point to make with an electorate that wasn't paying much attention to our race. Of course, everyone paid attention when he got killed, and I was able to get a lot of free TV time."

"You won the seat, so maybe you would have won anyway."

"No, not a chance. If Junior hadn't died I would have lost, but Junior's party had to scramble to find someone to run against me and the best they could come up with was a retired county commissioner that nobody liked much. Senior never forgave me for taking Arnie's spot in Congress. Next time around, he tried to bury me under his money again. I was better prepared and I won reelection, but it was close and he came at me every two years until he finally got me after my third term."

"Do you miss being in Congress?" Kate asked sympathetically.

"I did but I'm over it. Life's been pretty good to me. I dealt with the setback and put it behind me."

"I understand you were at the Westmont the evening Junior was killed."

Day nodded.

"What can you remember about the fight and the shooting?"

"Boy, that's a tough one. It was dark and very chaotic, and I didn't have a real clear impression of what happened even then."

"That's okay. Just give it your best shot."

"Okay, well, I didn't go to the club to hear the guru. I wasn't into all that self-improvement stuff. I came to be seen, part of the politicking. I got to the Westmont just as Marsh's entourage arrived and I parked in the lot. I was almost at the front entrance when the fight started."

Day stared into space for a moment, his expression blank. Then he brightened.

"I do remember a big black man fighting with a security guard. People were pushing to get out of the way and I was shoved back from the action. Then I heard a shot. When I turned I saw Junior staggering. I remember Sally running to him, but I didn't see much of what anyone else was doing, because I was focused on Junior."

"Can you remember anyone else in the crowd, a witness we can talk to who may have seen something?"

Day's brow furrowed as he tried to remember the twelve-year-old scene. After a while, he rattled off a few names Kate recognized from the police reports.

"That's all the people I can recall right now. I'll think about it some more and if . . ."

Day paused. "Oh, I've got one more. Tony Rose was there."

"You saw Rose?"

"He was on the edge of the crowd almost in a line from where I was but much closer to the pro shop."

"Near the spot where you saw the guard and the black man fighting?"

"Right. He may have had a better view of the shooting. You should ask him."

"I'll be sure to do that," Kate said.

"IT LOOKS LIKE the interview was a bust. Day doesn't know much," Dennis said.

"Yeah, but we didn't know that before we talked to him," Kate answered, concealing from Dennis the conflict between what Tony Rose had told her about his location when Junior was shot and Day's recollection.

"You know, I feel bad about the way I acted when we were on our way to see Day," Levy said. "I'd like to make it up to you."

"Forget about it. I have."

"No, seriously, how about dinner, tonight? You can pick the restaurant. I'm on an expense account. Make it someplace expensive and romantic."

Kate turned her head for a second and Levy flashed a wolfish grin. The investigator made a note to ask Amanda for hazardous duty pay.

"Thanks, Dennis, but I'm living with someone."

"He doesn't have to know. Tell him it's a business meeting."

"Dennis, let me ask you directly. Are you hitting on me?"

Levy's grin shifted from wolfish to sly. "Maybe."

"Don't."

"By this time next year, I guarantee you I'm going to be famous and rich. You could do a lot worse."

"Dennis, I'm trying to be nice and I'm trying to be clear. I'm in a serious relationship and it's not with you. Furthermore, it won't be, ever. Do you understand what I just said? And while you're thinking about your answer, remember that I carry a gun and I know how to use it."

Twelve years ago, Sally Pope had made a vivid impression on the college student who was watching her father try his biggest case from the spectator section of a Washington County courtroom. The media portrayed Sally as a "femme fatale" and she embodied the secret fantasies of every schoolgirl who stayed on the straight and narrow. Women like Sally populated television soap operas and the romance novels serious young women read when no one was watching. Her looks were breathtaking and her figure was an advertisement for sex; she was mysterious *and* she may have been a murderess.

Something else had riveted Amanda's attention on Mrs. Pope. Frank's daughter could not help noticing the way her father's eyes strayed to his client and the way Sally Pope's hands strayed to her father's forearm when they leaned close to confer. Amanda was living with Frank that summer. After the trial ended, he was conspicuously absent at night, often arriving home in the early hours of the morning.

Amanda had been fiercely protective of her father and not comfortable with the idea that he might be having a serious relationship with anyone. The possibility that the woman he was seeing could have murdered her husband ramped up the dread Amanda felt each time Frank disappeared.

Amanda never knew for certain that her father was romantically involved with Sally Pope and she never got up the nerve to confront him. Amanda almost forgot about Sally when she returned to the rigors of her college studies and the demands of the swim team, and she was very relieved when Sally left for Europe. But Amanda's old emotions had resurfaced with the resurrection of the charges against Charlie Marsh.

A powerful sun was directly overhead when Amanda parked her car in the turn-around in front of Sally Pope's house. She squinted to avoid the glare as she hurried into the shade of the front porch. Gina, Sally Pope's personal assistant, showed Amanda into a large living room that looked out on a colorful flower garden through a set of French doors. Sally Pope entered the room a few minutes later.

"It's good to see you again, Amanda," Sally said with a pleasant smile. She was wearing tan shorts, sandals, and a yellow T-shirt, and her blond hair was pulled back in a ponytail. Amanda could see signs of aging but was still impressed by her beauty and poise.

"I'm surprised you remember me," Amanda said as they shook hands.

"Of course I remember you. You were in court every day and Frank talked about you all the time. He's very proud of you."

Amanda blushed and Sally pointed toward a long, beige couch. "Why don't we sit? Do you want coffee or an iced tea?"

"Iced tea sounds good," Amanda said.

Gina had been waiting unobtrusively near the door to the living room. She left as soon as she heard what Amanda wanted to drink.

"I understand you saved Charlie's life," Sally said.

"I just pushed him down when the first shot was fired."

"That was quick thinking."

Amanda shrugged.

"Is Charlie okay?"

"He was shaken up but he's not hurt."

"Good. Frank said you wanted to talk to me about his case."

"Is that okay?"

"Of course, but I don't know what I can say that will help."

"Let's start with how you and Charlie met."

Sally laughed. "He 'rescued' me from Tony Rose after one of his seminars at an estate in Dunthorpe. It really wasn't necessary but he put on this macho act. He even punched Tony in the nose."

"Was this when Rose says you asked him to murder your husband?"

Sally stopped smiling. "There was not

one shred of truth in anything that bastard testified about."

"Then why do you think he said it?"

"Isn't it obvious? Senior paid him to lie. Who do you think bankrolled Mercury?"

"Can you prove that?"

Sally shook her head. "Senior is like some mythical beast when it comes to his business practices. You might think you've spotted a partial footprint in the snow but you never see the beast itself. Then the wind comes up and obliterates the track and you're left with nothing."

"If I call you, will you testify that you never asked Charlie to kill your husband?" Amanda asked as Gina returned with her iced tea.

"Of course. The only evidence Karl Burdett had was those photographs and the note, and Frank proved that was a setup."

"But you and Charlie were lovers?" Amanda asked.

"Amanda, there were a lot of things I've done that I'm not proud of, and sleeping around is at the top of the list. Before I married Arnie, I did it because I thought that my body was the only thing I had going for me.

After I married Arnie, I slept around to get his attention. Charlie was a roadside flare, that's all. We never meant anything to each other."

"What did you see at the Westmont?" Amanda asked.

"I didn't see the person who shot Arnie, if that's what you're after."

"Just tell me what you do remember."

Sally closed her eyes for a moment and Amanda took a sip of iced tea.

"John Walsdorf, the club manager, and I were outside the front entrance when Charlie's limo pulled up."

"Before the limo arrived, did you have a conversation with Tony Rose?"

"That's right! I forgot about that. Only it wasn't a conversation. He wanted to talk but I didn't. Especially not then, with the guest of honor arriving."

"What happened?" Amanda asked.

"I told Tony I couldn't talk to him and he left me alone."

"Did you notice where he went?"

Sally's brow furrowed. After a few seconds, she shook her head.

"I'm sorry. As soon as Tony walked off, Charlie's limo pulled up. Then Arnie started causing trouble and there was the fight. I forgot all about Tony."

"So you don't remember seeing him after he tried to talk to you?"

"I'm pretty certain Frank asked me who I remembered seeing and where they were standing soon after I hired him. He probably made notes."

"I've seen them. I wanted to get your impressions now."

"I remember Charlie getting out of the car. There was some trouble with a man who looked like a biker. He testified at the trial, but I don't remember his name. Then Arnie came storming up and threw the photos in my face. That's when the fight started."

"Did you see your husband get shot?"

Sally nodded. She looked sad. "I was watching him during the fight so I did see him get shot, but I didn't see who did it because my eyes were on Arnie."

"And you don't remember who was near him?"

"Just people. It was dark, there was a lot of confusion."

"What about the guy who looked like a biker? Did you see him?"

"Yes. He was fighting with one of the security guards. So was Charlie's bodyguard, Delmar Epps."

"Were you close to Mr. Epps at any time that evening?"

"I was right next to him when he got out of the limo. There was some problem with a man who opened Charlie's door. It wasn't his driver. I can't remember his name. He wasn't a witness at the trial.

"Anyway, the driver was coming around to do it, but this man walked up to the car and opened the door. Then Delmar got out and it looked like there might be trouble, so I walked over to the car to cool things down."

"How close were you standing to Mr. Epps when you went to the car?"

"I was in front of him, almost touching."

"Did you notice whether he was carrying a gun?"

"In his hand?"

"Anywhere on his person."

Sally closed her eyes and concentrated. After a short time she opened her eyes and shook her head.

"I don't remember seeing a gun, but I

wasn't really looking. He could have had a gun under his jacket."

"What about Charlie? Where did he go when the fighting started?"

"I'm not sure. I didn't see him in a fight with anyone, but that doesn't surprise me. Charlie was a talker, not a fighter. He wouldn't have hit Tony if his bodyguard wasn't right behind him. Quite honestly, I can't imagine he would shoot someone, either."

"Your husband had just hit him and was running toward him."

"I know, but I just don't think Charlie had that kind of violence in him."

CHAPTER 35

Amanda decided to spend the rest of the day reviewing the file in *State v. Pope*. Dennis Levy was no longer in the conference room and she thanked God for small favors. By the time she was done for the day, she was working on her third mug of coffee and everyone else in the office was gone. Mike Greene called to see if she wanted to grab a bite to eat, but she was so tired she decided that a quick dinner, a warm bath, and an early bedtime was what she needed.

Amanda ordered sushi to go at a restaurant near her office. A little before eight, she parked in her spot in the garage of a converted redbrick warehouse in Portland's trendy Pearl District and took the elevator to her loft. It was 1,200 square feet of mostly open space with hardwood floors, high ceilings, and tall windows that gave her a view of the metal arches of the Freemont Bridge, the traffic on the Willamette River, and the snow-covered slopes of Mount St. Helens, an active volcano. Most of the art that decorated her condo had been purchased in the galleries scattered among the restaurants and coffee houses that were so easy to find in the Pearl. She loved living someplace where she could walk to work or take the trolley on days when she didn't need her car.

Amanda opened the front door and started to punch in her alarm code. The alarm wasn't on. She paused, her fingers over the keypad. Amanda hadn't slept well because of the events at the courthouse. She decided that she'd probably been so tired that she'd forgotten to set the alarm when she left for work. She flipped on the lights, left the sushi on the kitchen counter, and headed toward her bedroom to change. Halfway through her living room, she froze. A slender black man was watching her from her couch.

"Not to worry, Miss Jaffe," Nathan Tuazama said in his lilting African English. "I have no intention of hurting you."

Amanda took a closer look at her visitor. His suit was expensive and his shoes were shined. She thought his tie might be silk. This was definitely not the attire of a cat burglar.

"I think you should explain why you broke into my apartment before I call the police," Amanda said, keeping her voice calm while she scanned the area around her for potential weapons.

The intruder's lips curved upward but there was something unnatural about his smile. Amanda was reminded of the rictus she'd seen on the faces of corpses in autopsy photos.

"I assure you that Charlie won't want the police to learn of our conversation."

Amanda pulled out her cell phone. "I just punched in a nine and a one. If I don't get a good explanation for this break-in, I'm finishing the call."

"Please, Miss Jaffe, sit down. I know it

must be unsettling to find someone in your home but I won't be here long and you are perfectly safe. It's your client who should be worried."

"If you want to talk to me about my client, I have an office and business hours."

"Long hours, to judge from the time I've spent waiting for you. I'm pleased to see that Charlie has such a dedicated advocate. But let's get to business. It's late and you must be tired.

"I am Nathan Tuazama, the director of President Jean-Claude Baptiste's National Education Bureau." Amanda felt her stomach roll. "You have heard of President Baptiste?"

Amanda nodded. "Charlie's also mentioned you."

"I imagine he has."

"What do you want with me?"

"President Baptiste would appreciate some assistance with a problem."

"And that is?"

"Charlie took something that did not belong to him when he left Batanga, something that belongs to President Baptiste. If Charlie was still in Batanga I would be having this conversation with him in the basement of the executive mansion, and the problem would be solved quickly."

Charlie had told Amanda what happened in the basement of the mansion, and it took every ounce of Amanda's courtroom training to maintain her composure.

"Unfortunately, I am in America, so I am here to ask you, on behalf of my president, to act as our intermediary and convince Charlie to return what he has taken."

The box! Tuazama had to be referring to the contents of Charlie's box.

"Assuming I can get this property to you, what happens to Charlie?"

"Once I have the property, President Baptiste will have no further interest in your client," Tuazama lied. "Charlie is an insignificant and easily forgettable individual, but he will become significant to me should he try to retain the president's property. Tell him that. Tell Charlie that he will become someone of great interest to me if I do not get what I want. And tell him I am not a patient man when it comes to my president's interests."

"What is it you think Mr. Marsh has?"

Tuazama stood. "That need not concern

you. In fact, the less you know, the better off you are. Believe me, you do not want to involve yourself in this business other than as a messenger."

"How will I contact you to tell you what Mr. Marsh wants to do?"

"Don't trouble yourself about anything but communicating President Baptiste's wishes to your client. I know the number of your cell phone. Rest assured, I'll be in touch soon. It's been a pleasure meeting you."

Amanda set her alarm the moment her door closed behind Tuazama. Then she sat down until her nerves settled. Amanda had no idea what Charlie was into but she was convinced that Tuazama had been responsible for the chaos in Charlie's hotel room. Amanda wondered if Tuazama was the sniper and if he'd missed on purpose to frighten Charlie. He'd certainly frightened her.

HALF AN HOUR later, Amanda was seated on the sofa in the sitting room in Charlie's suite.

"Do you remember telling me about Nathan Tuazama, the head of Baptiste's secret police?"

Charlie's eyes shifted nervously and a sheen of sweat appeared on his forehead.

"I just got a chance to meet him, Charlie. He broke into my apartment."

"He didn't hurt you, did he?" Charlie asked with genuine concern.

"No, but he made it pretty clear that he's going to hurt you unless you return what you stole from President Baptiste."

"I didn't steal anything."

"Then what is Tuazama doing here?"

Charlie looked ill. "He's after the contents of the box I gave you."

"And that is?"

"Some diamonds I smuggled out of Batanga," Charlie answered, his voice barely above a whisper.

"How many diamonds?"

"I don't know exactly."

"Guess."

Charlie looked down, unable to meet her eye. "A lot. I haven't had a chance to show them to anyone who can tell me what they're worth."

"Do the diamonds in the box belong to President Baptiste?"

"No, not really."

"Then why did Nathan Tuazama say they did?"

"Uh, it's a law thing."

"Humor me, Charlie. Pretend I'm a lawyer who might be intelligent enough to understand what you have to say."

Charlie licked his lips. "Well, in the U.S., women have a lot of freedom. I mean, look at you. You can vote and go to law school. Stuff like that. In Batanga they have all these tribal laws. Husbands sort of own their wives and once they're married anything the wife owns becomes the husband's property."

"They were Bernadette's diamonds?"

"He treated her like shit, Amanda. He can't get it up, so he'd take it out on her. When we were in bed, she would cry. I saw the marks."

"And you took advantage of her and got her to give you these diamonds?" Amanda said, not even trying to disguise her disgust.

"It wasn't that way," Charlie protested. "They belonged to Bernadette and she gave them to someone who gave them to me."

"Who?"

"I can't tell you."

"Why can't you tell me?"

"I can't tell you that either. Believe me, I would if I could, but I swore I wouldn't talk about it."

"You don't think I've earned the right to the information after Tuazama's visit?"

"Please, Amanda, don't ask me anymore about the diamonds."

"Am I in danger, Charlie?"

"If Tuazama thought you knew anything you wouldn't be here. As long as he doesn't know I gave you the diamonds, you're safe."

"Would Tuazama have the nerve to kill you in the States?" Amanda asked.

"Oh, yeah. This guy is pure evil. I'm not completely convinced he's human."

"Do you think he was the sniper?"

"He could have been. I wouldn't put it past him to miss on purpose to put the fear of God in me. Did you know he was in the courtroom?"

"At the bail hearing?"

Charlie nodded.

"Why didn't you tell me?"

"I didn't want you involved."

"Well, I am. You involved me when you gave me the diamonds."

Amanda thought for a moment. Then she looked directly at her client.

"Let me give him the diamonds, Charlie, if it will make him go away. They won't be worth anything to you if you're dead."

"What if I don't? What can we do? Can't you report him for breaking into your apartment?"

"The only crime Tuazama has committed is trespass. He didn't break in to commit a crime. He just asked me to ask you to give back the diamonds. Trespassing is a misdemeanor. He'd be out on bail immediately and a lot madder than he is now. Don't screw around with this guy, Charlie. Baptiste may have a legal claim to the gems. Give him the diamonds."

Charlie worried his lip. He looked at the floor. Then he shook his head.

"I can't do it."

"Why, for God's sake? Are they worth your life?"

"If I give back the diamonds it's like Bernadette died for nothing. Baptiste thinks he's invincible, that he can hurt people on a whim without any consequences."

Charlie stopped to take a deep breath. Then he looked directly at Amanda. "If I keep his diamonds it won't be much, but it will be something."

"Charlie, there are diamond mines in Batanga and Baptiste controls them. He can get all the diamonds he wants."

"But he can't have these diamonds. I know it doesn't make sense to you, but I know Baptiste. He can't stand the idea that someone might stand up to him or outsmart him. That's why my diamonds mean so much to him. Not having them will drive him crazy."

"From what you've told me, he's already crazy and he has no respect for life. If Tuazama is as dangerous as you say, there's a good chance he'll kill you."

Charlie broke eye contact with Amanda. His shoulders hunched and he wrung his hands.

"I just can't do it."

"You might have to if it will save your life. Tuazama will be calling me to learn your answer and I don't think he'll wait long."

Charlie stared at the floor.

"There's something else we should discuss," Amanda said when it was clear that she'd make no more headway with this subject tonight. "I was going to talk to you about it tomorrow, but I'm here, so we might as well talk about it now. What do you want to do about Mickey Keys?"

"What do you mean?"

"I had a talk with him in the hallway when he was leaving. He's really upset and he seems desperate. He threatened to go to Burdett if you didn't make things right with him. Is there something he can tell the DA that can hurt you?"

"I don't think so."

"Keys was in the limo with you on the ride to the Westmont. Would he know what happened to the murder weapon between the hotel and the club?"

"I . . . I don't know."

"Is there something you're not telling me about the gun, Charlie?"

"No. I don't know what happened to it after I got out of the car. I just know I didn't have it."

"Can you do anything to placate Keys so he'll talk to Kate?"

"You mean like give him a cut of my earnings? That's what he wants."

"Keys gave me a copy of his contract

with you. Contract law isn't my specialty but we have attorneys in the firm who can look at it to see if it's binding. If you're going to lose in court, we might as well cut a deal with Keys and keep him happy."

"The bastard sold me out to the feds."

"From what I know about Inner Light, the feds would have found out everything he told them anyway."

Charlie rubbed his eyes and sighed. "I'm beat, Amanda. Let me get some sleep. I can't think straight."

"All right, we'll talk in the morning, but you're going to have to decide what I'm going to tell Tuazama. I don't think we can stall him."

36

Kate Ross shut the door to Amanda's office before sitting next to Mickey Keys on one of Amanda's client chairs.

"Thanks for coming to see us," Amanda said.

"No problem. So, is Charlie going to honor his contract?" Keys asked eagerly.

"Mr. Keys, it will be impossible for you to continue as Charlie's agent. You must see that."

"I don't see that at all."

"Agents can help a client because of contacts. You haven't been an agent for a dozen years. How many people do you still know in the publishing industry?"

"With Charlie as a client, making contacts won't be difficult, believe me."

"You're also a potential witness against Charlie. If he's prosecuted for his part in the Inner Light scam, there will be a conflict of interest."

"I don't care about any conflicts of interest. Charlie hung me out to dry when he split. I lost everything. He's loaded and he owes me."

"I've had an attorney in my firm look at your contract and he doesn't think it's enforceable."

"Well, he wouldn't, would he, since he's working for Charlie?"

"Agents have a fiduciary duty to their clients," Amanda said calmly. "When you told the feds that Charlie was involved in tax fraud and revealed your business dealings with him, you breached that duty and lost the right to be his agent."

"I had no choice."

"Of course you did. You could have protected your client by refusing to cooperate."

"Yeah, and gone to jail for ten years."

"In any event, we don't think you can enforce the contract."

"We'll see about that."

"You can hire an attorney and go through lengthy litigation you'll probably lose," Amanda said.

"I'll take my chances."

Keys started to get to his feet.

"Or we can resolve this problem another way," Amanda said.

Keys sat down. "I'm listening."

"Charlie doesn't recognize any legal obligation under the contract but he's not unsympathetic to your situation. He's willing to settle your claim without going to court."

"How much are we talking about?" Keys asked, trying to look nonchalant and failing miserably.

"Charlie is willing to give you a check for fifty thousand dollars if you relinquish all claims under your old contract."

"Fifty! That's nothing. I read *Variety*. I know how much he got from the publisher."

"A good part of his advance will be used to fund his legal defense. And don't forget the IRS. They'll come after Charlie just like they came after you. So he might not end up with anything. Fifty thousand dollars is much more than fifteen percent of zero."

Kate and Amanda sat quietly while Keys weighed his options. His body language broadcast his anguish better than words ever could. When he finally spoke, his shoulders sagged with resignation.

"Make it seventy-five," Keys said.

"Done," Amanda said after hesitating long enough to make Keys think she was struggling with her decision. That morning, Charlie had given her authority to go as high as one hundred thousand dollars to buy off Keys.

"I want a check today."

"That won't be a problem. Are you willing to answer a few questions about Charlie's case after I give it to you?"

"Yeah, ask away," Keys answered. He sounded tired.

"I'll draw up the check while you read this," Amanda said as she handed Keys a document in which he agreed to give up the right to be Charlie's agent.

As soon as he signed, Amanda handed Keys the check. Then it was Kate's turn to take the floor.

"Mr. Keys, how did you and Mr. Marsh meet?"

Keys laughed. "That's a good story. Charlie was a hot property after the prison standoff, but no one could get to him. Technically, he was still a prisoner and the cops had him under wraps in the hospital." Keys flashed a proud grin. "Know what I did?"

"I can't begin to guess," Kate answered.

"I slipped a nurse a few bucks for the number of his room and one of those ID tags you clip on. I switched my photo for the photo of the doc on the tag. Then I dressed up. I had this clipboard and stethoscope and the white coat." He shrugged. "It was easy as pie. The cop on the door took a quick look at the ID tag and I was in. Charlie liked my moxie. I guess he figured if I could con my way past the cops I could con the publishing and movie people. And I already had some good ideas for merchandise."

Keys paused. He looked thoughtful. "Charlie made the right choice. I did great by him. I mean, we made out like bandits." Keys paused again. "I guess I shouldn't use that phrase, huh? What with the IRS and all."

"Whose idea was the Inner Light scam?"

"I thought it up. I had the accounting background."

"Did Mr. Marsh ever protest?" Kate asked.

"You want to know if I had to twist Charlie's arm?"

Kate nodded.

"Don't forget why Charlie was in prison. He's been a con artist his whole life. He'd just never operated on this scale before."

Amanda asked Keys to outline the scheme. When he was finished, Kate asked Keys about the evening of the shooting.

"Who was with you and Charlie at the country club?"

"Let's see, it was me, Charlie, Delmar Epps, and . . . there was someone else."

Keys thought hard for a moment. Then he rolled his eyes. "I forgot Moonbeam."

"Who?" Amanda interjected.

"This groupie." Keys shook his head. "She was an obnoxious little twit who attached herself to Charlie. I have to believe she was the greatest lay in history because I can't think of any other reason Charlie put up with her. Anyway, she was in the car with us."

"What do you remember about the fancy revolver that was used to shoot Congressman Pope?" Kate asked.

"Some broad Charlie banged in Texas gave it to him. Her husband was an oil tycoon who was ancient and he collected guns. Charlie saw it when he was at her house and took a shine to it. She gave it to Charlie when he was leaving. I bawled him out about taking it. He was on parole, for Christ's sake. Possessing a weapon could have sent him back to prison."

"How did the gun get to the Westmont?"

"Delmar Epps brought it. He loved toting that gun around, pretending he was Wyatt Earp. I remember him twirling it on his finger in the car, because the limo hit a bump and he dropped it. I almost had a heart attack. The damn thing was pointing at me when it bounced off the floor. I thought it would go off. I yelled at Delmar to put the damn thing away and I have a clear picture of him putting it on the seat next to him while we were driving."

"Did he have the gun when he left the car?"

Keys's brow furrowed. "Delmar usually

had the gun stuck in the waistband of his pants, but I don't know if he had it on him when he got out of the limo. Some guy Charlie knew opened the door to the limo instead of the chauffeur and Delmar got in his face. I was concentrating on that while I got out of the car. Then I moved back as fast as I could because I didn't want to be in the way if a fight started."

"Do you know where Epps is now?" Kate asked.

"Actually, I do. He's dead, killed in a car accident. They had a story in the newspaper about it because of his involvement with Charlie."

A knock on the door interrupted Kate as she was about to ask her next question.

"I'm sorry to interrupt, Miss Jaffe," the receptionist said, "but there's an FBI agent in the waiting room who'd like to speak to you."

Amanda frowned. She had a few cases going in federal court but she couldn't think of any reason for an agent to be contacting her.

"You two go on," she said before leaving the room.

A stocky, broad-shouldered man with

wavy black hair, whom Amanda didn't recognize, was standing in the reception area. He was wearing a navy blue pinstripe suit, a crisp white shirt, and a tasteful dark blue tie with narrow red and yellow stripes.

"I'm Amanda Jaffe," she said as she offered him her hand.

"Agent Daniel Cordova from the FBI office in Seattle," he said with an easy smile. "I'm pleased to meet you. They say good things about you in the Portland office."

"Uh-oh. That means I'm probably not doing my job very well," Amanda answered with her own smile.

"From what I hear, you do it too well."

"What can I do for you, Agent Cordova?"

"Is there someplace private we can talk?"

Kate was still interviewing Mickey Keys, and the *Pope* file still covered the table in the conference room. Frank was in court, so Amanda led the FBI agent to her father's office.

"You're representing Charles Marsh on a state murder charge," Cordova said when they were seated.

"Yes," Amanda answered cautiously.

"In the course of your representation,

have you come across the name Gary Hass?"

"He was a criminal associate of Werner Rollins, one of the witnesses against Sally Pope, wasn't he?"

"That's right. And Mr. Hass is still a criminal, someone we are very anxious to arrest. A few days ago, a Russian drug dealer named Ivan Mikhailov was tortured to death in Seattle. Mikhailov was trying to take over territory serviced by Julio Dominguez, another dealer with ties to a South American cartel. An informant told us that Hass murdered Mikhailov on orders from Dominguez."

"What does this have to do with Charlie?"

"Hopefully, nothing. But we searched Hass's hotel room. He'd collected several articles about Mr. Marsh and his return to Oregon to stand trial. Do you know if Hass and Mr. Marsh had a falling-out before Marsh fled the country?"

"I can't reveal attorney-client confidences, but why do you want to know?"

"Hass is a peculiar person. He's very smart, very violent, and he's known to harbor grudges for years. It's possible that he's in Oregon seeking to even an old score."

"Have you heard that a sniper tried to kill Charlie after his bail hearing?" Amanda asked.

"That's why I'm here."

"You think Hass was the sniper?"

"We have no evidence to support that but I'd like to talk to your client to see if he knows anything that will help us catch Hass. If Hass is trying to kill your client he'll benefit by cooperating."

"Why don't you wait here and I'll call Charlie."

Amanda closed the door and started down the hall to the conference room when her cell phone rang.

"Have you spoken with your client, Miss Jaffe? " Nathan Tuazama asked. Amanda's pulse began to race. She hated to admit it, but the Batangan frightened her.

"He's thinking about your request."

"I will be calling you this afternoon. If you don't have a positive response for me I will go to plan B."

Tuazama disconnected. Amanda swore

and hurried into the conference room. She dialed Charlie's hotel room from the phone on the credenza. Marsh picked up on the second ring.

"I called you for two reasons, Charlie. Both serious. There's an FBI agent named Cordova in the office. He wants to talk to you about Gary Hass."

Amanda heard an intake of breath on the line. "Charlie?"

"What about Gary?"

"They think he was in Seattle recently. He's a suspect in a murder up there. When they searched his hotel room the FBI found articles about you. Would there be a reason he would try to kill you?"

"The FBI thinks he's the sniper?"

"I don't think they have anything concrete, but Cordova wants to talk to you about Gary to see if there's a reason he might be in Oregon looking for you. What do you want me to tell him?"

"Oh, man. This is all I need, Tuazama and Hass after me."

"That's the other thing I wanted to talk to you about. Nathan Tuazama just called. He wants an answer by this afternoon."

"If I talk to the FBI, will they protect me?"

"I don't know, Charlie. I don't think they can do anything while you're facing a murder charge unless you have some amazing evidence about some huge case the feds need help with. I get the impression Cordova just wants to find out if there's a reason Hass might be in Oregon. Do you want to talk to him? I'll make sure he doesn't ask you anything that will hurt your case. If the FBI arrests Hass, that's one less thing you have to worry about."

"Okay, bring him over. It'll give me something to do."

"I'll be right there. By the way, the problem with Mickey Keys is settled. He signed a waiver to any rights he may have had as your agent."

"How much did it cost me?"

"Seventy-five."

"Damn, I'm bleeding money."

"Think of it as one less problem you have."

"Yeah, right."

"Do you know what you want me to tell Tuazama?"

"No, not yet. I still want to think about what I'm going to do and this stuff about Gary isn't making that any easier."

"MR. MARSH, DO you know why Gary Hass would have newspaper articles about you in his hotel room?" Agent Cordova asked as soon as the introductions were completed.

"Gary and me go way back and he was there when the congressman was killed, so it's natural he'd be interested in reading about me and the case."

"Other than curiosity, why would he be interested in you? Does he have a reason to want to hurt you?"

Charlie thought about that. "He might. The day Pope died, Gary came to one of my book signings and threatened me."

"About what?" Cordova asked.

Charlie suddenly looked uncomfortable.

"Don't answer that if you were talking about something criminal," Amanda cautioned.

"Miss Jaffe and Mr. Marsh, I'm not taking notes on this and I promise you I will not use anything Mr. Marsh tells me to get him in trouble. The Bureau wants Hass badly. This is strictly background."

Charlie looked at Amanda. She nodded.

"Gary said there were incidents in the book from his life and he wanted to get paid."

"What kind of incidents?" Cordova asked.

"There was a chapter about a bank robbery. That's the one I remember."

"What about a bank robbery?"

"I wrote about one where I was robbing a bank and everything got messed up and some people were killed. He said I wasn't there and he wanted to get paid because he said I was taking credit for something he did."

"What did you do when he asked for the money?" Cordova asked.

"I told him that I wasn't going to give him any."

"How did he react to that?"

"Gary was pissed off. He doesn't deal well with rejection. He said he was going to give me time to think and we'd discuss the money later at the country club. He showed up but we never got the chance to talk because of the murder."

"Did you see him after that?"

"No. I was in Africa until a few days ago. I never even thought about Gary."

"Do you think Hass would hold a grudge all these years?" Cordova asked.

"Gary's brain doesn't work like a normal person's brain," Charlie explained to the agent. "He doesn't believe in forgive and forget. So he might."

"Would he be angry enough to try and shoot you?"

"You mean the sniper?" Charlie shook his head. "I can't see him doing that. Gary likes to hear his victims scream. Also, I never heard of him being a great shot. A knife is more his style. Or a handgun. He'd use one of those but he'd be close when he used it."

"WHAT DO YOU really think about the possibility of Hass being the sniper?" Amanda asked when Cordova was gone.

"I meant what I said. I just don't see it. Gary is a psycho. He wants to see suffering up close. A long-range shot doesn't sound right."

"What about Tuazama?"

"Oh, he'd do it all right. He doesn't kill for pleasure. I don't think he knows what pleasure is. He's a technician. If a person needs to be dead, Nathan kills them. It's like fixing a flat tire for him."

"If he's that dangerous, what do I tell him about the diamonds?"

"I can't do it. It would dishonor Bernadette's memory."

"If that's your decision, I think we should use some of the money I have in trust to hire a bodyguard."

"That's not going to help. If Tuazama wants me dead, nothing's going to stop him. That's another reason why I can't give him the diamonds. Once he has them, he won't have any reason to let me live. Those stones are the only thing keeping me alive."

CHAPTER 37

Charlie was going stir crazy but he didn't dare leave his hotel room with Tuazama on the loose. He called room service for dinner, watched an in-room movie, then tried to get to sleep. The moment he closed his eyes, he thought about Tuazama, and his pulse rate accelerated. He finally fell asleep from exhaustion at 1:30, after downing several small bottles of booze he found in the minibar. At 2:17, the jarring ring of the bedside phone cut into Charlie's brain like a razor.

"Who the fuck is this?" he asked after fumbling in the dark for the receiver.

"Charlie?" a woman asked. It was a voice he would never forget. Charlie sat up and turned on the lamp on his end table.

"Sally? What's going on? It's two in the morning."

"I have to see you."

"When?" Charlie asked, still groggy from the shock of being jarred out of a deep sleep.

"Now, tonight."

Charlie thought Sally sounded desperate but he had no intention of leaving the safety of his hotel room in the dead of night.

"Didn't you hear me? It's two in the morning. I was sound asleep."

"It has to be now."

Sally's voice trembled and that made Charlie pause. The Sally he knew was never out of control.

"What's so important that it can't wait a few hours?"

"It's about your case. There's something I have to show you. It can't wait until morning."

"I don't even know where you live. I don't have a car."

"Get a taxi. I'll drive you back."

Sally gave him directions to her house.

"That's in the middle of nowhere," Charlie said. "I'm not going to hell and gone tonight. Besides, if this is about my case, I want my lawyer along."

"No! This can't wait until morning. It has to be now," she repeated. "And you have to come alone. I know something that will help you get your case dismissed."

"What do you know?"

"I can't tell you over the phone. I have to show you. Please."

Charlie was wide awake and wise enough to know that there was no way he would be able to get back to sleep. If he didn't go, he'd be up all night imagining what Sally wanted to show him.

"All right, I'm coming, but this better be good."

"Thank you, Charlie. Thank you."

Sally hung up and Charlie sat on the edge of the bed reviewing what had just happened. She'd said she could show him something that would get his case dismissed. It sounded too good to be true. What could she possibly know now that she didn't know twelve years ago?

Sally hadn't sounded happy or confident.

She'd sounded desperate and panicky, emotions he would never have associated with her. What was she afraid of and why couldn't she wait until morning to show her evidence to him? It was very confusing, but he was too tired to work out the problem and too revved up to fall asleep. He called the front desk, asked them to get a taxi for him, and got dressed.

THE CABBIE WAS a grizzled, talkative Ukrainian who spent the early part of the ride giving Charlie his unsolicited opinion of the current state of soccer in the United States. Much to Charlie's relief, he shut up after they left the highway and the signs of civilization faded away. It was spooky driving through the sparsely populated farm country in the dark.

Even with Sally's directions the driver almost missed the narrow entrance to her estate. The woods closed around them as soon as they passed through the break in the stonework, giving Charlie the unsettling, claustrophobic feeling that he was inside a coffin of leaves. His anxiety didn't ease when they drove out of the forest. In daylight, the colorful flower beds and bright green lawn made Sally's antebellum mansion look cheerful. At night, with only the pale rays of a half moon to illuminate it, the house resembled a skull.

When they drove up to the front of the house, Charlie looked for some sign of life and finally spotted dim yellow light seeping through the curtains in a downstairs room.

"Stop here," Charlie said when the cab reached the front door.

"You want me to wait?" the driver asked.

Charlie thought about that. Sally had said she would drive him back to town, and he had a cell phone.

"No, you can go."

Charlie got out and the cab drove off. There was a soft breeze, a faint smell of freshly mown grass, night sounds, and nothing else. He was spooked, so he turned in a slow circle to make sure no one was behind him. He had almost completed his turn when he thought he saw movement where the woods ended and the lawn began. He peered into the darkness. The space between the low branches of a tree seemed to disappear and reappear. He strained to find the cause but heard and saw nothing. He blamed the phantom on his imagination and climbed the porch steps.

No one had left a light on, so it took Charlie a moment to find the doorbell. The chimes echoed hollowly in the downstairs hall. As Charlie waited for Sally, there was a faint sound behind him. He turned toward the yard but still saw nothing. When he turned back, his eyes had grown accustomed to the dark and he noticed that the front door was not flush with the frame. He pushed and it opened. Charlie hesitated before stepping inside. There was a glow at the end of a long hall. Charlie inched toward the light and called Sally's name. He was waiting for an answer when he saw the dog. It lay on its side partially hidden by a low cedar chest that stood against the staircase to the second floor. Charlie assumed the collie was sleeping. Then it dawned on him that, sleeping or not, the dog would have come awake when he called to Sally.

Charlie walked to the chest and peered over it. The collie's head was in a shadow and it took him a moment to see that it was resting in a puddle of blood. He jumped back, almost tripping over his own feet. If Charlie's DNA contained a gene for common sense, he would have fled. Instead, he picked up a brass candlestick from the top of the chest and started down the hall toward the light. His feet made no sound on the carpet and he could hear his heart beating rapidly. Charlie's heightened senses focused on the open doorway at the end of the hall. As he inched closer, he could see a rug, the end of a couch, and part of a table.

Charlie pressed his back to the wall and slid sideways toward the room, brandishing the candlestick like a club. When he reached the doorway, Charlie paused and took a deep breath. Then he spun through the door, his arm raised above his head.

He was in a large living room and the light he'd seen from the end of the hall came from a table lamp that stood next to a phone. Next to the end table was a straight-backed, wooden chair. Sally Pope was secured to it by duct tape. Her head had fallen forward. She was wearing a white nightgown that showed the blood that drenched the front of it to maximum effect.

Charlie also took in the body of a dark-haired woman sprawled on the floor in front of a long couch. He couldn't tell if she was dead or unconscious. He was about to go to her when a muffled sound brought him around. A wild-eyed teenage boy was lying on the floor near the fireplace, tied tight by the same gray duct tape that bound Sally to her chair. He was trying to tell Charlie something but his words were muffled by the tape that sealed his mouth.

Charlie started toward the boy, who jerked his head violently toward the drapes hanging on either side of French doors that opened onto the patio. The drapes moved and a man appeared. He was dressed in black and his face was hidden behind a ski mask.

"Who . . . ?" was all Charlie got out before the man raised the gun he was holding. Charlie heard someone moving behind him just before he was shot. As he fell, he heard more shots and the sound of shattering glass. Then he passed out.

CHAPTER 38

Dad," Amanda said as soon as Frank Jaffe answered the phone, "Sally Pope is dead. She's been murdered."

Amanda waited for a response. "Dad?" she repeated when she got none.

"I . . . I'm just . . . What happened?"

It was 6:38 in the morning. Frank was getting ready for work and had just finished in the bathroom. The unexpected ring of the phone had startled him. Now his daughter's words stunned him and he slumped on the edge of the bed.

"I don't know all of the details, but Charlie Marsh was shot. That's how I found out. He had someone call me from the hospital. Sally was murdered in her house. He was there."

"What was Marsh doing at Sally's house?"

"I don't know. I'm going to the hospital. I'll let you know what I find out."

Amanda hung up. Frank held the receiver for a moment. It took an effort to return it to its cradle. Suddenly Frank felt very old. His shoulders sagged. A sob escaped his lips and he was consumed by grief.

THE POLICEMAN WHO was guarding Charlie's hospital room checked Amanda's ID before letting her in. Charlie was propped up in bed connected to monitors and IV bags by an array of wires and plastic tubing. His tan was a few shades paler and his left arm was in a sling.

"How are you feeling?" Amanda asked as she dragged a chair to the side of the bed.

"If I'd known how good morphine felt I would have gotten shot a long time ago," Charlie answered with a sloppy grin. Then he sobered. "They wouldn't tell me anything. Is Sally dead?"

Amanda nodded. "And Gina, her personal assistant. Sally's son wasn't harmed physically but he's so traumatized that the doctors won't let the police interview him. You're the only other survivor. The detective in charge of the investigation is in the waiting room. He wants to interview you. I told him I'd ask you what you want to do."

"This is so terrible. I liked Sally."

"Will you talk to the detective? I'll be with you to protect you if he gets too far afield."

"Yeah, I'll do it."

"One thing they'll want to know is why you're not dead."

"That's easy. Someone saved me."

"Who?"

"I don't know. I never saw him."

"What were you doing at Sally Pope's house in the middle of the night?"

"She called me. She wanted me to come alone, right away. She claimed to know something that would get my case dismissed."

"What was it?"

"She wouldn't tell me. She said she had to show it to me."

"How did she sound during the call?"

"Shaky, panicky."

"Do you think she was being forced to say what she did to lure you to her house?"

"I'm sure of it. The killer probably threatened her kid to force her to call me."

Amanda nodded agreement. "Go on."

"I took a cab. When I got there, the house was dark. I went in, saw that someone had killed the dog, and noticed light coming from the living room. When I walked into the room Sally was taped to a chair. Her head was down, so I couldn't be sure she was dead, but there was blood all over her nightgown. There was another woman sprawled on the floor."

"That was Gina."

"Sally's kid tried to warn me, but the killer had taped his mouth shut so I didn't know what he was saying. Then this guy came out from behind the curtains and shot me."

"You're certain it was a man?"

"Pretty certain. He was wearing a ski mask and gloves, but he had a man's physique."

"Okay, what happened next?"

"Just before I was shot I heard someone behind me, but I was shot before I could turn. There were more shots behind and in front of me and glass breaking. I'm guessing that was the French windows. Then I woke up here."

"So there were two shooters," Amanda mused. "That might explain the 911 call."

"What 911 call?"

"It's why you didn't bleed to death. Someone made an anonymous call to 911. Otherwise you wouldn't have been found in time to save you. When the medics arrived you were almost dead from blood loss. I'm guessing that the person who saved you also made the call."

The door opened and the police guard stepped in. He didn't look happy.

"There's a man out here who insists he's part of the defense team. He wants to talk to Mr. Marsh."

"Tell this cop I work with you and I'm entitled to see our client," Dennis Levy yelled angrily from the corridor.

"Excuse me," Amanda said to Charlie. She stepped outside and grabbed Levy by the elbow.

"Come with me," she said as she led Dennis down the hall until they were far enough from the officer so he couldn't hear them.

"You are not a member of the defense team," Amanda said. "You are a reporter and you have no legal right to talk to Charlie."

"Now wait a minute. This story is huge," Levy said as he bounced in place with excitement.

"Aren't you the least bit concerned that Charlie was shot?"

"Hey, I'm sorry he was hurt. Really, I am. But you have no idea how big this story is. I mean, *no idea!*"

"I know how big you think it is because you've told me several times. What you haven't shown me is any compassion toward any of the people involved. Has it gotten through to you that several people were murdered last night? They're dead, Dennis."

"Hey, reporters deal with death all the time. If I got emotionally involved I couldn't do my job."

"Your lack of emotional involvement is pretty obvious, but I can't shut off my emotions. I do care about Sally Pope and Gina and Charlie, who are all human beings. Charlie could have died. I bet that would really have messed up your plans. Now go to the waiting room and don't bother the police officer anymore. I'll tell you what I can when I come out."

Amanda waited until Dennis turned the corner, before approaching the guard.

"I apologize for Mr. Levy. He gets over-zealous at times."

The officer nodded but he still looked angry. When Amanda reentered Charlie's room he was staring at his blanket, deep in thought.

"There's something I want to tell you," Charlie said.

"Go ahead."

"I was lying here thinking about how I almost died and what I've done with my life. Before Freddy went nuts and kidnapped those hostages I was nobody, a petty crook. Then I got to be somebody but it was because I lied."

"It was because you saved the hostages."

"You know why I threw myself over that guard? I didn't give a shit about him. I did it for me. I knew I'd be in jail for life if Freddy killed him. That's the only reason I did it, to save my skin, not his.

"And that inner light bullshit. That's all it

was, bullshit. I didn't see any lights when I got shot just now and I didn't see any when I was stabbed. Mickey Keys thought up that gimmick because it would get me on TV. And he was right. Everyone ate it up, but it never happened. Neither did half the stuff I wrote in my book. Or at least it didn't happen to me. Freddy committed most of those crimes and was in the fights. I'm a coward. I've never gotten into a fight I could run from and I never used a gun or . . . Well, you get the picture. So, I've been thinking. I should set the record straight in my new book. I should tell the truth. If I do, what do you think Dennis will say?"

"I don't know and, frankly, I don't care. In the end, you have to do what you think is right, no matter what Levy thinks. Right now, however, you should talk to the police so they can catch the person who killed Sally and tried to kill you."

Amanda left and Charlie thought about what he'd just said. He could tell the truth about some of the things that he'd lied about, but he wouldn't tell the whole truth about what had happened at the Westmont Country Club the night Arnold Pope Jr. died, unless he had no choice.

CHAPTER 39

The day after Sally Pope's murder, the PI in Denver called Kate to tell her he'd located Werner Rollins. Until a month ago, Rollins had been serving time in the Colorado State Penitentiary for armed robbery, but he was currently on parole. Kate talked to Henrietta Swift, Rollins's parole officer, who called back an hour later to tell Kate that Rollins had agreed to meet her.

During the two-and-a-half-hour flight from Portland to Denver, Dennis Levy didn't hit on Kate once or brag about how great he was, and he never mentioned how famous he was going to be. He seemed preoccupied as he worked on his laptop or stared out the window. Kate wondered why the reporter was so quiet, but she didn't want to press her luck by asking.

The meeting with Rollins was at a sports bar near Coors Field. They had a late flight back to Portland, so Kate rented a car at the airport and drove into Denver. It was a spectacular summer day and it took a moment for Kate's eyes to adjust from the bright midday sunlight to the dim light in the bar, but it didn't take long to pick out Rollins in the crowd of lunchtime patrons. He was the only man sitting alone at a table in a wheelchair.

Rollins's parole officer had briefed Kate about the high-speed chase that had led to a prison term for armed robbery and cost Rollins his legs, but she hadn't prepared Kate for the real toll the accident had taken on the gangster. The Werner Rollins of Kate's imagination was a meaner version of Conan the Barbarian. There was nothing menacing about the man in the stained Denver Broncos T-shirt who was working on his second pitcher of beer. Despair had beaten the life out of Rollins and hard living had changed the sharp planes of his steroid-enhanced physique into flab.

"Mr. Rollins?" Kate asked as they drew close to his table.

Rollins looked away from the ball game airing on one of the large-screen TVs that were scattered around the bar.

"This is Dennis Levy and I'm Kate Ross, an investigator working for Charlie Marsh. Thank you for taking the time to meet with us."

"Yeah, well, my social secretary was able to find time for you on my busy schedule, and Henrietta said you'd spring for my beer. It was a no-brainer."

Kate smiled. "May we?" she asked, indicating one of the chairs at the table.

"Be my guest."

"Dennis is a reporter. He's covering Charlie's trial for *World News*. Do you have a problem with him sitting in on our conversation?"

Rollins shrugged. Kate had the impression that he didn't care much about anything anymore.

"So how's old Charlie doing?" Rollins asked.

"He's had a rough time. I don't know how closely you've been following his case, but there have been two attempts to kill him. He was shot during the second attempt and he's in the hospital."

"That's tough," Rollins said without much conviction.

"I understand that you were Charlie's friend," Kate said.

"You got that wrong. We were never buddy-buddy. I tolerated him because of Freddy."

"Freddy Clayton?"

Rollins nodded. "They were like Batman and Robin. Freddy took the little punk everywhere. If I didn't know Freddy real good I woulda thought they were faggots." Rollins tossed a quick glance at Dennis, smirked, and added, "No offense."

Levy reddened but didn't respond.

"But you knew Charlie pretty well?" Kate said.

"Yeah. It's like that nursery rhyme, anywhere that Freddy went Charlie was sure to go."

"Is that why you were at the Westmont Country Club on the evening Congressman

Pope was killed? Were you and Gary Hass reconnecting with an old acquaintance?"

Rollins laughed then took a drink from his mug. Kate waited while he used his forearm to wipe the foam from his mouth.

"That thing with Charlie was Gary's deal. He wanted to shake him down, see if he could scare him into parting with some cash. When Freddy was alive no one would touch Charlie, but Charlie was a rabbit and Gary figured he'd be an easy mark with no one to protect him."

"You testified for the prosecution at Sally Pope's trial."

"I had to, didn't I? Burdett was threatening me with hard time for fucking up that security guard. With my record, I couldn't afford to go down again. Charlie was out of the country, so what I said couldn't hurt him, and I didn't owe the broad anything." Rollins shrugged. "It was her or me and I chose me."

"Mr. Rollins, the state will want you to testify again, and this time what you say could send Charlie to death row. So, let me ask you, if you testify at Charlie's trial, what will you say?"

Rollins eyed Kate warily. "If I said something I didn't say the first time I'd be looking at a perjury charge, so I guess I'll have to say that I saw Charlie shoot Pope."

"The statute of limitations has run out, Mr. Rollins. You can consult a lawyer on that if you don't believe me, but I checked. No one can prosecute you if you lied under oath at Sally Pope's trial."

Rollins thought about that. "I might say something different," he told Kate.

"Like what?"

Levy leaned forward, his eyes riveted on Rollins.

"That depends," Rollins said. "As you may have noticed, I ain't doing very well. In fact, I've got no fucking legs, which makes it hard to get a job."

Rollins paused and the blatant bribe attempt hung in the air between the convict and the investigator like a Goodyear blimp hovering over a football stadium. Kate smiled and turned her head toward Levy.

"This is off the record, Dennis," she said.

When Dennis didn't object, Kate turned back toward Rollins. She had no illusions about the type of man with whom she was dealing. Rollins was a career criminal and a sociopath. Appealing to his better nature was hopeless, because men like Rollins didn't have better natures. But they were human and they didn't have to be evil twenty-four hours a day. Kate looked Rollins in the eye and held his gaze long enough for him to figure out she was not someone who scared easily.

"I don't know what your experience has been with other attorneys," Kate said in an even, nonjudgmental tone, "but my firm doesn't pay witnesses for their testimony. We want the truth. If it's what you testified to at Sally Pope's trial we'll have to deal with that. You, on the other hand, will have to live with Charlie's death sentence if you help convict him and you're lying.

"I don't know if that would be easy for you to do, because I know very little about you, but I do know that you've suffered and, if you're a normal human being, I can only hope that you would want to keep someone you know from suffering if you could help them without hurting yourself."

"I'm not a charity, lady."

Kate laughed. "I've read your rap sheet and a few police reports of your exploits, Mr. Rollins, so I know that's for sure."

Rollins hesitated for a moment. Then he smiled. "Yeah, I guess no one would ever confuse me with the Red Cross."

"They did make for interesting reading," Kate told him with a conspiratorial grin.

Rollins stopped smiling and his eyes lost focus. "I was something before this," he said, pointing toward the place where his legs had been.

"Amen to that. And you'll be something again when Charlie's case goes to trial. Everyone will be listening to you because you will be a key witness in the case. My question is whether you'll be the star witness for the state?"

Rollins took a thoughtful sip of beer, then stared at the table top. When he looked up his expression was serious.

"The DA ain't going to like what I'm going to say. He's gonna be pissed. But I owe him one because he forced me to lie about Charlie. The truth is I don't know who shot the congressman. I saw him shot but I was looking at him and not at Charlie, the broad, Gary, or the nigger."

"What about the gun? Did you see who had the gun?"

Rollins shook his head. "I heard it but I

didn't see it. The shot came from my right so that's where I looked, but before I looked I heard the gun bounce off the ground and I never saw who tossed it."

"So you have no idea who fired the shot? No one acted like they had?"

Rollins laughed. "You think I was playing Sherlock Holmes, looking at everyone with a magnifying glass and working out the clues? I know how cops think. They'd have taken one look at me and thrown away the key. Pope's body hit the ground and Gary and I took off. So did everybody else."

"Thank you for your honesty, Mr. Rollins," Kate said.

"So, what happens next?" Rollins asked.

"Nothing from our end. You haven't said anything that helps or hurts Charlie. Karl Burdett will probably be in touch soon because he'll think you're going to make his case. Tell him what you told me and he may threaten you but I don't think he can do anything to you if you stick to your guns. Don't take my word for that, though. I'm not a lawyer. I'd advise you to check with one before you talk to Burdett."

Rollins nodded. "You paying for my beer or would that be some kind of bribe?"

Kate slapped fifty dollars on the table. "It's been a pleasure, Mr. Rollins. Have some nachos on me."

Kate blinked when she stepped into the sunshine. Dennis was right behind her. She was surprised that he had not tried to question Rollins for his magazine article. A key witness retracting his story was big news.

"How do you think that went?" Levy asked as they walked to the car.

"It couldn't have gone better."

Levy grinned. "My feeling exactly."

Kate studied Levy closely. Something Rollins had said had gotten Levy excited but she had no idea what it was.

IT TOOK ALL of Dennis's self-control to keep from bouncing in his seat from excitement during the ride to the airport, but he couldn't keep his foot from tapping. Kate returned the rental car and they rode the shuttle to the terminal. Then they had to check in and go through security. By the time they got to their gate, Dennis was ready to explode.

"I'm going to hit the john," he told Kate, forcing himself to sound calm. As he walked down the concourse toward the restrooms, he thought about what he was planning to do and he began to feel light-headed. As soon as he was certain Kate couldn't see him, Dennis took a few deep breaths. Then he started to punch in Martha Brice's number on his cell phone. Halfway through, he stopped. If he made the call, there was no turning back. Did he really want to do this? Sure he wanted to be rich and successful, but was this the way to get there?

Dennis's courage failed him. He cut the connection. His heart was pounding in his chest. Thanks to Werner Rollins, he was certain he knew who had killed Congressman Pope, but how was he going to use that knowledge?

Amanda had a tough time reconciling the colorful flower beds and emerald green lawns that encircled Sally Pope's mansion and the clear blue sky above it with the bloodshed that had taken place inside. It seemed impossible that life could go on as if nothing had happened, when a tragedy of this proportion occurred, but violent death had been a large part of Amanda's life long enough for her to know that it did. Even so, she was a little disoriented when her father parked in front of Sally's home.

Moments after Frank rang the bell, the door was opened by a thick-chested man with unkempt red hair, who looked more like a lumberjack than a writer of literary fiction. He also looked exhausted and terribly sad.

"Thank you for coming," Liam O'Connell said. "I would have gone to your office but I don't want to leave Kevin alone. He's very fragile and I need to be close by."

"Don't think about it," Frank said. "It was no trouble for us to drive out."

"Let's talk in the den. I can't go in there," O'Connell said, nodding in the direction of the living room.

Amanda couldn't help casting a quick glance toward the place where Sally Pope had died and she had sat sipping a cold drink and enjoying Sally's company so recently.

"Do you know about Sally's will?" the Irishman asked when they were seated in the den.

"No," Frank answered.

"Jimmy Pavel drew it up. He told me that Kevin inherits everything but Sally named me his guardian."

"That makes sense," Frank said. "I visited her while you were in Berkeley. She told me Kevin is very fond of you."

"It's mutual. He's a great kid."

"On the phone you said you had a problem you wanted to discuss that involved the will," Frank prodded.

"One of Arnold Pope's lawyers called me. Pope wants custody of Kevin."

"What exactly did the lawyer say?"

"There were condolences. Then there was some patter about how difficult it would be to raise a teenage boy by myself, given that I travel so much for my books and my teaching. All very sympathetic but I could see where he was going, so I told him it would be no trouble and I thanked him for his kind thoughts."

"I'm guessing that the conversation didn't end there," Frank said.

"Oh, no. It went on some with a heavy emphasis on Mr. Pope's concern for me and his grandson and the financial benefits that would accrue to me if I let Mr. Pope raise Kevin."

"I bet the amount the lawyer mentioned was substantial," Frank said.

O'Connell nodded. "And it grew as we discussed the matter."

"What happened when you turned down the offer?"

"Ah, that's when the threats commenced, all very subtle but unmistakable."

"What type of threats?"

"A custody battle that would certainly be hard on the poor lad and which I, not being blood kin or even married to Sally, could not possibly win."

"How did you respond?"

"I told the lawyer that Mr. Pope would be responsible for any psychological harm Kevin endured if he brought the suit and that his attempts to intimidate me or make me feel guilty had failed completely. Then I hung up.

"Fortunately, Sally foresaw the possibility of Pope trying something like this. There's a provision in the will that specifies that under no circumstances may Arnold Pope Sr. be allowed to have any contact with Kevin. The will permits Kevin's guardian to use estate funds to protect Kevin in case of a lawsuit, which brings me to my reason for asking you here. Sally had great faith in your legal abilities. She told me how you saved her when she was accused of murdering her husband and she told me how you stymied Mr. Pope's first attempt to get custody of Kevin. I want you to stop him again."

"It would be my pleasure, Liam. I can't think of anything more harmful to Kevin than living with Arnold Pope Sr. I'll do everything in my power to prevent it."

O'Connell flashed a smile of relief and the tension that had bunched his shoulders dissipated. "Thank you, Frank. I knew you wouldn't let Kevin down."

"Or Sally. I know how much she detested Senior."

Frank opened his attaché case and took out a legal pad. "If we're going to prevail, we'll have to convince the court that there's no reason to overrule Sally's wishes. Senior is going to go after you unmercifully, so you'll have to tell me how he might attack your character and how we can defend it."

"Mr. O'Connell," Amanda interjected. "I came here with my father because I'm representing Charlie Marsh. What happened here may impact his case. I'd like your permission to talk to Kevin while you two are conferring."

The Irishman hesitated.

"I know how badly he's been affected. But Charlie Marsh is facing the death penalty and Kevin might know something that can help him. I promise I won't push Kevin. I'll back off as soon as I see the first sign of a problem. But I'd really appreciate the chance to try to find out if he knows anything that will help clear Charlie's name."

O'Connell sighed. "Kevin spoke with the police yesterday. He seemed able to handle it. Go ahead, but please be gentle. This has been awful for him."

KEVIN WAS LYING on a chaise longue at the side of the pool, dressed in a swim team T-shirt and khaki Bermuda shorts. He had a paperback science fiction novel with him but it was lying facedown across his thigh and he was staring across the water and into space.

Amanda took off her flats and walked barefoot onto the pool deck. The sun was behind her shoulder. Kevin squinted at her then shaded his eyes. Amanda sat next to him on the edge of another lounger.

"Hi, I'm Amanda Jaffe. I was out here

about a week ago but we didn't get a chance to meet."

Kevin watched her but he didn't say anything.

Amanda pointed at the T-shirt. "What's your stroke?"

"The fly," he answered without enthusiasm.

"Are you varsity?"

Kevin nodded.

"You on a club too or do you just swim for the high school?"

"I work out with Tualatin Hills," he said, this answer no more animated than his others.

"I swam for them and Wilson High. My best distance was the two-hundred free."

Kevin looked Amanda in the eye. "Who are you?"

Amanda smiled. "Tired of my small talk?"

Kevin didn't answer.

"I'm a lawyer. I'm representing Charlie Marsh. Do you know who he is?"

"He was charged with killing my father but he ran away."

"That's right. Charlie is the man who

came to your house the evening your mother was murdered. You tried to warn him."

Kevin looked away at the mention of his mother's murder.

"He's very grateful, Kevin. A lot of people would have been too scared to try to warn Charlie but you risked your life to do it. That's the important thing."

"He still got shot."

"Sometimes events are out of our control and the best we can do is try."

Kevin looked away and sobbed. "It's not fair. She was so good."

Amanda wanted to say something to comfort Kevin but she knew Sally's death was too recent for anything she said to help. After a while, the tears stopped. Kevin lay quietly with his eyes shut and his chest heaving.

"Can you tell me what happened in your house?" Amanda said when Kevin's breathing eased.

"I don't want to talk about it."

"I know you don't, but someone has made two attempts to kill Charlie. The police are certain he'll try again. The person who murdered your mother is the man who is after Charlie. You may know something that will help the police catch him."

"I told them everything I know."

"Can you tell me?"

Kevin closed his eyes. Then he took a deep breath. "He came into my room. It was dark and he had a mask on, so I can't tell you what he looked like."

"That's okay."

"He put tape over my mouth. That's what woke me. I tried to yell, to warn Mom, but I couldn't."

"No one could have."

"I tried but my mouth was taped and he . . . he had a gun. He said he'd kill Mom if I tried to warn her. I . . . I believed him, but he killed her anyway."

Kevin sobbed again and Amanda waited.

"What did this man sound like? Was there anything distinctive about his voice?"

"He whispered when he talked to me. He was trying to disguise his voice."

"Okay. What happened next?"

"He tied me up and left me. I tried to get out of the tape but I couldn't. When he came back he told me that he wouldn't harm me if I did what he said. Then he brought me down to the living room. Mom was tied to a chair. Gina was . . . she was on the floor."

Kevin licked his lips and looked off across the pool.

"What happened then?"

"He made Mom call Mr. Marsh. He said he'd shoot me if she didn't. He told her what to say and she called him. Then we waited. We heard the front door open. That's when . . . when he . . ."

"You don't have to say it. I know what happened."

Kevin nodded. He started to cry again.

"Kevin, what did you see when Mr. Marsh came into the living room?"

"I tried to tell him there was a man behind the drapes. I was trying to warn him when the man stepped out and shot Mr. Marsh. Then there was a shot from the front of the living room and the French windows shattered and everyone was shooting."

"Did you see who saved Mr. Marsh?"

"When the shooting started I threw myself down on the floor. I was facing toward the French windows. I never looked at the door but I saw a reflection in the glass. It was wavy and there wasn't much light but I think I saw a black man."

"How sure are you that he was black?" Amanda asked as she tried to picture Nathan Tuazama as Charlie's guardian angel.

"I'm pretty sure," Kevin said hesitantly.

"What happened to the man who killed your mother?"

"He ran away. He got out through the windows."

"Do you know if he was wounded?"

"No. My face was pressed to the floor. I only saw his sneakers when he ran out."

Amanda could see that Kevin was exhausted and she decided he'd had enough.

"Thank you for talking to me," she said.

"Did it help?"

"Yes. You've cleared up a few things for me."

But the truth was that Kevin's story had only muddied the waters. It made sense for Tuazama to keep Charlie alive so he could get the diamonds. But how had he known Charlie would go to Sally's house in the middle of the night? She guessed it was possible that Tuazama had Charlie's hotel staked out but it didn't really make sense that he would be watching the hotel at two in the morning. Tuazama had to sleep.

And why didn't the killer murder Kevin? Maybe the killer had planned on murdering Kevin and the person who saved Charlie had forced him to run before he could finish off the last witness to his crime. That made sense, but Amanda could think of another explanation for Kevin's survival that was equally viable.

Amanda went to see Kate as soon as she returned to the law office.

"How did it go in Denver?" she asked.

"Excellent. Rollins admitted lying at Sally Pope's trial. He claims Burdett pressured him to say he saw Charlie shoot Pope by threatening to go after him for assaulting the security guard. He told me he never saw who fired the shot. There's a report on your desk."

"That's fantastic news. Rollins's testimony was the only solid evidence against Charlie. Now that he's retracted it, Burdett may have to drop the charges."

Suddenly Amanda smiled wickedly.

"Did you have any trouble with the boy wonder?" she asked.

"Not a bit. He didn't come on to me once during the trip and he didn't tell me how fantastic he is or brag about how rich and famous he's going to be. Actually, he kept pretty much to himself."

"Don't look a gift horse in the mouth," Amanda said.

"Yeah, you're right. So what have you been doing while I've been winning your case for you?" Kate asked. Amanda sobered instantly.

"I was at Sally Pope's house with Dad. Senior is going to sue for custody of Kevin. Liam O'Connell wants Dad to represent him."

"Did you get a chance to talk to Kevin about what happened when Charlie was shot?"

"Yeah. The poor kid is a mess. He was so upset I cut our talk short."

"Could he identify anyone?"

"Kevin can say that a man killed his mother, but it was dark and the murderer wore a mask. There was one interesting thing that came out of the interview. Kevin thinks that the person who saved Charlie was black."

Kate frowned. "There aren't any African-Americans involved in this case, are there?"

Amanda decided to keep Charlie's confidences about Nathan Tuazama to herself.

"No African-Americans I'm aware of," she answered honestly.

Amanda stood up. "I've got to work on my other cases or I'm going to get disbarred."

"See you later," Kate said.

Amanda started to turn when Kate remembered something she'd meant to ask her friend.

"Say, did you do something with the photograph of Charlie and his entourage at that Dunthorpe estate seminar?" Kate said.

"What photograph?"

"Someone took a picture of Charlie and his people at the seminar in Dunthorpe; the one where he met Sally Pope."

"I don't remember seeing it when I went through the file but Burdett will have the original. We can get a copy if you need it."

"No, it's not important. I just can't find it and it's bugging me."

"Sorry."

"I probably put it in a file with a lot of other stuff and just missed it."

"I'm sure it will turn up. See you later."

CHARLIE'S CASE HAD come at Amanda so fast that it had dominated her practice. Unfortunately, her other cases had not disappeared and some of them required immediate attention. Amanda worked on a motion for a schoolteacher accused of possessing cocaine until hunger pangs drove her to a nearby Chinese restaurant for takeout. While she shoveled General Tso's chicken into her mouth in a distinctly unladylike manner, Amanda read through the discovery in a securities fraud case she was handling for a stockbroker who had initially appeared to be honest and forthright but was now looking decidedly shady.

Amanda finished the discovery just as the last rays of sunlight faded behind the West Hills. She was deciding whether to call it a night or tackle another file when her cell phone rang.

"Is this Amanda Jaffe?" a man asked, slurring his words enough so Amanda had a hard time understanding him.

"Who is this?"

"It's Karl, Karl Burdett. Thank God I caught you. I know it's late, but we have to talk."

Amanda frowned. The DA sounded frightened and she was certain he'd been drinking.

"Is something wrong?"

"I need legal advice. I'm in over my head. I didn't see it until Cordova called me tonight."

"The FBI agent?"

"You've got to help me."

"Can you tell me what this is about?"

"Not over the phone. Meet me in the parking lot of the Tillamook Tavern."

"Why there?"

"That's where I am now. I'm afraid to go home. I'll be in my car in the last row in the back. It's dark. No one will see us."

"I don't think I can be your lawyer, Karl. We're adversaries in Charlie's case."

"This concerns Charlie. That's why I called you. Please, you have to help me."

"Okay, Karl. Calm down. I'll be there in twenty minutes."

"Thank you. Hurry."

As SHE DROVE to the tavern, Amanda tried to figure out why Karl Burdett would ask her for legal advice. After her father, she was the least likely person Burdett would consult if he had legal problems. Before she'd left her office, it had occurred to her that someone might be using Burdett to lure her into a trap similar to the one that had snared Charlie, so she'd slipped a handgun into her pocket. Amanda had been attacked a few times while working a case and she wasn't going to this meeting unarmed.

The Tillamook Tavern was a squat, one-story workingman's bar situated on a side street near an industrial park. On the same street were a rundown twenty-four-hour market with bars on its windows, which sold beer, cigarettes, and junk food, and a vacant, rubble-filled lot. Streetlights cast a pale yellow glow over one side of the bar but the only other light came from the neon sign with the tavern's name and smaller neon signs in the narrow front windows, advertising brands of beer. There were two pickup trucks and a weather-beaten Chevy scattered around the tavern lot. Karl's car was alone on the edge of a sea of asphalt in the last slot in the last row. When Amanda was a few rows from the DA's car, she made out Burdett's silhouette staring through the windshield into the darkness. Amanda parked a car length away. The DA did not look at her. She got out of her car and closed her hand around the grip of her gun. As she drew closer to Burdett's car, Amanda noticed that the driver's-side window was down.

"Karl?"

Burdett didn't react. Amanda's gut tightened. Something was wrong. She said the DA's name again. Then she saw why Burdett hadn't answered. He was staring straight ahead, slack-jawed, and there was a blood-rimmed bullet hole in his temple.

MIKE GREENE'S BLUE eyes were usually clear but were presently bloodshot, because he'd been awakened from a deep sleep. He parked on the street in front of the Tillamook Tavern, then walked around back, where he talked to the first officer on the scene and the forensic experts who were processing it. When he'd seen enough, he went inside the tavern and found Amanda in a booth in the rear of the bar. Sitting across from her was Billie Brewster, a slim black woman with close-cropped hair, dressed in jeans, a black Tupac Shakur memorial T-shirt, and Mercury running shoes. Billie, one of the top homicide detectives in the Portland Police Bureau, had been the investigating officer in several of Amanda's cases and they had become good friends.

"This is a pretty extreme way of getting a date, Jaffe," Mike said as he pulled a chair up to the booth and straddled it.

"Hey, bozo, your woman's shook up," Brewster said, "so can the gallows humor."

"How are you doing?" Mike asked, suddenly serious.

"I'm okay. It's not like I haven't seen a dead man before. It was just a shock finding him." Amanda shook her head. "I never liked Karl. He could be a pompous ass. But I'd never wish anything like this on him. If only I'd gotten here sooner, I might have scared off the person who shot him."

"Or gotten yourself killed," Brewster said.

"How did you happen to be the one who found him?" Mike asked, and Amanda told him about the phone call.

"And you have no idea what he wanted to tell you?" Greene asked when she was through.

"Only that it had something to do with Charlie Marsh."

Amanda paused. "There is something." She hesitated.

"Yes," Mike prodded.

"Burdett has been acting . . ." She paused again. "I guess 'weird' is a good way to describe his behavior."

"Weird?" Mike repeated.

Amanda told Mike and Billie about the bail hearing.

"I was really surprised when he didn't fight Charlie's bail and I couldn't understand why he seemed upset when he conceded the issue. If he didn't want Charlie out on bail all he had to do was contest my motion. What with Charlie skipping the country initially and this being a murder case, Karl would have had a good chance of convincing Judge Berkowitz to deny bail altogether."

Amanda paused again as she reran

Burdett's actions at the bail hearing through her memory.

"You know, now that I think about it, Karl behaved more like a subordinate who was carrying out an order he didn't agree with than the district attorney of the county, the man in charge. And there was the way he acted when he learned that a sniper had taken a shot at Charlie. He was much more upset than I would have thought he'd be."

"I'd be very upset if someone tried to commit murder in front of the Multnomah County courthouse," Mike said.

"I know. Anyone would. But Karl . . . I don't know how to describe it. I just had the feeling that there was more to his reaction than simple anger or sympathy for Charlie."

Amanda closed her eyes and sighed. "I'm beat, Mike. If you and Billie don't need me I'd like to go home."

"I took her statement," Brewster told Mike as she stood up. "And I know where to find you if I need anything else," she said to Amanda, "so I'll leave you lovebirds alone."

"Do you want me to stay over?" Mike asked as soon as the detective was out of earshot.

"Yeah, that would be nice. I really don't want to be alone tonight."

"Okay, let me check with the ME. Then we can head out."

AMANDA PEELED OFF her clothes as soon as she was in her condo. Then she flossed and brushed her teeth as quickly as possible before staggering into bed. Mike tucked her in and she fell into a deep, dreamless sleep. The prosecutor made a few calls in the living room to check on the progress of the investigation before going back to the bedroom. Mike and Amanda had grown close during the past year and he smiled as he watched her sleep. Then his exhaustion caught up to him and he crawled into bed beside her, falling asleep soon after he closed his eyes.

Shortly after three in the morning, Amanda's subconscious set off an alarm that jerked her awake. Karl Burdett had said something during his call that Amanda had forgotten to tell Billie Brewster and Mike Greene and she suddenly remembered what it was. She was tempted to wake Mike but he was sleeping so soundly that she crept out of bed, not wanting to disturb him.

Her cell phone was in her purse on the kitchen counter along with the card Daniel Cordova had given her. Amanda walked as far from the bedroom as she could and used the light from the phone to read the number on the card.

"Agent Cordova, this is Amanda Jaffe," she said as soon as the FBI agent answered the phone. "Have you heard what happened tonight?"

"Happened to what?" Cordova answered. He sounded groggy and annoyed, which didn't surprise Amanda.

"Karl Burdett was shot to death."

"Dear God!" Cordova said, instantly awake.

"I was working late. Karl called me. He was very upset and he sounded like he'd been drinking. He said he was in over his head. He also said that he hadn't realized that he was in over his head until he talked to you. Can you think of something you said to Karl that frightened him?"

"No." Cordova sounded puzzled. "I did talk to him but it was a courtesy call."

"I don't understand."

"We arrested Gary Hass in Sacramento. He was part of the muscle for a large heroin sale and we swept him up when we made the collar. It turns out he was in California when the sniper shot at your client. I called so Burdett wouldn't waste time on a dead end."

"And that's all you talked about?"

"Yes. It was a short conversation."

Amanda talked to the agent for a few more minutes, then she hung up. It wasn't obvious at first why Cordova's information about Hass had shaken up Karl Burdett but the germ of an idea was beginning to form.

MIKE GREENE BEGAN to get suspicious when the aroma of freshly brewed coffee woke him from a sound sleep. His suspicions grew when he wandered into the dining area of Amanda's loft and found a glass of orange juice waiting at a table setting. A full-blown alarm sounded when Amanda asked him what kind of omelet he wanted for breakfast.

Amanda wasn't a terrible cook but Mike knew she didn't like to spend time in the kitchen. When he stayed over, they usually ate out or he fixed breakfast. If she was up early cooking for him, Mike was certain it meant she wanted something he wouldn't want to give her.

"What's going on?" he asked.

"Can't I make you a nice breakfast without you getting suspicious?"

Mike folded his arms across his broad chest and stared at Amanda until she blushed.

"Okay, I do have an ulterior motive, but I also wanted to thank you for being so nice to me last night."

"Taking care of you was my pleasure. Now, please drop the other shoe."

Amanda plopped down across from Mike. She looked sexy with her hair mussed, dressed only in a T-shirt and panties.

"You know Karl's murder is connected to the *Marsh* case, right?"

"That's a possibility. But it could be a random killing," Mike said.

"Was Karl robbed?"

"He had his wallet, rings, and an expensive watch, but you could have scared off the killer when you drove into the lot. The killing could still be coincidental."

"You don't really believe that, do you?" Amanda asked.

"I don't know what to believe. It's too

early in the investigation to draw any conclusions."

"You should get Karl's files in Sally Pope's and Charlie's case. There may be notations in them that will explain why he called me."

"I was intending to do just that."

"Why don't you let me see them so I can point out things you might not realize are important."

Mike looked shocked. "You're kidding, right?"

"I'm dead serious."

"Is there some reason you want me fired and disbarred?"

"What do you know about Charlie's case?" Amanda asked.

"Not much. I know it was a big deal up here, and I remember reading about it when I was living in California."

"I've been living this case almost nonstop and my Dad tried *Pope*. I can spot things in the file you might miss."

"Amanda, you may be shocked to learn that I've actually gotten up to speed on other people's cases before. And I've done it without violating the rules of professional conduct. Do you understand what would happen if anyone discovered that I let you read the files of the attorney who was prosecuting your client? And I wouldn't be the only person in trouble. You'd be riding the elevator to hell with me."

Amanda smiled coquettishly. "That's so literary."

"Don't try your womanly wiles on me. Flattery, the batting of eyelashes, and come-hither stares are not going to work. This is too serious."

Amanda stopped smiling. "Now you've got it, Mike. This is damned serious. Someone's tried to murder Charlie twice and they succeeded in killing Sally Pope, her personal assistant, and her dog. Now they've killed the DA prosecuting Charlie's case. You need all the help you can get and I'm willing to risk my career to get the bastard who's doing this. If I help nail him, I don't care what rules of professional conduct I violate."

CHAPTER 42

Derrick Barclay had not changed much over the years, Frank thought, as Arnold Pope's personal assistant ushered him into a sitting room at the rear of Pope's mansion.

"Make yourself comfortable. I'll tell Mr. Pope you're here," Barclay said before shutting the door. The curtains were drawn and the subdued lighting from a small ceiling fixture gave the room a closed-in, musty feel. Most of the furnishings were antiques and Frank would not have been surprised to learn that white sheets had covered them until shortly before his visit.

He also thought that he should probably not be here, but his curiosity had gotten the best of him. When Barclay invited him to meet with his employer, Frank had been surprised and suspicious. Barclay claimed to know only that the meeting concerned Kevin Pope and Pope's lawyer in the custody matter would not be present. When Frank told Barclay that it was improper for him to meet with a represented party without the party's lawyer, Barclay said that Mr. Pope had prepared a notarized waiver in anticipation of Frank's objection. Frank had thought that over, then agreed to come. Now he wondered if he would regret his decision.

Frank waited for his host in a comfortable armchair across from a small marble fireplace. After a while, he glanced at his watch and realized that only five minutes had passed. There was a narrow, floor-to-ceiling bookshelf next to the fireplace. Frank was about to inspect Pope's library when the door opened and Pope hobbled in.

"Thank you for coming, Mr. Jaffe."

Frank noted the tremor in the older man's voice and the difficulty he had navigating across the room to the armchair opposite Frank. When he lowered himself onto the chair, he grimaced.

"Why am I here, Mr. Pope?"

Senior stared at Frank, irritated that his guest had taken control by skipping the usual pleasantries that preceded a business meeting.

"I see you like to get right to the point."

"Which is?"

"You are ideally situated to perform a service for me, which will bring me great satisfaction and will bring you a substantial reward."

"Go on."

"I understand you're representing Liam O'Connell in the guardianship contest."

Frank nodded. Pope shook his head slowly.

"What a sad affair. Poor Sally. We definitely had our differences, some quite vehement, but she was a fighter and I admired her spunk. She probably didn't know that."

Frank didn't respond. If Pope was trying to convince him that he was sorry that Sally was dead, he was failing. Frank knew how Pope really felt about his daughter-in-law and no phony show of sympathy was going to change his mind.

"I regret very much that Sally saw fit to cut herself off from me after my son's tragic death," Pope continued.

"If I remember correctly, Mr. Pope, you had something to do with that."

"You're completely correct, Mr. Jaffe. My son's death was a crushing experience. I was not rational at times after he passed and my grief interfered with my judgment. When Sally was indicted for Arnold's death I focused my hatred on her and I saw the dismissal of the charges against her as a personal affront.

"After the dismissal—after I had gotten my emotions in check—I hired a team of investigators to review the case. They concluded that there was a strong possibility that Sally had been unjustly accused."

Frank noted that Pope had conveniently managed to forget his involvement in the false accusations and the manufactured evidence that had led to Sally's indictment. He was tempted to remind him about the photographs and the note that had lured his son to his death, as well as the strong evidence that Otto Jarvis had been bribed to lie at Sally's trial, but he decided to hold his tongue.

"I made numerous attempts over the years to apologize and I made many offers to renew our friendship, all of which, to my sorrow, she rebuffed." Pope lowered his eyes and made a show of contrition. "I can't say I blame her."

"Where is all of this breast-beating leading, Mr. Pope?"

A flash of anger was Frank's reward for his blunt question, but Pope mastered his emotions quickly.

"I am very concerned about my grandson. Sally kept us apart as punishment for the way I treated her, but I love Arnie very much . . ."

"Sally's son is named Kevin," Frank interrupted, eliciting another flash of anger from Pope.

"Yes, Mr. Jaffe. His legal name is Kevin. My son wanted to name him Arnold Pope III but Sally named him Kevin to spite me. I bear her no grudge for that but he will always be Arnie to me."

"You were getting to the point of our meeting," Frank prodded.

"Sally designated Liam O'Connell as

Kevin's guardian in her will, but he has no right to be the boy's guardian. He and Sally never married, he's not kin."

"Kevin looks up to Mr. O'Connell and he's very fond of Kevin. From what I've seen, Mrs. Pope made a good choice."

"Kevin may be fond of this Irishman, but he has my blood in his veins."

"If I remember correctly, you and I discussed the possibility of you becoming Kevin's guardian shortly after Mrs. Pope's trial. Have you forgotten why your attorney advised you to drop your plans for a custody battle?"

Senior flashed a malevolent smile. "You mean your contention that I bribed Otto Jarvis and had something to do with that Rodriguez person, who took the pictures of Sally and her convict friend? Maybe you haven't heard, but Otto Jarvis passed away, a heart attack, I believe. And Mr. Rodriguez was shot to death in an alley. Something to do with a drug deal gone bad. So you would no longer be able to produce witnesses to support your allegations. But why bring up Sally's trial? It's old news."

"I still don't understand why I'm here."

"You're representing Mr. O'Connell, so you are in an excellent position to influence him. I want to adopt Kevin. He would be my heir. Surely you see the advantage to the boy in that. I want you to convince your client to turn down the guardianship and support my claim to be the boy's adoptive father."

"Why would I do that?"

"I have occasional need for an attorney with your talents, Mr. Jaffe. Obviously, I couldn't retain you or your firm while you're representing Mr. O'Connell in this matter, because of the conflict of interest that would create. However, if this business is concluded swiftly and favorably, the conflict would cease and I would be able to put your firm on a very healthy retainer."

Frank stared directly at Senior. Senior didn't blink.

"You don't see anything wrong in the offer you just made?"

"None whatsoever."

"Some people might interpret it as a bribe."

"Nonsense. It's to my advantage to have the very best legal talent at my disposal."

Frank smiled. "I appreciate the compliment, Mr. Pope, but I'm going to turn you down."

"That might not be wise. If you don't assist me I may have to contact the bar with some disturbing information I've had in my possession for some time. I would be very upset if I was unable to retain you because you were no longer permitted to practice law."

All of Frank's tolerance for Pope's clumsy attempt to corrupt him disappeared instantly, and Frank fixed his host with an icy stare.

"Why wouldn't I be able to practice law, Mr. Pope?"

Senior pulled a photograph of Frank and Sally Pope going into her home at night out of his inside jacket pocket.

"The bar frowns on affairs between a lawyer and his client. I have numerous pictures of you and Arnie's wife together during and after her trial and investigators who will swear before a disciplinary panel that you left my daughter-in-law's house in the small hours of the morning on many occasions."

Frank stood up. "You're going to have a

hard time convincing the bar that I wasn't conferring with Mrs. Pope about her legal affairs, but do your worst. I've never sold out a client and this definitely will not be the case where I start."

"You're making a big mistake."

"No, Mr. Pope, you are. If you come after me, do not think for one moment that I won't come right back at you."

CHAPTER 43

I can't believe I'm doing this," Mike Greene said as he carried two duffel bags loaded with Karl Burdett's files in the *Pope* and *Marsh* cases into Amanda's condo shortly after seven in the evening. Amanda gave him a big kiss on the cheek.

"You're a prince," she said as she picked up one of the bags and carried it into the living room. Amanda's romance with Mike Greene had been rocky at times, but that had always been her fault, especially when she'd been traumatized by the events in the *Cardoni* case. What made her love

Mike was his consistency. He was always there for her and he never judged her, even when she was at her worst.

"I would have been over earlier but I had to wait until everyone left, so no one would see me smuggling this stuff out," he told Amanda as he hauled his bag to the couch and opened it.

"I'll go through these files and you go through yours," Amanda said as she sat on the floor. "Then let's switch."

"I assume you made coffee," Mike said as he started pulling folders out of his bag, "because we have to get through this tonight so I can get the files back to the office in the morning before anyone gets in."

"Fresh coffee and doughnuts are on the counter. I even bought some maple bars," she added, naming Mike's favorite guilty pleasure.

"It's going to take more than a maple bar to get back in my good graces," he grumbled.

"I'll see what I can do, if we're not too tired," Amanda promised as she stacked manila folders in front of her.

. . . .

IT WAS TEN o'clock and several cups of coffee later when Amanda and Mike got ready to swap.

"Did you find anything in your files or Burdett's notes that was helpful?" Mike asked.

"No," she said, disappointed, "though I did find something that I don't understand."

Amanda carried a folder to the couch and sat next to Mike. He opened it.

"This looks like a master file," Mike said. "It has copies of the pleadings, correspondence."

"That's what I figured, but what's this?" she said, pointing to a line on a log sheet that was stapled to the left inside cover. "A lot of the entries were made twelve years ago, but look at this entry." Amanda pointed at the numbers and letter: 1253X. "It was made yesterday. Do you know what it means?"

"Sure. Washington County wanted to have a copy of the file to work on while we were looking at Karl's original file. That's a record of the number of pages that were copied. The file is a little more than twelve hundred pages long."

"Okay, that's what I figured. But look at this entry," Amanda said, pointing to an earlier, recent entry that read 1209X.

"That probably refers to another copy of the file," Mike said.

"Yeah, but see the date and time the copies were made? That's the afternoon of the day I visited Hillsboro and told Burdett that Charlie was returning to Oregon to face the charges against him."

"I don't see where you're going. I usually make a copy of my file so I can break it up when I make files for individual witnesses."

"If the office had a duplicate file when you asked them to make a copy, why did they need another one?"

Mike's brow furrowed.

"On the day I told him Charlie was returning to face trial, I think Karl made a copy of his complete file for someone who is not in the DA's office."

"Who would want something like that?"

"Remember I told you how upset Burdett was when the sniper took his shot at Charlie?"

"Yeah."

"I think Burdett might have been killed

because he put two and two together and came up with Arnold Pope as the man behind the assassination attempt on Charlie and the murders at Sally Pope's house."

"That's some stretch, Amanda."

"With Gary Hass out of the picture, who other than Senior would want Charlie dead? Revenge is an obvious motive for the attack at the courthouse. Arnold Pope Sr. could order Burdett to make a copy of the case file and expect to be obeyed. He could order Burdett to set free the man he held responsible for his son's murder so he would be out of jail, where an assassin could take a shot at him."

Mike frowned.

"I'm certain Sally Pope was used to lure Charlie out of his hotel so he could be killed after the first attempt at the courthouse failed," Amanda went on. "If Charlie's mysterious savior hadn't appeared on the scene, Sally and Charlie would have died. Pope is the only person I can think of who would want both of them dead."

As she spoke, an image of Nathan Tuazama flashed through her brain, but she decided to keep that information confidential. Besides, Tuazama wouldn't kill Charlie before he had the diamonds.

"It's a stretch, Amanda, and you haven't given me any hard evidence to work with."

"You're right about the proof part but you have to admit my idea makes sense. When Agent Cordova told Burdett that Gary Hass couldn't have been the sniper, I think Burdett realized that Pope was behind the attempt on Charlie at the courthouse. What if he confronted Pope? What if Pope became worried that Burdett would tell someone his theory? Pope could have had the same person who murdered Sally take care of Burdett."

"That's a lot of what ifs."

"What about Kevin?"

"Sally's son?"

"Why isn't he dead, Mike? Arnold Pope Sr. is obsessed with getting custody of his grandson. The person who killed Sally also killed her personal assistant and her dog but he never hurt Kevin. I think Kevin is alive because Arnold Pope ordered the killer to make certain that he survived unharmed."

"You've given me a lot to think about," Mike said.

Amanda thought of something else, the photograph of Karl Burdett and Tony Rose carrying hunting rifles that she'd seen in the DA's office.

"Are you ready to switch files?" Mike asked.

"Yeah," she answered, still distracted by her epiphany. She decided that she would keep this idea to herself until she talked it over with Kate.

"Why don't we just trade places?" Mike said.

"Good idea."

Mike sat on the floor and Amanda went to the couch. At 11:25, she was going through a stack of photographs when she came across the original of the photograph of Charlie Marsh and his entourage at the Dunthorpe mansion, which Kate had told her was missing. She picked it up and studied it. She had met Mickey Keys and Charlie but it was interesting to see what Delmar Epps looked like. As she studied Epps, her eyes strayed to his waist. The bodyguard was wearing a loose jacket. He was in mid-stride and the movement of his body had brought the fabric out and back. Amanda brought the photo to eye level. Yes, she could make out the butt of a revolver. Then she saw something else in the photograph. Her breath caught in her chest and she knew why the photograph was missing and who had taken it. When Mike wasn't looking, Amanda slipped the photograph under the cushion on the couch.

CHAPTER 44

Mike and Amanda got to bed a little before one, too exhausted for the second night in a row to do anything but sleep. The couple kept changes of clothes at each other's condos and Mike was showered and shaved at five in the morning so he could get into his office with the files without being seen.

Amanda tried to go back to sleep after Mike left but questions raised by last night's revelations bombarded her. Was Arnold Pope the mastermind behind these murders? Was Tony Rose the sniper? And there was the photograph from the Dunthorpe seminar. Charlie could help her there, so

Amanda showered, dressed, and headed for the hospital.

When she arrived, Charlie was sitting up in bed.

"Have you heard about Karl Burdett?"

"It was on the news but they didn't say anything except that he'd been shot and you found him. How did that happen?"

Amanda told Charlie about the phone call.

"Do you have any idea why Burdett wanted to see you?" Charlie asked when Amanda finished her recap of the night's events.

"He didn't say."

"But he said it was about me, about the case?"

Amanda nodded.

"What's going to happen now that Burdett is dead?"

"You're still under indictment. An interim DA will be appointed—probably Wanda Simmons, the chief criminal deputy—and someone will be assigned to prosecute the case."

"They'll still go after me after all that's happened?"

"Werner Rollins did retract his testimony,

so they don't have any direct evidence that you shot Pope. I'll try to convince the DA that enough questions have been raised to warrant a dismissal."

"What about all these people who've been trying to kill me? Shouldn't that make them think they've got the wrong man?"

"You're on trial for a murder that happened twelve years ago. There's no hard evidence that the current rash of murders has anything to do with the congressman's murder."

"Come on. It's obvious."

"The only thing that's obvious is that someone is after you. That could be because they think you murdered Arnold Pope Jr. and they want revenge."

"You mean Arnie's father?"

Amanda nodded. "I think there's a good possibility that he hired someone to kill you."

"Who?"

"I don't want to say right now, but I've seen the list of witnesses Pope is calling at the guardianship contest, so I might know more after the hearing."

"You think there's a tie-in between Senior's attempt to get custody of Kevin, Junior's murder, and the attempts on my life?"

"I think it's possible, but I'm open to suggestions. Besides Senior, can you think of someone else who might want you dead?"

Charlie looked nervous. "No. I mean there's Tuazama, but—like I said—I don't think he'd kill me until he got the diamonds."

"So, you can't think of anyone else?"

"No."

Amanda opened her attaché case and took out a manila envelope. Inside the envelope was the photograph she'd stolen from Karl Burdett's file. She took it out and laid it on top of the blanket on Charlie's bed.

The Honorable Maria Gomez took the bench and the parties in the case of *In re Kevin Pope* stood until she was seated. Judge Gomez was in her mid-forties. The wiry six-foot jurist had played on the LPGA tour until she gave up golf for law school. Then she'd brought her competitive drive to the legal profession, where she'd been one of the top domestic-relations lawyers in Oregon before the current governor elevated her to the bench. She was a no-nonsense judge who liked to move cases along and she disliked lawyers who were unprepared or wasted her time.

Sitting at one counsel table next to Arnold Pope Sr. was Andrew Curry, a stoop-shouldered, balding attorney with a skeletal build. Curry was nicknamed "the Vampire" because of the ruthless way he practiced law and a bloodless complexion that was the result of long hours spent indoors working on ways to win divorce and custody battles for his clients. Curry wore the nickname with pride. Nobody liked him but everybody recommended him to a spouse who wanted an ex destroyed, destitute, and demoralized.

Frank Jaffe sat across the aisle from Pope and Curry, and Amanda sat next to her father so they could confer. Liam O'Connell was next to Amanda. Kevin was not present, because custody hearings were often wars of character assassination and the accusations of biased witnesses were best left unheard by the child who would have to live with one of the maligned parties.

"Let me see if I understand the background of this case, Mr. Jaffe," Judge Gomez said. "Sally Pope was Kevin Pope's mother and Arnold Pope Jr. was his father. Mr. Pope passed away twelve years ago and Mrs. Pope raised her son until her recent death.

Mr. O'Connell lived with Mrs. Pope and Kevin for approximately five years before her death. In her will, Mrs. Pope named Mr. O'Connell as Kevin's guardian and Mr. O'Connell filed a petition requesting me to appoint him Kevin's guardian."

"That's correct, Your Honor," Frank Jaffe said. "I also want to make sure that you know that it was Mrs. Pope's specific wish—which she spelled out in her will—that Arnold Pope Sr. never be allowed to be Kevin's guardian. She was adamant while alive, and in her will, that Mr. Pope Sr. should never have contact with her son."

"I'm aware of that and I will consider Mrs. Pope's wishes very seriously when I make my decision. But I'm not bound by them. My main concern is the best interests of the child, Kevin Pope."

The judge turned her attention to Senior and his attorney. "Mr. Curry, your client filed objections to Mr. O'Connell's petition seeking guardianship and today I'm going to decide who will be appointed Kevin's temporary guardian until a full-fledged hearing can be held. Is that correct?"

"Yes, Your Honor."

"Then it seems to me that Mr. Pope has

the burden of proof, since the will asks the court to appoint Mr. O'Connell as Kevin's guardian."

Curry stood so rapidly that Judge Gomez had the impression that she had missed part of the transition from seat to feet. It was like watching a film from which several of the frames had been removed.

"Your Honor, I respectfully disagree with your holding. We believe that Mr. O'Connell should bear the burden of convincing this court that he should be appointed Kevin's guardian. Oregon law recognizes that grandparents have substantial interests in their grandchildren. A sexual partner with no blood ties to the child should not be granted superior rights to a grandparent.

"Furthermore, we take issue with Mr. Jaffe's position that Mrs. Pope's rabid and unjustified dislike of my client should play any part in the court's decision."

"I appreciate your position, Mr. Curry. I may be wrong on the issue of who bears the burden. If I am, the appellate court will straighten me out. But you brought this petition challenging the will, so I'm holding that you have the burden of convincing me that Mr. O'Connell should not be appointed

Kevin's temporary guardian. Are you ready with your first witness?"

BEFORE THE NOON recess, a child psychiatrist, who had been hired by Senior, testified that he would make an excellent guardian for Kevin. Then Curry called several prominent Oregonians, including one of Oregon's United States senators, who testified to their belief that Arnold Pope Sr. loved his late son and his grandson and would make an excellent guardian for Kevin. During cross-examination, Frank Jaffe established that each witness was biased by a financial or personal relationship with Senior. He also got them to admit that they knew nothing about Liam O'Connell's fitness to raise the boy.

As soon as court reconvened after lunch, Judge Gomez told Curry to call his next witness. Tony Rose straightened the jacket of his charcoal black pinstripe suit, adjusted his maroon silk tie, and walked to the witness stand looking every bit the successful business executive.

"Mr. Rose, what is your profession?" Curry asked after the witness was sworn.

"I'm the president of Mercury Enterprises. We manufacture sporting equipment."

"Your company also sponsors the Mercury training program for our Olympic athletes, does it not?"

"Yes, sir. There are several American athletes who have earned Olympic medals after taking advantage of our training facilities."

"Can you please tell the judge a little about the activities of Mercury worldwide?"

"That won't be necessary, Mr. Curry," Judge Gomez said. "I'm well aware of who Mr. Rose is and what Mercury does. I doubt that there's a person in Oregon, or the United States for that matter, who can't identify the Mercury logo."

"Very well, Your Honor. Mr. Rose, are you acquainted with Arnold Pope Sr.?"

"I am."

"How long have you known him?"

"More than ten years."

"What is Mr. Pope's reputation in the business community of this state?"

"Well, if I might, I think 'state' is too narrow. I would say that his reputation for integrity is something people across the nation are aware of."

"Have you ever had occasion to discuss Arnold Pope Jr. with him?"

"Yes, sir. He was devastated by the loss of his son. He still is."

"Has he ever discussed his grandson, Kevin Pope, with you?"

"Yes, sir. I am hard pressed to say what has affected him more, the death of his son or Sally Pope's decision to cut off all contact between Mr. Pope and his grandson."

"Do you think Mr. Pope would make a suitable guardian for his grandson?"

"Unquestionably. He loves the boy very much and would be able to give him all the advantages of his name and position."

"Your witness, Mr. Jaffe," Curry said.

"Your Honor, my co-counsel will handle the cross-examination of this witness."

"Very well, Miss Jaffe," Judge Gomez said.

"Thank you, Your Honor," Amanda replied before turning her attention to Tony Rose.

"Mr. Rose, your company's brochure, television commercials, and magazine and Internet ads portray you as a sportsman. Is that accurate?"

"Yes."

"You were a top high school tennis player before you joined the army?"

"Yes."

"And you were good enough to reach the quarterfinals of the NCAA Division I championships as a senior at Ohio State?"

"That's true."

"Then you played professionally for two years before becoming the club pro at the Westmont Country Club?"

"Also true."

"There are television commercials for Mercury Enterprises that show you volleying with Wimbledon and U.S. Open champion Gary Posner."

"Yes, but I don't do nearly as well when the cameras aren't rolling," Rose answered. Judge Gomez smiled and several spectators laughed.

"Don't other commercials show you hunting and fishing in the forests of Oregon?"

"That's true."

"Do you enjoy those sports?"

"Yes, I do."

"Are tennis, hunting, and fishing types of activities that interest adolescent boys?"

"Some boys enjoy them," Rose answered cautiously, sensing a trap.

"Mr. Pope isn't capable of playing tennis, is he?"

Rose hesitated. Then he said, "No."

"He can't hunt or fish or engage in any type of strenuous activity because he's in his seventies and has a number of physical infirmities?"

"Objection," Curry shouted. "Mr. Rose is not a doctor."

"I'm asking Mr. Rose to testify about what he's seen," Amanda argued. "A layman can tell if someone limps or is blind."

"Overruled," the judge said. "You can answer, Mr. Rose."

"Mr. Pope is not as spry as he was when I first met him."

"When was that? When did you first meet Mr. Pope?"

Rose frowned. "I'm not sure of the exact date."

"It was after his son was murdered, wasn't it?"

"Yes, I think that's right."

"And before you started Mercury?"

"Yes."

"That's about twelve years ago, right after his son was murdered?"

"Yes."

"Is it fair to say that twelve years ago Mr. Pope was a captain of industry and you were an unemployed tennis instructor?"

"That's fair," Rose agreed.

"Then how did you meet? You didn't exactly run in the same social circles."

"I . . . It's been a while. I don't actually remember."

"You must have hit it off pretty well, because Mr. Pope gave you the start-up money for Mercury."

"I can't really discuss that. We're a privately held corporation and our books are not open to the public."

"They are now, Mr. Rose. You're under oath in a court of law and I asked the question to show possible bias on your part in favor of the party who called you to the stand."

"Objection," Curry started.

"No, Mr. Curry," the judge ruled. "Miss Jaffe is entitled to show bias on the part of the witness you called. Please answer the question, Mr. Rose."

Rose looked very uncomfortable. He shot a quick glance at Senior, but the old man looked right through him.

"Mr. Pope did help me start Mercury."

"Does he hold a controlling interest in the company?"

"Yes."

"So you serve as its president at his will? He could fire you if he wanted to?"

"The company is doing very well and I'm its spokesman, so there would be no reason for him to do that."

"But he could if he wanted to?"

"I guess he could."

"Was Mr. Pope's initial investment in Mercury substantial?" Amanda asked.

"Yes."

"Without giving a specific figure, would it be correct to say that Mr. Pope's initial investment was in the seven-figure range?"

"Yes. That sounds correct."

"Why would Mr. Pope give you so much money?"

"He liked my idea for a sporting goods company. He was farsighted and was able to see the company's potential."

"I didn't make myself clear, Mr. Rose. I meant, wasn't it strange, if he truly loved his son, that he would give so much money to the man who was sleeping with his son's wife?"

Rose colored but kept his composure.

"I'm not proud of that and I told Mr. Pope I wasn't. But I also told him that Mrs. Pope had asked me to kill his son and I refused. I believe Mr. Pope appreciated that."

"We only have your word that Sally Pope asked you to kill her husband, don't we?"

"Objection, Your Honor," Curry said. "The question has no relevance to a custody proceeding."

"I'll tie it up, Your Honor," Amanda promised.

"I'll let you go on a little more," the judge ruled.

"Didn't Mr. Pope hate his daughter-in-law?"

"They didn't get along."

"He wanted her executed for his son's murder, didn't he?"

"I don't know anything about that."

"Your testimony was the strongest and most dramatic evidence directly tying Mrs. Pope to her husband's murder, wasn't it?"

"I'm not sure. I don't know all of the evidence the district attorney had."

"Was the start-up money for Mercury a payoff for lying at Sally Pope's trial?"

"No! Absolutely not."

"You would certainly have benefited if

Sally Pope had been found guilty, wouldn't you?"

"I don't see how."

"That would have closed the case, as far as the police were concerned. The authorities would peg Charlie Marsh as the shooter and Mrs. Pope as his coconspirator and they wouldn't look any further."

"I'm not following you."

"Permission to approach the witness," Amanda said.

"You may," Judge Gomez said.

A good cross-examiner changes the direction of her questions frequently to keep the witness off balance. Amanda handed Rose the photograph of him and Karl Burdett holding their hunting rifles that she'd seen hanging in Burdett's office.

"Do you recognize this photograph?"

"Yes. It shows me hunting with Karl Burdett."

"You're quite a good shot, aren't you?"

"I'm okay," Rose answered nervously.

"Don't be modest, Mr. Rose. You were given the grade of marksman in the army, were you not?"

"Yes."

"So you know how to hit a target with a sniper rifle from a long distance?"

"Well, I did, many years ago."

"Are you rusty?"

"I don't think I can make some of the shots I made in the military."

"Is that why you missed Charlie Marsh when you tried to kill him at the court-house?"

Rose looked shocked. "I did no such thing!"

"Objection," Curry bellowed so he could be heard over the din in the courtroom.

"You're on very thin ice here, Miss Jaffe," Judge Gomez said. "These are very serious accusations."

"I will tie this up, Your Honor," Amanda promised.

"I'll let you continue, but I will cut you off if I conclude you're fishing."

"Your Honor, Mr. Rose can cut me off by pleading the Fifth," Amanda shot back.

Judge Gomez considered what Amanda had just said. Then she turned to the witness.

"Miss Jaffe is correct, Mr. Rose. If at any time you believe that your answer to Miss

Jaffe's question would be an admission of criminal wrongdoing, you are permitted to assert your Fifth Amendment right not to incriminate yourself. Do you understand that?"

"I do," Rose answered as he sat up straight in the witness box and smoothed out his suit jacket. "But I have nothing to hide, Your Honor."

"Very well. You may continue, Miss Jaffe."

"Did Mr. Pope order you to kill Charlie Marsh when Mr. Marsh left the courthouse after his bail hearing?"

"No."

"Did he threaten to kick you out of your position at Mercury Enterprises if you didn't murder Charlie Marsh and Sally Pope?"

"No."

"But he was briefing you about Mr. Marsh's case?"

"No, he wasn't."

"Do you remember being interviewed by Kate Ross, my investigator, the day before Mr. Marsh flew back to Portland?"

"Yes."

"Toward the end of the interview she

asked you if you were still mad at Mr. Marsh."

"Yes."

"And you said that was water under the bridge and you asked her to tell Mr. Marsh that you had no hard feelings when she saw him the next day."

"So?"

"How did you know Mr. Marsh was flying into Portland the next day?"

"I . . . I don't know." Rose eyes shifted nervously. "I must have heard it on the news."

"Mr. Marsh flew to Portland on a private jet. His arrival time was a tightly held secret. The media knew nothing about the flight until the day after Ms. Ross interviewed you. That's when a reporter for *World News* tipped them off. Mr. Marsh was in New York before he flew to Portland. I can produce everyone in New York who knew Mr. Marsh's flight plans. They will swear under oath that they did not reveal this information to you.

"Aside from my father, Kate Ross, and me, Karl Burdett was the only Oregonian who knew when Mr. Marsh would arrive. If you knew the date, the information could only have come from Mr. Burdett or from someone he told, like his biggest contributor, Arnold Pope Sr., a man with a burning interest in the case of the man who allegedly killed his son. So, I ask you again, did Arnold Pope brief you about Mr. Marsh's case?"

"Objection," Curry shouted. "This line of questioning is totally irrelevant to these proceedings. Miss Jaffe doesn't have a shred of evidence to support her accusations."

"I might have an eyewitness," Amanda said, "if Mr. Pope thought that Mr. Rose killed his son."

"What!" Rose shouted.

"You told Kate Ross that you were at your car in the parking lot of the Westmont when Arnold Pope Jr. was shot, but Ralph Day will testify that you were in the crowd watching Delmar Epps fight with one of the security guards. The gun that was used to shoot the congressman was large and unwieldy and Mr. Epps usually kept it in his waistband. If Mr. Epps was carrying the gun and the gun fell out when Mr. Epps was fighting, you could have grabbed it."

"Why would I want to kill Arnold Pope Jr.? I'd never met the man."

"What if you didn't mean to kill him? What if you meant to kill his wife, Sally Pope, who had dumped you and refused to talk to you shortly before the shooting? What if you aimed at Sally Pope and killed her husband by mistake? If that happened, you could have tossed the gun away after you killed the congressman. Then you could have lied to Mr. Pope and told him that you refused Sally Pope's request to kill her husband and you could have agreed to testify against the woman Mr. Pope hated. If Mrs. Pope went to prison the police would stop looking for the congressman's killer. If Mr. Pope gained custody of his grandson a very wealthy man would be in your debt."

"Objection!" Curry shouted. "This is pure speculation. Miss Jaffe is making a jury argument in a criminal case. She's supposed to be asking questions in a custody matter. Her entire line of questioning is irrelevant."

While Curry was talking, Rose stole a look at Arnold Pope. The old man was leaning forward, his eyes riveted on the witness. Beads of sweat formed on Rose's brow.

"I'm inclined to agree, Miss Jaffe," Judge Gomez said. "Your allegations are very serious and I won't let you pursue them unless you can assure me that you have very strong evidence to support them."

"May we have a minute, Your Honor?" Frank asked.

"Go ahead," the judge said.

Frank leaned close to his daughter so no one would hear what he said.

"Amanda, do you have a shred of evidence that Rose killed Junior?"

"I never accused him of killing Pope. I just asked a lot of questions beginning with 'what if.'"

"You can't just toss around accusations of murder like that. I think you should drop this line of questioning."

"Don't worry, Dad. I've accomplished what I wanted to achieve."

Amanda stood up. "I don't have any further questions of Mr. Rose," she told the judge.

"I think this would be a good time to recess for the day," Judge Gomez said.

Amanda sat down and watched Tony Rose hurry out of the courtroom. Then she shifted her gaze to Arnold Pope, whose eyes were following Rose's retreating back with a look of pure hatred. Several rows behind Senior, a black man stood up and worked his way toward the door to the courtroom. Amanda's heartbeat accelerated. Then she calmed down. She'd thought the man was Nathan Tuazama but Tuazama did not wear tortoiseshell glasses.

"Do you really think Rose murdered Sally?" Liam O'Connell asked as the courtroom emptied out. He looked stunned.

"Someone wanted Charlie and Sally dead and that person went to great lengths to have them killed. The only person I can think of who would hate them that much is Senior. He couldn't do the job himself but he could have forced Rose to do it. If Rose were kicked out of Mercury Enterprises he would lose a fortune, and he's skilled enough as a marksman to have made the attempt on Charlie at the courthouse.

"The day I told Karl Burdett that Charlie was returning to Oregon, he copied his file. No one in the DA's office knows anything about that copy, so who did he give it to? The only person who would be that interested would be Senior."

"And you think Pope told Rose when Marsh was flying in?" O'Connell asked.

"Who else would Burdett have spoken to?"

"Will the police arrest Rose?"

"Not unless they dig up more evidence," Amanda said as she packed the last of her papers in her attaché case and headed out of the courtroom. "You can't get an indictment with guesses."

"That was straight out of Perry Mason," Dennis Levy said as soon as Amanda stepped into the hall.

"Except Rose didn't break down and confess. In real life, Dennis, witnesses deny, deny, deny, no matter how much evidence you throw at them."

"Then why did you cross-examine him like that?"

"To create doubt in the judge's mind about Senior's suitability as a guardian and to drive a wedge between Senior and Rose that might be useful at Charlie's trial."

"Would you give me an exclusive interview about the custody case? If I write this up now I can get my story in this week's edition of *World News.*"

"Sure, Dennis," Amanda said as soon as Liam and Frank were out of earshot. "I wanted to talk to you about the photograph from the Dunthorpe seminar, anyway."

Dennis turned pale. "What photograph?"

"Please don't play games with me. Kate saw it when she went through the file but it wasn't there after you went through the file. I know what it shows. I've seen the original. If you return it to me with any copies you've made I'll let you stay on the inside in Charlie's case. Keep the photograph and I will do everything in my power to make sure that someone else writes Charlie's book. So, what will it be?"

"You can't intimidate me," Dennis said, but the quiver in his voice contradicted his words.

"Blackmail is a felony, Dennis."

"What are you talking about?"

Amanda stared hard at Levy. Sweat formed on the reporter's brow.

"I'm going to my office. When you know what you're going to do, let's talk. You've been telling everyone what this book will do for your career, the notoriety you'll achieve, the money you'll make. Achieve your fame and fortune honestly, Dennis. Give back the photo."

Amanda turned and walked away. Dennis watched her leave. He suddenly realized that he was shaking. There was a bench a few feet away. He needed to sit down. Then he needed to decide what he was going to do.

46

Tony Rose was desperate to talk to Arnold Pope but reporters mobbed him when he left the courthouse and hounded him all the way to his car. Rose barely avoided destroying a reporter's handheld microphone when he slammed the door of his Ferrari. He was wondering if he could back out of his parking space without running over someone when the reporters suddenly disappeared. Rose looked out of his back window and saw the mob rushing toward the courthouse to ambush Pope and Derrick Barclay.

Rose had no idea what was going on in

Pope's twisted mind, but he knew that he had to convince Senior that Jaffe's accusations were crazy. He closed his eyes and followed the deep-breathing routine he'd used to calm himself during tense moments in his tennis matches.

Pope's limousine stopped in front of the courthouse and Barclay helped his employer into the backseat. They were probably going to Pope's estate. Rose was debating the wisdom of following the limo when his cell phone rang.

"Mr. Pope wants you at the house at ten o'clock tonight," Derrick Barclay said in that imperious tone that set Rose's teeth on edge.

"He doesn't think . . . ?" Rose started but Barclay had already hung up.

Rose swallowed hard and reversed out of his space. He was so intent on his problems that he didn't notice Pierre Girard's nondescript brown Toyota follow him out of the lot.

AT EXACTLY TEN o'clock, Tony Rose parked his Ferrari in front of Arnold Pope's mansion. He was still shaken by the summons. Rose made a lot of money but he'd spen plenty over the years. His cars and his houses cost a fortune to keep up and he was always inches away from bankruptcy. Only his king-size salary and overly generous bonuses kept the wolf from his door. That's why he'd agreed to kill Charlie Marsh and Sally Pope. Senior had known he was a marksman when he suggested the hits to Rose. When Rose balked, Senior used the threat of firing him from Mercury as the stick and a seven-figure payoff disguised as a bonus for his work as Mercury's president as the carrot.

Now Rose felt helpless. Who knew what Senior was thinking after hearing the ravings of O'Connell's lunatic attorney? If Pope believed everything Jaffe said he might kick him out of Mercury and he'd be back where he was when the Westmont fired him. And he had nothing with which to bargain. He couldn't threaten to implicate Pope without implicating himself. Besides, the police would only have his word that Senior was involved.

When he could put it off no longer, Rose got out of the car and walked to the front door.

"What does he want?" Rose asked

Derrick Barclay as Pope's lackey led him to the back of the house.

"You'll have to ask Mr. Pope."

The first thing Rose noticed when Barclay opened the door to the den was that the heavy curtains were drawn and the only light came from the low-wattage bulb in Senior's desk lamp, leaving Pope's features cloaked in shadow.

"Come in," Pope ordered from his seat behind his desk. Tony had taken a few steps into the room when he heard the door close behind him. He started to turn but his feet tangled in the drop cloth that Barclay had spread over the floor at Pope's request. Tony looked down and realized that every square inch of the beautiful hardwood flooring was covered.

"You killed my boy," Pope said.

Rose's head jerked up. "No, Mr. Pope. You can't believe what that lawyer said. She was just trying to prejudice the judge. That was nonsense. Why would I hurt Junior?"

"As soon as she said it I knew it was the truth. I sent those photographs to Junior so he'd show some spine and get rid of that bitch, but she couldn't have planned to kill Arnie, because she didn't know he was coming to the Westmont. And my investigators told me that Marsh is a coward. But the gun was found where he was standing and he'd been fighting with Junior and he ran away. All these years I was certain that Marsh killed Arnie. Now I know I was wrong."

"It wasn't me. I swear it wasn't me."

"Were you in the crowd like Jaffe said?"

"That's true."

"Then why did you lie to Jaffe's investigator and say you were at your car?"

Rose broke out in a sweat. "I didn't want her to know I was anywhere near Arnie."

"Did you think you were the only witness Jaffe would have interviewed? Didn't it dawn on you that someone else could have seen you?"

"I was under a lot of stress when Jaffe's investigator talked to me. That was the day before Marsh returned to Oregon. I was thinking about the best way to take care of him, just like you wanted. I wasn't thinking clearly."

"Is that your excuse for shooting my boy?"

"I didn't. I saw Epps fighting and I saw

him kick that guard. If he had that gun it must have dropped out earlier, because I never saw a gun come out of his waistband and I never saw a gun on the ground near where Epps was fighting. You have to believe me."

"Well, I don't," Pope said. "And even if I did, you're the only person who can link me to Sally's murder and the attempts on Marsh."

Suddenly, Tony realized that the drop cloth was covering the floor so his blood wouldn't stain Pope's precious hardwood. That flash of insight occurred simultaneously with the flash from the muzzle of the gun Derrick Barclay had aimed at his brain while Senior was distracting him.

"Get rid of his car and get this garbage out of my sight, Derrick," Pope said without a trace of emotion.

DERRICK BARCLAY WAS much stronger than he looked but it was still a strain to drag the drop cloth–wrapped corpse through the house and out the back door where an old Cadillac was waiting. He was sweating profusely by the time Rose was loaded into the trunk and he took several deep breaths before getting into the driver's seat.

A timber baron had a terrific advantage in a situation like this. Pope owned vast acres of forest land where a corpse could be buried with little chance of discovery. There had been other occasions when Barclay had disposed of unwanted items like Tony Rose, and he had found a lovely spot in the middle of an old-growth forest for the dearly departed. If there was life after death, Barclay hoped that Mr. Pope's victims appreciated his choice of a final resting place.

As soon as he had taken care of Rose, Barclay planned to use the dead man's credit card to buy a one-way ticket to Germany. Then he would leave Rose's car in the long-term parking lot at the Portland airport and take public transportation into town. With luck, the police would think that Rose had panicked and fled the country.

Two hours after leaving Washington County, Barclay turned off a two-lane state highway onto a dirt logging road that had not been used for many years. Twenty minutes later, he stopped the car near a narrow trail that would be invisible to someone who didn't know it existed. Barclay walked around to the trunk. He flexed his knees, took hold of the body through the drop cloth, and hauled Rose out of the car. Then he hoisted the corpse over his shoulders in a fireman's carry, grabbed the shovel he'd leaned against the side of the car, and tramped into the woods.

Barclay had walked a short way when he heard a rustling in the underbrush. Rose's dead weight hurt his shoulders and legs but he paused to listen for any indication that someone was stalking him. When he didn't hear anything, he decided an animal had caused the sound. Shortly before he reached his destination, Barclay thought he heard a twig snap. Was someone following him? No, that was impossible. He would have seen a car on the sparsely traveled country roads. His shoulders ached and he hurried the rest of the way so he could unload his burden. As soon as the body was on the ground, he flexed his back and shoulders. Then he paused to listen again, still spooked by the sounds he thought he'd heard. Except for the wind and the leaves it rustled, all was quiet.

Digging a grave was hard work and it required focus. That's why Barclay didn't hear Quentin Randolph and his partner, Nathan Rask, until they were almost on him. The sheriff's deputies were responding to a 911 call relayed to them by their dispatcher. The caller had a funny accent but he had given very specific directions to a site where he claimed a man was burying a body. Quentin thought the report might be a prank, but it was a quiet evening and checking out the call gave him something to do.

CHAPTER 47

Wanda Simmons, the acting district attorney for Washington County, was a severe-looking career prosecutor with frizzy red hair and a perpetually harried expression. Simmons, who had no life away from her cases, always wore identical rumpled navy blue skirts and jackets over identical wrinkled white blouses. Amanda suspected that Simmons put up with the time it took to get dressed only because she wouldn't be allowed in court if she was naked.

"Who wants to tell me why we're having this secret meeting?" Marshall Berkowitz asked as he looked back and forth between Simmons and Amanda.

"I'm going to dismiss the case against Mr. Marsh," the DA told the judge. "Neither party wanted a media circus."

Berkowitz raised his eyebrows in surprise as Amanda nodded her assent. Charlie Marsh, whom Amanda had ordered to speak only when she told him to, sat quietly at his lawyer's side.

"Care to tell me why you're dismissing?" the judge asked.

"You know that Derrick Barclay, Arnold Pope Sr.'s assistant, was arrested while he was burying Tony Rose on forest land owned by one of Pope's companies."

The judge nodded. The arrest of Arnold Pope and Derrick Barclay was the talk of the county.

"Barclay has been cooperating since his arrest and he's told us a lot we didn't know about Senior's involvement in this case. Twelve years ago, Senior pressured Karl to prosecute Mr. Marsh and his daughter-in-law. Karl had no intention of charging Mrs. Pope until Senior turned the screws. Barclay also says that Pope wanted Rose murdered because he believed that Rose killed his son.

"I've had a chance to study our evidence and I see a number of serious problems with the case. I had no idea how weak it was until I went through the file after Karl was murdered. Our biggest problem is that Werner Rollins has retracted his statement that he saw Mr. Marsh shoot Congressman Pope. Rollins was the only witness who put the murder weapon in Mr. Marsh's hand. Rollins tells us that he said he saw Mr. Marsh shoot the congressman because Karl threatened to prosecute him for the assault on the security guard if he didn't. Without Rollins's testimony, we don't have a case. Any number of people, including Tony Rose, could have shot the congressman. Now that Rose is dead we'll never know if he's guilty, but he's now as viable a suspect as Mr. Marsh and several other people who were standing near Mr. Marsh when the fatal shot was fired.

"Then there's the problem of the note and the photographs. Twelve years ago, when Sally Pope was prosecuted, it was the state's theory that Mrs. Pope and Mr. Marsh lured the congressman to the Westmont by sending him several scandalous photographs showing the two of them in situations that suggested that they were lovers, and an anonymous note saying that Mr. Marsh and the congressman's wife would be at the Westmont for one of Mr. Marsh's seminars. Frank Jaffe developed proof that Senior was behind the photographs and the anonymous note that lured Junior to the Westmont."

"I never knew that," Judge Berkowitz said.

"It's not public knowledge. In fact, the evidence and the transcript of the hearing where the information was revealed were sealed. Amanda told me about the evidence soon after I was given Mr. Marsh's case.

"I've given this matter a lot of thought and I've decided that I would have a reasonable doubt about Mr. Marsh's guilt if I was on his jury. I can't go forward in good conscience feeling that way."

"AM I FREE?" Charlie asked as soon as he and Amanda were alone in her car.

"It's over, Charlie. Of course, there's no statute of limitations on a murder charge. Theoretically you could be indicted again if new evidence implicating you turned up. But I doubt that will ever happen, since we both know what really took place at the Westmont."

"What's going to happen now?" Charlie asked.

"Whenever you're ready, Brice's corporate jet will fly you and Levy to New York so you can work on the book."

"Levy is going to be pissed when he hears the case is over," Charlie said with a smile. "He was counting on my trial and dramatic acquittal for the last chapter."

CHARLIE'S EUPHORIA LASTED as long as it took for Nathan Tuazama to slip into the elevator when it arrived in the hotel lobby.

"Good evening, Charlie," Tuazama said as the steel doors sealed Marsh in with the assassin.

Charlie's heart rocketed into his throat. He had been so distracted by the day's events that he'd forgotten the Batangan. With Tuazama a knife blade away, Charlie was too frightened to speak. Tuazama sensed his terror and smiled as he pressed a button that stopped the car between floors.

"Did you think I'd forgotten you?"

"What do you want?"

"I want the diamonds. You will give them to me now."

"Why should I?" Charlie asked with unconvincing bravado.

"If you choose to keep them, Charlie, I will kill you. I assume that argument is very convincing. I will call you tomorrow to tell you where to bring the stones."

Tuazama started the car again. The door opened on the floor below Charlie's.

"Wait," Charlie said.

"The time for waiting is over," Tuazama said as the doors closed and he disappeared from view.

Charlie was shaking when he locked the door to his room. As soon as he settled down, he called Amanda and asked her to bring the diamonds to her office in the morning. She asked no questions, assuming that Charlie wanted to have the stones with him in New York and she was perfectly happy to have them out of her possession.

As soon as Charlie hung up on Amanda, he made a second call.

48

Amanda handed over the diamonds an hour after Tuazama called Charlie with instructions. As soon as he had them, Charlie returned to his hotel and waited for midnight.

Washington Park, 130 acres of forest featuring attractions like the Oregon Zoo and the Japanese and Rose Gardens, overlooks downtown Portland from the West Hills. During the day, it is a feast of colors and a place for thousands of visitors to play. At night, it is deserted: a place for drugs to be dealt, lovers to meet, and the occasional act of violence. At midnight, it is no place for a law-abiding citizen but it is a perfect place to transfer diamonds worth several million dollars to a trained assassin without being seen.

Charlie had no idea where Tuazama was lurking when he parked his car in the deserted lot near the Rose Garden and walked along a shadow-shrouded path to the amphitheater, but he was certain that the Batangan was close enough to protect his property from the predators who roamed the park at night.

During the summer, concerts and plays were performed in a meadow surrounded by trees and shrubbery. Tonight, the only light illuminating the grassy field was from a half moon. Charlie stepped onto the platform that served as a stage, as he had been told to do. His heart was thudding in his chest. He closed his eyes for a moment in an attempt to control his breathing. When he opened them, Nathan Tuazama was standing a few steps away.

"I brought them," Charlie said, his voice shaking.

"I knew you would," Tuazama answered confidently as he started toward Charlie. He'd taken two steps when a man stepped out of the space between two trees. His first shot caught Tuazama in the chest. The Batangan stumbled backward and reached under his jacket for his gun. More shots hit him from behind as two other men materialized out of the shadows. The rebels had used silencers and the shots had been mere whispers in the night. Tuazama tumbled onto the grass and the three men surrounded him. Charlie joined them.

"Hello, Nathan," Pierre Girard said. Tuazama stared at him but didn't reply. Blood trickled from his lips. "Do you recognize me? I'm Bernadette's brother and I'm sorry I don't have time to make you suffer the way Bernadette must have suffered."

Pierre turned to Charlie. "Would you like to finish him?" he asked.

Charlie shook his head. Pierre turned back to Tuazama and shot him between the eyes. Charlie shuddered. He was relieved that Tuazama was dead but he didn't feel any sense of satisfaction. Killing Tuazama hadn't brought Bernadette to life.

"Did you bring the diamonds?" Pierre asked.

Charlie handed him the box.

"Thank you," Pierre said. "We will always be grateful to you for the risks you took for us."

"I'm the one who should be thanking you for saving my life here and at Sally Pope's mansion," Charlie said.

"We had to protect you until you could bring us the diamonds. We need them to buy the weapons that will bring Baptiste down."

"Good luck in Batanga."

"Thank you, Charlie. We will escort you to your car, then we must go," Pierre said. "I will always remember what you've done for us."

A lump formed in Charlie's throat and tears filled his eyes. "I did this for your sister, Pierre. I did this for Bernadette."

Moonbeam

The din of the noisy crowd in the living room of Martha Brice's penthouse dissipated when Amanda Jaffe shut the sliding door to the terrace behind her and Brice. It was a cool night in Manhattan and the threat of rain was keeping the guests inside. The party was in honor of the publication of *Violent Homecoming*. The reviews had been ecstatic and there was already a buzz about the book that cast it as the next *In Cold Blood* and *Helter Skelter* combined.

Earlier in the evening, Amanda had spotted Dennis Levy putting the moves on a stunning fashion model who had recently graced the cover of a sister magazine of *World News*. The girl appeared to be listening to Levy with rapt attention but Amanda suspected that she was only pretending to find him interesting. Dennis had been interviewed on network shows and written up as the next great writer of his generation, which meant that he was officially rich *and* famous, but fame and fortune did not miraculously transform a jerk into a decent human being. None of that mattered, of course. Amanda was certain that Levy would be in bed with the model before the night was through. A gorgeous woman could ignore unfortunate personality traits if a celebrity had enough money.

And maybe Dennis deserved to go to bed with a fashion model tonight, as his reward for doing the right thing. He had returned the photograph the morning after the custody hearing, even though Amanda could see that the decision had not been easy for the young reporter. But Levy's virtue appeared to have been rewarded many times over and it was now Amanda's turn to do a good deed.

"What did you want to talk about that we

couldn't have discussed inside?" Martha Brice asked Amanda.

"There are some things you need to see and I don't think you'd appreciate my showing them to you if anyone else was around."

"Why don't you complete your show-and-tell so we can go back to the party? It's chilly out here."

"Okay, Moonbeam."

Amanda expected a reaction and she wasn't disappointed. The color drained from Brice's face and she stared at Amanda for a moment before regaining her composure.

"Moonbeam? Why did you call me that?"

"Isn't that the name you invented for yourself when you followed Charlie Marsh to Oregon from Yale?"

Amanda took two photographs out of her purse. The first was the picture of Charlie's entourage that had been snapped at the Dunthorpe seminar. As soon as Amanda handed it to Brice, the editor's shoulders sagged.

"I'm not crazy about the shaved head," Amanda said.

"Where did you get this?"

"It was in Sally Pope's case file. No one would have seen it if Charlie hadn't come back to stand trial."

"I look so young," Brice said as she stared at the picture.

"How did it happen?"

"How did what happen?" Brice asked cautiously.

"To put your mind at ease, the authorities are half-convinced that Tony Rose shot Pope and I have no reason to change their mind. I can't prove you killed the congressman, anyway, and I have no interest in telling my theory to the police now that Charlie's case has been dismissed."

"What about Charlie?"

"He's going to keep his mouth shut, Delmar Epps is dead, and Werner Rollins didn't see you. I don't know what Gary Hass saw but no one would believe him, assuming that he even saw you shoot Pope. If he did, I doubt he'd ever make the connection between the hippie he saw in Oregon in the dark for a few minutes twelve years ago and the successful businesswoman who runs *World News*."

"You think I killed Arnold Pope?"

Amanda smiled. "No one is listening to

our conversation, and you don't have to admit a thing, if you're worried."

"I have nothing to worry about. I'm just curious to know why you think I'm a murderer."

"The gun has always been the key. If Delmar Epps had it when the fight started, any number of people could have shot Junior, but it had to be you if Epps left the gun in the limo. Mickey Keys, Charlie, Delmar Epps, and you drove to the Westmont in the limo. Mickey Keys remembers Epps dropping the gun during the ride to the country club. It freaked out Keys because the barrel was pointing at him when it hit the floor of the car and he thought he was going to be shot. He got very upset and yelled at Epps. Keys had a very clear memory of Epps putting the gun on a seat in the limo after he yelled at him, but he can't remember what happened to it after that and no one else can say what happened to the gun once the limo stopped at the Westmont.

"Keys couldn't have shot the congressman because he was behind him near the entrance to the Westmont.

"Epps is dead, so he can't tell us whether

he took the gun out of the car, but he acted instinctively to protect Charlie when Gary Hass opened the limo door and probably left the gun on the seat.

"Werner Rollins remembers you standing with Charlie, Gary Hass, and Delmar when Junior was shot. But no one has said where you were between arriving at the country club and the shooting."

Amanda showed Martha Brice the other photograph she'd brought from Portland, a crime scene picture taken on the evening of the murder.

"This is the turnaround in front of the entrance to the country club." She pointed to a section of the picture. "Someone trampled the flower beds on the far side. When the limo stopped at the front entrance to the Westmont, the driver went around to the passenger door to open it but Gary Hass beat him to it. Werner Rollins was also on the passenger side of the car. Delmar Epps got out on the passenger side when Gary Hass opened the door. Charlie and his agent got out on the passenger side right after Epps. No one saw you get out. I think that's because you went out the rear door on the driver's side while everyone was distracted by the commotion on the passenger side. I think you trampled the flower bed when you ran away from the fight.

"Charlie told me how concerned you were that someone would report him to his parole officer for handling the gun. I think you took the revolver with you to keep it from Charlie so he wouldn't get in trouble when the fight between him and the congressman started. You joined Charlie and Gary Hass when they went to the far side of the turnaround. Then you heard Congressman Pope threaten Charlie and run toward him. I think you shot Pope to protect Charlie."

"That's an interesting theory," Brice said.

"I always wondered why Charlie contacted you of all people when he needed money to escape from Batanga."

"He knew I'd pay him for his story."

"There's that too. You sent him seventy-five thousand dollars as soon as he asked. That's something you might do if you were worried that someone might expose a long-buried secret. But, as I said, you can put your mind at ease. Charlie has no intention of revealing your secret. He wants to put the past behind him. And I have no duty to solve the murder of Arnold Pope Jr. When Charlie's case was dismissed I lost all interest in what happened twelve years ago at the Westmont Country Club.

"There's no mention in any of the articles written about you of your brief disappearance from Yale and I assume few if any people know about your Oregon adventure. Killing Pope must have been a pretty sobering experience. You excelled at your studies after you returned and you've excelled in your professional life. Now that Charlie's case is closed I intend to destroy these photographs, because I can't think of a single reason to destroy the life you've made for yourself."

Brice smiled. "If I had any doubts before, you've convinced me that I made the right decision when I told Charlie to hire you. You are one smart lady."

CHARLIE MARSH WATCHED Amanda Jaffe and Martha Brice through the picture window. He knew why Amanda had brought Martha outside. When Martha came back in, he would tell her that she had nothing to fear from him.

Over the past few months, Charlie had thought a lot about his life and had come to the conclusion that he was at a cross-road. The murder charge had been dismissed and Amanda had gotten the IRS to agree that they wouldn't pursue any federal charges if he paid the taxes he owed. For the first time in years, Charlie was not in trouble with the law.

Two weeks ago, rebel forces had fought their way into Baptisteville and Jean-Claude had fled to Libya. Charlie had worried that the president would send someone after him to avenge Tuazama's death, but no one had shown up and now Baptiste had more pressing matters to think about.

On paper, Charlie's life looked pretty good. He was free of Baptiste and the law, he was a celebrity, and he was set financially. With the book royalties and the amount still sitting in his Swiss account he would be fine even after he paid off the IRS.

Charlie should have felt great. Instead, he felt like someone drifting in a lifeboat with no safe port in sight. What did you do when you had everything any rational person could want and it wasn't enough, because you'd lost the one person who had made your life worth living? The riches and the notoriety Charlie had wallowed in a decade ago now left him cold. And he still grieved for Bernadette. He would never forget her and he hoped one day he would find someone he could love as much as he loved her. At least he knew that he was capable of love.

Charlie felt he'd been given a fresh start and he needed a plan for the rest of his life, only he didn't have one right now. But he vowed to work on that, and this time it would be a good plan that didn't involve lies and violence. He had no idea how the plan would look but hopefully it would be illuminated by the light he hoped he had inside him.

Acknowledgments

For me, writing a novel is a team effort. After I outline my novel, I make a list of areas where I need the help of an expert. I want to thank Chic Preston, Steve Perry, and Joe Copeland for educating me about subjects of which I knew nothing. Carolyn Lindsey and Robin Haggard researched questions on the Internet for me, because I remain a techno-idiot.

Pam Webb, Jay Margulies, Karen Berry, and Jerry Margolin read drafts of *Fugitive*, and I appreciate their input and the time they spent.

When I finish my draft, I send it to my editor, who points out all the problems with the book that I missed, and suggests ways to improve it. If you like *Fugitive*, thank my editor, Sally Kim, for making it a better book than the one I sent her. Thanks also to Sally's intrepid assistant, Maya Ziv, and to Heather Drucker, and to everyone else at HarperCollins for their support.

There is a reason why I always thank my agent, Jean Naggar, and everyone at the Jean V. Naggar Literary Agency, in the acknowledgments section of each novel. They are the best.

Last, but most important to me, is Doreen, my muse, who still inspires me to do my best.